To Victoria,

the
LADY IN
BLUE
A MARIA CHAVEZ MYSTERY

A NOVEL
BY JEANNE BONACA

You will write your own story some day!

Jeanne Bonaca
Sept. 25, 2011

ISBN 978-0-578-06947-0

Book design by **HOWARD DESIGN GROUP,** www.howarddesign.com.

acknowledgements

ONLY THE REMARKABLE CONTRIBUTIONS of a great many friends made this book possible. When I was still struggling with a first draft, John Merrow of PBS gave me the courage to keep going. Helpful suggestions for revision came from a multitude of generous readers, such as Alison Coolbrith and Barry Lastra; Ann Skelton; Margie Aronson; Randi Ashton-Pritting; Ali Baird; Cristina Bonaca; Lauren Cullings, Marianne Callahan; Elisabeth Coleman; Sam Douglas; Pat and Karen Hatcher; Dianne Harrison; Dave Killian; Nancy Mather; Lois Muraro; Sandra Ploch; Marilyn Rossetti; Martha Ellis-Vasquez; Iran Nazario; Carolyn Siegel; Mal Stevens; Eloise Tencher; and from storytellers in the Southwest who wish to remain anonymous.

For their patience and support, I thank my family, especially Mario, my mother, Anne Robertson, and my brother Jim Robertson. For his kindness and generosity, Arthur G. Schaier. For technical expertise, I'm grateful to Tom Anderson, Marc Bonaca, Bill Shack, and especially Tommaso Missoni.

For her wise advice about writing and her unwavering encouragement, I would like to thank the poet, Sandy Sergio, and writers William H. Young, Allan Johnson, and Rich Holtzin.

For the generous gift of their time and talent, I owe a special thank you to the copy editors who helped proofread the final version: Ann Skelton; Mary Lawrence; Ceila Robbins; and Sandy Sergio.

Most important, I am grateful for the advice and support of the following members of law enforcement: Officer Kristina Vetrano; Agent Bruce Nickerson; Richard Rodriquez, President of The Hartford Police Union; Border Patrol Agent Larry Unger; and above all, Master Police Officer Marc Zifcak of the Montgomery County, Maryland, Fraternal Order of Police, Lodge 35.

about the author

IN ADDITION TO HER TEACHING, writer-photographer Jeanne Bonaca has traveled extensively in the American Southwest, documenting in words and images the landscape, culture, and borderland human drama that inform *The Lady in Blue: A Maria Chavez Mystery,* her first full-length novel. Her translation of the work of Italian poet Marcello Fabbri, *The Light of Memory,* was awarded Italy's *Il Premio Casalguidi.* She and her husband have two children and one grandchild. They live in Connecticut and Florence, Italy.

AUTHOR'S NOTE: The places described in this book are loosely based on cities and towns in the American Southwest. The place names, like the characters and the story itself, come from the author's imagination. Any reference to actual places or persons is purely coincidental.

A DEDICATION

*To the women and men of the
American southwest who entrusted
me with their stories.*

the LADY IN BLUE

A MARIA CHAVEZ MYSTERY

A NOVEL
BY JEANNE BONACA

JULY 1984 | Purgatorio, Mexico
Lastup, USA

BY THE TIME THE BUS LET THEM OFF in the Mexican border town of Purgatorio, the sun was high overhead. As she watched the bus drive away, the little girl could feel the pavement burning under her feet. It had been a long ride north from their village.

Her father bent down and pushed back the damp hair clinging to her cheeks. "I know you're tired, Soli," he told her. "But we still have to go on to the city of Ciudad Nueva *en el norte,* in the north. A little longer, that's all. Then we can rest."

"I can do it, *Papi,*" she told him right away, her dark eyes shining. "I want to go to Ciudad Nueva. And if anyone asks my name, I will tell them I am Maria Soledad Chavez, but my *Papi* calls me Soli, and I am four years old, and I come from...."

"Would you like something to eat, *mi niña*?" he interrupted her gently.

She nodded and took his hand, braiding her tiny fingers through his big ones. They walked over to the bench where her mother was sitting with her little brother, Pablo. He was two years old.

Her father reached into his *trique* bag, his knapsack, and pulled out two cans of sardines and a stack of tortillas. While he wrapped the sardines in the tortillas, Soli sang a lullaby to Pablo, *Duérmete mi niño,* "Sleep my little one." It was her favorite.

When the sandwiches were ready, she ate hers without talking. Then she asked her father, "Where do we go now?"

He pointed to a paved road leading away from the town. A black pickup truck was parked down the road near a water tower.

"Are we going to ride across the border in the black truck?" she asked.

Her father didn't answer. He was talking to her mother.

The little girl took some long swallows of water from a plastic gallon bottle painted black. The bottle was heavy, but she knew how to drink from it without spilling. Before they left home, she asked her father why he was painting the bottle black. He told her, "So it looks like the night."

"Are we going to ride in the black truck, *Papi*?" the little girl asked again, pointing to the truck.

"Yes, Soli," he said. "That's the truck that will take us to our new country." He turned to her mother, "Are you ready?" Her mother nodded.

They set out down the road together, walking close to each other, her mother with Pablo in her arms, the little girl in the middle between her parents. As they came up to the truck, Soli saw two men sitting inside. The one in the driver's seat made her think of a turtle. The way his head was sitting on his shoulders, it looked like he had no neck. The other man had long yellow hair pulled back into a ponytail.

"Stay in back of me," her father said as they came up to the truck.

"Are those men *coyotes*?" the little girl whispered to her mother.

"Yes, Maria, those men are *coyotes*, our guides," her mother said. "Now be quiet."

A third man was leaning against the back of the truck, watching them. He was wearing a straw cowboy hat and sunglasses and smoking a long brown cigarette. There were a lot of cigarette butts on the ground where he was standing.

When the little girl saw the man's smooth face, she thought, "Maybe he'll be friendly." But the man only looked at her, silent and unsmiling.

"These are not the right ones," her father said, coldly sizing up the young man.

The turtle-man in the driver's seat got out of the truck. The yellow-haired man in the passenger seat got out at the same time. He was very tall.

Soli hurried to hide behind her mother's back. She wanted to see everything, but the *coyotes* frightened her. She found a small opening in her mother's sweater and looked through it, trying to keep completely still.

Yes, now she could see them. All three *coyotes* were standing behind the truck, staring at her father in an unfriendly way. The turtle-man smelled like he hadn't taken a bath in a long time. Soli wanted to hold her nose, only she didn't dare move.

But when the tall man took off his sunglasses and rubbed his eyes, she couldn't keep from shivering. His eyes had no color. They were so pale, he seemed blind, and he was looking at her father as if he could see through him. After a few moments, the tall man squinted and put his sunglasses back on.

The little girl wanted to ask her mother about the tall man's eyes, whether the sun could burn his eyes since they had no color, but she knew this was no time for talking.

The young man kept smoking and kicking small stones around on the ground. Only once did he look up, and that was at the hole in her mother's sweater, as if he knew Soli had been watching him. She held her breath.

Her father was arguing with the turtle-man. "No! No!" her father said loudly, shaking his head. He turned his back on the *coyotes* and grabbed her mother's arm, trying to pull her away with him, but she planted her feet on the road and refused to move. There was a hurried, whispered conversation between them.

"These are not the right ones," her father said again. "Already the smell of liquor is heavy on their breath."

"You paid the first ones?" her mother asked.

Her father nodded, his face dark and unhappy. "Most of it."

"Then we must go," her mother said. "Otherwise we will have lost everything. In the north, we have jobs. In the village, we have nothing. How can we go back now?"

Her father stood there, no longer speaking, but not moving either. Finally he went back to talk with the *coyotes*. After a few more words, he pulled some folded money out of his pocket and gave it to the turtle-man.

When her father picked up the little girl and set her down in the truck bed, he was holding her so close, she could feel the tears on his cheeks. After he helped her mother and Pablo into the truck, he climbed in and stood beside them.

The truck followed the village road for a long time before it turned onto a narrow dirt road leading into the desert. The truck went speeding down the dirt road, a cloud of dust following in the air behind them. A crow flew silently overhead. The little girl followed it with her eyes until it disappeared into the distance. The sun kept moving down the sky until it was completely invisible behind a line of purple mountains.

It was dark when the truck took a sharp turn off the road, bumping heavily over the uneven desert ground, tossing all of them from side to side in the open bed. The little girl held on tightly to her mother's arm while her mother brought Pablo closer to her chest, trying to soften the jolting motion of the truck.

"Close your eyes, Soli, close your eyes," her mother said. Her hands were trembling as she covered the little girl's back and shoulders with a blanket. Soli pulled the blanket up higher so it covered most of her face. She loved this blanket, a birthday gift from her *Tia Rosita*. Its deep red color was divided by four wide, pink stripes, and each pink stripe was outlined in a beautiful green color that always made her think of new leaves in the spring. And it was warm, protecting her from the cool night air.

But the blanket could not keep out the fearful sounds falling wildly around them, her mother's frightened questioning, her father's desperate words. "We should not have left the road. We are heading into the middle of nowhere. God help us! What can we do? What can we do?!"

The little girl looked over at her father, frightened. His arms were stretched up towards the sky, and he was weeping.

Last night he had explained that it would not be an easy trip, but when they got to their new home, they would have good jobs and enough to eat. Again that morning, he had warned her to be ready for hard times. "You will have to be brave, Maria," he'd told her. "We will all have to be brave."

The little girl understood that she would be tired and hot. But she never thought she would see her mother sobbing with fear or her father pleading with God to save them. Now she felt a sharp fear twisting inside her stomach. She let out a sharp wail.

She could hear her mother praying, but the words kept floating away on the dusty night wind. Then her mother was speaking to her, up close to her ear. "Pray to the Lady in Blue, my little Soli, pray to the Lady in Blue. And never give up hope. Remember, the Lady in Blue will always be with you."

The truck shuddered to a stop, and the doors opened. The turtle-man walked around to the back of the truck and motioned at them to get out. The tall man stood next to him with a thick metal pipe in his hand.

Without any warning, her father leaped out of the truck and drove his feet straight into the tall man's stomach, knocking him to the ground, smashing him in the face with his fists. The tall man let out a ferocious yell. There was so much blood on his face, it was dripping over his shirt.

"Run! Run!" her father screamed at her mother, but the turtle-man had already pulled her out of the truck, his arms wrapped tightly around her neck. Her mother was struggling to free herself, but she had Pablo in her arms, and the turtle-man was too strong.

Frozen in place, the little girl stood alone in the truck bed trying to understand what was going on around her. She couldn't make sense of anything. Too much was happening all at once. Her mother and the baby were screaming, and her father was trying to free her mother, punching the turtle-man around the neck and shoulders, but the tall man had stumbled back onto his feet, and he was coming up fast behind her father with the iron pipe in his hand.

The little girl screamed a warning, but it was too late. Before her father could turn around, the tall man brought the pipe down on his head. The blow was so hard she could hear his head crack. He fell forward into a heap on the ground.

"*Papi*" the little girl cried out, "*Papi*," but he didn't move. Her father wasn't moving. The tall man turned and studied the little girl with his pale eyes.

"Come here and take the woman," the turtle-man said. The tall man walked over to her mother and held her prisoner with one arm around her neck. Then the turtle-man headed towards the little girl.

"I'll take care of her," the young man said, appearing out of the darkness and moving fast towards the back of the truck. His hard voice made Soli shiver with fright. He jumped up into the truck bed and grabbed her, lifting her feet off the ground. She tried to get away from him, twisting and turning as hard as she could, but he had trapped her inside her blanket. She could hear the other men laughing as the young man threw her like a blanket roll over one shoulder and climbed down from the truck.

"Wait a minute," the turtle-man said. He came over to the little girl and pulled the blanket away from her face. She closed her eyes, but she could feel him make a mark on her forehead with his fingernail. Her skin burned where he made the mark. "You can have her for now," he said to the young man, "but remember, she's mine."

The young man took off running with the little girl over his shoulder, his breathing loud and noisy. It felt like he was running up a hill. When he stopped, he took off the blanket before he put her down on the ground. She could feel the rough sand and grass under her back.

She looked for the truck, but everything had disappeared. All she could see in the darkness was the young man. He had one of his knees across her legs, and he was holding her shoulders to the ground.

"*Mami! Papi! Estoy aqui!*" she screamed, but the man pressed his hand hard over her mouth and said roughly, "Listen! Listen to me, little girl. You have to stay here and you can't move. Do you understand? If you get up and try to find your *Mami*, you will die." He pulled her face sharply towards him. "Don't move, and don't make any noise, understand?"

He stood up and looked down at her. "*Dios te cuide,*" he said under his breath. Then he turned and started running fast, as if something was chasing after him. She lay motionless, looking up at the sky. The moon was so bright it hurt her eyes.

She heard her mother and Pablo screaming in the distance. She wanted to scream back, but the man's words had taken away her voice. She closed her eyes and lay very still. After a while, the truck doors slammed shut. The shattered silence of the desert returned.

"I love you, *Mami*, I love you *Papi*," she whispered into the night. "I'm here, waiting for you. Please come back and find me soon."

1 | MAY 2009
Ciudad Nuevo
Vereda
Friday

THE SPRAWLING WESTERN CITY OF CIUDAD NUEVA moves along at a
steady pace under the hot springtime sun until May arrives. Then the sun gets an attitude. It sits
stubbornly in the blazing summer sky and burns everything in sight. It shallows the river that
runs through the heart of the city. It heats the air until the ground cracks and even the most
pungent scents from the high chaparral fade away.

Movement in the city slows to a crawl. By afternoon, children at play have vanished from
view. The sidewalks empty. People hide from the scorching heat wherever they can. They dissi-
pate into shadows behind the curtain. They surrender to the dark of houses, small apartments,
unsavory alleys.

The blistering summer days limp along until evening when the overheated sun finally burns
out. Then the darkening sky opens up the city like an invitation. People spill outside to live night
on the street, where the air moves along with the mariachi music, and guitars send their lone-
some notes out of bars until dawn.

By Friday afternoon, the sun had forced most of the city to a standstill. Only the *barrio* of
Vereda, a low-income neighborhood tightly packed into the city's south end, continued in full
swing. Spring or summer, day or night, Vereda never slowed down.

On Vista Drive, a narrow strip of pavement that separated the southeast corner of Vereda
from the desert, the usual cars kept moving along the road with their slow, bumpy rhythm, and
the usual people gathered outside, talking in small groups or walking from one house to another
through the thick hot air.

Ten years ago, Vista Drive had been utilized as a service road while the city's major highways
were under construction. But when the work was finished, Vista Drive was seen as a blemish in
the soaring, brightly colored highway system now serving Ciudad Nueva. Cheap desert scrub
was planted on both sides of the road to hide it from view, and it was officially put aside.

The neglected pavement quickly disintegrated into cracks and potholes. There were no sidewalks and no street lights. But Vista Drive also had some advantages. It was easily accessible
from several highways and well hidden behind the desert scrub planted around it.

Not long after the new highway system was completed, a large four-story apartment building appeared on Vista Drive, set back on a barren, fenced-in lot where the road began to climb
into the higher elevations. Across the street from the apartment building, there was a derelict

auto repair shop with a thriving junkyard behind it that stretched far out into the desert. From the back of the junkyard, all that was visible of the highways were streams of headlights during the night.

Houses continued to crop up along Vista Drive, mostly one-story single houses, peeling paint and full of holes where boards were missing. Fugitives on the run used some of the houses as hiding places. Other houses were used as safe houses, where illegal immigrants could hole up for a night or two before moving on.

The most important activity on Vista Drive was the pharmaceutical business. A local gang, *Los Viboras*, was in charge of supplying and selling narcotics in Vereda for the Gil Gomez-Gil drug cartel, the major cartel in the Southwest and one of the largest in the country.

The apartment building served as the center of the Vista Drive narcotics trade. On the street it was called *la finca*, the farm, because that's where it all begins. The building had a thick steel front door, and there were always gang members in residence to safeguard the large cache of drugs, cash, and guns inside.

The gang paid special attention to *la finca* because the trade in narcotics on Vista Drive was good, very good. For over six months, there had been no interruptions. People were starting to take it for granted that Vista had fallen off law enforcement's radar. Once in a while a customer would disappear, but it didn't matter. No one came to Vista by accident.

Inside the Vereda District Police Station, Vista Drive was seen differently. The police chief had let it be known that he was feeling pressure from above. Vista Drive had to be cleaned up and soon.

Detective Al Diaz, the senior officer in charge of informants, had picked up a rumor that the usual protection on Vista Drive would be missing Monday night. Al wanted to investigate further, but the chief wanted action now. The Narcotics Unit would have to serve a warrant on the Vista Drive *finca* on Monday night.

2 | MONDAY NIGHT
Vista Drive
Vereda

A FEW HOURS BEFORE MIDNIGHT, a dark blue van jumped the curb on Vista Drive and headed across the desert for the junkyard. It parked inside with its front end pointing towards the opening cut in the fence by the advance team. Ten figures sat in the van. They were dressed in dark jeans, long-sleeved black shirts, and black caps. In spite of the van's darkened windows, someone might notice them sitting inside. They would have to leave the van and sit outside on the hard desert floor. It would be a long, hot, uncomfortable wait.

Toby "Dan" Danforth, supervisor of the Major Crimes Unit, was first out the door. He watched as the rest of the team silently exited the van one by one. The two from his unit were noticeably different from the others. The large, square shape was Cali. In the dim yellow glow of desert night, he looked like a block of cement moving across the sand on short, thick legs.

Maria was one of the last to step out of the van. Her slender figure looked like an afterthought next to the burly men who made up the rest of the team, but she caught up to Cali with an easy stride and sat down on the ground beside him.

Danforth saw her checking out the rest of the team as soon as she sat down. She was obviously tense, but there was nothing strange about that. Everyone got nerves on their first assignment outside the building.

What bothered Danforth was his own uneasiness. No matter how hard he tried to convince himself otherwise, he still thought Maria was too inexperienced to be part of a night raid on Vista Drive.

She was looking over at him. He nodded in response and gave her the victory sign, ignoring the hollow feeling in his stomach. She smiled, visibly more relaxed, and leaned back against the van, talking to Cali in a quiet whisper. It looked like a conversation that would last a while. That was good. Cali was a reassuring presence for Maria.

Cali was a loner, much like Maria, and his conversations with others in the unit were usually short and to the point. But Cali knew a lot about working the street, and as Maria's unofficial mentor, he held nothing back. Maria listened to him carefully. After a while, they stopped talking and sat quietly, lost in their own thoughts.

Maria studied Danforth, standing next to the van, checking his watch, scanning the junkyard, the desert, the sky. He was close to fifty and still an impressive figure, broadly shouldered and lean. But under the yellow light of the sky, the lines on his face seemed deeper than usual. He would never admit it, but she suspected he was there for her.

"He's worried," she said to Cali. "It's my fault. He's putting himself at risk."

"No," Cali said forcefully. "Not your fault."

She was silent, thinking about Danforth. He was a Boston transplant who had put down roots in Ciudad Nueva as a rookie over twenty-five years ago. He could go back East anytime. His two daughters were grown and out on their own, and his wife had died from cancer a few years ago. But by now Ciudad Nueva was his home.

Maybe he's feeling protective because he's alone now, Maria thought to herself. Maybe it's because he felt helpless while his wife was dying. She would never know. He didn't allow that kind of closeness with anyone except Cali. And Cali was a closed book where Danforth was concerned.

"Soli," Cali said, interrupting her thoughts. "Dan knows better than anyone just how good you are at your job, you know that, right? He works hard to find the right people for his unit. He handpicks all of them."

Maria nodded. Cali meant well, but he wasn't very subtle. He was trying to reassure her about the raid, that was obvious. Still, he was her only real friend in the unit. She even let him call her by her nickname, Soli. No one else could do that.

But it bothered her that he saw her as being "alone."

"You call me Soli as if that's how you see me," she couldn't help saying to him now. "But what about the rest of you? Always inside your cars, with your scheduled walk-throughs. I get out of my car, I walk through the parking lots, I go into buildings, I talk with the kids on the street. Maybe, you're the ones who are *soli*."

"I suppose you're talking about the Alvarez kid. You got a break there, that's all."

"Bullshit!"

"OK, I'll give you that," Cali admitted with his usual sardonic grin. "You were at the right place at the right time because you're always out there."

She relaxed slightly.

"That must have been something," Cali added. "Seeing the 'little snakes' with their lead pipes getting ready to take down that kid, just for the fun of it."

Maria nodded. She would never forget it. She'd been walking through the parking lot behind N. Building in the Hildalgo Housing Project when she saw a small boy surrounded by the bullies of N. Building, *los culebritas*, "the little snakes," who worked for an important cartel lieutenant named Snake Baby.

She'd pulled "the little snakes" off the boy with full force, bouncing them hard against the pavement. Anywhere else someone might have complained about excessive use of force, but not there. Most of the residents hated the "little snakes." What Maria was still trying to digest was that the "little snakes" were only eleven and twelve years old, still in elementary school.

"I asked you a question," Cali said, looking at her as if he were trying to read her thoughts from her face. "You know how Dan finds people for his unit?"

"I know he has more power than most supervisors to handpick the members of his unit," she said, trying to ignore the way Cali was staring at her. He was checking her out. She was a young recruit, and they were going on a tough raid. It was inevitable. "I'm fine, by the way," she added to make her point.

"Good. So listen up. Dan usually finds the people he wants by keeping track of the new officers, their reports, their arrest records, and so on. But he noticed you when you were in the academy. Number one academically. A smart woman who could outrun and outshoot the rest of the class. Just look at your hand. It's like it was shaped for the grip of a gun."

"Then why he is worried tonight?"

"Because of you."

"But you just said...."

"I said it's not your fault, but you're right about the rest, there is something about you that gets to him. Maybe it's what happened to your family, I don't know. But if Danforth is feeling protective, that's his problem, not yours."

Maria looked hard at Cali. He had jet black hair and black eyes that could hold you in place when he stared at you, but she had learned how to challenge him. "You did this," she said, accusingly. "You set it up."

"Guilty as charged," he admitted.

"Explain."

"I thought you were ready to move on. I was afraid Dan would hold you back, that his protective feelings could cloud his judgment. So I proposed the raid. I told him you were ready to go outside the building, that it was time for you to earn your street degree. Maybe I'm wrong, but that's how I see things."

"What did Danforth say?"

"He wasn't enthusiastic. Thought it was too soon. Said I should talk to you, find out how you felt about it."

"He decided to leave it up to me," Maria said, resigned. "That's the problem. He decided to leave it up to me. And now he regrets it."

3

MONDAY NIGHT
Vista Drive

DANFORTH STOOD NEAR THE VAN, going over each step in their preparations one more time. The raid was far from being a sure thing. The informant's tip had been ambiguous, no real information about why there would be less protection tonight, and the Narcotics Unit hadn't had much time to prepare. So when Danforth had volunteered to lead the raid, everyone had been surprised. It didn't seem to make sense. Senior Sergeant Detective Toby Danforth was the supervisor of the Major Crimes Unit and a senior officer. A senior officer was supposed to stay in his office, not go on a night raid in the most dangerous part of town.

The supervisor of the Narcotics Unit had been more than willing to let Danforth take the lead. He couldn't understand why Danforth wanted to be part of the raid, but like everyone else at the district station, he had learned to expect the unexpected from Danforth.

Danforth was widely admired at every level of law enforcement. He was a "cop's cop," and there weren't many of them around anymore. He knew how to work the street, and he stood up for his people regardless of the political fallout. He even looked like a Senior Detective with wary gray eyes and graying red hair cut so short it bristled. His leadership had been recognized at both the local and national level, and he had unusual latitude in his decision making. His Major Crimes Unit was a success, protected by its reputation. At least for now.

Danforth didn't explain why he was going on the raid, and the speculation continued. Some people thought the boss wanted to relive the glory days. Others said maybe there was an unknown target on Vista Drive.

Only Cali Martinez, Danforth's second-in-command, knew why Danforth was going on the raid. Cali and Danforth were about the same age, and they had gravitated towards each other from their first days together on the force. They worked together effectively, and they had remained close personal friends. By now they had no secrets from each other.

Cali knew Danforth was going on the raid to keep a protective eye on their unit's newest recruit, Maria Chavez. Danforth had seen something unusual in Maria while she was still in the academy, and he'd been watching her closely ever since.

When an opening in the unit came up in January, Danforth talked with Cali about offering the position to Maria. "Her performance over the past six years has been consistently outstanding," he told Cali. "The way she interrupted that 7-11 robbery last year? When that guy came at her with a knife, and she took him down by shooting out his knee? That was something else!"

Cali nodded. "Isn't that also against regulations?" He gave Danforth a wicked smile. "But then she was the best shot in the Academy. That probably gave her the confidence she needed to go her own way. You do remember those regulations, Dan, don't you? You know, like take no chances, come home alive?!"

Danforth brushed off Cali's comments. "With her skills, she wasn't taking chances."

"She can shoot, no doubt about it," Cali agreed.

"And given what happened to her as a child, you could say that Maria has had a personal encounter with evil," Dan continued. "She knows it from the inside, and it shows. We need more cops like that."

"That's what you're always telling us," Cali reminded him with another sardonic grin. "Evil in the world and all that."

Danforth ignored Cali's comment, but he knew he had a persistent belief in the existence of evil. He wasn't shy about letting people know how he felt either.

"I'm not saying you're wrong about Maria," Cali added quickly. "I agree with you. But from what I hear, even though she can outperform almost everyone else in the unit, there's something about her that puts people off."

"I have one answer to that," Dan said. "Like most cops, Maria takes a tough stand when she's working a case. She can't allow herself to become emotionally involved with the victims. She has to stay focused on the predators until the case is solved.

"And Maria does that as well as anyone. Her problems develop after the case is closed, when she continues to keep her distance from the others in the unit, even if they've just finished working a case together. It's not fair, but some in the department see her reserve as a real drawback. I keep telling them, give her time."

"I agree," Cali said. "Maria gets my vote. She's in great physical shape, she's smart, and she's an unusually skillful shooter. She brings other things to the job too. She connects to the community in a big way. People in Vereda know her. She's like a hero to them. She can help create the link we need if we're ever going to get a handle on what's happening out there. It's on our side of the border now, too." Cali paused. "Did you ever think it would get this bad?"

"It's bad," Dan said. "Definitely bad."

"So it's Maria for the unit?" Cali said when they'd finished talking.

Dan nodded. "Yes. You OK with that?"

"Absolutely."

Cali had encouraged Maria to put in for the opening in Major Crimes, and by the end of January she'd been temporarily assigned to their unit. That way she could try it out, see if it was a good fit. So far things had gone well even though she was too reserved to connect to her colleagues. Cali was still her only real friend. With everyone else, she kept her distance. No happy hour with the rest of the unit after work, no informal socializing.

No major problems either, at least not until last Friday. But Cali was creating one. Danforth hadn't expected it. He hadn't expected Cali to propose that Maria be temporarily detailed to Narcotics for the Monday night raid on Vista Drive after only six months in the unit. "It seems on the early side to me," Dan told him. "I don't like it."

"I disagree," Cali said forcefully. "I think she's ready. She needs to grow, she needs to push herself beyond what she thinks is possible. It's time for her to earn her street degree." He paused. "She's got what it takes, Dan, I'm sure of it."

"I don't know about that," Dan had told Cali. "But I'll think on it. In the meantime, talk to her, tell her what's involved. Let's see how she feels about your proposal."

4

MONDAY NIGHT
Vista Drive

DANFORTH PACED BACK AND FORTH IN FRONT OF THE VAN. The hot air sent sweat dripping down his neck and back. And the noise from all directions was constant and irritating. Barking dogs everywhere. That was inevitable. But the crunching of little teeth and the rapid, rustling movements all around him!? How many mice, rats, squirrels, and who knows what else had made nests inside the discarded engines and cars that filled the junkyard.

He could see the silhouette of a rat on top of a junked car not far from the van. Instinctively he bent down to get a stone. He straightened up, his hand empty. No noise. He knew that. But what a relief it would have been.

Last Friday Maria had come to Danforth soon after talking with Cali. She wasn't unusually tall, but she held herself straight, and even sitting down, her eyes met Danforth's directly. "Cali wants you to detail me to Narcotics," Maria told Danforth.

"What'd he tell you about the assignment?"

"He said Narcotics was going to execute a warrant on the Vista Drive *finca* Monday night."

"And Vista Drive?"

"He said Vista Drive is one of the most dangerous parts of Vereda. One side of the street borders the desert."

"How do you feel about that?"

"A little spooked, I guess," she admitted.

"This is your sixth year here in Vereda, right?"

She nodded.

"Why are you in this line of work, Maria?"

Silenced at first by the unexpectedness of the question, Maria considered her answer. Cali and Danforth had become her unofficial mentors. She'd only been working with Danforth for six months, but she had come to trust him. She would try to explain.

"I wanted to be involved with the illegals," she began hesitantly. "That's one reason anyway. The *coyotes* take their life's savings and agree to bring them across the line. Then when they're lost somewhere in the mountains or the desert, once they can't go back, the *coyotes* force them to become *mules*, carrying drugs in their backpacks, or else make them take amphetamines so they can keep going no matter how tired or thirsty they are.

"And then there are the bandits on both sides of the border who rape the women and young

13

girls or rob the whole group and leave them for dead. When that happens, the *coyotes* run away. The illegals have no defense.

"Someone once called the illegals the bravest of the poor. I agree. I feel strongly about human trafficking. How could I not? Only please don't get me wrong," she interrupted herself. "I don't condone breaking the law under any circumstances, you know that. But what happens to the illegals on their way to a job, that's a high price to pay for unemployment, don't you think?"

Danforth was silent, but Maria thought she saw a flash of sympathy in his eyes.

Embarrassed at speaking so openly, she stared down at the table. "I was also looking for a place where I could belong," she admitted after a moment, looking up to meet Danforth's eyes.

She's lonely, Danforth realized. He'd understood that she was a loner, but not how lonely she was. "Why Vereda?" he asked cautiously.

"I don't know." She felt even more embarrassed now. "A Border Patrol posting or a city like Tucson or Phoenix would probably make more sense as far as the immigrants are concerned. But Vereda feels right to me. So does the District Station. I grew up near here in Sandy Hills." She stopped, started up again. "I don't have anyone anymore, you know that, right? Even my adoptive parents have passed on."

Danforth remembered. A bad car accident. The other driver was DWI but had walked away with minor injuries. Both of Maria's adoptive parents had died before reaching the hospital. He had often wondered why she never talked about them.

"I loved my adoptive parents," Maria said, as if in response to his unspoken question. "But I try not to talk about them. It's too hard to explain that I've lost my parents twice. It makes me feel like I'm jinxed or something. But I still think about what happened to my family in the desert."

Danforth remained silent.

"I don't remember anything," she went on. "But from what I've learned, there were two or three men, supposedly *coyotes*, but the Border Patrol Agent who investigated wrote that it looked more like they were young men pretending to be *coyotes*, young men who got drunk and decided to have a good time.

"Whoever they were, they were hired to bring my parents to jobs in the orchards Northside. Instead they stopped in the desert to have some fun. They beat up my father and raped my mother before they drove away. The report says my father must have died right away from his injuries. But according to the agent, my mother found the strength to find me and my baby brother and take us with her as far as she could go. She gave us all the water she had, and she pushed us under whatever green bushes she could find. She didn't last long after that. By the time they found me, even my little brother was dead. He was only two."

Maria spoke calmly, unemotionally. Danforth had to work at keeping his voice steady when he answered her.

"It's none of my business, and you don't have to tell me anything," he said, "but I can't help wondering. Do you ever worry that if they're still alive, those men might be watching you? Afraid you'll start remembering?"

Maria's reply was emphatic. "No, absolutely not. If they were worried, I'd have been dead a long time ago. And the doctor was very clear. The memory dump from a trauma like that, especially at such a young age, is almost always complete and permanent. The only things I know are from what I've read. And anyway, no one would ever bring forward a case based on the recovered memories of a four-year-old."

Danforth nodded.

"I think about those men sometimes," she admitted after a moment, rubbing her forehead. "But I didn't join law enforcement to find any answers, Sarge. I'll never know who those men were or why they killed my family. It's past history. I've accepted it."

She's strong, Danforth thought to himself. Stronger than she knows. Her story moved him. "Now about that raid," he said.

"Yes?" She looked at him intently.

"Cali's interest in you is a compliment," Danforth said, choosing his words carefully. "If Çali thinks you're ready, he's probably right. But you also need to understand that you're free to refuse. Going on the Narco raid, that's a proposal from Cali, not an assignment from me."

She nodded. "I'd like to give it a try. If you agree, that is."

"It's your decision," he told her. "Think about it." Then he was quiet, unsure about how much weight he should give to his instinct that the mission would be dangerous for her. She made the choice for him. "I'll do it, Sarge. I want to. I'll tell Cali."

Well, she had made her decision. Now there was nothing to do but wait. He was sick of waiting. Time was dragging. He looked up at the sky. How strange that it had been the moon to finally decide things. Tonight there was only a thin slice of moon in the sky. The sun had disappeared hours ago, but the sky looked as if it had been bleached out by the heat. Dark nights near the desert were rare in May. Even a few hours before midnight, the sky was still light. Far below the horizon, the sun had angled its rays to shine off the sand. Then the brilliantly shining sand turned the desert into a glass surface reflecting invisible rays upwards. Its rays made the sky glow with a pale golden light, like a halo over the earth. An unending May day.

In another hour, the desert light would disappear. The sky would darken. With just a slice of moonlight in the sky, the team had a decent chance of getting close to *la finca* before anyone saw them. Before anyone could start shooting.

5
MONDAY NIGHT
Vista Drive

MARIA STOOD IN A POOL OF SHADOWS near the back door of *la finca*. It was past midnight and slightly cooler, but only because the sun had finally slipped out of sight. She was soaked through with perspiration, and her own breathing sounded loud enough to wake up the whole building.

By now her eyes had adjusted to the dark. She studied the back of the building. There was an external staircase near the back door that ran from the ground up to the roof. The informant had told them that most of the dope was on the first floor in the pipes, under the ceiling panels, even in tunnels under the floor boards.

A slice of moon in a dark sky. Distant stars. *La finca* itself was quiet and completely dark except for a pale light in one of the second-story rooms. There was hip-hop music blasting out of a house somewhere in the distance, and dogs up and down the street kept up an incessant howling. A clump of tumbleweed twisted and rustled on the razor wire fence next door.

Something came out of the silence and hit her shoulder with a heavy thud. A breath brushed across her cheek. She dropped to the ground, her heart racing. Cali was by her side before she could say his name. They stared. About ten feet away, they could see the pale outline of a great horned owl grabbing a small animal with its talons. There was a shriek before the owl lifted off as silently as it had descended.

"You OK?" Cali mouthed at her.

She managed to nod before Cali disappeared again into the shadows across from her.

She couldn't stop shivering. She slid into a sitting position on the ground, trying not to make any sound. Cali didn't say anything. He hadn't heard her. Good. She put her head down and started breathing deeply. She would not faint. She would not get sick. She was determined not to let Cali see how badly frightened she was.

The owl lived in her most terrifying childhood nightmares. An owl bumping into her in the middle of the night was one of the worst things she could imagine. And yet tonight of all nights, a great horned owl, intent on its prey and going too fast to suddenly change course, had unexpectedly found her in his path. His enormous, strong wings had come so close that she'd felt the breath of his feathers across her face, and the impact of the collision had knocked her to the ground. It was like finding herself in the middle of a nightmare.

She stood up carefully. Cali was still quiet. At least she'd been able to pull herself together before he realized how badly frightened she was. She tried to focus on the real dangers facing her. How many dogs were in the house? How many guns? How many shooters? Even with her vest on, she made an easy target if anyone bothered to look closely into the dark area around the back door. The team had come out in the dead of night to execute their search warrant because the usual protection was missing. Supposedly. But what if the informant was lying? What if it was a trap?

She and Cali were the guards behind the building in case someone tried to make a run for it through the back door. They were waiting for the TAC team to bust open the front door. She knew Cali had chosen to guard the back of the house in order to stay close to her. Danforth was somewhere nearby as well.

She could barely make out Cali's shape in the shadows, but she knew what an intimidating figure he was. That broad chest. Those muscular arms and legs. She thought he looked like he could take down a freight train.

She'd never seen it, but people said that the most frightening thing about Cali was the expression on his face when he was after you. Supposedly you could tell just by looking at him that whatever happened, the usual rules wouldn't apply, that he would be absolutely unrelenting. She didn't know whether it was true or not, but she was glad he was on her side.

The night silence was suddenly broken by a deafening crash. The front door had gone down. The reverberations of metal against metal echoed up and down the street. After that, things happened fast.

Screams and yells spilled out of the building. Lights came on. She heard a window shatter in the front of the house. Someone started shooting. Two men came running out the back door and straight into Cali. A third man followed them closely and deliberately caught Maria hard under the ribs with his elbow. The sharp blow took her breath away, and she doubled over in pain.

"You OK, Maria?" Cali called out to her.

"Fine, just catching my breath," she said, pushing past the pain. She straightened up and searched the darkness, trying to follow the sound of footsteps.

Cali was pulling the two men he'd taken down towards the front of the house. Maria kept searching in the direction of the footsteps. When she caught sight of the man who'd pushed past her, she saw that he was heading for the street. Before she realized what she was doing, she found herself running after him.

"He's going for his car," she screamed at Cali over her shoulder. As she approached the street, she saw two large black figures with flashlights in front of the auto repair shop where a dog was growling ferociously. There were gunshots. The growling stopped.

Maria followed the sound of footsteps ahead of her in the darkness along the street. She ran past an old man standing in front of one of the houses. A light from the house was shining directly on his face. She glanced at his hands. They were empty. In the same instant she saw his broken teeth, the swollen red bumps on his face, the flat bridge of his nose. By the time he picked up a rock and threw it at her, she was past him, but the rock caught her on the back of her neck. A small, sharp pain, but for a moment it made her dizzy.

Strange cries and whistles filled the night. Shadows seemed to be moving everywhere. She ignored them and concentrated on the sound of the footsteps ahead of her. She passed one small house, then another. Suddenly a shadow from one of the houses came at her as fast and silently as the owl. He held his knife against her throat and pulled her into the house, running down the hall, kicking at doors until one of them opened. He pushed her into the room and wrestled her to the floor, ripping away furiously at her clothes. Even as her mind froze with disbelief, her training kicked in, and she fought back, trying to jab his eyes with her fingers, twisting away from him with all her force.

Seconds later, Cali came crashing into the room. He cracked the man's wrist, sending the knife onto the floor. Then he grabbed the man by the neck and held him twisting and dangling in the air while he looked closely at Maria. "You OK?"

She nodded and turned away from him, trying to pull her clothes together. Cali's fists were already talking. The conversation didn't last long.

"It's over," she heard Cali say. "Maria, it's over."

She looked up. Her attacker was lying motionless on the floor.

"You sure you're not hurt?" Cali said, looking her over.

"No," she said. "Nothing. Just a few bumps and bruises." But it wasn't true. Inside she was hurting all over. She couldn't stop thinking about the feel of the man's hands on her skin. What if Cali hadn't come in when he did?

The next thing she knew Cali had pushed her out the door and was running with her down the street, practically carrying her with one arm. He hurried her into his car and took off.

"What now?" she managed to say as they went flying down Vista Drive.

"Leave it alone," Cali said forcefully.

She shook her head in refusal.

"Leave it alone!" Cali said again. He was angry. "Look, Maria, was it a dumb thing to do? Yeah, it was a fucking dumb thing to do. You satisfied now?"

She bit her lip.

"And is it something everyone does their first time out? Yeah! It fucking is!!! It's built into us. Every rookie officer goes charging after the one that runs away, especially if he's knocked you down first. You can't help it. Next time you'll know better. Next time you'll wait for backup."

She was too tired to argue further, but when they got to her house, she refused to get out of the car until he answered her questions. "I have to know," she said. "Did the guy I was chasing get away?"

Cali nodded.

"Any idea who he was?"

Cali shook his head.

"Why did that other man attack me?"

"I'll answer your question," Cali said. "But first I want to show you something." He bent his head down so she could see his scalp. It was crisscrossed everywhere with tiny, fine white scars.

"Cali! What happened?"

He lifted up his head and looked into her eyes with deadly seriousness. "That's what happens when you're a little kid and someone in your house smashes bottles on your head."

She didn't know what to say. She felt a stab of pain, thinking that Cali had been hurt like that in his own home when he was little, but what did it have to do with her question?

"That must have been rough," she said finally.

"It was. It was very rough. But those scars taught me early on that there are people out there who will hurt you if they can. They taught me that there is no free pass through life. Everyone gets hurt sooner or later, Maria. Everyone carries scars with them. Most scars are inside where other people can't see them, and that makes it easier to forget about them or pretend they're not really there. But some of us, like you and me, we have scars on the outside too, scars that show. That means..."

"What are you talking about?" Maria interrupted him. "I don't have any scars. On the inside maybe, but not outside. You mean the scar on my forehead? I had an accident when I was little, that's all. You're not talking about accidental scars, are you?"

"No, you're right, I'm not taking about 'accidental' scars although there are people who would say no scars are accidental. But that's something else. What I'm talking about are the scars that come from someone hurting you on purpose. And the point I'm trying to make is that how we feel about those scars can make a big difference."

"I don't get what you're trying to say, Cali. And you still haven't answered my question.

"Look, when you asked me why that other man attacked you, I thought I heard something in your voice that was asking, is there something about me that attracts danger? Am I marked in some way? I wanted to be sure you understood the difference."

Maria shook her head. "I don't know what you're talking about."

Cali was silent, reconsidering. Then he said, "OK, I got off track. What I wanted to say is that scars can make some people feel "marked." If you feel that way, if you feel you're marked for disaster, you'll feel helpless, and then bad things really will happen to you.

"But scars can also serve as warning signals, they can serve as reminders that you always have to be on guard. At least that's how it works for me. I'm not afraid of the battle, Soli. But I want to be ready for it when it comes. You need to do the same."

"You still haven't answered my question."

"I'm getting there. There are reasons why that man attacked you, concrete, practical reasons that have nothing to do with you or any scars you might have. Those cries and whistles you heard? Those were signals. That guy probably got an order to slow you down so the other one could get away."

"But you stopped him. Now the gang will be out to get you."

"Look, the guy who pulled you inside was one of the gang's lookouts. Now he's on his way to the hospital with some broken bones and a concussion. He's lost face, that's how it works with the gangs, so there's a chance he'll try to get back at me someday. I'm not worried. I'll be waiting for him. Then business will go on as usual."

"Will there be trouble with Danforth?"

Cali shook his head. "No problems there. The guy attacked you. He had a knife. All I had was my hands. Besides, no one is going to care about this one. He doesn't have any friends in the neighborhood to complain for him. Your biggest problem is the press. Too many people in Vereda know your story. Dan will make sure the reporters keep focused on the raid itself, not on what was happening down the street."

Cali got out of the car and walked with her up to the door. "Danforth wants to talk to you tonight," Cali said. "That OK with you?"

She nodded numbly. "I need to go inside for a few minutes first."

"Go ahead. I'll tell you when he gets here."

Maria went into the bedroom and lay down on her bed, staring up at the ceiling. She had to regain control before Danforth arrived. Cali had been introducing her to the unspoken rules of working the street. She saw that now. It wasn't for everyone. There were plenty of cops at high levels who had never written an arrest report, never worked the street at all. But Cali thought she could do it. For him, Vista Drive had been an initiation. He had saved her tonight, but he wouldn't always be there. If she wanted to do that kind of work, she would have to learn to hold her own.

A short time later, she heard Danforth's car coming down the road. She went into the bath-room and slapped cold water on her face. Then she headed outside to meet Danforth.

"I'm going to take a look around the garden," Cali said. "Call me when you're through talking."

Danforth nodded. He turned to Maria. "How's it going?"

"Sarge, about what happened," she said right away. "I know I had no business taking off like that. I blew it!" Her voice was heavy with discouragement.

"Maria, when you talk like that, it really makes me wonder whether you're cut out for this kind of work at all," Danforth said sharply. "You think you're the only one who got caught up in what happened tonight? A lot of people got hurt. One of the men from Narcotics could lose his eye. What do you think happens on a raid anyway?! It's not about you, don't you know that yet? Let it go, Maria. You'll be more careful next time, that's all that matters."

She nodded. Danforth's words gave her a sense of relief.

"Cali, I'm off," Danforth called out as he headed for his car. "Get some sleep, Maria," he said to her over his shoulder. "You don't have to come in tomorrow, you know that, right?"

"I'm planning on coming in, Sarge," she told him.

"Your choice," he said. "But knowing you, you'll be there, no matter how you feel." He shook his head as he got into his car.

After Danforth drove away, Cali said, "I'll be here all night if you need me."

"You don't have to sit outside," she said, but he didn't answer. "I'm planning on coming in tomorrow," she added as she went inside.

"Lock the door," he reminded her as he pulled it shut. "I'll see you tomorrow at the station."

6

TUESDAY MORNING
Vereda District Station
Hidalgo Housing projects

BEING CAUGHT IN RUSH HOUR TRAFFIC made Maria edgy and impatient. Even when there was no scheduled appointment, she would start to feel she was losing the race against time, that it would be too late when she got there.

But this morning she had good reason for wanting to get to work as soon as possible. She wanted to know what people at the station were saying about the raid.

The traffic was worse than usual. Construction was forcing her to merge early into the long line of cars moving towards the city, and the whole lane had slowed to a crawl. She rubbed the back of her neck. It still ached where the old man's rock had hit her. The bruising was painful and the cut deeper than she'd realized at first.

She twisted uneasily in her seat, fiddling with the radio dial. Nothing about the raid on Vista Drive. Weather reports dominated the stations. Everyone was talking about the heat wave that would come in tonight. The temperature would break records.

The Squad Room on the second floor of the station was crowded. Maria headed straight for her desk without making eye contact with anyone. If people were looking at her critically, she didn't want to know about it. She picked up the stack of reports waiting for her on her desk and started going through them, but it was useless. She was just shuffling paper, not absorbing anything. She couldn't concentrate. Her mind kept going back to the desert sky, the owl, the man who'd attacked her.

Involuntarily she looked up. Jamison, the man at the desk next to hers, made a point of catching her eye. "Welcome to the club," he said with a smile. "We've all been there, going after the one who got away."

"That's for sure," added Pezda, a veteran female detective, who had always seemed critical and distant. "We lose ourselves in the chase and then get clobbered."

"Take me with you next time," an attractive younger officer named Hatcher, pleaded dramatically. "Let's go into the woods together!"

Everyone in the room started laughing, even Pezda. Maria couldn't believe it. There was actually a good feeling in the room. It began to rub off on her. She leaned back in her chair and relaxed slightly. It was the first time she'd really felt at home in the unit.

It was close to noon when Al Diaz walked into the Squad Room and headed for Danforth's office. "Good work, kid!" he called out to her over his shoulder. A compliment from Al! Maria felt like she'd crossed some sort of an initiation line.

It had taken her time to feel comfortable working with Al. He was a small, wiry man who dressed carefully for work in a three-piece suit, and he wore his dark hair neatly pulled back into a ponytail. But the rest of his appearance was in sharp contrast to the elegance of his suit and his hair.

What you noticed first was his left hand. It was badly scarred, and with the middle two fingers missing, it looked more like a claw than a hand. And he always had a cigarette. If it wasn't hanging out of his mouth, it was sitting in the curved grip of his hand.

Cali knew the story behind Al's hand, but he wouldn't give her the details. "That's Al's story to tell if he wants to," Cali said when she asked him about it.

It wasn't Al's smoking or even his hand that bothered her. She could get used to those things. It was the color of his eyes, a light brown flecked with gold of such clarity that his eyes seemed more yellow than brown, almost animal-like in nature. At first his yellow eyes had unsettled her. They made her think of the bad dreams she'd suffered as a child, dreams of coyotes, wolves, and owls.

Like everyone else in the station, she knew that Al had been married and divorced twice, but that was all she knew. He was formal in his manner, an intensely private person, and she had been careful to keep her distance.

After lunch, Danforth called her into his office. Cali and Al were already there.

"We've been talking about the raid," Danforth told her. "Trying to figure out who tipped us off about the lack of surveillance on Vista last night. We assumed it was a rival cartel, but Al's been out there all morning, and he says no one's claiming credit. Not only, he can't find his informant."

"Crossed signals?" Maria asked. Gil Gomez-Gil ran the city's major cartel, but he spent most of his time in the small border town of Lastup. His lieutenants ran the business for him in Vereda. "Maybe *Los Viboras* got the wrong info," she added.

"Possible," Cali said. "How well did you know this guy?" he asked Al.

"He's someone I worked with a long time," Al said in a bitter voice. "He was part of Gil's cartel or at least I thought he was." He dug into his pocket for a cigarette but came up empty-handed. Danforth was tolerant, but no one could smoke in the building anymore.

"Let's not forget one thing," Danforth said. The satisfaction he was feeling about the raid was clearly visible on his face. "The chief is happy. Al came through for the unit in a big way. We picked up a large cache of drugs, cash and guns. And *la finca* on Vista Drive is down for good, with most of the guys who were running the business in jail."

"You suggesting it was the chief pulled off the protection?" Cali said with a wicked grin.

Even Al had to crack a smile at that one.

"Now let's see if our mysterious benefactor can help us out with the other hot spot in town," Dan went on. "With Vista Drive out of action, the Hidalgo projects on the west side are going to be the only place in town to do business. That means all our attention is going to shift over there. And since the projects are Gil's home base when he's here in Vereda, all our attention is also going to be on Mr. Untouchable Gomez-Gil."

"And on Snake Baby," Al interrupted. "Snake Baby and *Los Viboras* run the cartel business for Gil everywhere in Vereda. Not just Vista Drive. Out at the Hidalgo projects too. That means more pressure on Snake Baby."

"Snake Baby," Cali said, spitting out the words as if they had a bad taste in his mouth. He looked disgusted. "He's gotta be busy these days. Drugs. Dogfights. Cockfights. Human trafficking. Anything that gives him a chance to hurt people or animals. It's his specialty. Could be why Gil's put him in charge of business in Vereda. But Gil is usually smarter than that. Snake Baby is *loco*. Everyone knows it. He loses his head over nothing. Always fighting with the *coyotes*. Rumor has it he even went into the ring to fight with a cock."

"Could be," Al said. "But we'll get him. Cali's right. Gil's made a mistake this time. Snake Baby is unreliable. He's nuts. He'll bring them all down sooner or later."

"There's something else," Danforth said. Maria looked at him curiously. All the satisfaction she'd seen in him earlier was gone.

"Homeland Security called me this morning," Danforth said. "A joint Federal Task Force is investigating the possibility of a high-level mole in one of their organizations. They want someone from local law enforcement on the task force. They want Cali in particular. The task force is operating out of Lastup. I don't like the idea of losing Cali even for a week, but I don't have much choice. Cali, go ahead and fill in the details for Maria and Al."

Maria swallowed hard. Ever since she'd been in the unit, Cali had always been somewhere nearby.

Cali nodded. "I've already spoken with the Fed heading up the task force," he began.

As Cali went on to explain more about the task force investigation, Danforth thought about Maria. The raid on Vista Drive had made *Los Viboras* nervous. Angry. This wasn't the best time to send anyone from his unit into the Hidalgo projects. But at least he'd been able to refuse the Fed's request to send Maria out there alone. "She can go with Al," he'd argued over the phone. "Both of them were assigned to the Juan Alvarez missing person case. That gives them a motive for a visit."

"Al, why don't you and Maria take a trip out to the Hidalgo projects this afternoon?" Danforth said unexpectedly, interrupting Cali.

Al looked at him, surprised.

"You up to it?" Dan asked Maria.

"Yes, Sarge."

"And Al, you and Maria handled the Juan Alvarez case, right? The pilot for G&G Airlines who disappeared?"

Al nodded.

"OK, then. You and Maria are going out to Rosa Alvarez's apartment in N. Building to ask if she's heard anything from her husband. Let her know we're still looking for him. And while you're there, take a casual look around. See if you can learn something that explains what was behind the tip on the Vista Drive raid."

"That'll work," Maria said. "I've been stopping by to visit with Rosa and...." Her face was growing hot. She didn't need to explain. She stood up to leave.

"I'll follow you over there," Al said. "I'll take my own car."

They were almost to the projects when she got Al's call. "I'll meet you in a few minutes," he said. "I have to make a stop first."

"OK," she said. "See you soon."

The Hidalgo Public Housing Project took up an entire block. It was the largest housing complex in Vereda. Two police cruisers sat parked 24-7 in front of each of the four housing units that made up the project. The police presence was as much a part of the project landscape as its four dreary housing units and the intense graffiti on the walls.

Maria drove slowly past N. Building. The two patrol cars near the front door were empty. Four or five homeboys stood on the sidewalk near N. Building, smoking and talking, punctuating their conversation with their hands. They were wearing red beads, and their clothes were red and black, the colors of *Los Viboras*. Only homeboys with status could wear that much red. These men were part of the leadership.

Maria turned left to circle the block. The streets of the *barrio* were burning in the afternoon heat. As she came up to N. Building a second time, she slowed to a crawl. Al wasn't there. The homeboys were still standing in a group on the sidewalk, but the patrol officers were back in their cruisers. Maria pulled over and parked next to them.

One of the officers opened his car window and leaned out to talk to her.

"I'm waiting for Al Diaz," she told him. "We're going into N. Building to talk to some of the residents."

"Got it," the officer said and closed the window.

Maria sat in her Jeep, thinking about Al. There was a lot he could teach her if he wanted to, but it wasn't easy to work with him. It still angered her that he was so often late. Half the time he didn't show up at all. He was completely unpredictable, but that was the secret of his success. For years he'd managed to keep the identity of his informants secret in spite of the inevitable leaks and double agents in the informant game, in large part because he would meet them at odd hours and in unexpected places, and he never confided anything about them to anyone, not even to Danforth.

Once Al had told Maria that information couldn't be protected anywhere, not even at the station, not even in the Squad Room. "You have no idea how easy it is to corrupt people," he'd told her. "I have to assume the worst about everyone, no exceptions."

Running informants meant he had to keep his work completely separate from the rest of his life. It was the nature of his work. It was a matter of survival. She understood all that, and she had tried hard to adjust to his way of doing things, but still, he was late, he smoked in the car, and most of all, to her he seemed cold-hearted in his dealings with people. Once she'd accused him of not caring enough. He'd pushed back, accusing her of getting too involved, like stopping by on a daily basis to see Rosa Alvarez.

"Not true," she'd told him. "It's not our case anymore, for one thing. I'm just trying to keep in touch with the family in case they get new information."

"I see," he'd said sarcastically.

She wasn't surprised when Al called her on his cell a few minutes later, bypassing radio contact. He told her he would be late. She closed her phone with a snap, angry and frustrated. Al was the only person in the unit who could consistently disobey instructions and get away with it, but he was careful not to advertise it. She checked her watch. By now it was obvious. Today he was with an informant. Today she would be on her own.

But she would not go back to the station empty-handed. She could go in and talk with Rosa and her little boy Ramón by herself. She'd done it before, and there had never been any problems.

The Hidalgo Housing Project was Snake Baby's turf. In the projects, he had lookouts and protection. He was untouchable. But in the projects, he was also working for Gil. He had to follow Gil's orders, and everyone knew that Gil told his people to leave the cops alone as long as they didn't interfere with business. Gil tried to avoid unnecessary confrontations with the cops. That meant she had some protection as well.

She got out of her car and looked around. The gangbangers on the sidewalk stopped talking and stared at her, their faces closed and sullen. They'd already recognized her as a cop even though most people didn't see her that way. In the short-sleeved shirt and slacks she wore to work, she usually passed as a civilian unless the gun and spare magazine on her belt became visible. But not here. Homeboys like the ones staring at her knew how to recognize cops no matter how they were dressed.

Someone had scrawled the letters "HH" in fluorescent red over the front entrance of N. building, shorthand for "Hidalgo Hell." Angry black graffiti covered everything else you could reach.

One of the patrol officers got out of his car and walked over to her.

"I'm going ahead," she told him. "Al will be here soon."

"You want company?"

She shook her head and headed over to the front door of N. Building, carefully scanning the top of the building. She made a point of looking up when she was working. Even a jar hurled out of an apartment could be dangerous.

She caught the edge of a shape moving out of sight from one of the windows on the upper floor. Today the apartments up there would be like a furnace, but a lookout would be posted there anyway. There were always lookouts posted around the projects. They were probably checking her out right now.

The front door of N. Building had been propped open with a wooden crate. Maria went inside. The lobby was empty. A list of apartment numbers was taped to the front wall. No names. Rows of mailboxes lined the wall to her right. Most of them stood open, their doors missing or broken. A pile of mail sat stacked in the corner on the floor. Maria picked up a few envelopes and read the postmarks. Last week's mail.

She looked outside. The homeboys had moved closer. Now they were standing near the front door, looking in at her with undisguised hostility. She could hear the patrol cars open and close. The four patrol officers were walking over to N. Building to check on her.

Not another incident, she couldn't help thinking. Not after last night. If only she could get back to her car before things turned ugly.

She heard someone running down the stairs. It was Luis Santiago, the building manager. He went past her, through the lobby, and out the door without slowing down, yelling at the homeboys even before he reached them.

Luis was a small man with thinning hair, and he looked even smaller next to the young, muscular gangbangers surrounding him. His clothes were just as unimpressive, a sleeveless undershirt and a pair of shorts, with some middle-aged paunch hanging out above the waistband. But he moved with the agility of a much younger man, and he had a penetrating yell, a ferocious way of spitting out words. Finally, after some last threatening glances at Maria, the gangbangers began to move away from the building.

Luis stayed outside until the homeboys were back on the sidewalk. Then he came into the lobby to talk to Maria. As usual, he was jangling a large key ring in his pocket. When he started talking, you could see the spaces where he was missing teeth, but gold flashed from his mouth when he smiled.

"*Hola Luis*," she said, returning his smile. She studied him curiously. "How'd you do that?"

"Too hot for a fight," he said with a quick flash of gold. "You looking for Rosa?"

She nodded.

"She's out at the store with Ana Fuentes and the two boys."

"I'll wait," she said. She looked at the stack of mail on the floor. "I see things are still the same around here."

"First-class mail, second-class citizens, what do you expect?" Luis said.

Maria nodded. "Everything OK?"

He shrugged. "Summer means more new kids, you know?"

"I know," she said. "Anything else? Can you talk?"

Luis looked around again before he gave her a quick nod. There was no one else in the lobby or on the stairs.

Maria and Luis often talked like this, meeting in the lobby when it was empty. She didn't know how he pulled it off, the man in the middle on good terms with both the cops and *Los Viboras*. "Snake Baby must know that you and Danforth are old friends," she couldn't help saying.

"Can't keep something like that secret."

"Snake Baby doesn't mind?"

"I guess I'm the public face of the projects," Luis said carefully. "Gil wants order around here. His instructions are for his people to obey me. If I say move on, they do it quick. But I don't "see" anything around here either. I keep my mouth shut. Only if Dan asks. Then I try to answer if I think it's safe. I owe him my life. That puts me in his debt."

"You've got guts," Maria said.

"I've got that for sure," Luis said with an unhappy glance at his paunch. "What do you want, Detective?"

"Some information about the Vista Drive raid. We can't seem to trace the source."

"No one here knows anything about that either," Luis said. "All I can tell you is that no one is very happy."

He started moving down the hall towards the back door of the building. "I gotta go, Detective. But I have something for Dan to think about. One of my tenants wants her stuff from the storage building, you know, the one at the end of the parking lot? She's afraid to go there by herself. So are most of the other residents. I'm the only one who can come and go as I please. Take care, Detective. I gotta go." She heard the back door open and close. He was gone.

7

TUESDAY AFTERNOON
Hidalgo Housing Project
N. Building

MARIA LEFT THE BUILDING and walked over to the cruisers. Two patrol officers were standing there, waiting for her. "What's your name, Officer?" she asked the one closest to her.

"Bryan Robertson."

"Robertson, do you check out the storage building in back of N. Building?"

"Yes, always."

"Same time every day?"

He nodded.

The officer standing next to Robertson seemed uncomfortable with her questions. He kept looking at the homeboys on the sidewalk.

"Why?" she asked both of them. "You'll never find anything if they know you're coming."

Robertson had blond curly hair and fair skin. His face was covered with freckles. "Sometimes the storage building is used as a safe house," he said reluctantly. "As a hiding place where illegals can go when they hear that *La Migra*, Immigration officials, are on the way. We don't want to run into the illegals. It's bad publicity for us. Makes us look like we're hunting them down."

Maria was silent. She knew their orders came from above. No profiling, No questions for "good citizens" about their legal status, especially if they had information about a criminal investigation. She had mixed feelings about how easily illegal immigrants were able to merge into the community in Vereda, but she accepted the fact that much of her job involved trying to keep some semblance of law and order in the lives of all the residents, legal and illegal. Most of them trusted her, and that had come in handy for her unit more than once.

But she also knew that a controversial new ordinance was being considered in a neighboring state. It was an ordinance that would allow, even constrain, local police to stop and ask papers from anyone they suspected of being an illegal immigrant.

She didn't feel qualified to comment on the long-term results of such a law, but short-term? One thing she knew for sure was that law enforcement would lose a lot of valuable information, information that protected all the citizens of Ciudad Nueva, not just those living in Vereda. The connection was obvious. Drugs cost money. Trying to get money to buy drugs led to crime in all parts of the city. And she had worked hard to develop trust among the illegals who knew the most about what was really happening on the street and along the border.

She looked around. Still no sight of Al. No sign of Rosa either. She was already in her car and ready to leave when she heard the gangbangers on the sidewalk openly jeering at her. So much for unnecessary confrontations with the cops. Maybe Gil wasn't in charge of running things out here as much as he thought he was.

Maria stared back at the homeboys. The gangs were so damned arrogant. If they ended up anywhere near a jail, they lawyered up faster than she could write up her report. Almost none of the upper level dealers did jail time.

She got out of her car and walked back to the patrol officers still standing outside their cruisers. "I want to see the storage building," she told them.

There was complete silence. No one said anything.

"Robertson?" she said sharply. She could tell he was unhappy about her request.

"You can see it from here," he said. The storage building was in the far right-hand corner of the parking lot. Most of the parking lot was empty.

"All I can see from here is a front entrance," she said. "Can you get into that building from the back?"

"Not that I know of," Robertson said. "Like I told you, officers check out the building every morning and again at night. We walk around it and through it. If there's a back exit somewhere, it's well hidden." He hesitated. "But it wouldn't surprise me. We really don't know all that much about what goes on. We stay outside. Snake Baby and his gang are inside the buildings 24-7. That makes a difference."

She nodded. "Agreed. But I still want the two of you to check it out again. Right now. Look carefully, very carefully for any sign of a back entrance into the storage building."

"We'll get right on it," Robertson said. Nobody moved. "It's not the scheduled time," Robertson added hesitantly. His voice sounded very young.

"I know, but check it out anyway. And make absolutely sure no one's inside. I want to take a fast look around myself before I leave."

Robertson nodded. "Come on, Ben," he said to the officer standing next to him.. "Let's get it over with," he added under his breath as they walked away.

Maria studied the building while she waited for them to return. It was a rectangular-shaped structure with a peeling, corrugated tin roof. The back part of the building had external walls made out of plywood. The front part of the building consisted of vertical support beams covered by thick sheets of plastic. Even from where she was standing, she could see through the plastic sheets into the front of the building. It was filled with rows of vertical compartments going from floor to ceiling. The opening to each compartment was covered with something that looked like chicken wire.

"We checked it out," Robertson said when they came back five minutes later. "We didn't see anyone. But we'll keep you company when you go through it."

Maria considered his offer. His orders were to stay out of the building except for the regularly schedule walk-through. Why get him in trouble? "No, I don't think so," she said finally, "but stay close by in case I need you."

She walked quickly over to the storage building, anxious to get through the intense heat rising up from the asphalt surface of the parking lot. Inside the building, there was a semidarkness that left her almost blind after the glare of the parking lot. She had imagined there would be more light coming through the plastic walls.

She turned on her flashlight and started down the first row of storage compartments, peering into them through the chicken wire covering. She saw jars, a rug, boxes, bottles, some old pots.

Nothing out of the ordinary.

She walked down the second row, again looking into each compartment through the wire covering. Again, nothing unusual. No hiding places that she could see. Just storage compartments. As she walked down the third row, she heard a slight rustling from one of the rows ahead of her. When she aimed her flashlight in the direction of the rustling, she saw clearly that the remaining compartments were in the part of the building where the external wall was solid, not plastic. There the darkness was pitch black.

She wouldn't go any further by herself. She had an uneasy feeling about the dark corridor in front of her. She turned around and headed for the front door. She had unsnapped her holster and was reaching for her radio when she heard footsteps coming up fast behind her. She whirled around. The same homeboys who had been on the sidewalk were standing there, sneering at her. So there was a back door after all.

She faced them straight on. "*Ya,* that's close enough," she yelled at them and pulled her gun out of its holster, but before she could get it firmly into her hand, she was shoved hard from behind. The gun slipped out of her hand as her knees cracked against the floor. It was all she could do not to cry out.

The heavy heel of a shoe dug into the small of her back. Someone said, "Get the piece." Then she was being pulled up off the ground, her arms pinned so tightly behind her it felt like daggers twisting in her shoulders.

Now she could see the man who must have been waiting for her inside the building. He was holding a cigarette in his hand and wearing a simple eye mask, but she recognized him immediately. Snake Baby.

Shorter than the others and muscular, like a boxer, he was wearing a tight red body shirt, cut off at the shoulders. A tattooed snake slithered down his arm. She could see the head of the snake on the back of his hand. In the snake's fangs there were two interconnected hearts, one surrounded by roses, the other by thorns. The gang's highest symbol of power.

One of the men kept her hands pinned behind her back while Snake Baby and the others circled around her, rhythmically taunting her in a cruel sort of rap. Snake Baby kept staring at her through the mask with such burning hostility, she could feel it on her skin.

What was he waiting for? As if in answer to the question, the taunting unexpectedly stopped. The homeboys stood motionless in place. The dark stillness surrounding her seemed unreal, like a nightmare. Snake Baby took a step closer. He had her gun in his hand.

The sound of a cell phone broke the silence.

"*Qué?*" Snake Baby said into his phone, keeping his eyes fixed on Maria.

She could hear the voice on the phone yelling, "*Sal de ahí ahora!! La policia vienne.* Get out of there. The police are coming!" It was one of the lookouts warning them to go.

"*Está bien. Vámonos!* We're going, we're going!" Snake Baby screamed back into the phone. Maria could hear the patrol officers running across the parking lot. The homeboys looked at Snake Baby, waiting for him to make the first move.

Snake Baby kept his stare on Maria while he closed his phone, moving his eyes slowly up and down her body as if he had all the time in the world. She flinched involuntarily. He looked deliberately at her breasts, then hurled the gun at her face. "*Adiós puta, adiós baby,*" he spit out at her before he turned and ran down the corridor towards the back of the building. The other men followed him outside just as the patrol officers came storming into the building.

"Let's wait inside my patrol car," Robertson said, walking close beside her. Maria nodded. Her forehead was bleeding where the gun had hit her. She wiped away the blood with her sleeve.

She could already hear sirens coming closer. She knew that once the message went out that an officer had been attacked, every cop in the city would show up at N. Building. She was grateful for their loyalty. It was part of what she loved about her job. But then the press would follow. And the crowd of spectators. She wished she could disappear.

The first to arrive was Al Diaz. He came sweeping into the parking lot like the fiery tailwind of a thunderstorm.

"Maria, what happened?" he said as soon as he saw her sitting in the cruiser, blood on her face. He was as tense as a cat with its back up.

"I'm OK, Al. But when the medics get here, send them away, please?! Can you take care of things? Use your first aid kit? It's mostly just a bruise,"

When Al came back with his first aid kit, she got out of the cruiser and walked over to him, ignoring the fact that her knees felt like someone had hit them with a baseball bat. Her legs wobbled, and she found herself leaning on Al for support.

She studied his face as he put on the bandage, struck by how different he seemed while he was taking care of her. His hands were gentle, his eyes warmer than usual. Even the color of his eyes seemed changed, more golden brown than yellow. By the time the bandage was in place, she was standing steadily.

Al's phone was ringing. He took the call. "I've got to go," he said after he closed his phone. "Robertson and the other officers will stay with you. Dan is on his way." Then he took off, running fast.

Before long, there was so much activity swirling around the projects, Maria couldn't keep track of what was happening. It looked like every cop in the CNPD was there, running through the buildings and parking lots, questioning everyone in sight. In a few minutes the TV cameras and the reporters would join the crowd. So far she had escaped notice, but it wouldn't be long. She hated the thought of everyone staring at her, writing yet again about the little girl lost in the desert.

Just then, Danforth drove up. He left the engine running as he got out of his car and came over to her. "Can you walk to my car?" he asked.

She nodded.

"Good. I'll get you out of here before the press finds you, but first we're going to bring over the homeboys we've picked up so you can see them."

"You've got them already?!"

Danforth looked pleased. "Not bad, I got to admit. We were lucky! Al guessed where they'd be hiding out and led us in the right direction. He went after them like an avenging angel. They were completely off guard, like they never expected us to find them or get there so fast."

Maria's knees were shooting pain, but she kept up a steady pace with Danforth until they reached his car. He picked up his radio. "Keep the press away from me. Send those reporters and their cameras over to E. building where officers are chasing down other suspects. That should give them the action they're looking for. I'll be making an official statement as soon as we're sure what we've got here."

A group of officers came up to the car with the suspects, all in cuffs.

"Are these the ones who attacked you?" Danforth asked Maria.

She looked carefully at the men standing in front of her. She recognized them right away. "Yes," she said. "I'm positive. These are the men who attacked me."

"Good," Danforth said. He turned to the officers. "Throw the book at these bastards. Keep looking for the others. I'll be back in an hour."

Maria was silent as Danforth drove out of the parking lot and headed towards the highway. "We have some talking to do," Danforth said. "My men will follow us. They'll drop your car off, and a few of them will spend the night at your house."

She started to protest. Danforth interrupted her. "I'm running this unit, remember? There will be officers outside your house tonight. Period."

After that, they were both quiet. Maria was numb with disbelief. She had walked through the same storage building other officers walked through every day. But for her, a back door had materialized. For her, Snake Baby had been waiting in the building.

And once again, someone had silently come up on her from behind and pushed her to the ground. Even an owl had crashed into her! How many people had ever been knocked down by an owl?

When her adoptive parents died, she had fought hard against the feeling that some mysterious ill fate had attached itself to her life. She had worked hard to be a success at the Academy, she was dedicated to her job, and she went out of her way to be careful.

It seemed like she'd spent her whole life fighting the feeling that she was powerless to stop bad things from happening to her, that she was marked for failure. And yet they kept happening. A wave of fury and despair swept over her. Why couldn't she get out of it, this circle of misfortune that seemed to haunt her? Every accomplishment secretly devoured and such a lonely battle. Danforth and Cali were on her side, she knew that. But in the end, the battle inside was hers alone to fight.

"You look dazed, kid," Danforth said out of the silence, interrupting her thoughts. "I'm not surprised. Two attacks in two days. Most of the unit doesn't see that much action in a year! Let's talk. There was a fourth man, right?"

She nodded.

"Snake Baby?"

"I think so. No, I'm sure of it."

"You told Al he was wearing a mask?"

"Right."

"Could you make a positive ID?"

She shook her head. "No way, the mask confuses things too much.

There was a long pause. "Sarge, I took a chance," Maria managed to say finally. "But it was stupid, I know that."

Danforth nodded. "Yeah, it was stupid. But I can see why you did it. Using a set schedule to check out a storage building that everyone knows is used to hide illegals....that makes all of us look pretty stupid. He paused. "Where was Al?"

"He had to meet someone."

"That damn job of his." Danforth paused. "And you asked Robertson and the others to check out the building before you went into it?"

She nodded.

Danforth was quiet for a few minutes before he went on. "You need to put things in perspective, Maria. There was a lot of stupidity going around tonight. You don't need to take all the credit, you know."

"Thanks, Sarge. I'll try." This time her voice was steady when she spoke,

"You know we won't be able to get anything on Snake Baby for this attack, you understand that, right? The others will swear Snake Baby wasn't there."

She nodded. "I know. He always gets away somehow."

"You worried?"

"Not at all," she said firmly. And it was true. She wasn't frightened of Snake Baby. "He could have hurt me tonight," she added. "But he didn't. He was making a point, that's all. I wish I knew why."

This time after she locked the front door, she barely made it into her bedroom before she crawled onto her bed and fell asleep.

8 | WEDNESDAY
Vereda District Station

DANFORTH WAS AT HIS DESK early the next morning, making calls and pulling files right away. Things were happening fast, unexpected things, and the phone call late last night had caught him at a vulnerable moment.

He had learned how to live alone after his wife died, mostly because of his work. It kept him busy. But at home, the nights often felt heavy with sadness. He'd been feeling that way last night when the phone rang. He hadn't been able to sleep at all after that, and he was tired, but the issues raised by the phone call had to be clarified as soon as possible.

He began to read through the files on his desk. When the words began to blur, he forced himself to focus. He didn't want things slipping out of his control. Working with the Feds was always complicated. Now he'd been informed that Maria would be involved. He picked up a thick folder labeled "Snake Baby." If there was an evil seed in the world, that evil seed was Snake Baby. If only Snake Baby hadn't made things personal.

Danforth watched Maria come into the Squad Room shortly before ten. She went over to her desk without making eye contact with anyone. Typical Maria. She'd been through a lot over the past two days, anyone would feel defensive, but that wasn't a good reason to pull away. It wasn't helpful.

Maria's assimilation into the group had been difficult, in part because her appearance caught people off guard. She looked very young, far too young to work in a Major Crimes unit, and while her face was appealing with its high cheekbones and wide-set eyes, she was lean and slightly awkward in her movements, more like an adolescent boy than a mature woman. Unless she was running. When she was running, sure-footed and fast, she looked as if she had been freed from something.

By itself her appearance wouldn't have mattered. But Maria was one of only two women in the unit, and at 29, she was the youngest member of the unit as well. That meant she drew curiosity from all quarters. Her response was respectful but guarded. She did not invite closeness from anyone. It was hard to know what she was thinking. It was hard to know who she was. Danforth and Cali had mentored her closely over the past 6 months, and even they still saw her as a puzzle with missing pieces.

If you couldn't get by the shyness and the reserve, Danforth thought, you might think she lacked depth, that she was all technique and no feeling. But he knew differently. He'd seen her purposeful and angry, like the time she'd rescued the little boy out at the projects. And when she opened up about herself, her eyes spoke of such pain, it seemed they must belong to someone else entirely.

Around noontime, Danforth stood up and looked out the small second-story window in his office. Today the usually brilliant sky was in full retreat. The pressure of the heat was unbearable. Only the Sierras west of the city still flaunted their blue colors.

The heat wave had come in last night. Now the sky was white with heat, as if the summer blues had been sucked up into a white sheet stretched tight over the city. Heat didn't stretch, but if it did, Danforth would have said that it was stretched to the breaking point. All they could do was wait for it to snap.

He studied the burning white sky overhead. Its whiteness made him think of the great white whale in Melville's novel, *Moby Dick*. He'd been forced to read the book in high school, and at first, he'd hated everything about it. Too long. Too boring. Who cared about whaling anyway?

But when he finished it, he was surprised to find that something in the book had caught his attention. It had stayed with him ever since. Maybe it was because he became a cop. He didn't know why, not really, but one thing he did know. The longer he was a cop, the more truth he found in Melville's writing. A few hundred years ago, Melville couldn't have imagined what life in 2009 would be like, but that didn't matter. Melville knew the world for what it was.

Danforth had a lot of years under his belt, and what he saw never changed. Most people closed their eyes to the presence of evil in the world. They denied it existed even when it sat down at the table with them. Most cops ended up feeling like their eyelids had been taped open. They had to deal with the messy results of evil on a daily basis. After a while they couldn't avoid seeing it everywhere.

By now Danforth had read *Moby Dick* so often, he knew parts of it by memory. From time to time he even quoted passages from the book to the members of his unit, ignoring their loud sighs and moans. He still pretended ignorance of their secret nickname for him, "Toby Dick."

He didn't mind the teasing. Melville's novel had been his first great lesson. The character of Captain Ahab had taught him that sometimes you have to ignore the warning signs and keep on going anyway. Sometimes you have to die for what you believe is true.

But Melville's words also ripped away the false cover of the world, teaching him that if you looked at things straight, you could see the signs and symbols that warned of approaching danger. Like that white sky outside his window. Any sailor forced to steer his ship through water as white as that sky would be on high alert until he could find blue water again. Danforth felt the same way.

He looked around his office. It was a small room, too small for someone with his level of responsibility. His rumpled jacket hanging from a hook on the back of his office door was a permanent fixture in the room. It was too hot to wear a jacket anywhere, but he kept it there anyway, just in case he had to meet with the press or someone higher up in the scheme of things.

That didn't happen often. Danforth liked to work cases, and he was good at it. His unit admired and respected him. But he didn't waste time cozying up to administrators, especially the ones who had never worked the street. And even though it made his numbers look bad, he continued to take the cases nobody else wanted, the cases that didn't solve fast or easy. So the hats made him senior supervisor of his own handpicked Major Crimes Unit and set him aside. He couldn't find a good reason to retire, especially now that his wife, Nora, was gone, but in one way, it really didn't matter. Whether he retired today or ten years from now, he would finish up his career in this office.

He heard a light tapping on his office door. Maria was standing there signaling that she was leaving the station.

"Wait, Maria!" Danforth called to her. "Why do you want to go outside in this heat? It's hot, it's noontime, wait inside." But she was already gone. He could hear her flying down the stairs. He looked at his watch. He would let her go for now. There was still time to set things right.

That morning he had assigned her to go back to N. Building to see Rosa. "It's not great timing after yesterday," he'd acknowledged, "but your reputation with the residents makes your visit essential."

A short while later, she'd told him that Al had called. He wanted to go with her. He would pick her up at the station. Danforth had said nothing. At the time the situation had seemed too complicated to explain.

Now he looked back up at the sky and sighed. Maria was his best recruit by far, and the unit provided her with a family of sorts, something she badly needed. She'd had a rougher start than any child deserved, but given her history, she was making progress. Even if it took her longer than most to make her place in it, his unit should eventually be a good fit.

But the hunt for the mole and the unexpected discovery of the bodies in Lastup over the weekend meant that she would soon be severely tested. He sure as hell hoped she was ready. One way or another, she was going to end up squarely in the middle of things. "What a goddamn mess!" Danforth said out loud in frustration.

He looked at his watch again and took out his phone. It was time.

9 | WEDNESDAY
Vereda District Station

MARIA LIKED ASSIGNMENTS that took her out of the station. It was the atmosphere inside that disheartened her. The original building had been constructed with small windows and strong doors as a warehouse for the railroad. Ten years ago the city had renovated the building into the local police station, but the small windows remained. May or December, inside the station it felt gray.

With the cool air of the station still clinging to her skin, she'd rushed outside to meet Al a few minutes before twelve, but as soon as she stepped out the door, she'd felt strangely trapped by the scorching heat. She tried to clear her mind. Fighting the sun was wasted effort. And sometimes when the sun was very strong, sharp pieces of memory caught at her before she could protect herself.

From his window on the second floor, Danforth saw Al's car come into sight, taking the corner on two wheels. He hit the direct contact button for Maria.

She opened her cell phone. "Sarge?"

"Change of plans, Maria. I want you to go out and see Rosa Alvarez by yourself. She's there today. She'll be waiting for you."

Al pulled up to the curb, brakes screeching, and threw open the passenger side door. Maria stared up at Danforth's window with a puzzled expression on her face.

"Tell Al to park his car and come up to my office," Danforth told her.

She leaned into the car and spoke to Al. Then she stood up and spoke into her phone. "Al says he wants to come with me. After yesterday, he's worried about Snake Baby."

Danforth could feel his cheeks flush. The members of his unit were supposed to go out to the projects in pairs, and today Maria was in a bad spot. Everyone knew who she was, and yesterday had made it clear that there was bad blood between her and Snake Baby. He wasn't happy with the idea of Maria going out to Snake Baby's territory alone, but he had no choice. The phone calls had made that clear. In this case, the Feds had the final word.

"I need Al here now," Danforth said firmly. "Tell him to come up to my office. Maria, take your car and go out to see Rosa Alvarez. You can go home from there."

Al drove away slowly, looking unconvinced.

"What's going on?" Maria said, looking back up at his window.

"It's complicated," Danforth said after a brief hesitation. "A short time ago, Rosa Alvarez called

39

the office looking for you. She heard about Snake Baby. She wanted to know how you were do-ing. I told her I'd send you out there to see her. You've gone to visit Rosa by yourself more than once or twice over the past week, right? In spite of my advice to the contrary?"

"Right" Maria admitted, "but only on my own time."

"OK, Maria, make it clear that also your visit with Rosa today is personal, that you're on your own time as usual, understand? Everyone out there knows that you've been checking in with Rosa on a regular basis lately, so that shouldn't be a problem, right?"

Maria nodded. "Right."

Danforth pressed on. "But anything you learn when you talk to Rosa today, I want you to keep to yourself. You report back only to me."

In the silence that followed, Danforth imagined that he could see Maria wince.

"Got it, Sarge," she said after a moment. "I'll call you."

"Ok, then, later." Danforth closed his phone. He sighed heavily. He kept telling Maria not to get personally involved with her cases, then he used her involvement with the community to help solve cases. So did Al and the others. When they wanted information from the residents, they called on Maria. No wonder she was confused about where to draw the line.

Danforth sat down and stared at the wall. He felt deflated. It was one thing when Maria went out there on her own time. But today she was on the clock, and he had just assigned her to go out there again by herself.

At least they had a contact who could keep an eye on her. Quickly Danforth called Luis. When he'd explained what he needed, he closed his phone. Then he radioed the officers who were stationed in the patrol cars at N. Building.

After that, he felt better. He pulled the stack of informant files sitting on his desk towards him and began to go through them. He and Al had a lot of work in front of them. It was time to get started.

10 | WEDNESDAY
Hidalgo Housing Project
N. Building

MARIA FELT UNEASY AS SHE DROVE OUT to the Hidalgo Housing Project. Why had Danforth changed her assignment like that at the last minute? He was always reminding her to partner up when she went out to the projects. Yet today he was sending her there alone even after yesterday's encounter with Snake Baby.

In the distance off to her right, several gray hills bumped up along the horizon. Tourists often found them a suggestive sight, especially at twilight with the wide expanse of desert stretching out behind them. The residents knew the hills were just garbage dumps.

Maria thought about Lastup, where Cali would be working on the task force. Sooner or later, the violence from Lastup and the borderlands spilled over into the city. The *coyotes* worked near the border, but some of them lived in Lastup, and most of the upper echelon of the drug cartel lived in Ciudad Nueva.

Beyond the dumps was the desert, blazing white under the unrelenting sun. Maria always paid attention to the desert. It was the desert that had made her decide to become a cop. It was the desert that had changed her life forever.

When she got to N. Building, Maria parked near the cruisers, then headed straight for Rosa's apartment on the second floor. Before she could knock, the door opened and a little boy with curly black hair and a wide grin flew out of the apartment.

"*Pà donde vas chico?*" Maria said, scooping Ramón up in her arms. "You don't want to see me?"

Ramón put his arms around her neck. "I don't want to go, Detective Maria. It's my *Mami*. She's making me go play with Carlito."

Rosa came to the doorway. She was wearing sandals and a light cream-colored shawl over her shoulders. "Maria, welcome," she said, her deep black eyes shining with pleasure.

Rosa wasn't a woman who would stand out in a crowd. She was tiny, and she made herself seem even smaller by the way she kept her eyes down and her feet and arms close to her body. But Maria knew from experience how much the human face revealed, and once she'd had the chance to study Rosa's face close up, she'd been amazed.

Rosa's eyes, together with her wide cheekbones and smooth dark skin, spoke of an ancient tradition that somehow kept her isolated from the modern world around her. Even her grief over her husband's unexplained disappearance had entered her heart directly without leaving its traces on her face. Rosa seemed ageless, as if no matter what else happened, a part of her would always travel through life innocent and untouched by time.

Now Rosa looked sternly at Ramón, but there was laughter in her voice as she scolded him. "Ramón. Stop complaining! You are going to Carlito's house."

Maria put the boy down, keeping her hand on his shoulder. "I'll be back soon, *niño*," she told him before she gave Rosa a hug and a kiss on each cheek. "What the hell," she thought to herself. "And if this isn't procedure, so what?"

In spite of her resolution not to become personally involved in her cases, when Rosa reported her husband missing, Maria had found herself stopping by on a daily basis to see how Rosa was doing and to give her the same bad news: Juan was still missing.

By now Maria felt close to Ramón, and it was clear that Ramón felt the same way. He looked up at her and said, "You are our Lady in Blue, did you know that?"

"Why do you call me that?" Maria said more sharply than she intended. The Lady in Blue was a real person, a nun named Maria who lived in Spain a long time ago and always wore a blue habit. What made her a legend was that she was a cloistered nun who spent her entire life within the walls of her convent, completely closed off from the outside world. Yet she could accurately describe the landmarks and peoples of the American Southwest.

Equally mysterious were the reports from people living in the Southwest, reports that not only described Sister Maria's appearance perfectly but also recounted in detail all the times she had appeared to those in need, especially to lost travelers trying to cross the desert. And when death was inevitable, the Lady in Blue would come to offer consolation and grace to the dying. The story of the Lady in Blue was Maria's favorite childhood story. It reminded her of her mother.

"Why do you call me that?" Maria asked Ramón again.

"Because you're wearing blue?" Ramón said, giving her a wide grin.

He was right. Today she was wearing dark blue pants and a blue shirt. "But I don't always wear blue," she reminded him. "Besides lots of other people wear blue too."

"But you come to us when we need you, just like Sister Maria in the story," Ramón said.

"I'm no Lady in Blue," Maria said firmly. "But I did love that story when I was your age."

"I'm going to make a book for you about the Lady in Blue," Ramón said. His eyes were serious. "To thank you for coming to us."

Maria felt a lump in her throat. "It will be a fine book, Ramón. Thank you."

Rosa gave Ramón a gentle push out into the hall and watched him go to the second floor landing where Ana Fuentes was waiting for him. Ana smiled and waved before she put her arm around Ramón and started up the steps with him to her apartment on the third floor.

"I asked Ana to keep Ramón because I need to talk to you privately," Rosa explained.

"What's wrong, Rosa? Have you heard something about Juan?"

"No, it's not that," Rosa said, shaking her head. "I need to ask you something about Ramón. But first, are you OK? I heard about the storage building."

"I'm fine," Maria told her emphatically. "Snake Baby's boys were just trying to frighten me. It goes with the territory. Now tell me, what about Ramón?"

"Will you sit down?" Rosa asked her shyly. "I'll make us some tea."

Maria sat down. After Rosa put the water to boil, she pulled a chair up next to Maria. "The third graders at Ramón's school are supposed to go on a field trip to Riverside Park on Friday," she said. "It's the last day of school. Ramón's teacher sent me a letter and a permission slip to sign a few weeks ago."

Maria waited for Rosa to continue.

"I signed the slip," Rosa said unhappily. "I signed it, but now I don't want Ramón to go. I'm afraid for him, Maria. I think it could be dangerous for him to go to that park. What should I do? Should I keep him home because I'm afraid? How do I explain it to his teacher? How do I explain it to Ramón?"

"Why would it be dangerous for him, Rosa?" Maria asked gently. "Why would it be dangerous for him to go to the park?"

The tea kettle was whistling. "Let me make the tea," Rosa said. She stood up and went over to the stove. She poured the boiling water into a teapot and brought it over to the table. She put two teacups, some sugar, and some paper napkins on the table in front of Maria. Then she sat down again.

"You will think I am foolish," she said to Maria after a few moments.

"No, Rosa, I won't think you're foolish. Now, tell me, why is it dangerous for Ramón to go to the park?"

Rosa gave a little sigh. How could she explain her dreaming to this detective even if she was her friend? The police didn't believe in dreaming. These days almost no one believed in dreaming.

"It's my dreams," Rosa began slowly. "But I don't mean regular dreams, like everybody has. Like Ramón. He's always dreaming, but his dreams are what he wishes for. He still dreams that Juan will return. And he still runs to open the apartment door whenever he hears a man's voice in the hallway. But his dreams are different from mine. They are...I don't know.... hopeful dreams, I think. Do you know what I mean?"

"Of course," Maria said. "We all have dreams." She hesitated a moment before she added, "I have dreams too, Rosa, but my dreams are mostly pieces of memory that keep trying to reach me. So far, nothing I've dreamed has ever made any sense."

Rosa reached over and took Maria's hand. "Thank you," she said in a shaky voice. "I know you are telling me about yourself so that I won't be afraid. You are a kind person, Maria."

"It's nothing," Maria said, embarrassed.

"Oh yes, I think it is," Rosa said, smiling a little. "Not exactly police procedure, am I right?"

Maria couldn't keep from smiling back. "You're right, Rosa, I admit it. So you can see how much I want to hear what you have to say, isn't that right too?"

Rosa nodded. "Well, first of all, I have regular dreams, just like you. And some of my dreams are sad too." She paused. "We all have memories...."

Maria nodded.

"But there are also other kinds of dreams. Have you ever heard the tales of the old dreamers?" she asked Maria uncertainly.

Maria nodded. "I heard stories about them when I was little. I don't remember much. What about them? Why?"

"I think I am a dreamer," Rosa said, looking down at the floor. "My Grandfather was known as one of the old dreamers in the village where I grew up. I remember that people treated him differently, with respect but also like they were a little afraid of him at the same time, you know what I mean?"

Maria nodded.

"My Grandfather told me that I could be a dreamer. He said that dreaming was a hard gift but that the old ways of dreaming could bring you to faraway places. I don't understand how it works, but it's true, sometimes dreams come to me and it's as if I can see into the future, but only the shapes of things, like shadows in the dark. Nothing I can describe when I wake up."

Maria nodded again.

"Maria, I want to tell you a story about dreaming, OK?"

Maria nodded.

"My *Abuelito*, my Grandfather Nestor, was living with us when I was born. He and my mother were always arguing, but the worst time was on my fifth birthday. After ice cream and cake, my *Abuelito* and I started to play hide and seek. I was hiding under a pile of blankets on my mother's bed.

"Suddenly grandfather pulled away the covers. I was so excited. I looked up, expecting to see a smile on his face, but instead he was staring at me as if he had seen a ghost. I grabbed at his big hand and asked him, 'What's wrong, *Abuelito*? What's wrong?'

"Then my mother came by and started yelling at him. 'Don't be scaring the child with your visions,' she told him in an angry voice. She didn't like his ways. She didn't want him to live with us. He left our house soon after that."

"Did you miss him?"

Rosa nodded. "But before he went away, my Grandfather tried to teach me about dreaming. He gave me exercises to do."

"No!" Maria said skeptically. "You mean like homework?!"

Rosa flushed and looked down at the floor.

"I didn't mean to say that," Maria said quickly. "I do want to understand, Rosa. Please, tell me, what do you mean when you say he gave you exercises?"

Rosa looked at the large turquoise ring on Maria's hand. "You have to look at something at night before you fall asleep." she said. "Like your ring. Then you have to see yourself in a dream and remember to look at the ring while you're still dreaming." She sighed. "It's so hard to explain."

She started over. "You have to see yourself in your dream as if you are awake. If you can do that, after a while you can go places while you are dreaming or talk to someone who can tell you about the future. It's as if you become two people. One of you is dreaming. The other one is somewhere else."

Maria was very still.

"I tried the exercises, and one time I think I traveled to a city I had never seen before. It was the scariest thing that ever happened to me. Even now I don't like talking about it. I told my *Abuelito* that I didn't want anything to do with dreaming. He went away to live with my father's relatives before I was six. Like I said, my mother didn't want him around. We were good Catholics, not superstitious Indians holding on to the old ways like Grandfather Nestor."

Rosa stopped talking and stood up. "I'll pour the tea now," she said. She carefully filled both their cups. Then she sat down, staring at Maria as if she were trying to read her thoughts.

Maria sipped at her tea and smiled at Rosa. "Go on."

Rosa began again with her story. "When I was fifteen, I decided to run away with Juan and go north. I didn't tell anyone of our plans, but my grandfather found me waiting for Juan on one of the smuggling trails.

"'I won't tell your mother, don't worry,' Grandfather said. 'But I have something important to say before you leave. Will you listen to me?'

"I told him, yes, of course I will listen."

"What did he tell you?" Maria asked.

"I didn't understand what he meant," Rosa said. She looked embarrassed. "First he told me that you can't know what you will find in *el Norte*, and you can't choose your fate. No one can. But he thought I would have a good life in my new country. And he said I would have a beautiful son."

"Well, that's good, isn't it?"

"Yes," Rosa went on, "but after that, he said something else. I memorized the words, trying to figure out what they meant. He said, 'Someday you may have to do battle with evil, my child. I know you will never give up as long as there is hope, but when nothing else is left to you, remember your gift. Use your dreaming. If death comes for you, your dreaming will help you face your death with courage.'

"I loved my grandfather, but I didn't know what he was talking about. I was only fifteen. Juan and I came north. We worked hard to build a new life for ourselves, and I forgot all about what Grandfather Nestor told me. But since Juan disappeared, I think about my *Abuelito* more and more often. Now the old ways of dreaming come to me almost every night, and I see my grandfather. I hear him talking to me."

"What does he say?"

"He says, 'Look around you, Rosa, there are signs of danger everywhere.'"

"That must be hard," Maria said slowly. "I can understand how Juan's disappearance has changed the way you see the world. But what do the dreams have to do with Ramón? Do you think your grandfather is warning you about something to do with Ramón?"

Maria was trying to keep an open mind, but she didn't believe that anyone could know the future. If you could "read" the future, that meant everything was already decided. Then what would be the point of anything? Nothing you did would make any difference. No, Maria definitely did not believe that anyone could know the future. "We make the future happen," she'd often told herself. "It's what we do here in the present that makes a difference in the future."

Rosa's words broke into her thoughts. "I keep dreaming that danger is waiting for Ramón in the park," she said, burying her face in her hands. "Please help me, Maria. I could not bear to lose Ramón. I don't know what to do."

Maria sat silently, trying to think things through. She had a lot of respect for dreams. But the old dreamers, if they ever existed at all, lived a long time ago. In today's world, for a gifted child like Ramón to be denied the classroom experience in Riverside Park because of dreams? It didn't make sense.

And yet she couldn't help thinking that even modern doctors acknowledged the importance of dreams as symbolic messengers from the hidden parts of our consciousness. What if Rosa knew something her conscious mind didn't recognize as important?

"Have you heard anything new about Juan?" she asked. "Anything at all?"

Rosa shook her head.

Maria thought some more. "Would it help if you could talk to Ramón's teacher?" she said finally. "You could ask him some questions about the trip to the park. Who will be there to look after the children? Could you come too? Maybe then you could make up your mind."

Rosa nodded. "Yes," she said. "I could talk to his teacher. His name is Mr. Medrano, and I like him very much. He is a good man." Rosa was sounding more confident now.

"Will you go to the school and talk to him tomorrow? You can call him up now if you'd like to set up an appointment."

"Yes, I'll do that," Rosa said. "It would make things easier."

"Good, that's good," Maria said. "Then after you talk to Mr. Medrano, you should do what you think is best. Ramón will understand."

Rosa shook her head. "No, he won't. Not if I keep him home. But I will try to do what is best for him."

On her way home, Maria called Danforth and told him what Rosa had said. "She's worried about the school trip to the park. She thinks Ramón could be in danger. She doesn't have any specific reasons. Only dreams. That's natural enough after her husband just up and disappeared."

Danforth was quiet.

"Is it important?" Maria asked.

"I think you did the right thing," Danforth said.

"What's wrong?" Maria said. He was making her anxious. "And why the sudden interest in Rosa Alvarez? It's over a week since her Juan disappeared."

"It's complicated. We'll talk tomorrow. Come to my office as soon as you get in," Danforth said. "And remember, watch your back, understand?"

"I always do," Maria told him. She closed her phone and checked the rearview window. There were only a few cars in back of her. None of them stayed with her.

She got onto the expressway that would take her to Sandy Hills, the small village where she lived. Sandy Hills was only thirty miles north of Ciudad Nueva, but its open spaces and fruit orchards made it seem a world away.

Her shift was over. It was time to put the job aside. But Maria knew that the questions would stay with her until tomorrow. In spite of Danforth's constant warnings to the contrary, tonight she was bringing the job home.

11 | WEDNESDAY NIGHT
Sandy Hills

MARIA SPENT MOST OF THE NIGHT AWAKE, arguing with Danforth in her mind. She knew it was necessary to keep a firm line between her life and her work, and she had worked hard to keep that line well guarded from her natural tendency to be empathetic. But certain situations continued to come up, when it was as if an invisible button had been pushed. Then she couldn't seem to hold back her need to get personally involved.

She knew why it happened. It was that deep crack in her childhood foundation, a crack that threatened to undermine the life she had struggled to construct around it. But she didn't know how to mend it. Neither did Danforth.

"I know a lot about police work," he'd told her once over coffee at the local bagel shop. "But I don't know how to help people patch up their lives. All I know is that there's no good explanation for the evil in this world. Read Melville. Why did Moby Dick exist? To destroy the already miserable lives of sailors balancing on pieces of wood in dangerous waters? There's no explanation for evil, Maria. As a cop, you have to learn to accept that."

Danforth's words were good advice to new recruits, but in her case they didn't hold up. How could she forget the fact that her family had been left in the desert to die?

She had been truthful with Danforth about one thing. She didn't expect any answers, and she didn't become a cop to find answers either. She accepted what happened as past history. She knew there would never be an explanation.

But she never saw the desert without feeling haunted by the darkness of her past. The doctors said she was too young to have memories, at least not the kind of memories that could give her a consistent explanation. She knew it was true. All she had were confused images, fragments blowing around the edges of her thoughts, too small to form anything recognizable and as easily swept away as the desert sand.

Another time when she'd been finishing up some paperwork in the Squad Room, Danforth had come out of his office and said to her out of nowhere, "You know you'll never answer it."

She'd looked up at him, puzzled. "Answer what?"

"The question. You'll never answer it. There is no answer."

"Just what question am I trying to answer, Sarge?"

"Why? That's the question. You want to know why, why it happens."

"Why what happens?"

"Why whatever it is that gets into your gut, happens," he'd answered. "Every cop has a question like that. If you don't, you aren't much good to anyone in this job. It drives you to go beyond where you know the limits are. Sometimes it's good, sometimes no. But remember what I'm telling you, Maria, whatever it is that sets you off, there's no answer to why it happens. It just does."

"Yes, things just happen, that's true," she'd admitted to Danforth at the time.

But, she argued with him now in the silent hours of the early morning, it's also true that people make things happen. If Ramón goes to the school picnic, it will probably be because of something I do or don't do. All it would take to keep him home would be for me to tell Rosa, "Don't let him go. Listen to your dreams."

The question was, should she interfere in Rosa's life? On what basis? How could she know what was best for Rosa's boy? Worse yet, she carried with her the weight of being a police officer. That alone was dangerous for their friendship.

As of now, she was facing a hard choice, but not an impossible one. The real problem would emerge tomorrow if she learned something from Danforth that suggested Rosa's dreams might have a basis in reality. Then what? What if sharing her information with Rosa would put an important investigation at risk? How would she choose? Was there a right choice? And how could she know in time to make a difference?

For tonight, it was a guessing game she was playing with herself, pure and simple. She already knew that if she learned of any concrete danger to Ramón, her instincts would push her to keep the boy far away until things had been resolved. But how would she do that? Pick him up and move him away to a faraway land? That was a fairy tale, not real life. Her professional training, her logical understanding of what she should do, those told her in no uncertain terms, this is not your personal affair.

In real life, if you're a cop, you don't get close, you don't let any of it get inside. You can't have relationships with your cases. How can you when you have to tell the parents of a missing kid that their only child isn't coming back, when you have to attend an autopsy for a suspicious infant death, when you have to say something to the child molester to make him think you understand the attraction.

"You have to leave it on the outside," Danforth kept telling her. "Keep it at arm's distance. Just observe. Sometimes you have to let things play out in front of you, like watching a bad movie without reacting. Sometimes you have to swallow it in the moment, to throw it all up later. When you stop to taste it, that's when you get in trouble."

Well she was in trouble now, she knew it. She was too connected with the Alvarez family to think straight. "Never again," she promised herself. "Never again."

12 THURSDAY MORNING
Vereda District Station

THE DREAM THAT WOKE HER UP WAS FAMILIAR. She knew that even as she was dreaming it. The sky was burning hot, and she wanted to rest, but there was something she still had to do, and she had to hurry or it would be too late.

She woke up exhausted and soaked in perspiration. Her bedroom was always hot in the summer, and the heat wave that had come in yesterday made it even hotter. Maria glanced over at the clock on her night table. It was early in the morning, only 3:00 a.m. Too early to get up. She closed her eyes.

The next time she looked, it was already past ten. Damn! She dressed in a rush and drove pedal to the metal into Vereda. She was only a few blocks from the station when the longest stoplight in Vereda shot up in front of her.

All she could do was slam on the brakes and say a quick prayer. Her Jeep Cherokee shuddered to a stop just as the line of cross traffic took off in front of her, horns blaring, arms and fingers swearing in her direction. She glanced at her watch. She was going to be late.

She took a deep breath. She was stuck in front of one of the city's longest stoplights. But, she told herself, it could have been worse. She'd almost blown through one of Vereda's major intersections. The last thing she needed was an accident, even a minor one. She checked the traffic again. There was a break in the flow. Only a few cars in the distance were moving towards the stoplight. She could run the light.

She took another deep breath and tried to relax. She would wait for the green. Another flaw in her character according to Al. "What's the point in being a cop if you can't drive through the red and get away with it?" he'd ask her whenever she was driving.

This red light seemed endless. And apparently she wasn't the only one who felt that way. Across the street, a small brown dog was staring at the light as if he'd been waiting a long time for permission to cross the street.

Maria leaned out the car window. "*Dale perrito*, go on, boy, *dale*," she called out to him. "*Dale perrito*, you've got the green." At the sound of her voice, the dog turned in her direction. Now she could see his eyes. She looked at him more closely. His ribs were sharp under his skin, and his tongue was hanging heavily from one side of his mouth. She couldn't see a collar.

The light turned green. As she accelerated through the intersection, Maria flipped open her cell phone The woman who answered at the Animal Control Center told her they'd pick up the dog within an hour.

Maria took the next corner on screeching tires, her thoughts still with the dog. If he was lost, his owners would find him at the shelter. If he was lost. But if he had been abandoned? If they had dumped him out on the curb, like a broken toy or a used-up piece of furniture, and then gone away without a backward glance? How long before hunger or thirst would force him to leave his corner of the intersection? He was waiting for his owners. He was waiting for them to come back and get him. They were his family. Who else should he wait for? Where else could he go?

Now the dog would go to the shelter. She knew what would happen next. The shelters were full of abandoned dogs and cats in the summer months. If no one came for the dog, eventually he would be put down.

When she thought about the dog, blindly holding on to the vague memory of familiar hands and voices, an old anger began to grow until she could feel it burning under her skin. Abandonment was unforgivable. There could be no excuses, no mitigating circumstances.

By the time she made her way into the Squad Room, it was a few minutes past eleven. She headed directly for Danforth's office at the far end of the room. He was standing by the doorway.

"Inside, Chavez," he said as she came up to him. "I want you to meet someone." He stepped aside so that she could move past him, then followed her into his office and closed the door.

The man sitting on the other side of the room looked younger than Danforth, in his early forties, she guessed. He had weathered good looks, clear hazel eyes, and the kind of cheekbones that suggested Native American ancestry. His brown hair was short, but a cowlick in the center of his part seemed to tease the otherwise straight lines of his cut.

His chair was pulled up close to Danforth's desk in what seemed a familiar way, his long legs stretched out in front of him. A black zipper folder was on the floor next to his chair, and his large hands were resting loosely on his lap. If he was carrying, she couldn't see it. She couldn't see a ring anywhere either.

He was wearing cowboy boots, faded jeans, and a black denim jacket, but even without a uniform, she could tell he was law enforcement. She wondered if he and Danforth had worked together before.

When their eyes met, she realized he was carefully taking her in as well. He offered her a quick smile. She flushed in spite of herself and looked away.

"Detective Chavez, this is Border Patrol Agent Joe Carter. He's been temporarily detailed to our unit," Danforth said.

"Detective," the agent said as he unfolded his legs and stood up. He was well over six feet tall.

"Maria," she said returning his handshake.

As they sat down, Joe was careful not to stare at her, but it wasn't easy. Maria Chavez! He had just turned ten when her story hit the newspapers, and he'd been hooked from the start. He wasn't the only one. It was as if the entire country could think of nothing else.

There was an awkward silence. "Let me see if I can get hold of Al before we start," Danforth said. "I think he's outside smoking. Back in a minute."

With Danforth out of the room, Maria found herself acutely aware of Joe's presence. He had picked up his folder and was going through his notepad, but she could feel his interest. She looked down at her own folder while Joe went through his notes, but whenever she looked up, she found her glances bumping into his. Finally he looked directly at her and smiled. "You must be wondering what the hell I'm doing here in Vereda," he said tentatively. He had an appealing voice with a slight western drawl.

She smiled back. "And you must be wondering what the hell you got yourself into!"

He nodded.

"Have you ever worked with Danforth before?" she couldn't help asking.

Joe shook his head. "Heard about him though. All good."

Maria couldn't keep from glancing at his chair next to Danforth's desk.

Joe understood what she was thinking. "We felt comfortable with each other right away," he said. "As if we'd been friends for a long time."

"I wondered," she said. "Danforth is usually reserved."

"Not usual for me either," Joe said.

After a few more minutes of silence, he went back to looking through his notes. He would never tell her, but the truth was that Maria herself was the connection between them. An unlikely connection on the face of it, different reasons, different times, different places. But as they talked, they discovered that Maria Chavez was important to both of them.

"I head the Major Crimes Unit," Danforth had told Joe over the phone when he'd asked for details of his assignment in Vereda. "I handpicked every member of my unit. Most of them come from Homicide and Narcotics. They're smart and they're good at what they do, but what really sets them apart is that they're willing to work the cases that don't solve fast, the messy ones no one else wants.

"You'll want to keep in touch with Al Diaz on a daily basis. He can work the street like nobody else. He still goes in undercover if it's a place where nobody knows him, but most of the time, he runs informants. He's the source of most of the information we get from the street.

"You'll partner with Maria Chavez. She has her own style, but she's my best new recruit. She's tough when it counts, very tough. You can see it by the way she carries herself. Very, very effective." Danforth had hesitated. "You remember the little girl lost in the desert, right?"

Of course Joe remembered. He had heard the rumors that Maria Chavez was in law enforcement somewhere in the Southwest, but the thought had never crossed his mind that he might be working with her someday. Yet even though a lot of years had gone by, he'd recognized her as soon as she'd come into the room. Her photograph on the front page, day after day. Those dark, wide-set eyes, looking out warily at the world. They hadn't changed. They were still too large for her face. They still caught at you. At first you noticed nothing else.

13 | THURSDAY
Vereda District Station

DANFORTH CAME INTO THE OFFICE a few minutes later and sat down heavily in his chair. "Al won't be here for a while," he said in a tired voice to Joe. "But I filled him in as best I could. He'll be in touch with you later today."

Danforth studied Maria for a moment before he spoke. "This meeting is for you, Maria," he said. "Cali and the other members of the task force have been informed of what's at stake. Al knows most of what's been happening as well. Joe is going to explain things to you himself. You're going to be working with him."

Maria nodded. "I'm ready."

"Go ahead, Joe," Danforth said.

"I'm stationed in Lastup," Joe said. "Been there quite a few years now. I guess the best way to describe Lastup is to say that it's a small border town with big problems." Joe's voice was quiet, but the intensity that edged his words was audible. "Ten miles south of the border, it's like a war zone. The big money in drug smuggling means there's a lot at stake. The smugglers come at us with everything they've got, from "Molotov rocks" to assault rifles.

"But today I'm tracking a different problem. In Lastup, we work closely with the local police department. When Juan Alvarez was reported missing last week, I got the case."

Maria waited intently for Joe to continue.

"I beat out a few leads," Joe said. "They went nowhere. We had nothing, no witnesses, no fingerprints, no weapon, not even a body. It looked like we would have to suspend the case, but it stayed on my mind."

"Because Juan was a pilot?" Maria said, with a trace of irritation in her voice. "He flew computer parts, not drugs, you know that, right?"

Joe nodded. "Right. We know he worked for an American assembly plant just over the border in a Mexican town called Purgatorio. The G&G *maquiladora*, as they call it there, assembles computers from parts flown into Mexico from the U.S. Then the assembled computers are flown back into the U.S. to be sold.

"G&G has been in operation for over twelve years, and Juan had been working for them ten years when he disappeared. So we know that G&G was no fly-by-night operation, and Juan was no fly-by-night pilot. And as far as we can tell, Juan Alvarez never knowingly transported drugs." Joe hesitated. "But sometimes just being in the vicinity can be dangerous."

"Go on, Joe," Danforth said. He drummed his fingers on the desk impatiently. "Let's not drag this out."

"You may not want to hear this, Maria," Joe said slowly. "But when Juan and Rosa arrived in this country, they didn't have papers. They didn't have money. Otherwise they couldn't have gone to live in the subsidized housing of N. Building.

"Apparently Juan began doing small part-time construction jobs in Vereda. But someone must have noticed him, a smart, hardworking man, who kept to himself. A man who wanted to move ahead but had few opportunities. Always running from *La Migra*. How could he succeed?

"The next thing we know, he and Rosa somehow get green cards. Juan starts taking flying lessons. He gets a pilot's license and then a job working for G&G computers. There's no way he could fly in and out of this country without papers and a license. Without those, he never could have found a job as a pilot. You can connect the dots yourself."

"I don't believe you," Maria said firmly. "Rosa's husband would never have had anything to do with drug-trafficking."

"I'm not saying that Juan knew anything about the hidden cargo he was carrying," Joe said. "He flew computer parts and computers in and out of the country. That part is true. But he must have known something. Did you ever ask yourself how the Alvarez family managed to stay in N. Building when Juan was earning a pilot's salary?"

Maria was silent. She had never even thought about it. "Well, Rosa isn't earning any pilot's salary now," she fired back. "She has every right to stay in N. Building."

"Agreed," Joe said. "Let's move on. As you know, last week one of our agents on patrol decided to check out the backyard of an abandoned house in Lastup. When he kicked away at a garbage dump, he didn't expect to find a human hand. Didn't expect it to point the way to other bodies in the dump either."

Maria sat tensely in her chair, her hands balled into white-knuckled fists.

"You know that the Gomez-Gil smuggling ring has been operating out of Lastup for years, right?" Joe said.

She nodded. "What about it?"

"It started off small, but now Gil's cartel dominates the entire Southwest. We've made a few dents in it, but we've never been able to get anywhere near Gomez-Gil."

"And?"

"Three of the bodies we found in the dump heap belonged to the Gomez-Gil cartel."

"Gil's cartel?!" Maria said. "Not a rival cartel?"

"That's what everyone thought at first. But Gil is a psychopath and paranoid as hell. He suspects everyone. He's constantly on the lookout for betrayal, and sometimes he finds it. It's one reason he's survived. Al's sources tell us that a short time ago, Gil began to suspect three men, all cousins. He took action to find out what they were up to. I won't describe what happened to them."

"Were they actually working against him?"

"I don't think we'll ever know one way or the other."

"The three men from Gil's cartel.....they had ID's in their pockets?"

Joe nodded. "Right. We were meant to identify them. Gil wanted to get out the message. If anyone betrays him, they will pay a heavy price."

"What about the other body?"

"There were no IDs on the other two bodies, but we got lucky on one of them. Managed to lift some prints."

"The other *two* bodies?" Maria said.

Joe paused briefly before he went on. "We identified the fourth body as a longtime resident of Lastup, a man we called Pipé. He was an addict who ran a souvenir stand in the square near the church of Santa Teresa. He was one of my informants." Joe's anger was palpable.

"Sounds like he was more than an informant," Maria said cautiously.

Joe nodded. "I worked with him a long time. Last Friday, when I couldn't find him at his stand, I drove out to his place. It wasn't like Pipé not to show up. But his friends wouldn't give me much."

"They blamed you?"

"It happens," Joe said. His eyes darkened. "His friends did say that a few days before he disappeared, Pipé gave information to another agent. One of yours, they said. That was a goddamn shock, believe me, because there is no one else in any of our organizations who works with Pipé. If it's true that there's a mole high up in a law enforcement agency around here, and if Pipé gave information to the mole, that could explain why Gil took him."

"What about the other body?" Maria asked the question in a quiet voice, but her throat ached.

"The fifth body was buried separately in a deep ditch at the end of the property line," Joe continued. "We had to dig a while before we found it. Almost gave up in fact. But I insisted. I knew it had to be in the area somewhere. The dogs found the head and hands nearby. We're working on the identification."

Maria was so still, she hardly seemed to be breathing.

"That body hasn't been identified yet, but the chances are good that it's Juan Alvarez."

Maria felt the ache from her throat run through her body. It wasn't fair, but unexpectedly she found herself angry with Joe. "Just why are you here?" she said bluntly.

"I guess you could say it's a matter of connections," Joe said after a moment. Maria waited. Danforth was staring up at a point in the wall behind her.

"Our state has a relatively small border," Joe went on, "but over the past few years, a lot of smuggling activity has moved over our way. A short time ago we learned that the Office Supply Repository here in Vereda functions as the main drug warehouse for the Gomez-Gil cartel."

"The Office Supply Repository in the South End industrial park? The one with all the trailers in the back?" Maria found herself standing up as she spoke.

Joe nodded.

"But that's where they've put the elementary school classrooms until the new school is finished, in the trailers behind the Repository," Maria said, disbelief written all over her face. "That's Ramón's school!" she added before she could stop herself.

Joe looked at Danforth.

"One and the same," Danforth said. He didn't look happy. "Sit down, Maria. Let me give you some history. A few years ago, a certain member of our city council suggested renovating an empty building into an office supply exchange warehouse. Corporations and businesses would donate surplus office furniture and supplies to the Repository in exchange for a tax write-off. In return, state and city buildings could take the supplies they needed from the Repository free of charge.

"Amazingly it works. It saves money and everyone benefits. It's considered a real success story for the city."

"Once we learned that it was also being used as a drug distribution warehouse, we put the Repository under surveillance," Joe said without missing a beat. "And it's already clear that the building is the perfect cover for drug distribution. There's a constant stream of trucks and vans bringing supplies in and out of the building. We're trying to stay under the radar so we haven't stopped and searched any of the vehicles. But the timing, the trucking company, the extent of the traffic, everything suggests that your Office Supply Repository is also a Drug Supply Repository.

"We would need to get someone inside the operation to get any concrete evidence, but so far, no luck. It's a tightly closed shop. And Gomez-Gil always keeps his distance. Never comes near the place."

"If you really do have a high-level mole, wouldn't he have already informed Gil that you suspect the Repository?" Maria interrupted.

"Probably. But very few people know about it. We've played this one very close to the chest. Or maybe the mole thinks any kind of a leak is too dangerous. Risky tactic, though. Gil isn't the forgiving kind. Anyway, a guy named Angel is the man in charge of the operation at the Repository. Maria, did you ever meet him when you were out at the school?"

She shook her head." I knew he was there, but he must live in the Repository. I never even saw him."

"Go on, Joe," Danforth said impatiently.

"There's no evidence of any kind directly linking Gil to the warehouse, so it's beginning to look like all we'll be able to do is shut down the operation, arrest Angel and some of the lower level operators, and confiscate the merchandise. Our plans for the raid are already in place," Joe said. As soon as he mentioned the raid, he felt Maria's eyes burning a hole in his forehead. "After school is out for the year," he added quickly. "As I said before, we've kept this information very close, but Gil has plants everywhere. We don't want Gil closing up shop before we can act. We're racing against the clock. School ends Friday. We plan to raid the Repository soon afterwards. But who knows if we'll be able to pull it off with any element of surprise."

"Because of the bodies?" Maria said.

"Exactly. Because if one of the bodies is positively identified as Juan Alvarez, there's a direct link to G&G Computers, the company that employed Juan Alvarez. It's based here in Vereda, but it's owned by Gomez-Gil."

Maria took a deep breath.

"The point is that finally there's a connection to Gomez-Gil," Joe went on. "Once we identify the fifth body with complete certainty, we'll know officially that Juan Alvarez, pilot for G&G, was murdered. We'll want to know why, and Gil knows that we'll be asking ourselves that question. And even if Gil doesn't yet know that we have the Repository under surveillance, he knows that the discovery of the pilot's body, the place where it was found, the men he was buried with..... all that means we are now going to take a closer look at how the pilot lived, his family, his home, even the boy's school. And Gil may start to feel that we're getting a little too close to home."

Joe paused. "Did you ever see that movie, *Lord of the Rings*?" he asked Maria unexpectedly.
She looked at him, surprised. "What about it?"

"You remember there's this all-seeing eye that always turns in the direction of the ring?"
Maria nodded, intrigued in spite of herself.

"Well, that's how I see Gil," Joe said. "The identification of Juan Alvarez as one of the bodies will pull Gil's attention in this direction. Now Gil will be keeping a close eye on the Repository and everything connected to it. He'll be suspicious, maybe even nervous. Nervous enough to want to check things out for himself? I doubt it. But it's a possibility and it's one of the reasons they wanted me here on the scene as soon as possible.

"There's still a lot that's confusing about what happened last week," Joe went on. "For one thing, according to the medical examiner, the three cartel members and the pilot were all killed at approximately the same time, last Monday. But Pipé wasn't killed until three days later on Thursday. His body was dumped in the same place, but it looks like that was just a matter of convenience."

"But what connection could there be between Juan's death and Pipé's three days later?" Maria insisted.

"At first glance, it looks like no connection at all" Joe said. "No sense either. But what if the pilot had accidentally stumbled onto something at the airport or found out something incriminating about Gil. Maybe Gil just suspected that Juan knew something. That would have made Gil uncomfortable. Maybe he wasn't completely sure Juan would keep his mouth shut. So when the opportunity presented itself, maybe he decided to get rid of Juan along with the three cousins, just to play it safe...."

"I don't know," Maria said. She looked dubious. "That's a lot of speculation."

"There's another possibility," Joe said after a moment. "What if Juan talked to Pipé before he was killed? What if Juan told Pipé that he wanted to get away from Gil, that he wanted witness protection for himself and his family in exchange for some information, maybe even that he would testify against Gil?"

"Why would he tell Pipé?"

"Maybe he thought Pipé could help him contact someone in the government. Maybe he knew Pipé was an informant."

"Dammit, Joe," Maria said sharply. "If Gil learned from Pipé that Juan had something to use against him, we need to warn Rosa right away!"

Danforth shook his head. "We can't tell Rosa anything until we make a final ID."

"We can put surveillance on her."

"Already in place," Joe said. "We have people watching both her and the boy. New faces from out of town. It's safer for everyone that way."

Something was still bothering Maria. "You said you have credible information about the Repository?"

Joe nodded.

"Was the info from your informant, Pipé?"

"No. Source unknown, at least unknown to me."

"You can't say where?"

"Right."

"But it's somehow connected to the bodies?"

Joe nodded. "That's all I can say for now, Maria. I just found out about it myself yesterday."

"Do you think Juan had something incriminating he could use against Gil? That he hid it somewhere?"

Joe shook his head. "I don't know. I wish I did."

"From everything Rosa told me about Juan, he was a very smart man. If he did leave anything hidden somewhere, I'll bet it was for Rosa."

"For Rosa?" Joe looked surprised.

"Yes, for Rosa. If Juan was worried about Gil, if he thought there was even a small chance that Gil would take him out, he might have left something to explain things to her. So that if he did disappear, she would know he hadn't just up and left her for no good reason. So she and the boy would know it wasn't by choice. I think that would have mattered a lot to Juan."

"Could be," Joe said. "I hadn't thought of it, but it could be."

"Why don't I go out to Ramon's school right now?" Maria said. "I was thinking of doing that anyway. To see how the conference with Ramon's teacher went and what Rosa decided about the trip to the park. I was already planning to drive her home."

"That works," Danforth said. "Like you said, you were going to do that anyway. Take Joe with you. New kid on the block. Show him around. Someone out there may recognize him, but they'll assume he's here because of the pilot, the discovery of the bodies. That OK with you, Joe?"

"Works for me," Joe said. "And it gives me a chance to ask Rosa some questions. She may know more than she realizes."

Something was still bothering Maria. "Why haven't you been able to positively ID Juan Alvarez?" she asked Joe.

Joe looked at Danforth.

"What was left of the pilot wasn't easily identifiable," Danforth said briskly.

Maria felt another stab of pain in her stomach. Some part of her had known the truth from the beginning, but she had pushed it aside, not wanting to face it. Torture was standard procedure, a warning to potential rivals. Stay out of my territory. Show people what happens to them if they even think about betraying Gil. But Juan?

"No Maria, it doesn't look like Juan was tortured," Joe said quickly, reading her mind. She shot him a look of relief.

"In fact, that's one of the things that makes us think that Gil taking the pilot was as much an accident as anything. There's a bullet hole in his skull, and it was the bullet that killed him. That means he died quickly, easily in comparison to the others."

"Then why is it hard to identify him?"

"That's another part of the puzzle." Joe said. He looked uncomfortable. "His body was dismembered post mortem. His head and his hands were missing among other things, but as I said, there were no signs at all to indicate any kind of torture before he died. Maybe they wanted to make his ID impossible, or at least difficult. As I said, Gil doesn't want anyone paying attention to this part of his operation."

"But the way he was cut up, it must have taken a hell of a lot of anger to do that to someone who was there as an afterthought," Maria interrupted. "Why? Why would anyone do that?"

Again Joe shook his head. "We just don't know," he said in a tired voice.

"Those bastards!" Maria said. "What they must have done to Juan's body!" Instantly she made herself a promise. Rosa must never know what happened to Juan after he died. At least Rosa's memories of Juan would be whole.

14

THURSDAY

G. Washington Elementary School Trailers
Southside Industrial Park
Vereda

MARIA'S CAR WAS PARKED IN THE OFFICIAL LOT around the corner from the station. "Why don't you drive?" she said to Joe. "Best way to learn your way around. Follow the Avenue through the third stoplight. It's a big intersection with the longest red light in Vereda. You'll see the industrial park on your left immediately after the light. Go past the first driveway. Take the second one, also on your left. There's a bus stop directly across the street."

"No problem," Joe said sliding into the tight space of Maria's seat. In the close quarters of the car, Maria couldn't help noticing Joe's broad shoulders and long, lean legs. He was definitely in good shape. Deliberately she looked out the window. The last thing she needed was for him to notice her interest in him.

Joe pushed the seat back into a more comfortable position and confidently started through the after-school traffic clogging the Avenue. Before long he was drumming his fingers on the steering wheel. He was frustrated by the traffic, she could tell. His eyes had narrowed, and the little creases around his mouth had deepened.

"We'll get to the school before Rosa," she said. "Her appointment isn't until 3:00, and Medrano runs late with his appointments these days."

"We've got time then," Joe said. He flexed his shoulders and settled back into his seat. He seemed to be wrestling with his thoughts. After a few minutes, he added, "Sounds like Charlie Medrano's putting in long hours."

"He's been appointed interim administrator of the school for the summer while the Board of Ed decides on a new principal," Maria explained. "That means a lot of additional work for him."

"Why would a teacher be given an administrative position during the summer?" Joe asked cautiously.

"The system in this part of town is breaking down, Joe. Not enough teachers, not enough staff, not enough money. Besides Medrano knows the school better than anyone else. What's the problem?"

"I was wondering if Medrano volunteered for the summer job," he said. "The long hours would make it easier to run a second business out of the Repository."

Maria looked at Joe in surprise. "You have a problem with Medrano?"

"I've never met him," Joe said. "Sounds like a nice guy." He hesitated. "Maybe too good to be true?"

"I don't think so," Maria said. "He cares about those kids. When I was on patrol, I used to spend a lot of time here at the school. You know, 'Officer Friendly'?"

Joe grinned at her.

She ignored his grin. "I worked closely with Medrano. He's dedicated to his students. He wants them to succeed."

Joe gave her a skeptical look. "That's my point. I'm wondering just how far he would go for them."

"What do you mean?" she said, puzzled. "He's one of the good guys."

"Looks that way," Joe admitted. "But what keeps going through my head is that Medrano must have turned a blind eye more than once if drugs are being moved through the Office Supply Repository. Everything would be taking place next to the school trailers. He must have noticed something. Maybe he's just trusting. Maybe he's just too busy taking care of the kids. But whatever the reason, it seems to me that he doesn't want to see what's really going on around him. In my book, that's a kind of cowardice."

"That's pretty harsh," she said. "Medrano means well. I'm sure of it."

"Well, if he cares about those kids so much, maybe he needs to get his eyes checked. By now someone at the school ought to have noticed what was going on at the Repository."

Maria was silent. She'd obviously touched a sore spot with Joe. She looked out the window. They had come up to the third stoplight at Vereda's busiest intersection. The light was red. As they waited at the light, Maria watched the people on the sidewalk, the women straddling their kids to their sides, moving in and out of stores, the group of older men on the corner, talking and commenting with their hands. Not for the first time, she was struck by the incongruities of the barrio, the passions for religion and family walking the streets arm in arm with the imploding cruelty of the gangs, children raping other children, selling drugs, killing each other in the schoolyard with pipes and knives and guns, staining everything around them with fear and despair.

The light had turned green, but the car in front of them wasn't moving. The middle-aged woman behind the wheel couldn't seem to get her car into gear. "That piece of junk must be a hundred years old," Joe said, drumming his fingers on the steering wheel even harder than before. By the time the woman finally drove off, the light was red again, and the opposing traffic was moving through the intersection.

As they waited, Joe looked over at Maria. "What are you going to say to Rosa?"

His question caught her off guard. "I want to talk to her, find out what she's decided to do about the school trip to the park."

"You can't say anything about Juan," Joe said, his eyes back on the red light. "He hasn't officially been declared dead. You already know that, but I'm reminding you. This is my case too."

She didn't say anything.

The light turned green. Joe drove slowly past a long cement wall topped by barbed wire on the left.

"That wall separates the industrial park from the street," Maria said. "Go past the first driveway," she reminded Joe.

After the first driveway, the color of the gray cement wall along the street turned into a deep aquamarine. Fantastic sea creatures had been painted on the wall as well, but they were barely visible under the heavy black graffiti that covered them. Now it was impossible to see what flights of fancy might once have lived in that wide splash of blue.

"The teachers painted that wall," Maria said. "To make the industrial park more inviting to the children in the trailers. Take your next left."

Joe turned left into the next driveway. It was a broad road that ran along the back of the Office Repository, a large, nondescript two-story building. Several men in overalls were busy carrying boxes out of the Repository into the trucks parked by the loading dock.

"The school parking lot is straight ahead," Maria said, pointing to the small parking area at the end of the driveway. "You can park there."

They heard a loud siren start up from the direction of the Repository even before they got out of the car.

"What's that?" Joe asked. He looked irritated. "Some kind of an early warning system?"

Maria couldn't keep back a smile. "Usually they use radios or cells, but supposedly if there's a big load and the workers are scattered outside, they use the siren to get everyone together as soon as possible. The teachers hate it, but we haven't been able to stop it. Apparently it doesn't happen often."

Joe looked at her skeptically.

"Relax," she said. "There's nothing we can do about it."

"Fine," he said evenly. "Let's go. We can wait for Rosa inside the trailer. Which one is it?" He studied the six large white trailers evenly spaced in the large empty lot behind the Office Repository.

"The one on the far right, that's the third-grade classroom," Maria said. They walked across the field towards the trailers. She could feel eyes on her back. She turned around. No one else was in sight. She glanced over at Joe.

"I know," he said. "I feel it too. Probably someone in the Repository." He paused. "You know, these days it seems like everything that happens is being recorded. From satellite eyes in the sky to dashboard cameras. I try to ignore it, but I don't think I'll ever get used to it."

Maria studied him. No one she knew talked like that. Where had he come from? Maybe it was Joe Carter who was too good to be true.

"Just out of curiosity, earlier you said that there was no evidence linking Gil to the Repository, right?"

Joe nodded.

"But from what I hear, Angel's not quite right in the head. He must get instructions from Gil somehow."

"No doubt about it. They talk by cell phone all the time."

"Cell phone?!" She paused. "Couldn't you listen in?"

"We have some listening devices around the Repository, but we can't cover Angel all the time. He takes a different car every time he goes out, and he goes out often, early in the morning, in the middle of the day, even late at night.

"And he chooses different places to park whenever he's talking to Gil, seemingly at random. He might go into the large parking lot at the Nature Preserve or drive around the Olde Road where there's never much traffic. We can't get close enough to eavesdrop, especially since we're trying to keep a low profile. We've picked up some of his toss-away phones. Clean as a whistle. He must wear gloves to clean the phone he's using, even when he's taking out the batteries. We get nothing if we stop him except to warn Gil that we're on to the Repository."

"But don't people wonder about Angel going out like that all the time?"

"He's got a cover for that, too. Angel is an animal lover and a bird watcher. He even takes along a pair of binoculars."

"Eye in the sky but not on Angel?" Maria said. "That's hard to believe."

"I know, but it's true."

They walked past the first trailer. "What happens inside these trailers?" Joe asked her.

"Classes, the library, the cafeteria, some administrative offices. It's a bare bones setup, but it's only for another week. In September, the students will be in a new elementary school in the center of town." Maria stopped walking and looked directly at him. "Now it's your turn, Joe. Tell me more about what happens inside the Repository."

"Fair enough, but don't stop. Let's keep walking and looking at the trailers."

Maria nodded.

"The showroom is on the first floor of the Repository," Joe said. "In the basement they do a lot of restoration, some of it quite good, I understand. That area is off limits to the public. But if you're shopping for library shelves for your school, you can select a model from the showroom on the main floor, and most of the time they can come up with matching shelves. The Repository is a success in its own right. I hear it may even win a community service award."

Maria couldn't keep from laughing out loud.

Joe looked directly into her eyes. His squint lines had softened, and his clear brown eyes were warm and smiling. No one had looked at her like that for a long time.

"I notice that most of the silver moving vans over by the loading docks are from the same company," she said, keeping her eyes fixed on his.

"Good point," Joe said, holding her gaze. "It's a nonprofit moving company called *Helping Hands*. They have the exclusive moving rights for the Repository."

The image of helping hands sliding bricks of drugs into desk drawers and filing cabinets was too much to resist. She burst out laughing again. Joe laughed too and unexpectedly put his arm around her shoulders.

"What are you doing?" She stopped smiling. "That isn't funny!"

"At least we should hold hands until we get inside the trailer," Joe said seriously, although the look in his eyes suggested this wasn't just business. "Who knows? One of these days we may need a good cover story for being together."

"You're such a flirt, Joe Carter," she couldn't help saying even as she slipped out from under his arm. Uncertainly she took his hand. "You could never get away with a move like that in our unit."

"But I'm not in your unit," he answered her with a grin. "Plus I'm the Fed and I'm in charge."

She didn't know what to say, but their show was convincing to whoever was watching them, she was sure of that.

Brightly colored scenes of children at play had been painted on the outside of the third-grade trailer. In one scene, two boys were racing down a street. In another, girls were skipping rope. "Looks like someone really cares about this trailer," she couldn't help pointing out to Joe.

They climbed into the trailer. Maria looked down the hallway. Something had changed since her last visit to Medrano's classroom several months earlier. The hall felt strangely wide. Empty. Then she remembered. All the lockers had been removed.

She'd read about it in the newspaper. A teacher had found drugs in a fifth grader's locker. The next day, they'd found a gun in the locker of a fourth grader. The offending students had been expelled, and lockers had been banished from all the trailers, even the one with the kindergarten in it. She looked around. Only the surveillance cameras were still in place. They seemed to be everywhere.

15

THURSDAY
N. Building
Medrano's Third-Grade Trailer

THE SCHOOL BUS DROPPED RAMÓN OFF in front of N. Building at the usual
time. Rosa brought him up to Ana's apartment right away. Then she flew down the stairs to
the bus stop. She didn't want to be late. It was 2:30 when the city bus finally pulled up at her
bus stop. Rosa climbed into the bus and sat down. She could hardly contain her anxiety. Her
appointment was for 3:00. The temporary trailers that housed the school weren't far from the
bus stop, but the last time Rosa had gone out there, she'd lost at least ten minutes trying to
find them.

Maria had tried to explain to Rosa why Ramón's elementary school had been temporarily
housed in an industrial park on the southern boundary of the *barrio*. Rosa understood what
Maria wasn't saying. Most of the new children moving into the neighborhood were the children
of immigrants, legal and illegal. It was because of these children that the city had to build a new
school. For now, the children would have to make do with the trailers.

Rosa and three men got off at the bus stop. The man wearing a straw cowboy hat and sunglasses walked briskly away. Rosa crossed the street and started down the driveway. The other
two men followed closely behind her.

A small truck came racing down the driveway and blared its horn. Rosa jumped. The men in
back of her laughed. It made her nervous that they were so close to her, almost on her heels.

A tall man with blond hair and dark sunglasses was standing by the back door of the Repository. Several cats lay sleeping in the sunlight near the door. The tall man nodded at Rosa politely
as she approached.

"Sorry about that truck," he said. "Not one of our regulars. Ours know better than to drive like
that with children around. They're careful about the animals too."

"Yes, thank you," she said walking quickly past the Repository towards the trailers. She gave
a nervous glance over her shoulder, but the tall blond man had turned his attention to the two
men. He was talking to them as they went into the Repository. Rosa continued straight ahead in
the direction of the field and the school trailers.

Joe and Maria were already inside the trailer waiting for Rosa. On their left was a silent classroom. Its desks, neatly organized into five long rows, seemed to suggest something incomplete,
as if the room itself were waiting for the students to return. "Medrano's room is at the other end
of the hall," Maria said. "You mind waiting here?"

"No problem," Joe said. He went into the empty classroom and sat down at one of the small student desks. "Is this OK, Miss?" he teased Maria. "Can I use my cell? I've done all my homework."

He was making her laugh again. She couldn't believe it. She hadn't laughed with anyone like that in a long time. Inadvertently she checked his hands again. Definitely no wedding ring. "Definitely," he said grinning up at her. Damn! He didn't miss a thing.

She walked down the hall to Medrano's classroom. He was sitting in the front of the room talking with a mother and her daughter. "Hi Charlie," Maria said from the doorway. "I'm here to give Rosa Alvarez a ride home. It's not official," she added. "We're just friends."

"That's good, Detective," Medrano said smiling back at her. "I wish that kind of thing happened more often. Do you want to wait here?"

Maria shook her head. "No thanks, I'm with a friend. It looks like there's some nice artwork in the alcove by the front door. There's no hurry. Take your time."

When she went back down the hall, Joe was waiting for her by the empty classroom door. "I was getting cramps in my legs," he explained, straight-faced.

She couldn't help grinning. "Serves you right," she told him. "No phones allowed in school."

They walked into the alcove to look at the children's artwork. "Look at these pictures!" Joe said. His whole expression had changed. He was looking intently at the pictures, and his eyes were serious and sad. Maria couldn't stop staring at Joe. Was it possible he cared about the pictures of third graders?

Then she looked at the pictures. A line of drawings hung across all three of the alcove walls. Someone had drawn a laughing sun on a large piece of paper. Written under the sun were the words, "My Summer Vacation." Most of the pictures didn't show much sun or even much sky for that matter. One drawing was so finely composed, it looked as if it had been done by a mature artist. It showed a girl swinging on enormous hangers in a closet. In the background there were two men sitting on a worn-out sofa. There were bottles all over the floor near the sofa, and the men were sitting slouched over as if they were drunk.

"This is how I swing on birches," someone had written in a childish scrawl below the picture. Maria felt goose bumps on her arm. How did a third grader in one of these trailers even know Frost's poem about swinging on birches?

Another drawing showed two boys playing hide-and-seek in a parking lot. Nothing unusual about that except that most of the cars in the parking lot were filled with bullet holes, and most of the windows were smashed.

Maria kept searching until she found the drawing signed by Ramón Alvarez. His drawing showed two stick figures sitting under a mass of leafy green scribbles and a crayon blue sky. It wasn't hard to recognize Rosa in her apron, with her dark eyes and a smile on her face. Ramón was sitting next to her, wearing his favorite red and white striped shirt, laughing and pointing to something in the sky that looked like an airplane. A man was sitting in the pilot's seat. *"Mi Papi"* was written on the side of the airplane.

It was the figure of the father that caught Maria's attention. Joe was staring at it too. The father's face was completely empty. Maybe Ramón had run out of time or crayons, but she didn't think so.

"Damn!" Joe said and blew out a deep breath. Maria felt the same way.

16

THURSDAY
George Washington Elementary School
Third-Grade Trailer

ROSA CLIMBED INTO THE TRAILER with such concentration, at first she didn't even see Maria waiting for her by the door. A tall man who looked like a cowboy was standing next to her.

"Maria!? What are you doing here?" Rosa said.

"I'm here to give you a ride home, that's all," Maria told her in a reassuring voice. "This is my friend, Border Patrol Agent Joe Carter."

"Pleasure, Rosa," Joe said, shaking her hand. "I hope you don't mind me coming along for the ride."

"Thank you," Rosa said shyly. "Yes, I would like a ride home. But I haven't seen Mr. Medrano yet. You would have to wait."

"No problem," Maria said. "We've already checked in with Mr. Medrano. Take your time. We have some artwork to admire."

Rosa glanced into the alcove. "OK, I'll come back as soon as I can."

When Rosa got to the classroom, she saw Mr. Medrano sitting at his desk, talking to a woman she recognized as the mother of one of Ramón's classmates. Medrano looked up at Rosa and smiled. "I'm running late, Señora. I'm sorry. Can you wait?"

Rosa nodded and smiled back at him. Usually she found it hard to talk to people, but she felt comfortable with Mr. Medrano. She went into the back of the room and sat down at one of the student desks while she waited to wait for Mr. Medrano to finish.

"Can you keep an eye on the door, Maria?" Joe said.

She nodded and went over to the front door of the trailer. Through the glass window, she had a good view of both the Repository and the field where the other trailers stood.

Joe headed straight for the back wall of the alcove. He lifted the latch on the right-hand side of the wall, and a door swung open into a large storage closet. Wide shelves filled the entire space. There were baskets on the shelves, each labeled with a child's name. Joe pulled Ramón's basket down from the top shelf and quickly looked inside it before he put it back in its spot on the top shelf. Hurriedly he went through the other baskets, one at a time, checking inside each of them before replacing them. Some of the baskets were empty. Others were filled with books, notebooks, pencils, boxes of colored crayons, children's scissors. Joe took down Ramón's basket again and stared at it.

"What's the problem?" Maria said. "What's wrong with Ramón's basket?"

"I'm not sure," he said in a puzzled voice. "But it looks like things have just been thrown in here. Would you say Ramón is a disorganized child? Sloppy with his schoolwork?"

"Not at all," she said emphatically. "The opposite."

A movement outside the trailer caught her attention. "Joe, we're going to have company! A man is headed this way. It must be Angel, the manager of the Repository."

Joe closed the closet door and stepped out of the alcove just as a man climbed into the trailer. He stared at them. "You have business with Charlie Medrano?" he said, studying them as he spoke.

"Detective Chavez," Maria said holding out her hand. "And you are...?"

The man took off his sunglasses and shook her hand. "Angel Ramirez, manager of the Repository."

When Maria met his eyes, she had to struggle to keep her balance. The man's eyes were unusually pale, but what frightened her was that he looked at her as if he knew her. Something about him seemed terrifyingly familiar as well.

"Are you OK, Detective?" Angel said bringing his face up close to hers.

Joe stepped out between Maria and Angel and took Maria's arm. "I'm Agent Carter," he said to Angel. "We appreciate your concern, Ramirez, but there's no problem. Detective Chavez is just getting over a fever."

"What brings her out here?" Angel asked him suspiciously.

"That's not your concern, Ramirez. It has nothing to do with you."

Just then Rosa stepped out of Medrano's classroom and waved down the hall at Maria. "I'll have to wait a while longer, is that OK?" she called out.

"No problem," Maria called down to her. Then she turned back to speak to Angel. She had regained her equilibrium. "Rosa's a good friend of mine," she told him in a steady voice. "I'm here to give her a ride home. "

"She must be a good friend," Angel said in a carefully neutral tone of voice, but he was still thinking about how strongly Maria had reacted to seeing him. But then she had good reasons for being shocked by his appearance even if she didn't know why. "Nothing for Gil to worry about though," he decided as he studied Maria's face. He had caught her off guard, that's all. Nothing to do with the Repository.

"They've been friends ever since Rosa's husband disappeared," Joe added.

Angel relaxed slightly. That explained the BPA. "Oh yes, the pilot. I remember," Angel said, turning his attention to Joe.

"And you are here in the school trailer because...?" Joe asked Angel in a cold voice.

"Charlie Medrano is a good friend of mine," Angel shot back at Joe. A small smile played across his lips. "I help out around the school whenever I can. They are short-staffed now more than ever. It's very unfair to the children, don't you agree? Their artwork," he added before Joe could reply, "their artwork reveals so much about their lives. It's a shame. Well, I'll check in on Charlie before I go. Nice to meet you both."

"He's a smooth piece of work," Joe said in a low voice as soon as Angel left the alcove. "What is it, Maria? Are you OK?"

"I don't understand it," she said. "Nothing like that has ever happened before. Forget it, will you? I feel fine now, and we have more important things to worry about."

"No problem," Joe said. "Already forgotten."

While they waited for Angel to return, Maria found herself looking again at the closet door in the alcove. "Joe, what's the problem with Ramón's basket?"

"It looks like someone went searching through it in a hurry."

Maria tensed. "What do you think that means?"

"Here's one way it could have gone down," Joe said slowly. "Just speculation at this point, but let's say that Juan really did have incriminating evidence against Gil, evidence that he was hoping to use to buy freedom for him and his family, say in a Witness Protection Program."

"Go on."

"Let's say Juan told Pipé about it."

"No, that doesn't make sense. Pipé was killed after Juan."

"I know, but separate things for a moment. What if Juan made a threat to Gil's thugs right before they killed him? Not the smartest thing to do, but you don't always think straight when you're facing death. Maybe there was a gun barrel in his face, maybe he wanted to fight back by saying something that would frighten them."

"And?"

"And so they got frightened. But they weren't sure. Maybe it was just an empty threat. Now back to Pipé. If Pipé told the mole about Juan, Gil would know that Pipe was an informant. So maybe he tells his guys to take Pipé and find out what he knows. And Pipe tells them that Juan really did have some evidence. Now they are seriously worried."

"Do you think Juan really did have evidence?"

"It doesn't matter. What's important is that now it looks like Gil thinks he did."

"How do you know that?"

Joe dropped his voice. "We have an undercover agent who's been able to infiltrate Snake Baby's gang. They've been told to keep their eyes open for anything Juan might have left in N. Building or anywhere else around the projects."

Maria stared at him. "You could have told me," she said finally.

"I didn't have time, remember? You were headed for the school to see Rosa. This is the first chance I've had to tell you."

"You don't trust me," she said. "You don't trust me with Rosa."

Joe didn't say anything.

"What about the search out at the projects?"

"According to our agent, they haven't found anything, and frankly, I don't think they ever will. If Juan had hidden something around N. Building, finding it would be almost impossible. He would have left word with someone. No point in leaving evidence if no one can find it."

"Rosa!" Then Maria shook her head. "No, she doesn't know anything. I'm sure of that." She paused. "Do you think they found something in the basket?"

"I don't think Juan would have left anything with Ramón either, if that's what you're thinking," Joe said quickly. "Putting his family at risk is the last thing he would have wanted to do. But sometimes, if you're desperate enough and you don't have many choices....."

She nodded. "I agree. It's very unlikely that Juan left anything with Ramón. But then why did someone search Ramón's basket?"

"Because Gil will want to check out everything, even if it's a long shot."

Neither of them spoke for a few minutes. Maria broke the silence. "We need to talk more about the school picnic," she said with a determined look on her face.

"Fine with me," Joe said. "Let's talk."

17

THURSDAY
Mr. Medrano's classroom
Third-Grade Trailer

ROSA STUDIED MR. MEDRANO while she waited to speak to him, trying to decide how to tell him about her fears for Ramón. Mr. Medrano had a long, thin face and a bumpy nose that looked like it had been broken more than once. And he was so small and bony, he seemed to be floating around inside his clothes, everything several sizes too large. He was almost forty and not yet married. At least that's what Ana Fuentes told her.

Rosa wondered if it was because of the way he looked. Probably no one would describe him as good looking. But he didn't seem worried about his appearance. His glasses were still held together on one side by a safety pin, just like they were the first time she met him last fall. And there was still yellow chalk dust on his sleeve. She liked the way he looked. He had an honest face and kind eyes. She thought she could trust him. If only she could explain things well enough to make him understand.

When it was her turn, she went up to the front of the classroom. "Thank you for letting me come," she began. "I want to talk to you about Ramón." Before she could say anything else, the tall man with the light hair and pale eyes she had seen standing by the Repository walked into the classroom.

"Angel," Mr. Medrano said. "What are you doing here?"

"Just thought I'd see if you are all set for tomorrow," Angel said.

"Yes, we're all set, Angel, thanks." Medrano hesitated. "You talked with Detective Chavez?"

"Yes, I did, and Border Patrol Agent Carter as well," Angel said pleasantly. "It looks to me as if you have very good security, Charlie."

"No, that's not it," Medrano corrected him. "Maria is Rosa's friend. She's here to give her a ride home, that's all."

Angel stared at Rosa, waiting for an introduction.

"Señora Alvarez," Medrano said finally. "This is Angel Ramirez. He's in charge of the Repository."

"A pleasure, Señora," Angel said walking over to shake her hand. "I think we met earlier. So you're Ramón's mother." His voice was friendly, but Rosa felt a shiver go down her back when he touched her.

"Thank you," Rosa said in a voice so low, it was more like a whisper.

"See you tomorrow," Angel said to Medrano before he left the room. Rosa listened to his footsteps go down the hall.

"Now tell me," Mr. Medrano said with a reassuring smile. "You have something important to say. The reason you came to see me today is...."

Angel could not have interrupted them at a worse time. Now Rosa had to find her courage all over again. The words stayed stuck in her throat.

"Your son is a gifted student," Mr. Medrano said after a few moments of silence. "He's a bright, curious, boy. He works hard. He's popular with his classmates too. You must be a very proud mother." Rosa nodded. She needed more time. Something else to say until she could find the right words to explain.

"That man," she said hesitantly. "With the light hair and pale eyes?"

Mr. Medrano waited for Rosa to tell him what was on her mind, but she seemed lost in her thoughts.

"He has a somewhat strange appearance, I know," Mr. Medrano said, trying to fill up the awkward silence, "but he's become a real friend to us here at the school. His job requires him to be at the Repository at all times of the day and night, and more than once, he's been able to help us out in an emergency when no one else was around. By now everyone calls him Angel, Mr. Angel. He's certainly an angel to the abandoned dogs and cats that come around here looking for something to eat. Angel always manages to find food to put out for them."

Medrano paused, waiting for Rosa to say something. When she remained silent, he went on. "We're understaffed here. Overcrowded and understaffed. The truth is, I don't know what we'd do without him. Angel will cover a class if a teacher is late, and he knows first aid, which means that most of the time, he's the closest thing to a nurse we've got. He's generous too. He's offered to bring ice cream out to the park tomorrow as a special surprise treat for the children. He really is an angel in disguise."

Rosa scarcely followed what Mr. Medrano was saying. She was still trying to get up enough courage to ask him about the school trip to Riverside Park. Could she come too? That way she'd be able to stay close to Ramón and help look after the other children.

But she couldn't find the words. Probably the school had already invited the parents they wanted. She could feel her face growing hot.

Mr. Medrano rubbed his eyes. He looked tired. "What is it, Señora?" he asked patiently. "Is it about Ramón's father?"

Rosa worked hard to keep the knot in her throat from dissolving into tears.

Mr. Medrano waited. "Don't hurry," he said. "You're my last appointment today. There's plenty of time."

"I'm worried about Ramón," she said finally. "I'm afraid for him."

"Because of his father?" Mr. Medrano asked again.

Rosa still didn't know how to say what was really on her mind. "Yes," she said finally in defeat. "Yes."

"Do you want to tell me what happened?" Mr. Medrano asked. "The police would say only that he was missing."

Unexpectedly, the desire to tell her story to Mr. Medrano overwhelmed her. The words poured out. She told Mr. Medrano everything from the beginning. Ramón's father was a pilot for a computer company. That was the cargo he carried in his plane, computer parts and assembled computers. She wanted to be sure Mr. Medrano understood.

Last week, after Juan had left his plane to be unloaded at the airport in Mexico, he had hitched a ride into the town of Purgatorio and then crossed into the U.S. on foot through the official Port of Entry, the POE. It was only a five-minute walk into Lastup from the POE, and whenever Juan was in Lastup waiting for his cargo to be unloaded, he went into Lastup to look for new postcards for Ramón.

Rosa paused, fighting back the tears.

"Oh yes, the postcards," Mr. Medrano said right away, trying to give Rosa a few minutes to collect herself. "Ramón brought his shoebox full of cards to share with the class just last week. Those postcards are very special, Señora. The black and white photographs of the Rio Poderoso, the way it used to be. The pictures of the old highway, El Camino Real, before the interstate was built. And all those views of Ciudad Nueva as it was a hundred years ago. Real treasures, Señora."

Rosa felt a surge of pride. "Juan found those postcards for Ramón," she said. "Whenever he was in Lastup, Juan would go to see Pipé, an old friend of his who sold postcards and souvenirs near the church of Santa Teresa. Pipé was always looking for postcards for Ramón's collection." Her eyes filled up again with tears. Pipé had been a good friend to her husband. Now the police couldn't find Pipé anywhere either.

"Please go on," Mr. Medrano said after a moment.

She nodded. "I remember how excited Ramón was whenever Juan came home with new postcards or photographs of his plane. Ramón treasured those gifts. And Juan would always tell Ramón, '*La mejor fortuna eres tú, mijo.* But the best treasure of all, my son, is you!' Then they would hug each other and...."

Mr. Medrano looked at her sympathetically. "You were saying that your husband went into Lastup while his cargo was being unloaded at the airport?"

"Yes," she said. "The Point of Entry Records show that Juan walked out of Purgatorio and into Lastup at 11:05 am on 18 May 2009." She knew the time and date by heart.

"But since then," she continued slowly, willing herself not to start crying again, "no one's seen him, there's no sign of him anywhere. No body. No nothing.

"No explanation either," she started to add. Then she stopped. What was the point? She would never know the truth. All she would ever know was that Juan had gone out of her life forever, as if the earth had swallowed him up.

"When did you learn that your husband was missing?"

She tried to explain. While his plane waited for him at the airport into the night, she had waited for him at home with a heaviness in her heart that crushed all thought, all hope. Finally one of the men from the airport had called her just before midnight. They didn't know where her husband was. She didn't know either.

Early the next morning, she'd telephoned Rivera's Groceries where she worked mornings as a cashier. She had to stay home, she told them. An emergency. The school bus came and took Ramón to school. She sat down by the telephone to wait. But no one came. No one called.

"What about your family?" Mr. Medrano asked.

She shook her head. That was hard to explain too. Everyone else had family close by. But she was only fifteen years old when Juan had asked her to go away with him to find a better life in *el norte*. When she told her family what she was planning to do, they acted as if she had broken something sacred. Juan's family was just as hard. They blamed him for disgracing her. The whole village shut them out. Told them, if you don't get married before you leave, don't come back.

So she and Juan had come north alone. Once they had papers, they'd married, but they'd never seen their families again. She thought Juan might have a distant cousin in Lastup, but she wasn't sure. She'd never met him.

"Your friends?" Mr. Medrano said

Rosa shook her head again, embarrassed this time. She knew she was different from the other Latina women in the neighborhood. The women at work teased her. "Where's your Latina spirit?" they asked her.

She didn't know the answer to that. All she knew was that she'd always been this way. Different. Quiet. Shy. Juan understood her. But Juan worked long hours. When he came home, he was tired. She had one close friend, but her family was her life.

"I understand, Señora," Mr. Medrano said.

Rosa went on with her story. Later that morning, she told him, she went upstairs to talk to her best friend, Ana Fuentes. Ana had tried to help. She'd called the assembly plant and asked for help, but the operator told her personal calls were not allowed. Ana had even persuaded Rosa to call the police. They told her it was too soon to be worried, too soon to report a missing person.

But in the late afternoon, a policeman had come out to the apartment to ask her some questions. He didn't look like a policeman, with his long black hair in a ponytail and a cigarette in his mouth, so she'd asked him for identification. He'd showed her his badge and explained that he was a detective from the Vereda district station. Rosa paused. "At first I was afraid he would be angry with me for asking to see his badge," she admitted to Mr. Medrano.

"You had every right," Mr. Medrano said quickly. "Was he angry?"

Rosa shook her head. "No, no, not at all. He said most people thought he looked strange for a policeman."

"What was his name, Señora, do you remember?"

"Detective Diaz, Al Diaz," she said without hesitation.

Mr. Medrano nodded. "Oh yes, I know Detective Diaz. He spends a lot of time in the community, walking the streets, talking to people. He's not a cop who stays in his car looking out at us. Al's the right person to look for your husband here in Vereda. He'd know where to go, who to ask."

Rosa took a deep breath. "When I asked him why the police had decided to investigate Juan's disappearance, he said someone at G&G Computers had called his boss."

"What else did he say?"

"He asked me a few questions. Then Detective Chavez came out. She explained to me that Juan's case would be assigned to the authorities in Lastup. She said the police had to do their searching in the place where Juan disappeared."

Rosa paused and looked at Mr. Medrano. "Lastup is so far away," she said finally.

Mr. Medrano nodded. "I understand. Too far away for you to do anything."

"Yes," she said gratefully. "Yes. But that's not why I'm here," she said firmly. Talking about Juan had given her new courage. Now she would explain the real reason for her visit.

18

THURSDAY
Mr. Medrano's classroom
Third-Grade Trailer

"I KNOW JUAN'S DISAPPEARANCE has changed the way I see the world," Rosa began, remembering what Maria had said. "But it's not only that. I also have..." She paused, searching for the words that would sound right. "I have a mother's intuition, you know?"

Medrano nodded.

"I don't know how to explain it," Rosa continued. "But I am afraid for Ramón, that if he goes to the park tomorrow, something might harm him. Detective Chavez said maybe you could help me decide what to do."

Mr. Medrano was silent for a few moments. "I don't know exactly what to tell you, Señora," he said finally. "I can't promise you that nothing will happen to Ramón. But I can tell you that the park staff is very well trained. I will be with the class and some of the parents will be there too. School children visit the park all the time, and nothing has ever happened to any of them."

His voice softened. "Señora, this is an important trip for Ramón. He has been preparing for it all year. He will finally have the chance to see some of the animals he's been reading about, especially the Blue Herons, his favorites."

Rosa smiled back at him. It was true. Ramón was always talking about seeing the Blue Herons in the park.

"Ramón is a very fine student," Mr. Medrano continued. "But in my experience, to be successful in this country means that Ramón will also have to accept the culture of *el Norte*, its ideals, its values. Do you understand what I mean? He will have to fit in. That may mean giving up some of the values you grew up with. A bright future here in the north often comes with a price tag. In more practical terms, for example, that means he is going to have to explain to his friends why you kept him home from the park."

Rosa felt her heart sink.

"Dear Señora," Mr. Medrano said right away. "Please, don't be upset. That's just my opinion. I could be wrong. You must do what you think is right. If you keep him home, I will help Ramón explain to his friends. If you want, we can even say that Ramón is not feeling well."

"No," she said shaking her head. "That would not be truthful." They were both silent. But after a few moments, Rosa said in a confident voice, "I think I will let him go."

"What changed your mind?" Mr. Medrano asked. He looked puzzled.

"I want Ramón to fit in," Rosa explained. "This is his world. I want him to succeed. Old dreams should not ruin things for him."

When Rosa got up to leave, Mr. Medrano looked even smaller than before, as if the weight of her words lay heavy on his shoulders. He took her hand. "*Vaya con Dios*, Señora Alvarez," he said quietly. "I promise you, tomorrow at the park, I will do everything I can to look out for your son."

Medrano walked down the hall with Rosa to the alcove where Maria and Joe were waiting.

"Everything OK, Rosa?" Maria said.

Rosa nodded shyly. "Can we talk in the car?" she said.

"Of course," Maria said. "But Charlie," she said turning to Medrano, "before we leave, can we talk about the art gallery?"

"You enjoyed the children's artwork?" Medrano asked. He looked pleased.

"We sure did!" Joe said. "We were also wondering about the baskets in the closet," he added, pointing to the door latch on the right-hand side of the alcove wall.

"The closet?" He was surprised.

"And the baskets," Maria added.

Medrano looked uncomfortable. "You've discovered our little secret," he admitted. He walked over to the back wall and lifted the latch, opening the closet door.

"There's Ramón's basket," Rosa said, looking at a basket on the top shelf. Someone had pasted a picture of a Blue Heron next to his name.

"You might as well take it, Señora," Medrano said handing the basket to her. "I asked the children to start bringing their things home today. Less confusion tomorrow, you know?"

"Why is everything in Ramón's basket tossed around like that?" Maria asked.

"I think I know what happened," Rosa said. "Ramón probably tried to empty the whole basket into his book bag, but it didn't fit. He already has so many books inside that bag. He must have tossed everything back inside the basket and gone running for the bus."

Medrano nodded. "If you'll wait a minute, I'll get a bag from my room so that you can bring everything in his basket home to him today."

Rosa smiled. "OK," she said. "It's a big deal," she explained to Maria, proud of being able to use American slang in the conversation. "Tomorrow is Ramón's birthday. His father left him a special birthday gift before he...disappeared. They decided to leave the gift here at school in Ramón's basket. They were afraid that otherwise Ramón wouldn't be able to wait until his birthday before opening it. Rosa's voice trailed off. "I don't know why Juan gave it to Ramón so much ahead of time," she added, as if she was thinking about it for the first time.

Medrano was back with a large green plastic bag and a brown shopping bag. The shape of a shoe box was clearly visible inside the brown bag. "Ramón's postcards," he said holding out the bag to Rosa. "Please thank him again for bringing them to school. The students loved seeing them. So did I. But you might as well bring them home today. We don't want them getting lost in the confusion of closing up school tomorrow."

"I'll get that for you, Rosa," Joe said taking the bag from Medrano. "You'll have enough to carry."

Rosa didn't answer. She was busy searching through the contents of Ramón's basket. "Here it is, here's his present!" she said in an excited voice. In the middle of all the notebooks, paper, and crayons, there was a box with a large card taped to the outside of the package. The words "For Ramón" were written in large letters on the envelope. "I'm so proud of Ramón," Rosa said. "I know how anxious he was to open his present, but he left it here so he wouldn't be tempted to open it ahead of time."

Maria was surprised and curious about the new note of confidence in Rosa's voice. She seemed happier, more sure of herself, talking about the birthday present even though it was such a bleak reminder of Juan's absence. "Let me help you," Maria said. Rosa nodded and together they put everything from Ramón's basket into the green bag.

"One more thing," Maria said to Medrano. "Ramón's best friend is Carlito Fuentes. Where is Carlito's basket?"

Medrano's shoulders seemed to sag. "Yes, that's the problem," he admitted. "I know it's not exactly fair, but these baskets are only for the students in the honors program. When the administration took out all the lockers, there was no place for the honor students to leave their books. They have so many books and different projects. It seemed wrong to punish them for the action of a few older boys. Using the closet seemed to work. It's just a few more days anyway. Then we will have our new school!" He looked tired and serious. "The choices are difficult when you have so little of what you need," he said slowly. "I try to do the right thing."

"God bless you, Mr. Medrano," Rosa said unexpectedly taking his hand. "You are a good man."

"Thank you, Señora, I have to go now," he said. "There is a lot to prepare for tomorrow." He seemed to be limping as he walked back down the hall to his classroom.

"That is one exhausted teacher," Maria said quietly. "But God willing, tomorrow everything at the picnic will go well."

19

THURSDAY AFTERNOON
The Office Supply Repository

ANGEL WALKED BACK TO THE REPOSITORY, tormented by the headache scraping painfully at the inside of his head. The headaches came whenever he spent any time in the sunlight. His sunglasses were the darkest he could buy, but his pale eyes were unnaturally sensitive to light. "You have a disease. It's incurable," the eye doctor had explained to him. "All you can do is avoid bright light. And always wear sunglasses."

Thoughts of Gil tormented Angel almost as much as his headache. All his attention was focused on what Gil might want from him when he heard about the two cops in the trailer.

Angel went through the back door into the Repository. It was a dark cavernous building, and the air smelled closed, but it was a relief from the heat wave still in a holding pattern over Vereda. The main floor served as the showroom for customers. Desks, tables, and bookcases lined the walls. Chairs and file cabinets were left in whatever space remained.

Angel scanned the showroom. No one was there except for the two customers who had just arrived and the middle-aged woman sitting behind a counter at the front of the room. She was reading a magazine. A large computer filled up most of the counter space in front of her.

"Take care of them," Angel called out to her, pointing to the men in the showroom. "I'm going up to my office. Don't call me."

He headed over to the wide freight elevator that carried furniture to the basement level. Next to the elevator, a narrow flight of stairs disappeared into shadows on the second floor. Angel went up the stairs.

The Repository's second floor was a natural home for Angel. The only interior light came from a few rows of humming fluorescent lights on the ceiling. His corner office had two large windows that gave him a clear view of the traffic approaching the building, the loading docks, and the trailers in the back, but most of the time the windows were covered with dark heavy curtains. He opened them only when he needed to observe what was going on outside.

Angel went into his office and closed the door. The room was sparsely furnished. There was a large desk against one wall and a dark brown canvas knapsack on the floor next to the desk.

On the other side of the room there was a sleep couch covered by a gray blanket and a few pillows. Ignoring the stabs of pain to his eyes, Angel pulled open the curtains covering the windows and scanned the view outside for several minutes. Nothing. He closed the curtains. Then he went over to his desk and sat down.

The surface of his desk was empty except for a land-line telephone, a desk calendar, and an intercom. He opened the right-hand drawer. Inside were several drop phones and some plastic bags containing batteries. He took out one of the phones and pushed the direct call button. As soon as the connection was made, he hung up. In less than a minute the phone rang back once, then went silent.

After Angel had dropped the phone he'd used into the wastebasket beside his desk, he picked up the knapsack and checked inside. Everything he needed was there, his binoculars, an extra pair of sunglasses, and a hat.

He took a new phone and one of the plastic bags containing batteries out of the desk drawer and put them into the knapsack. Then he closed the knapsack and stood up, looking around his office one more time. Everything was in order. It was time for him to leave.

He walked down the stairs and went out the back door. The first car in line at the loading dock was his for the day. A bright red Mazda. Angel smiled. He never knew what kind of car would be waiting for him. All he knew for sure was that the car was "clean," that Gil's boys would have checked it out carefully for bugs or tracking devices of any kind. The keys were already in the ignition.

Angel drove off carefully. He didn't want to mess anything up by getting a traffic ticket.

Gil was crazy, no doubt about it. Crazy and paranoid, Angel thought to himself, as he turned onto the expressway. And Gil was bored. But it was Gil's money, Gil's organization, and he could do what he wanted. And what Gil wanted was to outsmart the cops while using Angel as a sounding board. It was insane, everyone said so, to talk so long and openly over a cell phone. But Gil was like a little boy, playing a game. It was Gil's game to play, and he was willing to risk everything to prove that he could win.

Angel took the exit for the Nature Preserve. He had to use a different location for each call. The Nature Preserve had a large parking lot, and in this kind of heat, it was usually half empty. All the same, Angel kept his eyes on the rearview mirror. No one had followed him.

He drove in and parked where there were no other cars anywhere near him. He took out his binoculars and put them around his neck just in case anyone asked what he was doing there. He had already decided that if anyone asked, he would say, "I'm going to observe the aviary." He liked the sound of those words.

He took the phone out of his knapsack and put in the batteries. Gil always made him keep the batteries separate from the phone until they were ready to talk. Then he punched in the direct call button.

"*Que?*" Gil said.

"It's me, man!" Angel said. Then he went silent, waiting for Gil to start with the questions.

"Everything quiet? Everything straight?"

"Yeah, man. Everything's smooth. But two cops went into Medrano's trailer this afternoon, Chavez from the CNPD and a Border Patrol Agent named Carter."

"Yeah, yeah," Gil said impatiently.

Angel wondered how Gil always knew things before he did, but he put the thought out of his mind. It wasn't his job to be curious.

"The kid's mother was there to talk with Charlie about her son," Angel said. "Chavez was there to drive her home."

"Believe her?"

"Yeah, I think so. The word out at N. Building is that they've become friends since the pilot disappeared."

"And the BPA Carter?"

"He works out of Lastup where they discovered the bodies. He got the case. I think he has something going with Chavez too."

"You were watching!" Gil snickered. "Good thing it wasn't Snake Baby on lookout."

Angel didn't say anything. Gil knew how much he hated Snake Baby. Finally he asked, "Have the cops ID'd the body yet?"

"They're sure it's the pilot. They just can't prove it."

"Why?"

Gil laughed. "Because we cut off all the important parts, that's why."

Angel was silent.

"You don't like Snake Baby's work?"

"I didn't say that."

"But you're wondering, aren't you? You're wondering why Snake Baby cut up the pilot."

Again Angel went quiet. But of course he was wondering. What the hell had happened down there?

"I appreciate you not asking," Gil said. He was angry now. "So I'm going to tell you. I'm going to tell you because this whole fucking mess is Snake Baby's fault. Goddamn little punk. I'm telling you, the whole, fucking mess is his fault!"

Angel waited.

"About the pilot," Gil said in his raspy voice. "I told the boys, tough luck, wrong place, wrong time. Just shoot him. Make it fast. I'm not a monster, after all." Angel couldn't help thinking about how much Gil loved to bullshit about what a good guy he was.

"I reward loyalty," Gil went on. "The pilot worked ten years for me, and he did good work the whole time. Too bad he came back from town early and saw what he shouldn't have saw. But that don't mean he has to suffer, you know?"

Angel nodded.

"So Snake Baby puts the gun to his head. Says 'good-bye pilot' and starts to pull the trigger. But just then the pilot makes a pronouncement, all serious-like. 'The truth will come out,' he says. 'And they will know what you did, you piece of shit.'

"So Snake Baby goes ballistic, you know how he is when he gets mad. He yells at the pilot, 'Piece of shit? Oh yeah?! Well eat this, you piece of shit' and pulls the trigger.

"The pilot falls to the ground, dead as only dead can be. But then Snake Baby starts to think. What did the pilot mean, the truth will come out? Only now there's no way he can ask what that means because the pilot is dead. So Snake Baby goes over the edge, cutting and swinging and swearing, take this you son of a bitch, take that you bastard, only at the end, all he's got is a bunch of body parts and no answers. What an asshole!"

Angel's mouth was too dry to form the words running through his head. He wondered why Snake Baby was still alive. Why did Gil put up with him? Why was Snake Baby so important to Gil? And what did the pilot mean, the truth will come out?

"Never mind, Angel," Gil said in a calm voice. It was like he could tell Angel was swimming in water over his head. "There's nothing to worry about. The pilot was just yanking Snake Baby's balls, you know that, right? And even if he wasn't, even if the pilot left something behind, we would've heard about it by now, right? Trust me. Our information comes from the top. All we're doing now is playing it safe, just keeping an eye open for anything unexpected. You OK with that?"

Angel nodded.

"I can't hear you nodding, asshole," Gil said, laughing at him.

"No problem," Angel said right away.

"Good. Now, what were the two cops doing in the trailer?"

"Waiting near the front door."

"Anything interesting around the front door?"

"Nothing except some pictures the kids made that Medrano taped onto the walls of the alcove."

"Do the surveillance cameras cover the alcove?"

"No," Angel said, shaking his head.

"Did the cops show any interest in the Repository?"

"Nah, nothing."

Gil was silent, but Angel could hear him thinking. "Call Snake Baby," Gil said finally. "Tell him to keep an eye on what happens when they bring the Alvarez woman back to her apartment. I'll talk to you later."

"Will do," Angel said. He hung up the phone without another word. He never questioned Gil's orders. Never even thought about them much. But he despised Snake Baby. That was a feeling he couldn't put down. It made him mad that Snake Baby could do whatever he wanted. He could even disobey Gil's orders. But Gil needed Snake Baby. There was no use getting mad about it. Gil was in charge.

The only thing Angel hadn't told Gil was that he had recognized the girl, the woman cop. And she had recognized him too, only she didn't know it. He could tell. He could see the fear in her eyes. But little kids didn't have memories, he'd read all about that. Why mention it to Gil? He'd probably just start laughing at him.

20 | THURSDAY AFTERNOON
Rosa's apartment
North Building

"CAN YOU STAY?" Rosa asked when they got back to the apartment.

Joe looked at Maria. She nodded her agreement.

Rosa put the paper bag full of postcards on the couch near the front door. She looked cautiously at Joe "Will you wait while I make some tea?" she asked hesitantly. "If we could talk...."

"Of course," Maria said. "Come on, Joe."

"Where should I put this?" Joe asked. He was holding the green bag with the contents of Ramón's basket inside.

"Anywhere on the couch is fine," Rosa said.

After Rosa had poured the tea, they sat in silence until Rosa said quietly, "I'm going to send Ramón to the park tomorrow."

"Ramón will be very happy," Maria said, careful not to let any of the uncertainty she was feeling show in her voice.

"What made you decide to let him go?" Joe asked Rosa.

"I want Ramón to succeed," Rosa said. "This new world is his world. Old dreams should not ruin it for him. And I want to dream too. I want to dream that he will succeed."

Joe smiled at her. "Ramón is a lucky boy."

"I am lucky too," Rosa said. "I have friends now, friends like Maria and Mr. Medrano. They care about Ramón, I know it. Maybe there is hope after all."

"Rosa, there's something else we need to talk about before Ana brings Ramón back," Maria said. "Joe thinks you might be able to help us. You remember when Juan disappeared, and his case was assigned to someone in Lastup?"

"I remember," Rosa said slowly. The glow of happiness faded from her face. "You?" she asked Joe.

He nodded.

"Has something happened?" Rosa said.

Joe didn't answer right away. He seemed to be looking inward for the right words, and Maria read something in his face she hadn't seen before, the shadow of an old pain, a flash of doubt. Then it was gone.

"Yes, Rosa, a couple of things have happened," Joe said. "And I think it's important we talk about them now before you make your final decision about sending Ramón to the park tomorrow."

Rosa sat quietly waiting.

"We've learned that Juan's employer, G&G Computers, is owned by Gil Gomez-Gil."

"I've heard of him," Rosa said in a low voice.

"Do you also know that Gil is head of one of the largest smuggling cartels in the country?"

Rosa drew back. "Juan would have never had anything to do with smuggling," she said, unable to keep the hurt out of her voice.

"We know," Joe said in a firm voice. "Juan Alvarez was an honest man."

Rosa nodded, her eyes glued to Joe's face.

"But while Juan was working for Gil, he could have accidentally seen something that put him in danger. Something that made him start thinking about moving away or working for someone else."

"Oh," Rosa said in a faint voice.

"Or he may have found something he thought could be used as evidence against Gil, something he left in a safe place, hoping that it might protect him or at least explain his disappearance to you and the boy."

Rosa stared at Joe, speechless.

"Think Rosa, did Juan leave anything in your keeping?" Joe said. "Did he ever suggest a hiding place of any kind?"

Maria stood up, resolutely pushing aside her desire to tell Rosa what they had learned about Juan's death and the rumor of a package. "Joe can explain things better than I can, Rosa, and I need to use the bathroom. Excuse me?"

Rosa barely nodded. All her attention was on what Joe was saying.

In the bathroom, Maria struggled to regain her composure. Her friendship with Rosa and especially her feelings for Ramón were eating away at her self-control.

Earlier in the trailer, while they had been waiting for Rosa, Maria had confided her plans to Joe. It was his case too. He had a right to know, especially if her decision dragged him into some unpleasant fallout.

"I'm going to tell Rosa everything," she told him.

Joe remained silent, waiting for her to explain further. After an endless minute, Maria decided she might as well finish what she'd started.

"Look, Joe," she began, dropping her voice. "We know Juan has been murdered, we know Gil is now looking for any incriminating evidence Juan might have left behind, and we know Angel was definitely checking us out here in the trailer. Gil is interested in everything that's happening in the vicinity of the Repository, including the school. Rosa should keep Ramón home from school tomorrow. It's too dangerous. Nothing must happen to that little boy."

Almost embarrassed, she had added, "I could tell Rosa to believe in her dreams. As a friend, of course, not as a police officer."

Joe studied Maria. The expression on his face remained neutral, but she could feel his concern. Then he was all business.

"Maria, you persuading Rosa to believe in her dreams, it would be based on information you got because you're a cop. That crosses the line."

Maria was silent.

"Cases like this are hard," Joe added after a moment. "Someday I'd like to tell you what happened to me in a situation much like this one. But for what it's worth, I agree with you in one respect. From the map, it looks like it will be a real challenge to protect the children in Riverside Park."

Maria nodded unhappily. "I know," she said. "A two-mile-long island is a lot of ground to cover."

"That's right," he said. "But what else can we do? At this point in the investigation, we don't know enough to say for sure that Ramón is at risk. All we have is speculation and hunches. We can't even tell Rosa her husband is officially dead."

Maria felt an anger that threatened to overwhelm her. "All these reasons you're giving me. They sound good, but do they really justify taking the chance that Ramón could be hurt or killed? I don't want us to make the wrong choice. It's not easy to live with the knowledge that you made a choice that cost someone his life."

"Do you hear what you just said?" Joe said. Now he was angry. "Believe me, Maria, I speak from experience. Try to keep this case isolated from anything else you've ever known. It's the only way to survive the work we do. Case by case. Otherwise you'll make yourself crazy. No one person is responsible for all the horrors in this world or for rescuing everyone at risk. No one! You could say the world has a mind of its own. And we probably have much less control over what happens than we think we do."

"What would you do?"

"I think we should let Rosa make the choice," Joe said. "She's Ramón's mother. She can keep him home if that's what she wants to do."

Now it was the day before the school trip, and here in Rosa's apartment, the time for making final decisions had arrived. Maria looked at herself in the bathroom mirror, searching for answers in her reflection. If she was going to tell Rosa about the discovery of Juan's body, the moment was now. Still undecided, she opened the bathroom door and joined Joe and Rosa by the kitchen table.

"Joe told me about Gomez-Gil," Rosa said as soon as she saw Maria. "But Juan never said anything to me about his work."

"I know, Rosa, that's OK," Maria said.

"And the day he disappeared, it was an ordinary day, just like any other day."

Maria nodded.

The door into the apartment opened. Ramón dropped his book bag on the floor and came running across the room followed by Carlito and a small, attractive red-haired woman. Ramón grabbed Carlito's hand and pulled him over to Maria. "Come on, Carlito, this is my friend, Detective Maria."

Carlito was taller and thinner than Ramón, with light brown hair and hazel eyes. Acutely shy, he looked down at the floor as Maria shook his hand. "*Hola*, Carlito," Maria said.

Carlito looked up, slowly meeting Maria's eyes.

"I already know your mother," Maria said. "Hello, Ana."

"Hello, Detective Maria," Ana said smiling. "That's quite a name Ramón has for you." She looked over at Joe curiously.

"This is my friend, Joe Carter," Maria said.

"Ana," Joe said with a smile. He took her hand. "I've heard a lot of good things about you from Maria. And this has to be Carlito," he added, putting his hand gently on the boy's shoulder. Carlito gave him a shy grin before he looked back down at the floor.

"I've been working with Maria to help find Juan," Joe said to Ana.

A shadow passed over Ana's face. "I'm glad you're here to help Rosa," she said quietly. "Juan was a good man."

"You've been working with Detective Maria?" Carlito asked Joe in a timid voice. "Are you a detective too?"

Joe hesitated briefly. "Actually I'm a Border Patrol Agent," he said. "I work in a town near the border called Lastup."

Carlito let out a sharp breath and stepped backwards. Ramón stepped back too and stood next to Carlito protectively.

"But for you, Carlito, I'm just a friend of Maria's," Joe added quickly. "When I'm not near the border, I'm just like anyone else. See, I'm not even wearing my uniform."

Carlito wasn't convinced. He grabbed his mother's hand and tried to pull her towards the door. Joe looked around the room for something to distract him. "What's that?" he asked, pointing at the brown paper bag that Rosa had left on the couch. "I wonder what's in that bag."

Ramón ran over to the couch and pulled the shoebox out of the bag. He held it up to Joe. "See? This is my postcard collection. *Mi Papi* helped make it for me."

Joe took the box. "Wow! That's one heavy collection, young man. Any chance I could take a look at it?"

"Sure, I'll show you," Ramón said pulling Joe over to the table. Joe sat down, and Ramón sat down next to him. Then he carefully opened the shoebox and spread the postcards out across the table, waiting for Joe's reaction. His eyes were bright with anticipation.

Joe was astonished. It was an amazing collection of old western postcards mixed together with a few black and white photographs mounted on postcard- size paper. "*Mi Papi*," Ramon said proudly pulling one of the photographs out of the pile and showing it to Joe. "*Mi Papi* and his airplane."

"And this is what was in your honors basket," Rosa said going over to the couch and picking up the green bag. She hesitated a moment, then went through it until she found the box with the card taped to it. "Ramón, look, here's your *Papi's* birthday present and a card for you."

Maria felt her heart skip a beat.

"I know, I know," Ramón said sliding off his chair and running over to take the birthday box from his mother. "But we're supposed to wait until my birthday to open it."

"It's been at the school all this time," Rosa said proudly. "Ramón kept his word. But now I don't know what we should do."

Ramón was hopping from one foot to the other, caught between his excitement at having the birthday present in his hands and his promise not to open it until his birthday.

"Ramón," Rosa said tenderly, "You have waited such a long time. It would be nice if you could open your present now with all your friends here. I think your *Papi* would understand."

"Oh boy! Oh boy!" Ramón said, trembling with excitement as he ripped open the box. Inside was a magnifying glass with a large lens and a finely worked silver handle.

"I've never seen anything like it," Rosa said. "What a beautiful gift your *Papi* left for you, Ramón."

Ramón stared at the magnifying glass, seemingly unable to touch it or even take it out of its box.

"Here's your card," Carlito said, picking it up off the floor where it had fallen. Ramón took the card and carefully pulled open the flap. Inside there were three photographs of Juan standing near his airplane at a large airport and another smaller card with the word "Rosa" written on the front of the envelope.

"Mami, here's a card for you too," Ramón said, giving the card to Rosa.

Rosa took the card and eagerly tore open the envelope to read what was written inside. Then she turned away and began to cry.

"*Mami*, what's wrong?" Ramón said, near tears himself.

"It's nothing, my son," Rosa said bravely. "Only your *Papi's* words. They make me miss him more than ever."

"What did he say?"

"We will be together soon," Rosa read out loud. "While we wait, dearest Rosa, you can use Ramón's glass to keep me even closer to your heart. I love you, Juan."

There was a long silence in the room. "Ramón, your *Papi* would not want you to be sad on your birthday," Rosa said, giving Ramón a long hug. "Let's be happy that he loves us so much. Now tell me, what did he write to you?"

Ramón took the three photographs out of the envelope and looked at each one carefully.

"Look, he wrote something on the back of this one," Carlito said pointing to one of them.

"Can you read it to us?" Rosa asked Ramón.

"Happy Birthday, my dear son," Ramón began to read. "Someday soon we will go flying together. Until then, keep exploring the world with your wonderful curiosity. I hope this lens will help you find all the hidden treasures that surround you. Much love always, your *Papi*."

Holding back his tears, Ramón picked up the magnifying glass and held it as if he was afraid it might break. The sunlight coming through the kitchen window passed through the lens and painted a rainbow across the ceiling. "It's magic," Ramón whispered. "It's beautiful. Thank you, *Papi*, thank you. I wish you were here."

"Wow!" Carlito said, drawn to the magnifying glass like a magnet. "Wow! What a great present. Can I use it, Ramón?"

Ramón nodded. Carlito took the lens and held it over the photographs. "Look, Ramón, look, you can even see the numbers on the planes."

Ramón took the lens and looked at the photographs. "You're right, Carlito, I can see everything, even the freckles on Papi's hands. It's as if he's right here in front of me." He tried to smile.

"Can I see your present too?" Joe asked.

"Sure," Ramón said and ran over to him with the magnifying glass and the envelope with the three photographs in it. He put them all on the table in front of Joe.

Joe picked up some of the postcards. "Here, Ramón," he said. "Hold the lens over the cards. Look at all you can see now. Even the stamp. Look at the picture on it."

Ramón gave a deep sigh. "It really is magic," he said. "It's wonderful. Come on, Carlito. Let's look at some of the other postcards."

The two boys went through the postcards spread out across the table, handing the magnifying lens back and forth, looking for the most interesting pictures.

"Look," Carlito said, holding up a card of the church of Santa Teresa. "Look, it's your Lady in Blue!"

"Let me see," Ramón said, putting the card under the magnifying glass. "Look, Detective Maria," he cried out. "Come here!"

Maria looked at the card. It was an interior shot of the church of Santa Teresa. In the center of the chapel was a statue of the Virgin Mary, dressed in blue.

"She's beautiful," Maria said. "Beautiful. We'll go to see her someday, would you like that?"

"Is it far?" Ramón asked, a worried look on his face. "We don't have a car."

"Yes, we'll have to drive there," Maria told him. "It's over four hours from here to the church of Santa Teresa. But I'll drive. We'll even bring a picnic lunch."

"Can Carlito come too?" Ramón said, giving Maria a long hug.

"Of course," she told him right away. "Everyone is invited."

Joe was studying the postcard collection with such concentration that his back and shoulders seemed to have turned to stone. Rosa looked at him anxiously. "Is something wrong?" she asked.

"Absolutely not!" Joe said firmly. "I was just thinking how valuable this collection is. Your *Papi* must have been a very smart man, Ramón." As Joe spoke, he asked Maria for a distraction with his eyes.

"I have an idea, Ramón," Maria said. "Even though tomorrow is your real birthday, we could celebrate it today, don't you think? After all, we opened the present. Why don't we all go out and get some pizza and ice cream?"

"And I'd like to offer Ramón a special cake," Joe said.

"Oh yes, please *Mami*, let's go get a birthday cake," Ramón pleaded with Rosa.

Rosa started to shake her head, but it was clear that Ramón would have his wish.

"That's a good idea," Ana said. "We need to be cheerful and celebrate. We can't be sad on Ramón's birthday."

"Ramón, you don't mind if I stay here and look at your cards, do you?" Joe said.

"Sure, that's OK," Ramón said happily. He was proud that someone as important as Joe was interested in his collection. "We'll be back soon, I promise."

"Get a very special cake," Joe said. "A ninth birthday is something important to celebrate."

Rosa waited until everyone was out of the apartment before she walked back to Joe. "We don't need charity," she told him in a low voice. "I have money for a cake."

"I know that, Rosa," Joe said, looking straight into her eyes. "But please let me do this for you. I lost a youngster a few years back. It would help me if I could do something for Ramón."

Rosa nodded. "Ok, yes, then. It will be a special party for all of us."

As soon as they were gone, Joe took a camera out of his pocket. It was a small camera with a large lens. He quickly began to photograph all the black and white photographs mixed in with the postcards. After he'd finished, he mixed the photographs back into the postcard collection.

When the group returned with the food and a huge birthday cake, Al Diaz was with them. "We captured Detective Diaz," Rosa said in a laughing voice. "He tried to get away, but Ramon and Carlito captured him. Ramón wanted him to be a part of the party."

"I'm happy to be here with all of you," Al said, looking shy and embarrassed.

"Come look at my postcards," Ramón said pulling Al over to the table.

"First the cake," Al said, looking severely at the boys. "I'm hungry." Ramón started laughing. Even Carlito was shyly grinning up at Al.

After the ice cream and cake, Ramón made Al sit down and look through the postcard collection with him, using the magnifying glass.

"It's wonderful!" Al said. "But I have to go now. Thank you, Ramón." Then he was out the door.

"We have to go too," Maria said, "But Joe and I will be checking on you two boys tomorrow out at the park, so you had better behave."

"You just want some more ice cream," Ramón laughed as he hugged her good-bye.

Maria hurried down the stairs, Joe close behind her. His cell phone was vibrating. He took the phone out of his pocket.

"Wait a minute," Maria said. "Wait. Before you talk to anyone, I want to know. What did you see?"

"I made copies of all the photographs," Joe told her. "But at first glance, it doesn't look like there's anything to implicate Gil or Angel or Snake Baby for that matter. There is one of Juan with his plane and in the back you can see Gil and Angel talking very clearly. But so what? Angel and Gil know each other; they grew up together in Lastup. They have the right to talk at Gil's airport. We can see Gil's airplanes in the background of some of the photographs, but we already knew that Juan was one of his pilots. We can see the numbers on the planes, but I can already tell you, there's nothing we can use."

She sighed. "I was hoping...."

Joe opened his phone. A familiar voice came through at the other end. "Joe, where the hell are you?"

"It's a long story," Joe said. "Maria and I are just leaving Rosa's apartment."

"I'll send someone out for you, Joe," Danforth said. Then he yelled so that Maria could hear him as well. "Go home, Maria. I mean it. Get some sleep. Go home!"

Maria took the phone. "I hear you, Sarge. I'm on my way."

"Maria, Joe!" It was Rosa running towards them. They stopped and waited for her. "I didn't want to say this in front of Ramón," she said, "but there is one more thing you should both know." Her face was animated now, almost joyful.

"Juan would never miss Ramón's birthday, not for anything in the world. I know in my heart that I will probably never see him again," she went on, pushing back the tears. "But I have a tiny, tiny hope. Because if Juan is alive, somehow he will get a message to me tomorrow so that I can be at peace."

21 | THURSDAY EVENING
Angel's office
Repository

AFTER HE'D FINISHED TALKING TO GIL, Angel drove back to the Repository. He went up to his office without speaking to anyone and lay down on the couch. He pulled the gray blanket up to his chin and, after hesitating, closed his eyes. He was too tired to stay awake, but lately he had been having frightening dreams whenever he tried to rest.

In his dreams Gil would turn into Snake Baby and go after him, his black eyes blazing with hatred.

"What did I do?" Angel would keep asking as he ran across an endless nighttime desert, looking for some way to escape. Soon Snake Baby would turn back into Gil, a laughing cartoon turtle with hooded eyes and a short, wrinkled neck. Then Angel would find himself alone and unable to move. All he could do was stare at Gil, trying to figure out why Gil never stopped laughing at him.

A phone in his desk rang once before it went silent.

Angel threw off his blanket and stood up. In a few minutes he would have to call Gil, but he found himself wishing the minutes would move more slowly. He wanted to think about the way he was feeling these days. Something was eating away at the satisfaction he had always found from working with Gil. He knew it was mostly because Snake Baby had become important to Gil, but it was also because Gil kept taking chances, dangerous chances.

Angel walked over to the windows and opened the curtains. Nothing unusual was happening outside. Long shadows were draped over the trailers. The big trucks were parked near the back as usual. The drivers would be somewhere downstairs, eating and talking. Gil always used the same drivers for his shipments. There was Felix, who gave the orders, the Kid, always in baggy jeans, and Smurf, older, with a dark handlebar mustache. They were Gil's most trusted lieutenants. They took care of the shipments, Angel's cars, and his cell phones too. None of them ever bothered Angel. Angel never talked to any of them either.

Angel opened his office door and listened. Everything was quiet downstairs, just as it should be. Business had closed for the night. Around seven the next morning, the big trucks, the 8-wheel vans, would leave the Repository to pick up furniture and make their normal delivery rounds to schools and city offices. Smaller trucks and cars would also come to the Repository during the day to order and pick up various office supplies.

In the afternoon Felix would drive one of the big trucks carrying furniture into Vereda. Unlike the morning shipments, the furniture in the afternoon truck was filled with unofficial merchandise for their regular customers. Felix would make a few discrete stops at businesses near the Hidalgo

Housing Project complex and on Vista Drive. Before Vista Drive went down, Angel corrected himself. No one had figured that one out yet.

After delivering the unofficial packages, Felix would slowly make his way back to the Repository. He made different stops along the way, to get something to eat at his favorite truck stop, or his favorite bar, or he would stop to visit with some friends in the parking area near the railroad, constantly checking to be sure no one was following him. By the time Snake Baby was telling his "little snakes" where to deliver the drugs, Felix was sitting comfortably in the Repository with the other drivers, and any connection between the packages and the Repository had vanished. Gil was brilliant, Angel had to admit it, and the Repository traffic was a gift.

Angel had read an old mystery story many years ago. He couldn't remember the title or the author, but it was something about hiding a letter by putting it out in plain sight. The investigators never found the letter they were searching for because it was right in front of their eyes. Angel had told Gil about that story, and Gil had remembered it. "You helped me discover the Repository," Gil used to tell Angel. Lately though, all Gil did was scream at him about Snake Baby.

Angel made his way down the stairs. A blue Volvo station wagon was parked in the place reserved for his car. He drove off slowly, trying to figure out where to go. There was a large gas station complex only a few miles away with an all-night convenience store. That would have to do even though it was close to the Repository. Gil would be getting impatient.

Angel parked the car near the gas station. Then he put the batteries into the phone and punched in the direct call number. Every call he made to Gil was to a different phone number already programmed into the new phone. Gil thought of everything.

"*Que?*" Gil yelled at him as soon as he got on the line.

Angel could tell from his voice that Gil was upset.

"*Que? Que fue?!?*" Gil said in the same tight voice. "I been waiting for your call for hours. What the hell is your problem?"

"I wanted to check things out first," Angel said defensively.

"And?"

"The two cops and the kid's mother left the trailer around 4:30. The mother was carrying a large brown paper bag with a box in it. It looked like a shoe box. I went over to talk to Medrano, to make final plans about when I should bring the ice cream out to the park. I mention the box. He tells me the box is the kid's postcard collection. The pilot used to buy postcards from Pipé whenever he was in Lastup waiting for them to load the plane."

"Pipé? The snitch?"

Again Angel wondered. How did Gil always know these things? How did he find out that Pipé was a snitch? Sooner or later Angel always heard the talk on the street, but there had never even been a whisper about Pipé.

"Angel? What are you thinking? That Pipé passed on information to the pilot?"

Angel snapped back to attention. "I got a headache," he lied. His second lie. What was wrong with him? What if Gil thought he was getting too curious for his own good? He had better shape up and fast.

"Are you thinking that Pipé passed on information to the pilot?" Gil said again. "Because I can tell you positively, he didn't. The pilot didn't know nothing. Pipé's contact was the BPA, Carter. You understand me, Angel?"

Angel nodded. Pipé would have told Gil's boys anything by the time they were through with him. "So it was just chance?" he found himself asking Gil. "Just chance the pilot got picked up?"

"Playing it safe," Gil said laughing. "It happens. Now back to business. What about this box of postcards?"

"Like I said, it was a collection of old postcards the pilot made for his kid. He bought the postcards from Pipé whenever he was in Lastup. The kid brought the collection into school a few weeks ago. Medrano left it out in full view on his desk for the other kids to look at whenever they wanted. Hard to believe the pilot would have slipped anything into the postcard collection. Who would know? And anyone could see them."

"Agreed," Gil said slowly. Angel could feel him thinking. Gil was like a computer, sorting through information piece by piece. And he never forgot anything. "OK." Gil paused. "So why did the pilot say, 'They will know'?" Gil said, interrupting Angel's thoughts.

Angel started. He felt caught off balance. Why was Gil jumping so fast like that from one idea to another? He tried to put his thoughts in order. "I don't know," he said hesitantly.

Gil was silent. Then he asked, "You ever look at the postcards, Angel?"

Angel felt a shiver run down his back. Gil wanted to know everything he did. He hoped he never forgot anything.

"Yeah, I did, when the kids first brought them in."

"And?"

"Nothing. Some old postcards, just like I said, and a few black-and-white photographs of the pilot next to his plane."

There was a long silence.

"What's the matter?" Angel said finally.

"What made you look at the cards?" Gil said.

"You told me to keep an eye on things."

Gil laughed. "Angel! You should have told me sooner, but it's OK, the thing is, you looked, you noticed. Pat yourself on the back."

Angel stopped himself just in time. He didn't need to hear Gil laughing at him again.

"So the mother left the trailer with the shoebox in a paper bag, right?"

"Right."

"What else?"

The BPA was carrying a large, green plastic bag with a lot of stuff in it. It looked heavy. They must have emptied everything in the kid's basket into the green bag."

"So after the mother and the others left the trailer, the kid's basket was empty?"

"Right. Medrano said he'd asked the kids to clean out their stuff, bring it home for the summer. Less confusion the last day of school. I guess some of them did and some of them didn't."

"What about the stuff that was in the kid's basket?"

"How could I know what was in the kid's basket? It was empty by the time I went to look at it. But I looked at the other baskets. Some of them were empty. Others still had school stuff inside, you know, notebooks, pens, pencils."

"The kid went straight home after school?"

"I know he did. I told Snake Baby's boys to watch him. He got off the bus and went to play with his friend, Carlito, while his mother took the bus out to the school for the conference with Medrano."

"So what do you think, Angel? Should I just leave this alone?"

Angel was silent.

"I've been thinking about something," Gil went on. "That cop, Chavez, she and her friend Cart-er spent a lot of time in the apartment tonight. What if the pilot left something in the postcard collection? What if Chavez found it?"

Angel felt sick. "No way," he said. "The pilot wouldn't risk it, putting his family in danger like that."

"Of course, we'll search the apartment," Gil went on, ignoring Angel's comment. "We'll search it subtle-like. No attention. But what if Chavez has already found the information? What if she's bringing it home?"

Gil's losing it, Angel thought to himself. He's not making sense. He's looking for trouble. That's why he likes Snake Baby. He feeds off trouble.

"Why would she bring it home?" he couldn't help asking.

"Shut up," Gil said. "No questions, remember?"

Angel was quiet.

"Anyway," Gil went on over Angel's silence, "I told Snake Baby he could have some fun with Chavez tonight." He gave a little laugh. "Why not?"

"Why can't you find out if there was something in the postcard collection from your source?"

"Shut up!" Gil said in an angry voice. Angel didn't like the sound of it. Whoever the source was, he would pay a high price if he was playing games with Gil.

"Maybe there hasn't been time," he said to Gil. "Your source is all the way down in Lastup, right?"

"Shut up, Angel. I warned you before, don't ask questions."

Angel shut up.

"Chavez is too nosey anyway," Gil said. "Always hanging around the projects, talking with the residents. She's interfering with business. So I told Snake Baby he could teach her a real lesson this time. First he should follow her home, but follow her so she knows it. No cop likes to think we can show up where they live. It's disruptive, you know? Then Snake Baby watches her house to see what happens. If half the force shows up, then we know she's got something important with her. If nothing happens, we know the evidence is still in the apartment."

"Right, but there's nothing in the postcards, I'm telling you. The postcards were in plain sight for weeks. Anyone could have looked. "

"Aren't you the one who told me about hiding a letter by putting it out in plain sight?"

Angel felt sick.

"Ok," Gil said finally after a long pause. "But you're going out to the picnic tomorrow, right?"

Angel nodded. "But not till lunchtime. Just to bring out the ice cream."

Gil went on as if Angel hadn't spoken. "OK, I want you to watch the kid, what he does, who he plays with, anything that looks different. Because it's like a one in a million chance, I know that, but if we find out that the mother has information, we're going to have to act, you know that, right?"

Angel felt his heart sink.....

"If I get the feeling that there is something to worry about inside the Alvarez apartment, and we can't find it, we can always take the boy."

Angel felt his mouth go dry.

"I don't mean hurt the kid, geez, you're such a ....anyway, what I mean is, we could always take the boy, all nice-like, so he doesn't even know it, like a trip to the candy store or something...." Gil burst into laughter.

Angel felt like throwing up. "The candy store?"

"Come on, Angel, what I mean is, we take the kid for a ride, tell the mother she gives us the package or else. If she doesn't have the package, we'll know it from her voice, then we say OK, and drop the kid back home. And if she does, we make the trade. Easy, OK?"

"OK," Angel said.

"Listen up, Angel," Gil said in a cold voice. "We're not looking to hurt the kid, got it? It's just that if the mother has information, the best way to get it is to take the kid. Not hurt him, understand. Just take him. We tell her, you give us the package, we give you the kid. That's all. No one gets hurt. The kid is just a chip in our pocket. Do you understand me, Angel?"

Angel nodded. "Got it. Just a chip."

"You can be my ears and eyes tomorrow, OK Angel?"

"Yes, I can do that," Angel said, feeling better. He could do everything Snake Baby did and better if he had to, and Gil knew it. Gil trusted him.

"Right," Gil said, relieved. Angel was a lot of work, no doubt about it, but who else would do what he did? Who knew as much as he did? And he always followed orders, like watching those fucking trailers day and night. Angel had a few weaknesses, but he was definitely worth the trouble.

"Good work, Angel," Gil said before he hung up.

Angel was feeling better than good as he headed back to the Repository. He felt great. Tomorrow he would show Gil what he could do when he had a chance to act on his own.

22 | THURSDAY NIGHT
Sandy Hills

MARIA PULLED ONTO THE INTERSTATE and headed north to Sandy Hills. Behind her the city lights receded into the distance. In less than thirty minutes she'd be home. The thought crossed her mind that she could swing by Animal Control and pick up the brown dog on her way. She wouldn't mind some company. But the temptation didn't last. This was no time for new responsibilities.

She checked the rearview mirror. A black car, a Cadillac El Dorado with dark tinted windows, was coming up fast behind her. She'd vaguely noticed the car when she left the N. Building parking lot after visiting with Rosa. When it followed her onto the interstate, she'd started paying attention. Now it was glued to her tail. Whoever was behind the wheel wanted to be noticed.

She couldn't see who was driving, but she could guess. Only Snake Baby would be screwing around like that on the highway. She decided to wait before calling in. If Snake Baby was really out to get her, she wouldn't have seen him until it was too late. So he was playing games. She'd try to figure out what kind of game he was playing before she called.

It was time to lose the snake if she could. She accelerated into the passing lane and stomped down on the gas. The air through the open windows of the Cherokee hit her face like a slap. She pushed hard, 70, 80, 90....The black car stayed with her easily, moving along behind her like a cat toying with its prey. She crossed into the right lane and slammed on the brakes. Now she was under the speed limit, crawling. The black car did the same.

A small piece of moon hung from the sky, cut in half by a long trail of black clouds moving across its face. The Cadillac was now less than a car length behind her.

She was almost past the turnoff for Sandy Hills before she cut to the right, taking the exit on two wheels. Without slowing down, she raced along the road that would take her into town. Only when the commercial district began to come into view did she take her foot off the gas. She checked her rearview mirror. Her Jeep was the only car on the road. That didn't surprise her. Sandy Hills was a sleepy town. Most of its citizens were home by nightfall.

She could feel the press of hot air through the windows of the Jeep. Sandy Hills was usually several degrees cooler than the city, but tonight the heat was unrelenting, a dry heat that made it hard to breathe.

She slowed down. Sandia Road, a winding strip of asphalt that led up to the small, one-story adobe house where she lived, was just ahead of her on the left. She checked her mirror. No other cars in sight. She made a fast left onto Sandia, killed the headlights, and pulled over to wait. A few minutes later a gray Dodge Charger steamed past her down the main road. She waited. The road remained empty.

She had just put the Jeep into gear to go up Sandia to her house when she saw the faint glow of headlights in the distance. She stopped and killed the lights again. The car moved steadily past the turnoff for Sandia. Moments later the taillights disappeared behind the curve of the road. But at such close distance, she couldn't be mistaken. It was the black El Dorado.

It was time to call Joe. "Did Danforth send someone out to follow me home?" she asked him as soon as he answered the phone. "Is he worried about me?"

Joe was silent for a moment. "Someone followed you?"

"A black El Dorado played games with me on the highway," she told him. "It followed me as far as Sandia Drive, but then it kept on going."

"I'll check with Danforth, but I don't think it's one of ours," Joe said. "Any ideas?"

"Snake Baby," she admitted reluctantly. "At least I think so."

"Looks that way," he said. "But keep your eyes open. I'll talk to Danforth. I'll come out as soon as I can."

She could hear the worry in his voice and instantly regretted calling him. "Snake Baby's just playing games," she said, trying not to let her exhaustion show. "Thanks, Joe. But no one else, OK? If it was Snake Baby, I don't want to give him the satisfaction of thinking that he frightened me. If anything else happens, I'll call."

"Agreed."

She closed the phone and barreled down the dirt road to her house, sending a cloud of dust fanning out behind her. She lived in a small guest house on a sprawling ranch called the Hacienda. Two years ago, the owners of the property had turned the main building into a luxury bed and breakfast. It had been an instant success.

The guest house where she lived was small and accessible only by a long dirt road, but Maria knew it was a gift. The house was invisible from the main complex, and it was set into the hillside in such a way that the rear windows and garden provided an uninterrupted, panoramic view of the river and the mountains.

When Maria first moved into the guest house, all of Sandia Drive had been a dirt road. But two years ago, except for the stretch leading to her house, Sandia Drive had been paved to satisfy the owners of the new bed and breakfast. Last year the town had put in street lights. Now Maria could hear the cars going back and forth along Sandia Drive late into the night. But at least from the back windows of her house, she had a wide view of the Rio Poderoso with the Blue Sierras in the distance. She still had the illusion of an open landscape even though with so much new development, landscape views in Sandy Hills were disappearing fast.

She parked the Jeep in front of her house and went inside. The air in the house was hot and stifling after being closed up in the sun all day. She threw open all the windows in the living room before going into the bedroom to change. She would close the windows before going to bed, but first she would cool off the house for a few hours. She would not let Snake Baby rule the way she lived in her own home.

She pulled on a pair of Khaki shorts and a white T-shirt, then tucked her sidearm into the back waistband of the shorts. It was uncomfortable, but she was in no mood to take chances. As she left the room, she glanced at herself in the mirror. A slender young woman with large angry eyes and long black hair clasped at the back of her neck stared back at her. She undid the clasp and shook out her hair, letting it fall loosely over her shoulders.

She walked down the hall into the kitchen and pulled a cold Dos Equis out of the refrigerator. Then she went out the back door into the garden, letting the kitchen door slam hard behind her. She needed a few minutes to cool down.

Two lawn chairs sat near the back door where they were shaded by the elm trees planted along the garden wall. She'd covered one of the chairs with the blanket her *Tia Rosita* had given to her when she was born. Four wide pink stripes, bordered in green, divided the deep-red background of the blanket. It had been hand dyed and woven in the central Mexican village where her family had lived. There weren't many like it around anymore.

The blanket had given new life to the chair, but rust was beginning to show through on the white iron table standing next to it. This whole place is falling apart, Maria thought to herself, wearily setting the beer down on the table. What else could she expect? She'd lived in the guest house for over ten years, and in all that time she'd never replaced anything. The house was more or less like it was when she first moved in. The only difference was that by now the worn edges were hard to ignore.

She took a deep breath and looked out at the flat expanse of sand and sagebrush stretching into the distance in front of her. The Blue Sierras standing solidly along the horizon were usually a reassuring presence in her life, but tonight that bruised purple mass rising up against a dark sky looked vaguely menacing.

She sat down and took a long swallow of beer, adjusting the blanket to relieve the pressure of the gun against her back. Over the past ten years, she'd learned how to live with a height-ened sense of danger as her constant companion. Only the small village of Sandy Hills, with its pastures and fruit trees and the *bosque* of tall cottonwoods lining the river bank, could offer her a temporary refuge from the tensions of her work.

But not tonight. Tonight threatening images clouded her mind, breaking into memories she'd thought were safely locked away. The sixth-grade boy who'd gone after her with a knife when she searched his backpack. The rookie officer a month on the job who'd been killed at a traffic stop. The random gunshots out of a speeding car in the *barrio*. Cali had almost been killed that night. They'd never found the shooters.

Maria took another swallow of beer and almost choked. Someone was walking through the garden in her direction. In a single movement, she leaned hard to her left and reached back for her gun, rolling off the chair and aiming as she hit the ground.

"Don't move!" she said in a voice so cutting and cold she scarcely recognized it as her own.

It was Joe, standing a few feet away from her. His face had gone white, and he was absolutely still.

"Joe! Why didn't you call?" she said as she lowered the gun and stood up.

"Can I move now?" he said evenly.

She couldn't speak. She put the gun down on the table.

"I did call," he said. "You didn't answer."

"I must have left my phone in the kitchen. I just wanted a few minutes...."

"I talked to Danforth," Joe said. His voice was heavy with anger. "He was worried about you. And frankly I can see why, sitting out in the garden, leaving your phone inside. Maria, what the hell is wrong with you?!"

She was dumbstruck. What the hell was wrong with him?!"

"Let's not fight, OK?" she said finally. "I had my reasons. Give me a chance to explain."

"No problem," he said, giving her a small smile, as if trying to take the sting out of his words. The tightness across his cheekbones softened. "I was worried, that's all. Let's go inside and talk."

She shook her head. "I want to stay in the garden. Just a few minutes longer. Now there are two of us. We can take turns."

Joe began to tense up again even before she'd finished speaking.

"Wait." She hesitated. "Tonight in the apartment, seeing Ramón and Rosa,...it wasn't easy."

"I know," he said. "I know. But...."

"And look at it this way," she persisted. "If Snake Baby wanted to take me out, I wouldn't be talking to you right now. He wouldn't have been so dramatic, coming up on my tail in a big black car. He wanted to spook me, remind me that he knows where I live. And it's a crummy feeling, I'll tell you. If he wanted to make me feel vulnerable, he's succeeded. But that doesn't mean he's dangerous, at least not right now. The opposite I think."

Joe looked around, considering. "Could you see who was driving?"

"No, the windows were too dark."

They were both silent.

"What are you thinking?" Joe asked her after a few minutes.

"This is something I have to tough out, Joe. I know that. But I want to know why Snake Baby followed me like that. Was it personal? Probably. But what if there was another reason, something to do with Rosa and Ramón? It could be more important than we realize."

Joe nodded. "It could be," he said. "It could be."

23 | THURSDAY NIGHT
Sandy Hills

"WHY DON'T YOU TAKE A BREAK?" Joe said over his shoulder as he took off

Maria didn't feel like arguing. She was tired of words. She sat down and closed her eyes.

A slight breeze rustled the leaves of the trees. She could hear an owl calling in the distance. Her thoughts began to slip away. Overhead the hot sky was bright with stars. The heat. The stars. She thought about another hot night so bright with stars it seemed a new kind of day, lit by millions of little suns. It made her ache, remembering the first boy she had ever loved.

They'd gone swimming to escape the heat. Under the stars, everything seemed magnified, enormous. How cool and smooth his skin felt when she touched it. His mouth tasted sweet, like fresh strawberries. And as he moved with her through the water, his long black hair lashed wet across his cheeks, she'd felt a sudden surge of joy. It was this she had hungered for all her life and never known it. It was her first real happiness, her first love, *su primer amor.*

He was just a boy when she'd known him. She hadn't seen him for over ten years, but she'd heard he was married. Two kids. He'd been able to move on. She hadn't had many chances to meet someone else. Tonight she realized more than ever just how lonely her life had become.

There was something about Joe that pulled at her. He made her laugh, and she didn't laugh easily. Other times he seemed more distant, strategic even, but that's what the job did to people, she knew that well enough. And sometimes when he let his guard down, there was a sense of weariness in his expression, as if the job had worn him down. But he still cared. The way he talked about his informant and how he'd gone out to his house trying to find him. The easy way he connected to Ramón and Carlito. He still cared. She was sure of it.

The sound of Joe's footsteps grew louder. "Find anything interesting out there?" she asked him as he came walking over to her.

"It sure is nice here," he said. "You live in a beautiful place, Maria."

"It's your turn to sit down for a while," she said. "It feels good to sit outside on a night like this."

He nodded and sat down. After a few minutes of silence, his breathing slowed. She looked over at him. His eyes were closed. The circles under his eyes were almost black. She wondered what he had been doing before coming up to Vereda. He hadn't had much time to prepare.

She stood up and started walking towards the back of the garden. Unexpectedly she felt a sharp anxiety. Now the noises in the garden seemed different. Something had changed. The shadows in the moonlight began to move slyly through the elm trees just outside the wall. She went back to her chair and grabbed her gun off the table.

It was after 2:00 a.m. when Joe drove away. He had offered to stay. She'd asked him to leave. She needed some time alone. He'd waited until she had closed and locked the windows and the kitchen door. She watched him through the front door. As soon as he disappeared into the darkness, she locked the front door. All she could think about was crawling into bed.

She was almost asleep when she heard strange noises coming from the back of the garden. She waited and listened. She heard the noises again. Animals often came into the garden at night, but these noises were different.

She forced herself out of bed. The thought of the little dog waiting at the intersection flashed through her mind. Now he was at the Animal Control Center. If no one claimed him, she could bring him home. He would be good company on a night like this.

She took her service weapon and a flashlight and went into the kitchen. She turned on the outside lights and stared outside for several minutes. She couldn't see anything in the garden or near the house. She turned off all the lights and quietly unlocked the back door, still intently scanning the darkness. When she pointed her flashlight at the elm trees, their leaves looked like little daggers.

Two coyotes silently appeared near the back wall of the garden. The coyotes were regular visitors. When she put her light on them, they looked back at her without fear. She wasn't afraid of them either. She knew their cries, their noises. She was looking for something more dangerous, a two-legged animal prowling around just out of sight.

After she had closed and locked the back door, she went down to the hall to her bedroom and collapsed on the bed. She fell asleep right away. Later the dreams would wake her up, but for a few hours she slept soundly. While she was sleeping, a cigarette glowed on and off in the darkness at the back of the garden until it faded away just before dawn.

24 | FRIDAY MORNING
Sandy Hills
Rosa's apartment

MARIA WOKE UP WITH HER UNDERSHIRT clinging to her chest. Even her hair was wet. The bedroom window was too small to cool off the room at night, and her dreams had been worse than usual.

She looked over at the clock. 5:00 in the morning. She could hear a car accelerating into the distance. The sound faded away. It was quiet again.

She closed her eyes and thought about Joe. She liked spending time with him. She wanted to see more of him. But what would happen when he went back to his regular job as a Border Patrol Agent in Lastup?

By now she wouldn't be able to fall back to sleep. Might as well get up. She walked down the hall to the living room. It was sparsely decorated. A blue overstuffed couch, a wooden table, and a brass floor lamp next to the couch were all that added definition to the whitewashed walls. What made the space come alive was the view from the back windows. It was breathtaking. It filled up the room.

Maria opened the windows. A warm breeze came rolling in like liquid across her skin. The heat wave had finally broken. In front of her, the patterned golds and purples of the garden seemed to unroll like an intricate carpet, stretching all the way to the fringed Sierras along the horizon.

In the distance, the blue peaks of the mountains began to glow against a bright orange sky. The garden slowly filled with sunlight. The light reassured her. In one of her dreams, she'd found herself in a darkened garden, searching for Ramón, silently stalking shadows until her flashlight picked up his tiny silhouette, almost transparent against the bruised sky. He faded away before she could reach him.

She called Joe at 6:00. "Any word on the ID?"

"Nothing, Maria."

"Then I guess it's the park. See you later." She hung up and dressed quickly. She wanted enough time to stop by N. Building on her way to the park.

It was a lazy May morning. The downtown streets were sleeping. Even the dust that usually moved in small swirls across the pavements had settled into motionless piles along the curbs. Only she felt immune to the relaxing call of summer. By the time she took the exit for Vereda, she could feel the tension coiling in her neck.

She found herself sitting in front of the long red light where she'd seen the little brown dog on the corner. She felt a twinge of guilt. Why hadn't she gone by Animal Control and picked him up? Then immediately, all the reasons. She was never home. She had no one to take the dog if she went out of town. What if he needed shots? She didn't have time. No, there wasn't time for a dog.

The light turned green. She accelerated, then slammed on the brakes. A drunk stumbled up against her car. She'd almost hit him! She watched him weave, zigzagging across the street. "What the hell are you doing?!!" she yelled at him. "What are the chances?!" she muttered to herself, trying to calm down.

She made it into N. Building just before 6:30. The lobby was empty. She took the stairs two at a time and went down the hall to Rosa's apartment. She knocked quietly at the door.

"Maria!" Rosa said when she opened the door. "Come in. Ramón is still asleep. Do you want me to wake him?"

"No, Rosa, that's OK," Maria said. She handed a small package to Rosa. "Here's a little something for his birthday. You can give it to him tonight."

Rosa gave Maria a long hug.

"I also wanted to check in with you," Maria said. "How are you doing?"

"I'm trying to be happy for Ramón this morning," Rosa said quietly.

"Rosa, if you have any doubts, say so! I'll talk to Medrano for you if that will help."

Rosa shook her head. "You don't understand, Maria. I know you mean well. But fate cannot be avoided. What's important is to face it with courage." Her eyes were serious. "I can't keep Ramón home every time I'm afraid for him. Ramón must follow his own dreams. This is a new world for new dreams. There is no other choice." Rosa hesitated." "Do you want to wake him up? It would be a nice surprise for him."

"Yes, I'd like that," Maria said, giving Rosa an encouraging smile. Rosa had decided to send Ramón to the park. She was Ramón's mother and that was her choice. All Maria could do was try to protect the boy out at the park if the danger Rosa feared turned out to be real.

Maria walked around the sheet that separated Ramón's bedroom from the rest of the one-room apartment. By now stubby fingers of light were pushing through his bedroom window, stretching one by one into the back of the room where he was sleeping. The shadows in the corner shivered and dissolved into a wooden table and a chair.

On the edge of the table was one of Ramón's school books. Its front cover was torn away, but the words, *Gifted Student Program*, were stamped in large red letters on the first page. A sheet of wide-lined yellow paper lay on the table next to the book. Maria went over to look at it. On the top line, Ramón had carefully printed his name in pencil. The rest of the page was filled with a column of words in English next to a column of words in Spanish. Students in the gifted program had homework even when there was a field trip to the park.

A stream of light reached across the bed where Ramón was sleeping. The full light on his face made him restless, and his legs began moving as if he were running, twisting his sheet into knots.

As Maria looked down at him, she found herself remembering the happiness in Rosa's voice when she told Maria about what she had done for Ramon's eighth birthday. She had painted his old wooden bed a bright blue, like river reflecting sky. Ramon had always dreamed of exploring the river, Rosa had told her. He still did even though this year in school he had learned that large sections of the great river had been tamed. Now that once unruly river passed through parts of the city in a straight line. Now the water was mostly brown. And in some places to the south, the river was drying up. But none of that mattered to Ramón. He was a hopeful dreamer.

This morning Ramón was dreaming about the Great Blue Herons who had come to live in Riverside Park. In his dream, one of the herons was standing motionless in the shallow water near the riverbank, almost close enough for him to touch it. Suddenly a voice startled it away.

"Wake up, Ramón! Wake up!" Maria said softly.

Ramón didn't move, and he kept his eyes closed, but Maria could hear him saying under his breath, "Please, please, don't let anything keep me from going to the park today." He opened his eyes. "The Lady in Blue," he whispered in surprise. He smiled up at her. "Now I know my wishes will come true."

He jumped out of bed, almost tripping over the bedspread that had fallen into a heap during the night, and hurried across the floor in his bare feet to look out the window.

A cloudless blue sky stretched out in front of him, and even at that early hour in the morning, the sun was shining brightly through the trees. Ramón felt a rush of happiness.

He dressed himself as fast as he could in the dark blue pants and red and white striped shirt his mother had put out for him the night before. They were his favorite clothes, the ones he saved for special days, like his birthday. Or going to the river where the herons lived.

While Ramón got dressed, Maria looked outside and thought about her little brother, Pablo. She was sure he would have been a hopeful boy like Ramón if he had lived. He would have felt the sunlight on his face in the morning while he was waking up. He might even have dreamed about herons. He had died a long time ago, but the passing of years had not brought any lessening of the pain. She felt the hurt of losing her little brother as if he had died just yesterday.

When Ramón finished dressing, he pushed aside the sheet that separated his room from the rest of the apartment and went into the kitchen.

Rosa was washing dishes when she heard the faint rustle of the sheet. Ramón had chosen the sheet himself. It was bright blue, like the sky and covered with tiny white clouds and colored birds. "You're a big boy, Ramón," she'd told him on his birthday last year. "You deserve your own room."

It had taken Rosa some time to figure out how to create a bedroom for Ramon from their one-room apartment. Eventually she bought four hooks that she could screw into the ceiling in front of Ramón's bed. By using one of the kitchen chairs and standing on her toes, she had been able to screw the hooks into the ceiling, about fifteen inches apart. Then she ran a wire through the hooks and attached the sheet to the wire with clothespins.

Ramón had been overjoyed with the result. The sheet failed by several feet to cover the entire width of the space between the apartment walls, and it hung six inches above the floor, but it afforded Ramón both privacy and an easy way around it. Over the past few days he'd pushed through the sheet instead of walking around it, as if to gently announce his arrival. He seemed to understand how easily startled his mother was since his father had disappeared.

Rosa looked up from the sink to see Ramón standing by the kitchen table, his eyes bright with excitement. She tried to smile back at him. "Happy Birthday, Ramón!"

His grin grew even wider.

"We'll celebrate your birthday again tonight with Ana and Carlito. They will come to eat ice cream and cake with us. And Detective Maria has a little gift for you as well."

Maria handed him the package. Inside was a keychain with a Blue Heron on it. Ramón was too overcome with happiness to speak. "I hear you Ramón," Maria said right away. She gave him a kiss on each cheek. "You'll have a great birthday out at the park!"

"I have to go to work," she told Rosa, and after a quick hug, she quietly let herself out of the apartment. She knew Rosa wanted some time alone with Ramón.

Rosa turned back to the dishes in the sink. She didn't want Ramón to see the tears in her eyes. She stared at the soapy water. Ramón was a big boy now, a third grader, but this morning she ached to keep him close to her.

Her friend Ana teased her about wanting to keep Ramón safe at home. "Most people would not call the Hidalgo Housing Projects a safe place," Ana would say in pretend despair. "Bad things happen here all the time. There is no safe place, Rosa, don't you know that yet?" Then she would give Rosa a hug. Ana understood.

The sprawling Hidalgo Housing Project complex was in one of the *barrio's* most violent neighborhoods. Gangs freely roamed the streets, and drugs were bought and sold in full view. The cops did what they could, but how could they compete with the gangs? A few years ago a newspaper reporter writing about the project had described it as Hidalgo Hell, l'Inferno Hidalgo.

But Rosa knew her neighborhood. Its dangers were familiar. And she knew Ramón's school even though it was over two miles away. Their daily routine was comforting. The school bus picked Ramón up where she could see him, right across the street. And in the afternoon, she could meet him when he got off the bus in front of their building.

Today the bus would bring him to the park. It wasn't easy for her to let Ramón go. Juan's still unexplained disappearance in a distant town near the Mexican border had darkened her view of the outside world, the world outside the small circle of places she knew: the Hidalgo Housing project, the grocery store where she worked mornings, and the school. Things happened to people in the outside world, unspeakable things. She knew Ramón would have to make his way into that world before long, but he was still so young.

She found herself stealing long glances at him over her shoulder. He was small for his age, and beautiful, with dark, curly hair and large brown eyes. He was smart too, smarter than anyone else in his class. If only he would watch where he was going.

But Ramón found it hard to concentrate on his feet. His dreams lived in the sky. Up there he might see a heron flying home to its nest or a pair of eagles following their ancient migration routes along the Rio Poderoso. He dreamed of exploring the river with the eagles, riding the air on their great wings all the way into Mexico.

Ramón had always searched the sky for signs of his father's plane. Whenever he saw a plane overhead, he would wave at it. Even now, after Juan's disappearance, he still waved at planes in the sky. If his father's plane should suddenly appear overhead, he didn't want to miss it.

Even Mr. Medrano had noticed. "Ramón seems to fall into dreaming the way other children fall into playing ball," was the way Mr. Medrano put it. But he had also tried to reassure Rosa, telling her that children eventually grow out of daydreaming. It just takes a little time.

Rosa dried her hands on her apron. The bus would come in a few minutes. She handed Ramón his lunch bag. "Have a good time, but be careful," she told him, trying to keep the worry out of her voice.

"*Bendicion*?" he said hugging her tightly. "Your blessing, *mami*?"

"*Que Dios te bendiga*. May God bless you, Ramón."

She watched him go out the door with a piercing sense of foreboding. She hurried over to the kitchen window and looked down. She could see her friend Ana below, waiting in front of the building with her son, Carlito.

Everyone noticed Ana. Everyone liked her too. She was small and curvy, with wavy reddish brown hair and a welcoming smile. To Rosa, it seemed like Ana was always doing something, talking, or laughing, or moving her feet around on the floor. Even when Ana was sitting, she jiggled her knees or made wide circles with her arms to go with what she was saying.

Ana was a hopeful person, like Ramón. Ana was always hugging her, trying to encourage her. Rosa wished she could be more like Ana, but she was happy they were friends. She was happy that Ramón and Carlito were best friends too.

When Ramón came out of the building, Ana bent down and gave him a hug. Then she took the two boys by the hand and walked them across the street to the bus stop.

As soon as the bus came, Ramón climbed into one of the front seats and looked up at her. Rosa waved back at him. And she kept the image of his smiling face pressed up tight against the school bus window close to her heart for the rest of the morning.

25 FRIDAY MORNING
Office Supply Repository

IN THE PARKING LOT NEAR THE REPOSITORY, Angel was loading an empty white Styrofoam container into the brown van waiting for him in his usual place. The school buses had already picked up the kids to bring them to the park. The ice cream wouldn't be delivered to the school for another hour, but Angel liked being well prepared.

He checked his watch. It was time to call Gil. He took the van and drove along the highway. Today he would talk while he was driving.

"You all set for today?" Gil's raspy voice came over the line.

"All set," Angel said right away. "And listen...." He wanted to tell Gil about the extra preparations he had made for the day in case an opportunity presented itself.

But Gil went on talking. "I hope so, Angel, I hope you're all set for today because after last night, I'm not feeling so good."

Something had happened. Angel felt his heart sink with disappointment. Now he wouldn't be able to tell Gil about his plans. Gil had to be in a good mood because Gil never trusted him to do anything right on his own. But this time, he was prepared. He had figured out how to fill the hypodermic needle with just the right amount of sedative for a little kid, and it was safely wrapped inside his pocket along with a pair of plastic gloves. And he had put a clean pair of pants, socks, and shoes into a waterproof bag that could fit inside the Styrofoam container along with the ice cream.

Angel knew that his preparations were useless. There was almost no chance he could take the boy. But still he hoped. If he could deliver the kid to Gil while he was still sleeping, too sound asleep to identify anyone, and they could get the package from the mother, if there was a package, then at least Gil would finally know what he could do on his own. Gil would know that Snake Baby wasn't the only one who could take action.

Angel especially wanted to tell Gil about the map. Gil could hardly read maps, but Angel had studied the map of the park down to the last detail. He was good at maps. And Gil would be amazed. It was the perfect setup. There were three different exits off the Olde Road onto the highway that led to Ciudad Nueva. Once the pickup car was on the highway, they were home free.

If he could figure out some way to take the kid without the cops seeing him, all he had to do was carry the sleeping boy up to the Olde Road. Then he could tell Gil where the boy was, and one of Gil's men could drive over there and get the boy into the car when no one else was on the road.

Once Gil had what he wanted, Angel could bring the boy back to the school himself. No one would notice his van, and he could sneak the boy into Medrano's trailer. As long as the boy was alive and unhurt when they found him in the trailer, even the newspapers wouldn't pay much attention to his disappearance from Riverside Park. "Brilliant," Angel thought, and for a minute he felt happy. Then the stabs of pain began. The sun was getting brighter. And Gil was yelling at him.

"Angel, what the hell is happening? Where are you?"

"Sorry. I was stuck in traffic. I'm back. Go ahead. What happened last night?" Another lie. Angel couldn't help noticing. It was getting easier.

"It was weird, that's all I can say, it was fucking weird. Something doesn't make sense," Gil said in an angry voice.

Angel was silent. "What happened?" he asked again after a minute.

"Don't ask too many questions," Gil said in a voice filled with menace. "But I'm going to tell you anyway because this whole thing is starting to make me nervous. I mean, at first everything goes smooth. Snake Baby takes the black car and follows the cop out to her house, all the way to Sandy Hills. He plays with her on the highway, makes her nervous, stays right on her tail like I told him to do.

"He takes the exit off the highway for Sandy Hills and follows the street through the town, just like she does, only now he stays back, out of sight. And when he comes to Sandia Drive, where she turns left to get up to her house, he keeps on driving. No point in going up the road while she's still looking to see if someone's on her tail, you know what I mean? She could turn around and come after him. And Snake Baby doesn't know yet if she's going to call for someone to come out and help her look around or not. So he goes on down the road and parks the car off to the side under some trees so you can't see it. Then he goes back to Sandia Drive on foot, keeping out of sight whenever a car comes by, and climbs up the hill to her house. By the time he gets into the woods at the back of her garden, the cowboy is there."

"So she did call someone?"

"Yeah, she must have called the cowboy. But the weird thing is they sit in the garden, talking. Don't sound like they were worried about nothing, not Snake Baby, not the black car, nothing."

"Maybe they were, you know, romancing...." Angel started to say.

Gil laughed so hard, he started choking. "Romancing?! Angel, you are really are one of a kind."

Angel didn't know what to do. Why was Gil always laughing at him?

"But here's what bothers me," Gil went on, his voice cold. "Snake Baby waits there in the woods for the cowboy to make up his mind, either go inside or leave. Finally the cowboy drives away.

"Snake Baby waits a little longer. He's a careful son of a bitch no matter what you think. Finally he decides. Chavez doesn't have any evidence with her. Otherwise there would have been a house full of cops or at least the cowboy would have stayed. So Snake Baby gets ready to leave. And right then he hears something. Someone else is moving around in the woods! Do you hear me, Angel? Someone else was waiting there in the woods, just like he was.

"So Snake Baby stays where he is, trying to see who it is, but he can't see anyone, it's too dark. So Snake Baby decides whoever it is, it's better not to go after him alone. What if it's Cali Martinez?"

"Martinez is in Lastup," Angel said.

"I know, I know, but the thing is, I want you to see that Snake Baby knows how to be careful, even if you don't think so. He has a bad temper that gets him in trouble, that's all."

Angel wanted to tell Gil, "...and I know how to act, even if you don't think so," but he knew better than to interrupt Gil. He stayed silent and waited.

"Finally Snake Baby decides to take off. But there's no way he can get out of the woods without being heard so all he can do is run like hell, moving in and out of the trees, and hope the other guy in the woods can't catch up with him. He never even looks back until he gets to the main road. But he could tell, even while he was running, that no one was coming after him. There was no noise in the woods at all. Just to be sure, he hides behind some rocks and waits. No one shows up. After an hour, he walks back down the road to his car and drives off.

"But here's the point, Angel. Whoever was in the woods stayed there instead of chasing after Snake Baby! Do you hear me Angel?! Watching Chavez from the woods was more important than running down Snake Baby. It don't make sense, but how else can you figure it?"

"Another cop?" Angel asked. "Assigned to keep an eye on Chavez?"

"It wasn't a cop. My source would know if it was," Gil said. "And any cop would have gone after Snake Baby."

Both men were silent for a few minutes.

"It don't make sense," Angel said finally.

"No, that's right, it don't make no sense at all," Gil said. "By the way, where were you last night, Angel?"

"I was here, like always, you know that," Angel said in a shaky voice.

"Yeah, I do know that, Angel. Don't wet your pants. That much I do know. So if the guy in the woods was another cop, he's keeping things private for some reason, so private even my source can't pick up information or...."

Angel waited.

"Or there's something wrong with my source."

Angel held his breath. When Gil talked that way, he was afraid to breathe.

"Maybe the cowboy doubled back," Angel said tentatively when he was sure Gil was through talking. "Just to keep an eye on things."

"Right. That's what Snake Baby thought too. But when he finally gets his car and starts driving back home, he slows down as he passes Sandia Drive, and what does he see? Some guy wearing a cowboy hat sitting in what looks like an unmarked cop car, parked on the side of the road. Snake Baby doesn't slow down, but he's sure it was the cowboy guarding the turn off for Sandia Drive."

"OK, that adds up," Angel said. "Chavez called for help. The cowboy came out, stayed a while, checked things out, and then decided to stay and spend the night in his car at the entrance to Sandia Drive. Like I said, when they were here at the trailer, it looked like there was something going on between them. So the cowboy decides to take some extra precautions, that's all."

"Right," Gil agreed slowly. "They probably figured out that it was Snake Baby following her on the highway, but they didn't think it was a planned hit. More like causing her trouble. And they were right up to a point. They know she's got skills, and they're betting Snake Baby won't actually try to get at her inside the house. So the cowboy settles for guarding the access road."

Angel was quiet. Then he said, "So now you know Chavez doesn't have the package, right? Otherwise the cops would be all over her place."

"Right. You got the point," Gil said. "Otherwise the place would have been crawling with cops." Gil paused. "But then, Angel, tell me this. If the cops weren't there, who the hell was watching her from the woods?"

26 | FRIDAY
Riverside Park

MARIA PULLED INTO A SPACE NEAR the front gate. She got out and looked around. No other cars in sight. The trees and brush clustered around the parking lot were silent except for an occasional thin birdsong, but the sky was clear and blue. At least the heat wave had broken in time for the school picnic.

Joe drove in a few minutes later and parked next to her.

"How's it going?" he asked, looking at her carefully

She thought briefly about telling him the nightmares that had kept her awake most of the night, then decided against it. "I'm OK," she said. "Just tired."

They walked out of the parking lot and onto the wide pedestrian bridge that crossed the Rio Poderoso into Riverside Park. From the bridge, they could see most of the island.

"It's amazing," Joe said. "I never imagined anything quite like this."

"We're proud of it," Maria said. "It's won national awards too."

"How did you do it?"

"Several years ago the city decided to dedicate some land near the river for a nature preserve. This was a small island fairly close to town with an unusual amount of vegetation on it. The city dredged up the river bottom around the island and then used the sludge along with some filler to create different elevations on the island.

"It worked. The landscape architects planted lots of trees, so by now the island is thickly forested. More important, the island has remained protected. No cars, no bikes, no dogs, no fires, no hunting. Officially the public can only enter the park over this bridge. That allows us to keep an eye on who is going and coming. I think it's made a difference.

"This bridge brings us directly into the park entrance on the northwest side of the island. You can see the Welcome Center over there, just to the right of the entrance. From the Welcome Center, there's a path that will bring us along the river to the south side of the island where the picnic areas and river classrooms have been set up.

"The only other building in the park is the small brown and lavender building known as the Lav. It sits in the woods on top of the ridge."

"Who's going to be in the park today," Joe asked.

"The park is closed to the public," Maria said. "The school buses will drive the children directly into the parking lot. Everyone will cross into the park using this bridge. At the same time, Al will drive along the Olde Road looking for anything or anyone unusual. And of course, we'll all be checking the river as often as possible to make sure no one tries to access the park through the water."

"Through the water?"

"In a few places where the water is shallow, it's possible to get onto the island by crossing the river on foot, but it's not as easy as it sounds. It doesn't happen often, believe me. The only ones we find trying to cross on foot are the all-day hikers in a hurry to get to their cars."

"So what you're saying is that most people, with the exception of a few hikers, come and go from the park across this bridge, is that right?"

"Why? You don't believe me?"

Joe smiled. "I believe you," he said. "But I'm always curious about the ones who don't follow the rules. Is there a place where hikers most often try to cross the river on foot? For example, it looks like the woods in back of the Lav go down to the river where the water is unusually shallow."

"They do and it is," Maria said in a tired voice. "We fought the planners tooth and nail, citing all the obvious safety concerns, but it was no use. So, yes, the hikers do wade across the river where it's most shallow, and from there, they can directly access the woods in back of the Lav. When the hikers splash through the water to get off the island, they either climb up to the back of the parking lot or they take the path leading to the Olde Road where someone is planning to pick them up. We try to catch them, and we hand out big fines when we do. It does absolutely no good."

"Talk to me about the Lav," Joe said.

"There is no back exit from the Lav. At least we got that much. There is only one way in and out of the building, and that door is in plain view of the picnic area at the bottom of the hill."

Joe didn't say anything.

"You've put someone near the Lav to keep an eye on the woods in back of it, right?" she asked Joe.

He nodded. "A retired agent, an older man, goes by the name of Cortez. Not from around here."

"Good. Now what can we do?"

"Cross our fingers," he said. He gave her an encouraging smile. The rumbling sound of school buses in the distance grew louder. He put on his sunglasses. "Get ready. Here come the kids."

There was no reason to be afraid. When they first got to the park, Ramón had been cautious and a little frightened. But Mr. Medrano had held his hand while they walked across the bridge, and then he had seen Maria waiting for him on the other side. She waved hello to him with a big smile. And once he had seen the park with his own eyes, he realized there was no reason to be afraid. The park was wonderful, and today was his birthday! He hadn't seen the herons yet, but Mr. Medrano said they would probably come out later in the afternoon.

Now the sun was blazing overhead in a bright, blue sky, and he was sitting next to Carlito at one of the long picnic tables set up so close to the edge of the river that you could even see the water bugs skating across the water.

The only way you could actually stick your hand in the water was to climb down the three wide steps that led from the picnic area to the edge of the river, but Ramón liked sitting at the picnic tables. It was close enough to see everything but far enough away so you wouldn't get splashed if one of the older kids decided to break the rules and start throwing big stones or sticks into the water. Some of the older kids were already bad boys, even if they were still in elementary school. People in his building called them "the little snakes."

Ramón wondered why his school was elementary. Was it because most of the kids were little? He thought the bigger boys should be in a different school. They were always picking on the little kids. Some of them had little snake tattoos on their shoulders where the teachers couldn't see them. But Ramón had seen the tattoos when the big boys took off their shirts after school and started fighting. Once they had tried to hurt him near N. Building, but Maria had taught them a lesson. Now they left him alone.

Ramón could tell that even out here at the park, "the little snakes," were planning something bad. There were two girls in his class that they always pushed around when the teachers weren't looking. He couldn't figure out why they didn't like the girls except that they were smart. But he was smart too and *los culebritas* never picked on him anymore. They were afraid of Maria. And they knew Carlito was his best friend, and Carlito was taller and stronger than the other kids in his class.

It was lunch time. The six long picnic tables for the third graders were crowded with children. Mr. Medrano and the other teachers began passing out cookies and small cartons of orange juice. Most of the other kids had started eating lunch, but Ramón wasn't hungry. He sat there twisting the top of his unopened lunch bag while he waited for Mr. Medrano to get to their table. It was taking a long time.

Finally Mr. Medrano made it over to their table. "Can I go to the Lav with Carlito?" Ramón asked timidly when Mr. Medrano handed him his juice and a large cookie wrapped in plastic. But Mr. Medrano wasn't looking at him. He was watching the "little snakes" at one of the nearby tables who were trying to push each other off the bench.

"He didn't hear you!" Carlito said.

Ramón felt even more anxious. There was so much laughing and shouting going on. Carlito was right. Mr. Medrano hadn't heard him. "Can I go to the Lav with Carlito?" he asked again, watching his teacher closely. By now Mr. Medrano had finished passing out food to the whole table. He looked at Ramón and smiled.

"Look, he's saying it's OK," Ramón told Carlito. "Hurry, let's go." He pulled Carlito away from the table, and together the two boys headed for the Lav.

"Where are you going boys?" It was one of the other third-grade teachers, Mrs. Longwood.

"Mr. Medrano gave us permission to go to the Lav," Ramón said.

Mrs. Longwood looked unsure, but when she turned to check with Mr. Medrano, he was trying to separate three of the mean boys who were fighting with each other at the table. "Charlie!" she called out to him, but the fighting boys were screaming at each other so loudly, Mr. Medrano didn't seem to hear her. "Is it really important?" she asked Ramón.

The expression on his face told her that he had to go in a hurry. "Well then, stay together," Mrs. Longwood said. "And come back right away. The ice cream is on its way," she added. She followed them with her eyes as they went up the hill to the Lav.

∞

Maria's phone began to vibrate. "Angel is crossing the bridge," Joe told her. "He's carrying a white Styrofoam container."

"The ice cream," she said.

"Right. Looks that way, but be prepared. I'm on my way."

"Thanks, Joe," she said, closing her phone. There was a loud splash in the water behind her. She turned around. What the hell were "the little snakes" doing in the water? Two young park staffers were heading towards them. She turned back to check the path along the river. Now she could see Angel approaching. The thought of one of Gil's men at Ramón's school picnic tightened the coils in her neck into a spasm of pain, and she couldn't help wondering once again, how they had ever ended up in such a situation. Then she stopped thinking and concentrated all her attention on Angel.

❦

At first the boys were quiet as they walked up the path covered with white stones that led up to the Lav. Carlito was walking much slower than usual, and Ramón knew why. When he was little, Carlito had been frightened by a man screaming at him with a raspy voice. And that morning on the bus, Mr. Medrano had told them there would be a man with a raspy voice sitting outside the Lav. Carlito knew it wouldn't be the same man who had frightened him when he was little, but he was afraid anyway.

"The man's name is Mr. Cortez, and he sits there to make sure the Lav is a safe place for you," Mr. Medrano had explained. The children knew what he meant. They had all learned about stranger danger in school.

Mr. Medrano had also warned them about the man's voice. "Don't act stupid when Mr. Cortez talks to you," he'd told them. "Mr. Cortez can't help the way he sounds. He has to speak through a tube because he smoked too many cigarettes." Mr. Medrano was always telling them how bad smoking was.

Ramón was still trying to puzzle out what Mr. Medrano meant when he told another teacher on the bus that the bathrooms were at an uncomfortable distance from the picnic area. Why was it an uncomfortable distance? The Lav was painted a bright lavender and brown. Nobody could get lost going to the Lav. Maybe it was uncomfortable because you had to walk up a long hill to get there.

"You know what Mr. Medrano said about the Lav?" Ramón asked Carlito as they came to the top of the hill.

Carlito nodded. "You mean about the man?"

"No, not the man," Ramón said. But before he could say anything else, they found themselves in front of the Lav, and a man was sitting there in a lawn chair, staring at them with a stern expression on his face. They were so close to him, the man could touch them if he wanted to just by reaching out his arm. He was wearing large sunglasses and a faded fishing hat that made it hard to see his face, but Ramón could tell that he was old. His large blue-veined hands were covered with brown spots, and the wisps of hair sticking out from under the fishing hat were a dirty gray.

"Your teacher know you're here?" he said in a raspy voice, pointing a bony finger at Ramón.

Startled into shyness, Ramón managed to nod.

"You sure about that?" the man said again.

"Come on, Ramón, let's go," Carlito said nervously, pulling at Ramón's arm.

"Boys room on the right," the man called out as they hurried past him into the building.

Inside the Lav it was quiet and empty. Ramón could see that Carlito was still nervous. "Hey, Carlito," he said. "When we're through, we can look at the woods behind the Lav. Mr. Medrano says the Blue Herons fly over those woods all the time on their way to their nest on the river."

"Cool!" Carlito said. Now he looked happy.

Ramón was still in the toilet stall when he heard the bathroom door swing open.

"Carlito?" he called out.

"Back in a minute," Carlito yelled. "Wait here for me." He sounded excited.

Before Ramón could answer, the bathroom door swung shut.

Carlito headed straight for Mr. Angel and his big box of ice cream. He wanted to get to the head of the line. He would explain that today was Ramón's birthday so he wanted to bring one of the first ice cream cones to Ramón. But by the time Carlito got up to Mr. Angel, the line of kids waiting for ice cream had disappeared. Something was happening by the edge of the river. He tried to see what was happening.

He could see the big boys fighting and throwing stones at each other. One of the boys was holding a steel pipe in his hand. Two other boys were lying on the ground, and it looked like one of them was bleeding from his head. He could see both Maria and Joe trying to separate the fighting boys, and he wanted to see more, but he forced himself to look away. He had to get back to Ramón.

"Two cones please, Mr. Angel" Carlito said shyly.

"Two cones?" Angel said, peering at Carlito through his sunglasses. "Isn't one enough?"

"One is for my friend, Ramón," Carlito said anxiously. "He's waiting for me up at the Lav. I promised I'd bring him some ice cream. Honest."

"I see," Angel said. "That's OK then. Here you go." He handed two cones full of ice cream to Carlito while he quickly glanced up at the Lav. And unbelievably, there he was, Ramón Alvarez standing all alone near the Lav looking into the woods.

Carlito started up the hill towards the Lav, but there was so much going on by the river. Everyone was there, screaming and yelling. There were police officers everywhere. He found himself being pulled like a magnet towards the excitement. He would stop for just a minute to see what was happening. Then he would run up the hill to bring the ice cream cone to Ramón.

Ramón had rushed out of the stall after he heard Carlito leaving. He was halfway to the bathroom door before he stopped and reluctantly turned around to wash his hands with soap and water. When he'd finished washing his hands, he hurried out of the bathroom even before his hands were dry, but by the time he got outside the Lav, Carlito was gone.

Ramón looked down at the picnic tables. Maybe Carlito had run down there to be first in line to get ice cream from Mr. Angel, but if Carlito was there, he couldn't see him anywhere.

Where were all the kids? He thought they'd be in a line waiting for ice cream from Mr. Angel. No, instead they were all crowded along the riverbank. Maybe Carlito was there too, in the middle of all those kids watching the bad boys fighting in the water.

Ramón looked again at the picnic tables. They were empty, and the place where he had been sitting with Carlito was empty too. Where was everyone? Even Mr. Cortez, who had been sitting in front of the Lav in a lawn chair, was gone.

Ramón wanted to run down the hill and join the other kids along the riverbank, but what if

Carlito was somewhere around the Lav waiting for him? They had promised to stay together. They weren't supposed to go anywhere by themselves.

Ramón felt a strange shiver along his back, as if someone was watching him. But there was no reason to be afraid, he told himself firmly as he looked around. He didn't see anyone anywhere near the Lav. And all the kids were lined up along the river watching the fighting. He decided that he would walk one more time around the Lav just in case Carlito was still there. Maybe Carlito was looking for the herons flying over the woods. Then if he still couldn't find Carlito, he would go down the hill, and in just a few minutes, he would be with his friends again.

Angel looked up at the Lav another time. Ramón was still standing there alone. How was it possible? Where were the cops? The screaming from the water answered his question. "They're pushing a girl into the river," someone yelled. Teachers and staff were running into the water or along the edge of the river trying to separate the groups of fighting boys. Angel could see the cowboy diving under the water. He must be looking for the girl who had been pushed into the water.

Quickly Angel began cleaning up the napkins and broken cones off the picnic table, pretending not to look at Carlito or the Lav, but out of the corner of his eye, he was tracking everything that was going on around him. Up by the Lav, Ramón was no longer in sight. "He's looking around the building for Carlito one last time," Angel said to himself. Angel was smart about things like that. He understood kids.

And Carlito? Angel scanned the group of kids who lined up along the river staring at all the people splashing around in the water. There he was, Carlito, standing in the middle of the kids, as if a witch had stuck him into the ground. Good. If he was lucky, Carlito would stay planted by the river and out of the way just long enough for Angel to run up to the Lav without being noticed.

Now all he had to worry about was the cop Chavez. Angel picked up the ice cream box and started to edge up the path to the Lav. If she noticed him, he would say he needed to use the bathroom before going to the parking lot. He was ready for her.

But Chavez was running towards the river. Angel froze in place. He watched her hesitate and glance over her shoulder. She sighted Carlito in the middle of the group of kids lined up along the water, Carlito holding two cones, one in each hand.

Angel felt his luck fill the air. He was so good at knowing what people were thinking. It was like magic. And today everything was working for him. It was like he could read Maria's thoughts. She saw Angel alone, in plain sight, getting ready to leave. She looked up the hill. She couldn't see anyone near the Lav. She saw Carlito by the river's edge with two cones. Two cones. Ramón had to be nearby even though she couldn't see him. Still she stood motionless, unsure.

A woman ran past her, splashing into the water, screaming hysterically, "Help! Help! Someone help me! My son is drowning."

Maria hesitated, looking everywhere for Ramón. Then the woman's desperation seemed to catch at her. She splashed into the river, then disappeared under the water. She came up for air, disappeared again. This time she came up with a small boy's body under her arm. Angel stared in a trance. The boy was so crumpled and still, he looked dead. To Angel, he looked just like Ramón except his hair was a light brown.

Angel watched Maria put the boy down on his back. She began to press on his chest. The boy took a halting breath, stopped, breathed, starting and stopping, starting and stopping. Quickly Maria turned him on his side. Now the boy was vomiting, his arms and legs jerking.

Angel couldn't stop staring at Maria and the boy. How had she done that? How had she brought him back to life?

All of a sudden, the "on" button came on somewhere inside Angel's brain. He stopped watching Maria. He couldn't see Carlito anymore, but he knew he was there in the middle of the group of kids watching the fighting. And he knew his good luck would keep Carlito planted there until he could get to Ramón.

Angel checked the Lav one more time. Ramón was nowhere in sight. No one was in sight anywhere near the Lav. All the cops were trying to control the kids fighting and splashing around in the water. Now was the time for action. No more thinking. No more watching. Ramón was alone somewhere around the Lav, and nobody else knew it. All he had to do was run fast enough to get to the boy before the cops could see what he was doing. Angel began running up the hill, sticking to underbrush along the side of the path so no one would notice him.

❧

But Carlito was no longer in the group of kids watching the fighting. While Angel was staring spellbound at Maria bringing the drowned boy back to life, Carlito had slipped away and started running up the hill to find Ramón.

Carlito ran as fast as he could, hoping no one would see him. The teachers had told the children they weren't supposed to go anywhere by themselves, but this was an emergency. He had left his best friend all alone in the Lav. And by now the ice cream in the cones was dripping all over his hands. "How could he have forgotten Ramón?" Carlito kept asking himself as he ran up the hill. He felt so ashamed! If only he could get there before the teachers noticed. Otherwise both of them would get in big trouble!

But once he got inside the Lav, Carlito couldn't find Ramón anywhere. "Hey! Ramón, where are you?" Carlito called out into the silence. No one answered. He started to feel frightened. Something was wrong. He hurried over to the large back window and stared outside. Then he remembered what he had learned about *La Migra*. "Never let anyone outside see you."

"I don't want anyone outside staring up at me!" Carlito said to himself right away. He quickly made himself as small as he could and squeezed into the space against the wall at the far right-hand corner of the window. That way he could peek out but no one could see him. He had learned a lot about becoming invisible when *La Migra* was coming to get them.

When he looked out, he saw Mr. Angel running up the hill towards the Lav with the ice cream box. Maybe he was in a hurry to go to the bathroom. Maybe Mr. Angel had seen Ramón. Maybe if he waved at Mr. Angel, he could catch his attention. He started to raise his hand. Then his hand froze in midair. He squeezed as far back as he could into the corner of the wall and slowly lowered his hand.

Angel looked up. Was that a flash of movement from the back window of the Lav? Angel stopped running and stared hard at the Lav. No, it was nothing. Besides Angel already knew no one was in the Lav. But what the hell was that raspy noise ahead of him? It sounded just like Gil. How could Gil have followed him into the park? The noise was coming closer and closer.

Now he could see what was happening. It was that old man, Cortez, the one who had been sitting in front of the Lav. Something had spooked him, and now he was trying to get down the hill, calling out for help, but with that raspy voice, who could hear him?

Angel got down on his knees, put on his plastic gloves, and hid behind a bush while he searched for a rock, just the right size for that old head. The old man came stumbling past him, his chest heaving as he struggled to breathe.

"You're not going anywhere, old man," Angel said when Cortez ran by him. He grabbed Cortez around the neck and punched him hard in the stomach. The old man doubled over and fell on the ground. Angel picked up the rock and brought it down hard on the old man's head. The labored breathing stopped almost immediately. Still hidden by the bush, Angel looked down the hill. No one had seen him, no one was coming. He had made it! Keeping as close to the ground as he could, he turned and zigzagged fast up the rest of the hill and dashed around to the back of the Lav. Then he went into the woods.

꠵

Ramón was in back of the Lav still looking for Carlito when something flying low in the sky caught his attention. He followed it wide-eyed. It was a large gray bird with enormous wings, its head pulled back on its shoulders, and it was slowly moving in his direction. It was in the air right above him. The Great Blue Heron! At the sight of the bird, Ramón wanted to shout with joy.

He began to run after the bird, trying to keep it in sight even where the trees made it hard to see. "Carlito!" he cried out as he ran. "Carlito!!" He was so excited he could hardly get the words out of his mouth.

In the distance he seemed to hear Maria's voice. "Wake up, Ramón. Wake up!" she was calling out to him, just as she had that morning while he was dreaming about the herons in the park, only this time her voice was louder, fearful. He stopped, confused. What was wrong?

Then he remembered how Maria's voice had frightened away the heron in his dream. That was the problem. He had to follow the heron as silently as he could. Ssshhhhh.....No noise. He had to be quiet! He had to stop calling out for Carlito. He didn't want to frighten the heron away. After he found the heron's nest, he could go back and tell Carlito.

Ramón started off again after the bird. He could see it just ahead of him, moving its wings heavily through the air. For a moment, the heron seemed to slow its flight, as if waiting for him to catch up. Then it floated down through the trees and disappeared. Ramón kept on running. The river was just in front of him, a thin shimmering ribbon lined with green. He was almost to the water when he fell.

He hit the ground so hard, at first he couldn't breathe. He scrambled to his feet, surprised to find that his legs were trembling. He looked at his stinging elbow. It was bleeding where he had scraped it when he fell. He wiped his eyes and tried to figure out what had happened. He must have fallen into one of the ditches along the river. He'd seen the ditches lots of times on walks with his father. They never seemed very deep. But this ditch had walls too high to climb, and the bushes at the top were so thick, he couldn't see the path.

But there was no reason to be afraid. He knew someone would come by soon to help him. He had to be patient, that's all, just like his mother had taught him. He took a deep breath and carefully brushed off his shirt and pants. Then he called out for his teacher in the loudest voice he could make. No one answered. He called out again and waited, listening, but there was only silence in the woods.

After a few more minutes, Ramón sat down and started to draw with his fingers in the soft soil. He drew the figure of the Lady in Blue and put in Maria's smiling face. He made the large outline of a car. Then, on the side of the car where the windows would be, he wrote: "*Ramón loves Mami, Papi, Maria and mi School.*"

When he finished drawing, he stood up and looked around, feeling the first twist of fear in his stomach. He began to call for help again, even louder than before. He waited and called again. This time a tall shadow appeared at the top of the ditch. Someone had come for him at last!

Ramón couldn't stop smiling as he squinted up at the shadow. He tried to see who it was, but the noonday sun slanting through the trees was blinding. All he could make out was a silhouette, black against the bright light. It didn't matter. Someone had come to help him. Happily, Ramón stretched out his arms and waited until he felt himself being pulled up slowly into the dark shadow overhead.

27 | FRIDAY
Riverside Park
The Olde Road

ANGEL HELD RAMÓN CLOSE to his chest as he sloshed through the river. He didn't want the water to splash on the boy's face. What if he woke up?

As soon as he reached the bank on the other side, Angel crawled out of the water and sat down under a spreading green bush a few feet away. He put Ramón down on his lap and studied the boy's face. His eyes were closed, but he was breathing. Good. That meant he was still sleeping. If he stayed asleep, it would be easy to carry him up to the road.

Angel pulled frantically at the top of one of the ice cream boxes, but his fingers kept fumbling around the edges. Calm down, he told himself. He pulled at the box top again, and this time he got it open.

As soon as he pulled out the new drop phone, he closed the box. Then he opened the phone and punched in the phone number he had memorized in case of trouble. He let the phone ring once. Then he disconnected and scrambled to his feet. Still holding the phone in his hand, he picked up Ramón and held him securely under his arm. He picked up the box with his other hand and started running up the hiker's trail to the Olde Road.

The phone rang. "I've got the kid!" Angel said as soon as Gil came on the line. He was breathing hard.

"Geez," Gil said.

Angel waited anxiously, but Gil was as silent as a stone. "Did you hear me?!" Angel yelled. "I've got the kid. He fell in a ditch, and I pulled him out. I crossed the river with the boy, and no one saw me, no one saw me! Now I'm on the other side."

Angel still couldn't believe how fast his feet had carried him across the river. He'd churned through the shallow water as fast as a motor boat.

Finally Gil said, "Is the kid listening?"

"No, I gave him a needle. He's sound asleep."

"What about the cops?"

"I don't see any. Maybe they're on the island where the kids are fighting in the water."

"Where are you?"

"I'm following the hiker's trail up to the Olde Road." Angel spoke in a rush, heaving for air.

"Angel, listen to me carefully," Gil said. He sounded strange.

"What's the matter? You told me to look for opportunities. Well, I found one. Here's the kid.

123

Isn't that what you wanted?"

"Yes, Angel, yes, that's good, very good. You're using a drop phone, right?"

"Right."

"Good. Now stay on the line and tell me when you get to the road, OK? Stay out of sight. And remember to clean this phone and toss it as soon as you can."

"I'm at the road."

"Any cars?"

"No, it's empty, like always."

"OK. Now put the kid down near the road but not in plain sight."

Not far from the side of the road, there was a patch of tall grass next to a tree. Angel ran over to the tree and put the boy down in the grass. The boy was so small, no one would be able to see him from the road. And he was still sleeping peacefully, almost smiling in his sleep.

In a small corner of Angel's brain, a tiny worry teased at him because the boy's chest wasn't moving up and down anymore. But the boy the woman cop had dragged out of the water, his chest hadn't been moving either at first. Angel had watched her very carefully. He'd seen how she brought the boy back to life. Gil could do that too if he needed to. There was nothing to worry about.

"Angel?!" Gil was yelling at him.

"I'm here."

"How am I going to find the boy, Angel? The road goes along the river for miles! What's the nearest exit to the highway?"

"Exit 6, I think. The one nearest to the park. I put the kid in some tall grass near a tree. You can't see him from the road."

There was a long pause. Then Gil said, "What tree, Angel?"

"It's called a hackberry tree."

Gil was silent again.

He doesn't know what kind of tree it is, Angel realized with surprise. I know a lot of things Gil doesn't know, he thought with satisfaction. Then he started to worry. What if someone saw him? He had to hurry. "I gotta go. I gotta get back to the van before anyone sees me. If I cut through the woods to the parking lot, I'll get there fast," he told Gil as he started to run back into the woods.

"Angel, stop! Listen to me, this is important," Gil screamed at him.

Angel stood still, shocked by the force of Gil's voice. "What's the matter?" he asked in a confused voice.

"You can't cut through the woods to the parking lot, Angel. You have to follow the hiker's trail back down to the river. Understand? You have to go back to the river the same way you came up to the road."

"Someone could see me," Angel protested.

"Shut up, Angel," Gil said harshly. "Do exactly what I tell you. This is an order! Don't go directly to the parking lot from where you are. You could leave a trail in the woods. Can you try to understand that?"

Angel didn't like the way Gil was talking to him, but he kept his mouth shut and nodded anyway.

"OK, first you need to follow the hiker's trail back to the river. Got it?"

"Got it. Back to the river."

"When you get down to the river, then you need to take the path that goes to the back of the parking lot. Know what I mean, Angel?"

"Yeah, I know that path. Everyone takes it. They go to the Lav, they cut through the woods, they cross the shallow part of the river, they climb out onto the other side, then they take that path up to the back of the parking lot...."

"Shut up!" Gil screamed at him. "Shut up!! What's wrong with you? We don't have all day here, you know?!"

Angel shut up.

"OK, now, listen and do exactly what I say. Follow the path into the back of the parking lot and get into your van. You parked the van in the back of the lot, right?"

"Right, but there could be a cop there," Angel said, breathing heavily. "And there's a fence at the back of the parking lot."

Gil was silent. "Angel," he said in a voice like ice "Listen to me. What were you planning to do after leaving the boy by the side of the road?"

"I was going to go back to the van through the woods and act like nothing had happened. If anyone asked, I was going to say that I crossed the bridge into the parking lot."

"What if people say they didn't see you?"

"I'll say that's their problem. Everyone was looking at the kids fighting in the water. No one was paying attention to me. No one can prove I didn't go into the parking lot from the bridge."

"Good, that's right. Now, when you made your plans, how were you going to get back to your van?"

"I was going to cut through the back fence into the parking lot."

"And if there was a cop?"

"I was going to wait until he wasn't looking."

"That's exactly right, Angel. Very good. I want you to do exactly what you planned to do except I want you to start from the river. Can you understand that?"

"From the river."

"Right. Then cut through the back fence into the parking lot, just like you planned. If there's a cop, wait until he isn't looking, OK? Just like you planned."

"OK. Just like I planned."

"Good. Now what about your clothes?"

"I brought the phone, dry pants, socks, and shoes in a bag inside one of the ice cream boxes," Angel said proudly. He had thought of everything. "I already changed. I left all my wet clothes, the syringe, and my gloves inside the bag, and I left the bag next to the kid. That's why I have dry clothes," he finished explaining triumphantly. "So no one can prove I didn't use the pedestrian bridge."

"Geez," Gil said. "Gloves?" He sounded completely lost.

"You didn't think I could do anything, did you?" Angel couldn't help saying as he ran along the hiker's path back down to the river, still carrying the ice cream box in his arms.

"You sure fooled me," Gil said. "Now I have to hurry, Angel, I have to find someone to pick up the kid and the bag before anyone else comes by. Did you ever think of that? I have about a minute, can you see that, you asshole?!"

But Angel had already closed the phone. All he could think about was running, running as fast as he could. He had to reach the van before anyone saw him.

He reached the river. He climbed up the hiker's trail to the back end of the parking lot, just like he had planned. There were already holes cut in the wire fence. Angel squeezed through one of the openings and looked around. The cop on duty in the parking lot was gone. Angel ran fast over to his van, pausing only to toss the phone into a trash barrel. He put the ice cream box inside the van, and then got into the driver's seat and sat there, trying to catch his breath.

He checked his clothes again. Everything was clean and dry. His luck had been good, Angel thought over and over again. And had Gil ever been surprised! Almost without words. That was a first! Now Gil knew that he could do things as well as Snake Baby. Angel smiled and took another deep breath. Yes, his luck had been good.

28 | FRIDAY
Riverside Park

CARLITO STOOD JUST BEYOND THE EDGE of the window. There was danger outside. He couldn't see it, but he could feel it in his stomach. He tried to imagine himself completely frozen, as if a magic wand had suddenly turned him into a block of ice. No part of him could move, not even his toes. Even his breath was an imperceptible shiver of air. Only the thoughts in his head kept moving, falling from one frozen spot to another just to melt away once he got close to them.

Carlito moved closer to the edge of the window trying to get a quick look outside. He couldn't see Ramón anywhere. But Mr. Angel was running into the woods. Was he trying to find Ramón? More minutes passed. Mr. Angel didn't come back. Neither did Ramón.

Carlito looked down at Mr. Cortez lying in the grass just below the window. Mr. Angel had smashed a rock on top of the old man's head. Now a stream of blood was leaking out of the old man's head onto the grass. Why would Mr. Angel hit an old man with a rock?

Finally Carlito couldn't stand it any longer. He turned and ran out of the Lav as fast as he could, not looking at anything, not even the walls. All he could think about was getting out of there and down to the picnic tables.

He could see Maria sitting on the ground at the bottom of the hill. He headed straight for her, without thinking, without knowing why, but before he could reach her, his feet stopped moving, and he nearly skidded and fell down. She was holding a boy in her arms, and the boy looked just like Ramón. Carlito stood motionless, staring at Maria, his thoughts lost in the emptiness of confusion.

Unaware of anything else around her, Maria let out a deep sigh of relief as the boy in her arms began breathing in and out, in and out. "I know, we almost lost him," Maria said to the boy's mother who was sitting on the ground beside her, sobbing. "But don't worry, he's going to be fine, he's going to make it just fine."

The boy's mother reached out to take her son, thanking Maria over and over again. Maria looked up. Carlito was standing there on the path in front of her, staring at her as if he had gone blind, his eyes open but not seeing, a melted ice cream cone in each hand. As soon as she saw him, she knew. The air around her turned yellow, Carlito receded into the distance. Then the world shifted, and she was back.

She jumped to her feet and ran towards Carlito, calling out for Joe as she ran. Carlito looked like a failed clown, upright but drifting from side to side as he moved forward to meet her, his face and arms smeared white with ice cream, his eyes vacant, his mouth hanging open in a wordless shriek.

"Carlito, Carlito, where is Ramón?" Maria said as she pulled him to her. As if it were almost too heavy to move, he slowly pointed his finger in the direction of the Lav.

Wordlessly, Maria held Carlito's trembling body close to her as she scanned the area around the Lav. Joe came charging up to her, took in the situation at a glance, ran past her, checking both sides of the gravel path as he headed towards the Lav. He was almost past the building when he stopped abruptly and bent down to look at something in the grass.

Medrano was already pushing through the crowd towards Maria. "Your teacher is here," she told Carlito. She put him into Medrano's arms. "He'll take care of you until I come back."

By the time she reached Joe, he was talking into his radio. "We have one down, it's Cortez," she heard him say before he snapped the phone closed.

Maria looked down at the ground. Cortez was lying face down, a stream of drying blood leading from his head onto the grass. Not far from the body she could see a blood-stained rock.

"He's gone," Joe said. His eyes were cold with fury. "I've updated dispatch. Secure the scene for me, will you Maria? We're going to do this one by the book. I want every available patrol car out here pronto. Every goddamn section of the Olde Road near the river needs to be saturated with cruisers, and they need to be on high alert for anything out of the ordinary, no matter how small.

"They also need to search on foot, on the chance the boy was picked up and then dropped off farther down the road. If we're in time, it may be our best chance at...." His voice trailed off.

"Wait a minute," Maria said. "Right now, we don't know anything for sure. Maybe Ramón is just lost."

"We can't wait," Joe said. "There's no time. I'll take full responsibility if this is a false alarm." There was an undertone of defiance in his voice she hadn't heard before.

"Explain," she insisted. "You think Carlito saw what happened to Cortez?"

"I don't know about that," Joe said. He turned to leave, his eyes already on the woods behind the Lav. "I don't know what Carlito saw. What matters is that I think someone took Ramón."

Maria repressed a shudder. "You think someone took Ramón from the Lav and brought him up to the Olde Road?"

"Maybe. Or else to the parking lot."

"But there's no one in the parking lot today," she began, stopped. "Angel!" Her stomach turned over. "No, he hasn't left yet, his van is still there."

"I called down to the parking lot," Joe said. "They're already on their way to check out the van."

"Where are you going?"

"I'm going down to the river. Then it depends on what I find. Probably I'll wade across to the other side and follow the hiker's trail up to the Olde Road."

Joe was running now. "Keep in touch," he yelled over his shoulder. A few moments later, he had passed the Lav and disappeared into the woods.

29

FRIDAY AFTERNOON
Riverside Park

AS SOON AS THE AREA AROUND CORTEZ'S BODY had been secured, Maria headed for the river, cutting through the woods behind the Lav. Close to the river bank, she saw where Joe had marked a deep irrigation ditch hidden behind a clump of juniper bushes. She studied the ditch as she took out her phone to call for someone to come and secure another crime scene.

She forced herself to look carefully at the childish scrawl in the sand in the bottom of the ditch, the scuff marks where it looked like little shoes had rubbed against the side of the ditch. She followed the broken twigs, the bent grass along the trail down to the river, refusing to think about what must have happened, concentrating all her thoughts on finding Ramón. She splashed through the shallow water and climbed up the hiker's trail to the Olde Road.

As she came out of the woods onto the road, she felt a sharp wind come up from the river and whip over her shoulders. She looked up. The sky was still blue, but the wind seemed to bring with it a light mist that dimmed the blue of the sky. Red-tailed hawks were circling overhead. Road kill was common along the Olde Road. The image of a Blue Heron, its sharp, pointed beak tearing into the flesh of a fish flashed into her mind. A bloodstained beak. Owls with cold yellow eyes. Coyotes gathered for the attack. She cleared her mind and walked over to Joe.

He was searching through a small area of tall grass near the side of the road. When he looked at her, his face was a mask of concentration. Only when she looked into his eyes did she see his discouragement and then only briefly.

He pointed to a faint indentation where something small had been lying in the grass.

"See the way the grass is bent there," he said indicating the area of indentation. "That's where a small body was lying."

She stared at him. Her ears would not stop ringing. She shook her head, trying to clear her ears. "A small body?" she said finally.

He nodded. "Where does the Olde Road lead?"

"I don't know exactly. It follows the curves of the river for miles, and miles, and goes at least as far as Ciudad Nueva. Most of the hiking trails in this area are marked by trailheads along the Olde Road, and most of the trailheads have small parking areas nearby. About ten years ago a four-lane highway was built that runs parallel to the Olde Road. Today most of the people who use the Olde Road are hikers."

"How many exits from the Olde Road onto the highway?"

"Every few miles or so."

Maria studied the road near the indentation. There was nothing to indicate a car had stopped there. Why would there be? It was a paved road. If a car had glided to a stop there and then pulled away just as carefully, there would be no tire marks. It hadn't rained in days. The wind from the river would have blown away any dust or sand that might have gathered by the side of the road.

Joe was on the radio talking to Danforth. He listened for a few minutes, nodding his head in agreement before he closed his phone.

"Danforth's at the park," Joe told Maria. "He'll send the K-9 unit to search this part of the Olde Road by foot once they've finished going through the woods in back of the Lav."

"Why would someone take Ramón only to drop off his body a few miles down the road? It doesn't make sense."

"I agree. But I want to look for a trail leading directly from here over to the parking lot. It's not likely, but just in case."

"Why not likely?"

"Because if a stranger took Ramón, there wouldn't be any trail," Joe said. "No reason. Whether he worked alone and left his car parked up here, or had a partner who picked him and the boy up, they would be miles away from here by now.

"But if Angel took the boy and left him for Gil to pick up? Angel could have panicked. The fastest route from here to the parking lot is straight through the woods, and if that's what he did, there would be a recent trail. Probably wouldn't mean anything, but you never know."

"You're saying that if it was Angel who left the boy by the road to be picked up, he could have been in such a hurry to get back to his van that he wouldn't even think about leaving a trail in the woods. By itself a trail wouldn't mean much, but if someone saw him coming into the back of the parking lot from the woods...."

"Exactly. Let's go."

Joe left the road and moved quickly into the woods that went up to the back fence of the parking lot scanning everything around him as he went. Maria did the same.

"Well?" she said when they got to the back end of the parking lot.

"I didn't see anything," Joe said. His face was dark with discouragement. "Let's go back to the Olde Road by the hiker's trail."

When they got up to the road, Joe said, "I can't be sure, but it looks to me as if someone ran along this trail fairly recently."

"Meaning?"

"Nothing. Nothing that would hold up in court anyway. Let's go." Joe started up the hiker's trail to the parking lot. Maria could see partials of big footprints that had gone off the trail, but Joe didn't seem to pay attention to them. When they were near the parking lot, she looked at Joe. "Still nothing?"

Joe's shoulders were tight with tension. "Nothing. Even if I find sign that suggests someone passed along this trail recently, what would it prove?"

Maria knew that Border Patrol Agents had their own kind of language. A border patrol tracker always refers to following sign, not signs like most city cops would say.

"My guess is that when we confront Angel, he will say that he went over the bridge into the parking lot just like he was supposed to do," Joe continued. "It takes him far away from the irrigation ditch and the possibility that he was involved with Ramon's abduction."

"And if no one saw him?"

"Doesn't prove he didn't go that way."

"If his clothes are wet? My shoes and socks, even the bottom of my pant legs, are wet from wading across the river."

"That might make a difference because then we would have caught him in a lie. Why would he lie? We could pressure him about that. It wouldn't prove anything, but it would be a pressure point. At least a place to start...."

"You want to go to the parking lot?"

Joe shook his head. "No, I'd rather stay out here. More chance of finding something. By now the parking lot and the van will have been thoroughly searched. Let's see if they found anything."

He took out his phone and called Danforth. "That son of a bitch," Joe said at one point, his face pale.

"What?" she said when he closed his phone.

"They found Angel sitting in his van. His clothes were dry. He said he was resting, keeping out of the sun for a few minutes before going back to the trailers.

"They asked if they could search the van. He agreed. It was clean as far as they could tell. He was calm and smiling the whole time. Asked what all the fuss was about. But when they invited him to go back to the station for some conversation, he refused. Talk to my lawyer, he said. Then he drove away. There was nothing we could do."

Maria was silent.

"Danforth wanted to let us know that Charlie Medrano called Rosa."

"Oh no," she said. "It's too soon. We still don't know anything for sure.... "

"Medrano insisted it was the right thing to do. Since Rosa would have come by taxi, Danforth agreed to send out a cruiser for her. We can meet her in the picnic area."

The thought of seeing Rosa added new weight to every step, but Maria pushed the thought out of her mind. For now Ramón was simply a lost boy about to be found.

30 | FRIDAY AFTERNOON
Rosa's Apartment
Riverside Park

ROSA HAD JUST OPENED THE DOOR to her apartment when the telephone in the kitchen began to ring. The key dropped from her hand. She could see it falling slowly onto the floor with a loud clang. No, that wasn't right, a key couldn't make a loud clang. But that's how she heard it.

She moved towards the phone, saying to herself over and over again, "It's nothing, don't worry, it's nothing." But in her heart she knew something bad had happened to Ramón.

When she picked up the receiver, she was surprised to see that her hand was steady. So was her voice. "Yes, I see," she said. "Yes, I will wait in front of the building. I'll be there right away."

As soon as she hung up, she seemed to float away from herself. She watched at a distance as another woman, her double, prepared to go out to the park. She could see the woman taking care not to look at Ramón's bedroom, as if she knew her strength could only cover so much territory. His bedroom was outside the protected area.

The woman used the bathroom. She carefully plaited her long black hair into a single braid down her back and straightened her collar. Then she picked up the key lying on the floor and left the apartment, locking the door behind her with care before she put the key into her pocketbook.

She couldn't remember going down the stairs. But by the time she got out to the street, she had floated back into her body. Now she was ready for the police in the cruiser waiting in front of the building.

"Rosa Alvarez?" one of the officers said as he got out of the front passenger seat.

"Yes," she said, nodding.

"I'm Officer Robertson," he said. "We're here to bring you out to Riverside Park." He opened the back door of the cruiser.

"Yes," she said again and got into the back seat. He closed her door and got back into the front seat. "Let's go," he said to the officer who was driving.

As the car began to move, Rosa found herself staring at the man sitting directly in front of her. He looked more like a boy than a man, with his short fuzzy hair, the smooth pink skin on the back of his neck.

When he looked back at her, she closed her eyes before he could say anything. She had to shut him out, she had to shut everything out, or she would shatter and break. With an enormous effort of will, she pushed away the grief rising in her throat. She had to focus all her attention on remembering. Maybe there was a sign, something to explain....

"Señora Alvarez! Rosa!" The officer in the passenger seat was trying to get her attention. She could feel the car slowly coming to a stop. She opened her eyes. "Are we there?"

He shook his head. "We're stuck at an accident. Can't get by until the ambulance clears. It'll just be a minute." He looked at her uncertainly. She stared back at him. What did he want from her?

"I thought you might want to know," he said hesitantly. "I called out to the park. There's no news. One way or the other," he added.

A sharp pain ripped through her stomach at his words. She had to struggle not to scream at him, "Where is my son? Where is Ramón?"

She shut her eyes again. Hurry! Erase the moment. Go back into remembering. Mr. Medrano had promised her that he would watch out for Ramón in the park. Oh! Why had she believed him?!

The movement of the police car starting up again cut through her anguish. The accident must have cleared. She heard the officer saying, "We're almost at the park, Señora."

Rosa opened her eyes. "I'm ready," she said, looking straight ahead at the road. "God willing, I am ready to find my son."

✂

Maria stood by the entrance to the parking lot. When the cruiser pulled up, she helped Rosa out of the back seat.

"You can go," she told the officers waiting in the car. "I'll take care of her from here."

For a few minutes, Maria and Rosa stood in a wordless embrace. Cars drove slowly past them into the parking lot at a steady rate. A helicopter clattered overhead.

"Rosa, let's go where we can sit down," Maria said. Rosa, mute and trembling, let Maria guide her across the bridge and along the river until they reached the picnic area.

There was a large group of children and teachers standing near the picnic tables. Officers were sitting at the tables writing on notepads, taking down information as each person came up to them.

Danforth was there too, talking to the K-9 sergeant. The dogs and their handlers were nearby, the dogs whimpering and straining at their leashes. Joe was talking on his cell phone. Al was with a group of reporters who had just arrived.

In the far distance, Maria could see a line of people moving through the woods around the Lav. She winced at the sight. The woods would be thoroughly trampled by the time the searchers reached the river.

Charlie Medrano came over as soon as he saw her. A hush spread over the picnic area as people became aware that Rosa was there.

"Come with me, Señora," Medrano said taking Rosa from Maria. He put his arm around her. "Come with me," he said again. "Maria has to work now."

Rosa nodded. "Thank you, Maria," she managed to say before she left with Medrano. Maria stared after them, Rosa stumbling over to one of the tables, Medrano with a steady arm around her shoulders. He helped her sit down on one of the benches. Then he sat down beside her and held her hand.

31
FRIDAY AFTERNOON
The Olde Road

THREE HIKERS STRAGGLED OUT OF THE WOODS and headed back towards the Bosque View trailhead, one of the most famous markers in the system of hiking trails along the river. The woodlands of willow and cottonwood trees growing along the Rio Poderoso had largely disappeared in other parts of the state, but here in Ciudad Nueva, full corridors of cottonwoods still lined the river banks. They were called with the old name, the *bosque*, the Spanish word for forest. The trailhead had taken its name from the wide view it offered of the river and the "bosque" along its banks.

By now the two girls and the boy, all teenagers, were walking slowly. It had been a long hike down to the river and back. The boy was perspiring heavily, and in spite of the sunburn on his nose and forehead, he looked pale.

The small parking area off the Olde Road where their parents were going to pick them up was only a few hundred feet away from the trailhead, but before they could reach the road, the boy collapsed onto the ground. He crawled towards the shade offered by a cluster of mesquite bushes planted near the edge of the parking area.

"I'm waiting here," he moaned, resting his head on his arms. "I'm not moving another step. Too hot! Too hot! I'm not moving."

"Teddy wasn't ready, Teddy feels unsteady," the two girls chanted in unison, giggling as they looked down at Teddy, prostrate on the ground under the bushes.

"Shut up! Give me some water, brats!" the boy said without moving. "I could die without water, you know."

Still giggling, one of the girls took a bottle of water out of her back pack and started walking over to Teddy. Before she could reach him, Teddy scrambled to his feet and starting screaming.

"What is it?" the girl said. Teddy had gone completely white.

"There!" Teddy screamed, pointing to the place where he had been lying on the ground. "There!"

The girls turned to look at the bushes.

"No, underneath," Teddy yelled at them, backing away. He pulled out his cell phone.

The operator came on line. "Ciudad Nueva 911, what is your emergency?"

"There's a body," Teddy said faintly. He was feeling sick to his stomach. "There's a body under the bushes near the Olde Road."

In the background the operator could hear the girls screaming. "Sir, I need you to remain as calm as possible. What's your name?"

"The girls saw the body too," Teddy mumbled incoherently. He was going to throw up.

"Sir, where are you exactly?"

The youngest girl ran up to Teddy and grabbed the cell phone from his hand. "It's a little boy," she sobbed into the phone. "Oh God! It's a little boy. And he looks like he's dead!"

✑✿✍

Danforth was standing with Maria when he got the call. A young boy's body had been found by some hikers near the Bosque View trailhead.

According to the officer who responded to the 911 call, there was a body lying under some mesquite bushes close to a parking area off the Olde Road, between exits six and seven. There were no apparent signs of a struggle on the body, but there was a visible puncture wound on the boy's arm. Best guess at this point was that the boy had died from a drug overdose. They would have to wait for the medical examiner and blood tests to be sure, but it looked like homicide, not an accident.

Danforth closed his phone. He looked shaken, as if he'd fallen and only just now pulled himself to his feet.

The thought of Danforth getting older flashed through Maria's mind, bringing unexpected sadness in its wake.

"What is it, Sarge?" she asked.

"I think it's Ramón," Danforth said in a low voice.

Maria looked over at the tiny woman sitting at the picnic table as still as a statue, staring blindly out at the water. "We don't know that," she said.

"I'll get Medrano to make the identification," Danforth said. "You stay with Rosa."

They walked over to the table where Rosa and Medrano were sitting, Rosa started shivering when she saw them. Charlie Medrano put his arm around her trembling shoulders. "Courage, Rosa" he said quietly. "May God be merciful."

"I'll stay with her," Maria said to Medrano. "Can you go with Joe?"

Medrano nodded. Before he could stand up, Rosa grabbed his arm and shook her head. "No, I want to go," she said. She pulled herself to her feet and tried to stand up, but her legs gave way. "Sit down," Maria said firmly. "Let Charlie take care of things for now."

Rosa collapsed back onto the bench. Maria sat down next to her. Neither woman spoke as they watched the afternoon sun send its flaming reflection across the water. Only the Blue Heron, barely visible against the deep blue shade of the cottonwoods along the riverbank where he was fishing, remained untouched by the falling light.

32

FRIDAY AFTERNOON
The Repository

THE PHONE RANG ONCE. Finally Gil could talk. Angel had been waiting to hear from him ever since he'd returned to his office. He couldn't wait to hear what had happened. Was the kid OK? When could he get him and bring him back to the trailer?

He called Gil from the gas station parking lot, anxious to hear his first words.

"Angel, you did fine," Gil said carefully.

Angel felt a chill down to his toes. Gil never talked like that to him. Something was wrong.

"We picked up the kid and the box," Gil said. Angel began to feel better.

"Now listen," Gil went on. "It's been a busy day. If for any reason the cops should come out to pay you a visit, you know nothing. You're clear, understand? There is nothing to link you to the kid, OK?"

"What do you mean?"

"You tell the same story. No matter what else happens, stick to it. You followed the path along the river and crossed over the pedestrian bridge into the parking lot. You saw nothing, you saw no one. That's right, Angel, isn't it? You saw no one?"

"Not exactly," Angel said with a slight twinge of hesitation.

"What do you mean?"

"I mean, there was an old guy up by the Lav who saw me coming up the hill so I had to rock him."

"You took him out with a rock?" Gil repeated.

"I had no choice. I had to move fast."

"I see," Gil said. Another pause. "And the Lav?"

"I don't have X-ray eyes, you know," Angel said, for once allowing some of his confusion and irritation to show through. "But I'm sure. No one was in the Lav."

Gil snickered. "Good for you, Angel. You can get mad once in a while, you know. It's healthy. But listen. Even if someone did see you, and I know they didn't," he added quickly keeping Angel from interrupting in protest, "even if they did, it's no problem, understand. Just say it's impossible and then call the lawyer. You remember his number, right?"

"Right."

"So don't worry, Angel. The cops have no way to hold you. They may threaten to arrest you, but they either have to charge you or let you go. Trust me. No one is going to say they saw you."

"So I did good?" Angel asked. He had to know.

"You did good," Gil said right away. "But listen, here's the thing, Angel. Things didn't exactly work out the way you planned."

"What do you mean things didn't work out the way I planned?" Angel asked, forcing himself to remain calm.

"Never mind the details," Gil said. He sounded angry. "No questions, remember?"

"I know, I know, but you said things didn't exactly work out the way I planned, and...."

"OK," Gil said with a long sigh. "It's not great news, but I gotta tell you now so you're prepared. See, here's the thing." He paused. "Angel, the kid was dead when we picked him up, I mean dead as dead."

"No!" Angel screamed into the phone. "No! I didn't make a mistake. I did everything exactly right."

"Maybe the stuff in the needle...."

"No," Angel insisted furiously. "It was right for a nine-year old. I checked."

"Well, the kid was small or maybe he had a defect of some kind, who knows, but what's the difference? He's just a wetback kid. No one cares. They'll forget all about him in a few weeks."

"What did you do with him!?"

"None of your business, Angel." Then Gil relented. "OK, you're going to hear about it on TV anyway so I'll make an exception this time and tell you. My guys went out there and picked up the kid and the bag with your wet clothes inside. They were just where you said they'd be. That was good work, Angel."

Angel couldn't trust himself to speak.

"But we were running out of time. Cop cars were on the way. We couldn't afford to get caught with a dead kid in the car, right? So my guys tore off down the road a couple of miles and dumped...I mean, they put his body under some bushes near a pull-off area. They tried to hide him as best they could, but they could hear the sirens coming closer, so they took off fast and got back onto the highway."

Angel still couldn't say anything.

"Angel, listen, the good thing is that some hikers found the body right away. They were coming from the other direction so the red and white colors of the kid's shirt stood out when they got close to the bushes."

Angel felt faint. That shirt. He remembered it perfectly.

"Listen Angel, like I said, the good thing is that now the body is safe. The mother can give it a proper burial. Do you hear me? The body will be buried in a church and all, no animals or anything like that."

Angel took a deep breath. "In a church?" he repeated.

"Yes, Angel, in a church. The important thing is no one can link the kid to you. Take a nap. Don't worry. I'll call you later." The phone went dead.

Angel sat motionless, thinking about what had happened. He had failed. His first and last action on his own. The feeling of defeat almost smothered him. He looked at himself in the car mirror. There were two empty holes where his eyes should have been. He moved his thoughts into the space in his chest where the pain couldn't touch him. Then he closed his eyes. If the cops came to the Repository, he would be ready. At least Gil would see that he still knew how to follow orders.

33 | FRIDAY AFTERNOON
Picnic area
Riverside Park

MARIA WAS WATCHING THE RIVER PATH when Medrano and two officers finally came into sight. Medrano was walking slowly, looking down at the ground.

"They're here," Maria told Rosa in a quiet voice. But Rosa remained as silent as a statue, staring out blindly at the river.

Danforth was standing with his unit at the far end of the picnic area. The officers headed in his direction. Medrano hesitated and looked over at Rosa. Her eyes were fixed on the river, and she seemed completely unaware of his presence. With a heavy sigh, Medrano turned away and followed the officers over to Danforth. After all of Danforth's questions had been answered, the two men walked over to the table where Maria and Rosa were sitting.

"I'm sorry," Danforth said to Rosa. His face had lost its color. Even after all his years on the force, he hadn't learned how to keep away the pain of telling a mother that her child was dead. "Charlie identified the body," he told her quietly. "It's Ramón."

Rosa looked at him blankly.

"Maria, we need you," Danforth said.

"I'll be right back," she told Rosa. "Charlie?"

Medrano nodded and sat down next to Rosa. He took her hand, but Rosa remained silent and unmoving. It was as if she didn't even recognize him.

Maria and Danforth walked over to their unit together. Neither of them spoke. Maria had put her grief over Ramón aside. She would let those feelings out later, when she wasn't on the job.

Danforth called the unit together for a quick briefing. "The most likely scenario is that the kidnapper took Ramón from the irrigation ditch and carried him off the island through the water, then brought him up to the Olde Road where a car picked up the boy and maybe the kidnaper too. Can't prove any of that yet, but it's a starting point.

"What happened afterwards? We can't find the sense in it no matter how we look at it. What was the motive? Why pick up the body and then dump it a few miles away? How could anyone plan something like that?

"We saturated the stretch of Olde Road between Exits Six and Seven with cruisers until we could get the roadblock set up. We got nothing."

"Someone was goddamn lucky is all I can say," Al interrupted.

Maria let out a long breath. "What do you think happened, Al?"

"Angel," Al said firmly. His voice was bitter. "It's the only scenario that makes sense. But some-one else had to be involved as well. Angel doesn't have the smarts to have figured something like this out." Al bit off his words with an angry intensity.

"Can we get anything out of Angel?" Maria asked.

"Doesn't look that way," Al said. "His van looked clean although we won't know for sure until forensics gets through with it. Right now we have no reason to bring him in."

"What about Carlito?" she asked Danforth.

"According to the doctor, he's fragile. He didn't see anything that could pin Angel to Ramón's abduction, but he's suffering because he thinks it's his fault, because he left Ramón alone while he went to get some ice cream. Poor kid. We sent a cruiser to bring him home, and we'll keep an officer posted outside Ana's apartment 24-7 until we understand things better."

Maria nodded.

"Another thing," Danforth said. "Rosa wants to go home, and she wants you to go with her, Maria. I know it means more involvement on your part," he added unhappily," but I think it's important. She trusts you, and if you can interview her in her own home, she'll feel safer than at the station."

"Yes, but I'd also like to try to interview Ana and Carlito while I'm there," Maria said. "If Carlito knows anything, if he saw anything, the sooner he tells us, the safer he'll be. We need to know what he knows as soon as possible."

"The doctor says no one can talk to Carlito without his permission," Danforth said in a serious voice. "The boy is way too fragile. The doc will call me as soon as he thinks the boy is up to it."

Maria nodded, but her reluctance was obvious.

Joe caught up to her as she walked back to Rosa. "Listen, Maria, I know how you feel, but will you listen to me, really listen to me?"

Maria stopped walking and waited.

"This is a complicated case and a very public one. It's going to be front-page news. We can't take any chances. I know you're worried about Carlito, but think about this. What if you inter-view him before he's ready and he loses it? What if he tries to kill himself?"

"That's ridiculous, Joe, and you know it," she said angrily.

"You're no doctor," he insisted.

"And you're not so smart either," she threw back at him. "I listened to you about Ramón and looked what happened."

His face remained impassive, but she saw from his eyes that her words had hurt him.

"I'm sorry, Joe," she said quickly. "That wasn't fair."

"You have to check with Danforth before you talk to Carlito," Joe said quietly as if nothing had happened. "Do you hear me?"

"I hear you," she told him. She wanted to say something else, but he had already turned away. She watched him walk back to Danforth with his long, steady stride, and it was all she could do not to call out after him. Why had she spoken to him like that?

She dreaded the thought of going back to Rosa's apartment without Ramón, but it was im-portant, and it was her job. She gathered up her strength and put a determined expression on her face. Then she walked over to Rosa.

34 | LATE FRIDAY
Rosa's apartment

BY THE TIME ROSA GOT BACK TO HER APARTMENT, she was a thin shell hollowed out by pain.

Maria and Mr. Medrano had stayed close to her the whole time she was out at the park. She didn't know what she would have done without them. So many people had been trying to talk to her, she'd felt battered by all the words.

When Ramón's body was found, she had wanted to go to him right away, but Maria had persuaded her to wait. Mr. Medrano had identified Ramón for her. She would go see his body at the station tomorrow.

They had brought her home after that. It was a silent drive. She had been in a daze, numb down to her bones. Nothing mattered anymore. Her life was over.

As soon as she walked into the apartment, she walked around the sheet into Ramón's bedroom and collapsed on his bed. At last she could cry. She knew Maria wanted to ask her more questions, but she could not stop weeping. She heard the police officers talking with Maria. Time passed. The apartment door opened and closed. It was quiet.

Rosa sat up on the bed, her head in her hands. Now she would have to answer questions. Maria came over to the bed.

"The other officers have gone," she said to Rosa in a quiet voice. "Can you answer some questions now?"

Rosa nodded and tried to think of something to tell Maria that could explain what had happened to Ramón, but it was impossible, she didn't know anything, and soon she lost all control, weeping helplessly.

Maria sat down beside her on the bed and took her hand. "We'll find the person who did this, I promise you, and we'll make him pay," she told Rosa in a firm voice. But for a long time Rosa was inconsolable.

I need to get through to her, Maria thought to herself. This is too important. Every minute lost could mean some small detail lost as well, and more times than not, it was the details that broke the case.

"I'd like to speak with Ana and Carlito," Maria said. "Would you call and ask them? It's important."

Rosa stopped crying and nodded. "Yes, I'll call them right away, maybe they know something," she said. She got up and went over to the phone in the kitchen.

"Now what am I going to do about Ana and Carlito?" Maria said to herself under her breath. Danforth's instructions and Joe's warning were very much on her mind.

She called the station and asked to be put through to Danforth's voice mail. "Sarge, Ana and Carlito are coming down to Rosa's apartment in a few minutes. I can't avoid speaking with them. I'll be very careful with Carlito." She disconnected right away and turned off her cell phone.

This time she was really up against it. She could lose her job. But if she were being honest with herself, she had to admit that it wasn't just to break through Rosa's grief that she'd asked her to call Ana and Carlito. Talking with Carlito had been her aim all along. She hadn't listened to her instincts about Ramón and look at what happened. Carlito knew something important. This time she would not be put off.

She radioed the officer outside Ana's apartment. "You can let them come down to the Alvarez apartment," she said. "I need to interview them now. Danforth has been informed." Her hand was shaking when she put back her radio.

"They're coming," Rosa told Maria after she hung up, "but something's wrong. Ana was different, almost unfriendly."

As soon as Ana and Carlito came into the apartment, Maria could see that Rosa was right. Ana's eyes, red from crying, were cold and defensive. "Just a few minutes," Ana said in an edgy voice to Maria. "Carlito is too upset. Ramón was his best friend."

Even after they sat down at the kitchen table, Carlito stood next to his mother, refusing to make eye contact with Maria. He was so pale, he looked like he was going to faint. What was wrong with him? Surely he trusted her. Ana was tense and still in her chair.

"Carlito, I'm sorry about your friend," Maria said trying to get his attention.

Carlito buried his head on his mother's shoulder, avoiding her eyes.

"I need to ask Carlito some questions," Maria insisted. Ana stared back at her, silent and distracted.

"Talk to the detective," Rosa whispered to Carlito. "She needs your help."

Carlito looked up at Maria. At last he met her eyes.

"Carlito, try to remember. What did you do when you first came out of the Lav?" Maria said to him in a gentle voice.

"I went to get ice cream for me and Ramón." Tears welled up in his eyes. "I didn't mean to leave him alone."

"That's OK, Carlito," Maria said, taking his hand. She could feel him trembling,

"Was Mr. Cortez in his chair when you first came out of the Lav?" Maria said.

Carlito nodded slightly, keeping his head on his mother's shoulder.

"You got two ice cream cones, right?"

Carlito nodded.

"But when you went back up to the Lav, you couldn't find Ramón?"

Carlito nodded again. "He probably got tired of waiting. I....I stayed in the picnic area for a while watching the kids in the water." Tears trickled down his face.

Maria squeezed his hand. "Did you see Ramón anywhere around the Lav?"

After a moment, the boy shook his head.

"Did you see Mr. Cortez?"

Again Carlito shook his head.

"Did you see anyone from the window inside the Lav?"

Carlito froze. A vacant look came into his eyes.

Maria was frustrated. There had to be some way to help Carlito feel safe enough to talk. What if he had seen something from the Lav? How could she protect him without knowing what he'd seen? What if someone had seen him?!

She glanced over at the postcards, still in a sprawling pile on the kitchen table. "Why don't you look at the cards with Ramón's magnifying glass," Maria suggested cautiously.

Carlito nodded.

"Here, take the glass," Maria said handing it to him. Carlito took the magnifying glass. After a few moments, he pulled an empty chair over next to his mother and sat down. Maria put a pile of postcards in front of him. "Go ahead, Carlito, you can look through the cards while I speak to your mother. We can talk later if you feel like it."

Carlito nodded, his attention already on the cards. Maria started talking to Ana, listening carefully to everything Ana said, but her eyes kept going back to Carlito. He seemed calmer now, but she was more convinced than ever that she had to find out what he knew. *Ese tiene la musica por dentro,* she thought to herself. This one has the music inside. He knows something.

"I want to speak to Carlito privately," she said to Ana. "Maybe that way he'll feel less afraid."

Ana gave Rosa a frightened look.

"What's wrong, Ana?" Maria said. "Tell me."

Ana sighed. "A short time ago a man telephoned. He said that if we help you, someone will turn us in to Immigration, *La Migra.*"

Maria had always imagined Ana might be without papers, but she hadn't thought much about it. Half the residents of Vereda were illegal. But now someone had threatened Ana specifically. No wonder she was so worried.

"Ana, we need your help in a homicide investigation. You and Carlito will be protected. I promise you," Maria said, trying to encourage her. "We need your help!"

"I'm frightened, Maria, I really am, but for Rosa's sake, I'll tell Carlito to talk with you," Ana said after a brief pause. She took Carlito aside and whispered something to him. Carlito turned to Maria. "I'll help you, Detective Maria," he said.

Maria took Carlito by the hand. "You can bring some postcards and the glass with you," she said. Looking relieved, Carlito grabbed a pile of cards off the table. Maria picked up the magnifying glass.

They walked together around the sheet that Rosa had used only a year ago to create a private space for Ramón's bedroom. Maria sat down on Ramón's bed, still holding Carlito's hand. He sat down next to her. The sheet hanging down in front of them kept them completely hidden from the rest of the room.

Rosa could hear Maria and Carlito talking in low voices. Then there was such a long silence, Rosa thought her ears would explode. What was Maria saying to Carlito with such a hurrying voice? And what was wrong with Carlito? He was shy, everyone knew that. But didn't he understand how important it was to tell Maria what he knew? Rosa wanted to grab him and scream in his ear, "Tell me, tell me, Carlito, what happened to my boy?!"

Clothespins suddenly went flying into the air. The sheet fell down, and postcards flew scattered across the floor. Carlito ran into the bathroom, slamming the door shut behind him. They could hear him throwing up. Shocked, Maria could only stare at the bathroom door.

Ana started to cry.

"Don't worry," Rosa said, trying to reassure her. "The sheet's easy enough to put back up."

Ana looked at Maria with frightened, questioning eyes.

Maria shook her head. "I don't know. He was just about to tell me what he saw from the Lav when he froze. The next thing I knew he had pulled down the sheet and was running for the bathroom."

"*Ay Dios mio*," Ana cried out. "What could have happened to him?"

There was a knock on the door. "I'll get it," Maria said. She snapped open her holster and let her hand rest on the Glock before she opened the door.

A huge figure with the solidity of a boulder filled the doorway, seemingly larger than the doorframe itself. Cali!

He barely acknowledged her before he pushed by her into the apartment and looked around.

"Cali, what are you doing here?" she asked him.

"Danforth called. Where's the boy?"

"In the bathroom."

Keeping his eyes fixed on the bathroom door, Cali began to pick up the postcards scattered across the floor.

"Cali, why are you here?" Maria asked again. She turned her cell phone back on. No messages.

Cali was slowly running his hand through his hair. When there was a difficult case, Cali would often do that, slowly running his hand over the scars on his scalp as if he were reading some kind of secret message in Braille. It was an odd mannerism, but as far as Maria knew, no one had ever asked Cali to explain what he was doing.

"What's going on?" Maria insisted.

Cali shook his head. The veins on his forehead were visibly throbbing.

Maria looked back at him, hurt and puzzled. All she wanted to do was find out what Carlito knew in order to protect him, and time was running out. What was wrong with Cali? Before she could ask him anything else, her cell phone began to ring. Rosa looked away while Maria was talking, trying not to listen, but the apartment was so small, you could hear everything.

"I'm not through here, Sarge," Maria was saying. "It's important." She listened for a few minutes. Then her face got hard. "You don't understand!" she said angrily, snapping her cell phone shut. She had turned pale, and her eyes looked dark and enormous against the pallor of her skin.

In the pause that followed, the bathroom door began to scratch against the floor. Everyone looked in the direction of the bathroom. The door opened, and Carlito flew out of the bathroom and into his mother's arms, his shoulders shaking with each long sob.

"He's had enough," Ana said in a shaky voice, wiping his face. "No more!"

"Yes, I know," Maria said, her face softening as she looked at Carlito and Ana. "I have to leave now, but I'll see you tomorrow, Carlito, OK?"

The boy looked up at her and gave her a small smile before leaving with his mother.

"I'll be right back," Cali said to Rosa. He touched Maria on the shoulder. "Maria, outside."

Maria went out into the hall with him. He gave her a strong look of reproach as he carefully closed the door to Rosa's apartment. "You disobeyed Dan's orders," he said in a low voice. "Dan is livid. He wants you to go home now. You should be grateful that's the extent of his response."

"But Cali, it was important...." she began.

"If the doctor gives his permission, you can talk to Carlito tomorrow," Cali interrupted her. His eyes were shuttered and angry. They closed her out. "You cannot talk to Carlito today, understood?"

Maria stared at him unbelievingly.

"You're not in charge," Cali said forcefully. "Dan is the head of our unit, remember? Take a break, Maria. I can take care of things from here on. Go home."

Without another word, he turned his back to her and went back into Rosa's apartment, leaving the apartment door open.

Maria stood in the hall watching Cali move around the apartment. It was as if she weren't even there. He hadn't given her a backward glance. He was already busy checking out Ramón's bedroom.

I don't understand it, Maria thought to herself. Danforth wants Cali to take over the case. Why? She could feel the hurt all the way down to her feet. And Cali! He was her best friend in the unit. And yet he had returned to Vereda without letting her know, and now he couldn't be bothered to say goodbye.

"Maria!" Rosa came running up to her. She looked tearful. "I didn't know you would have to leave so soon," she said, hurriedly wiping away the tears with her arm.

"Cali will be here," Maria told Rosa. "He'll ask you questions and search the apartment very carefully. And at least one officer will be posted outside Carlito's apartment all the time."

"Carlito's apartment?"

Maria tried to explain. "Just to be on the safe side. Because Carlito could have been the last person to see Ramón before he disappeared."

"Yes, I understand," Rosa said, interrupting her, disquiet written all over her face. "But Ana's apartment is on the third floor."

"What is it?" Maria said, looking at Rosa intently. "Are you afraid of something else, Rosa?"

Rosa was silent.

"Rosa, tell me. What is it? Do you think the same person who took Ramón is going to come after you?"

Rosa shook her head. "I don't know," she said embarrassed. "I have a feeling that some kind of danger is close."

"Tell me," Maria said again.

"It's not important."

"Yes, it is," Maria said. "If I can explain why you need help...."

Rosa didn't look convinced.

Maria found herself wanting to explain. It wasn't procedure, but Rosa had trusted her. She wanted to give something back.

"Part of the problem, Rosa, is that we only have so many officers we can assign to the case. To any case, not just this one. And my boss is probably thinking that if someone had wanted to hurt both you and Ramón, he wouldn't have waited. He would have moved in on you this morning, when you were alone, before all the attention that followed the discovery of ...." She couldn't say the words. She shouldn't have said anything.

Rosa looked at her helplessly.

"I could stop by after work," Maria said. "I could spend the night."

"No," Rosa said quickly. "No." That wouldn't be right. The danger she saw approaching was large and menacing. No, Rosa told herself, no, this was something she would have to face alone.

"No," Rosa said again. "My friend Ana wants me to stay with her tonight. I'll be fine."

Maria felt a surge of relief. It made no sense, but her instincts told her Rosa had good reason to be afraid. She would follow up with Rosa first thing tomorrow no matter what Danforth said.

"Cali will take care of things, Rosa. He's the best, you know that, right? If there is anything in this apartment that can explain what happened to Ramón, Cali will find it."

"Yes, I understand," Rosa said.

"You are willing to let him search the whole apartment?"

"I don't mind," Rosa said. "I want to help." Maybe the detective could find out why Ramón had been killed out at the park that afternoon. She knew she would never be able to make any sense of it.

Maria left the apartment, worried and apprehensive. She was concerned for Rosa. For Carlito too. The sooner they found out what Carlito knew, the safer he would be. She promised herself that somehow she would find a way to talk to Carlito tomorrow. No matter what the cost to her, she would not lose another boy.

35

FRIDAY NIGHT
Rosa's apartment

AFTER MARIA LEFT, Cali carefully searched Rosa's apartment. He asked her questions about everything. When it was late, he said he would come back the next morning. Rosa promised him she would go to her friend Ana's apartment. Cali stayed with her until she was inside Ana's apartment.

Ana insisted that Rosa spend the night there in her apartment, but Rosa refused. She could see that Ana had troubles of her own. And she didn't want anything to happen to Ana or Carlito. If someone was after her, and he didn't find her in her own apartment, he might look for her at Ana's. She wasn't convinced one policeman would be able to protect them. And anyway, what would be the point of spending one night away from home? If someone was after her, he would find her sooner or later.

But the real reason, she finally admitted to herself, was that she wanted to be home for Juan. What if he was in hiding somewhere and trying to get in touch with her? If she wasn't home, how would he be able to find her?

She explained all that to Ana. She would never be at peace, she told Ana, unless she was at home on Ramon's birthday. She had to know if there was any hope. She knew it wasn't likely, but just imagining the apartment empty while Juan was trying to find her made her feel faint. She saw the telephone in the kitchen ringing, Juan waiting for her to pick up. It would break his heart not to find her at home that night, the night when he had promised to call her if he could.

Ana understood. Rosa had no choice. She had to be home for Juan.

When the officer outside Ana's door came in to use the bathroom, Rosa quickly slipped away. Ana would say she was sleeping if he asked.

Now alone in her apartment, Rosa's sense of danger grew even stronger. She seemed to hear her grandfather's voice calling out to her, his words running through her head. "You can't choose your fate, Rosita. No one can. What's important is that when your time comes, you know how to face death with dignity."

Rosa locked the apartment door. Then she went back into the kitchen and took out the longest, sharpest knife she had in the house. It wasn't much, but it was all she had. What else could she do in this world?

She brought her cell phone over to the couch where she slept and propped the pillow up against the wall so that she could read. Then she got up again to take some blankets from the closet. Even though it was warm in the apartment, she found herself wanting to cover herself up under the blankets. They felt comforting and protective. She started reading, determined to stay awake all night. For a few hours she dozed on and off until unknowingly she fell into a deep sleep. Soon she was dreaming of herself as a little girl. She was waiting for her grandfather to tell her a story. He was looking at her, gesturing with his hands. Listen!

It was her favorite story about Sister Maria de Jesus, the beautiful young nun who wore a blue habit. Sister Maria lived in a convent far across the ocean in Spain, but the Indians in the American Southwest came to know her, as if she was living among them. They called her the Lady in Blue. When they were in trouble, the Lady in Blue would appear out of the air to comfort them. She was a vision of hope, especially to the desperate walkers struggling across the desert.

Her grandfather's voice faded away, and Rosa began to dream about the small farm house where she was born. Her mother was moving around inside the house, humming a song. She was outside playing with the white kitten. When she heard the faint click of a metal lock opening, she stopped playing with the kitten and looked up. A coyote was coming through the gate.

She grabbed the kitten and screamed for her grandfather, but her screams were soundless. They vanished into air. Terrified, unable to move, all she could do was watch as the coyote padded swiftly towards her, baring his sharp yellow teeth. When he was so close she could feel his breath on her cheek, he put his burning eyes on her, and she knew her death was near.

She heard her Grandfather's voice. At first she couldn't make out what he was saying, but his words grew larger and larger until the whole room was swirling in words. "Wake up! Wake up! Wake up!"

Rosa opened her eyes, staring into the darkness. Was she dreaming? No, she was sitting on her couch, and something in the apartment was moving. She reached for her knife just as a man rushed at her out of the darkness. Crying out for help, she struggled fiercely against the battering blows that fell on her from all directions, smashing bone, splattering blood across the sheets. The pain was blinding, unbearable.

Then the Lady in Blue appeared, floating down the air, long strands of roses trailing from her hands. Rosa felt the roses settle softly across her body, dissolving her pain, sending their sweet scent into the suffused blue light that filled the room. She saw Juan coming towards her, Ramón at his side, and with the lightness of a last breath, she rose to meet them.

36 | Angel's Office

ANGEL WAS SLEEPING WHEN the phone in his desk rang. He checked the illuminated dial of his watch. 3:00 a.m. He'd been expecting the call all night.

Gil had called him yesterday afternoon. "Snake Baby's going to search the Alvarez apartment sometime after midnight," Gil told him.

"Why?" Angel asked before he could stop himself. "What if she's in the apartment?"

"Don't ask questions, Angel!" Gil told him in a frigid voice. "Not your business."

After a long cold silence, Gil relented. "Snake Baby wants to check things out. He has his reasons. And the apartment will be empty. Rosa's spending the night with her friend Ana Fuentes. Besides, you're the last one to worry about anyone in the Alvarez family after what you did to the boy!"

At that moment, Angel hated Gil with a new passion. Snake Baby was always looking for an excuse to hurt someone. Angel wasn't like that. There was a big difference between him and Snake Baby.

After Gil's call, Angel tried to get some sleep. He kept reminding himself that the apartment would be empty. "Stop thinking about it," he told himself out loud every time he thought about Snake Baby in the apartment. But now the desk phone had rung, and it was 3:00 in the morning. Something was wrong.

Angel drove to the all-night gas station and punched in the direct call number.

"Snake Baby fucked up again," Gil said. "The apartment wasn't empty after all. Snake Baby lost it. Now the cops are after him. And we still haven't found any evidence."

Angel didn't say anything. He didn't want to know anything either.

"The projects are going to be crawling with cops tomorrow," Gil said. "It's not safe for Snake Baby. I'm sending him where he'll be safe. All that asshole has to do is lie low. You think he can manage that, Angel?"

"Lie low?"

"The doors and windows of the safe house will be locked, the cops can't go in without a warrant, and if they try to get one, I'll know ahead of time. Felix will be waiting in his car nearby just in case Snake Baby suddenly needs a ride. So what can go wrong? All Snake Baby has to do is lie low. You know what that means Angel? All he has to do is stay out of sight, keep his fucking mouth shut, do you hear me, Angel!?"

"Right, keep his mouth shut," Angel said slowly. "But Snake Baby...."

"Shut up," Gil screamed over the phone. "Shut up. If Snake Baby doesn't keep his mouth shut, I'll fucking kill him, you hear me?"

Angel took a deep mouthful of air.

"Listen Angel," Gil went on in a calmer voice. "I called to warn you. There's no school tomorrow so the trailers will be empty. You won't have a lot of customers. Everyone is going to lie low until we see what happens. You too. Just like Snake Baby, OK? You need to lie low. Stay in your office. Don't go out, don't do nothing. But be prepared for a visit from the cops."

"What?!!" Angel said, bewildered.

"You're not involved, Angel. I didn't mean that. I'm just trying to give you a head's up. You know what that means? It means be careful, be prepared. The cops might come by just to bother you, but just ignore them. They've got nothing."

Angel nodded.

"I can't call you tomorrow, Angel, so you gotta get comfortable being by yourself, OK?"

Angel nodded again.

"OK, then. I'll be in touch." The phone went dead.

Angel could hear what Gil was thinking even after he hung up the phone. "Time to clean up shop," that's what. Snake Baby was in real trouble this time. If the cops found him, Gil would have him killed in prison. And then? That's what worried Angel. Maybe Gil would decide to get rid of him too.

Angel drove back to the Repository and went up to his office. He stretched out on the couch and closed down his thoughts. All he could do was lie low, just like Gil said. The rest was up to Gil.

37 | EARLY SATURDAY MORNING
N. Building
Ana's Apartment

ANA WAS STILL IN BED WHEN SHE HEARD someone knocking. She grabbed her robe and rushed over to open the door. The officer who had been posted outside her apartment during the night was standing there next to Luis who was jangling his keys harder than ever.

"I said, keep it down," the officer told Luis, clearly irritated by the constant jangling. Luis stopped jangling his keys.

"This guy's the super, right?" the officer asked Ana.

She nodded.

"He says you told him your sink is clogged up and you've been after him to fix it. He says this is the only time he can do it."

One look at Luis was enough for Ana. He was crumpled, as if something heavy had rolled over him. There were dark pouches under his eyes, and his face was covered with sweat.

"Yes, it's OK, officer. He can come in," Ana said.

"Call me if you need me," the officer told Ana. He looked Luis over carefully another time before letting him go inside.

As soon as the door was closed, Luis pulled Ana into the back corner of the kitchen, as far away as possible from the front door of the apartment.

"Sit down, Ana," Luis said in a shaking voice. He pushed her down into one of the kitchen chairs and turned on the faucet in the sink. Then he came back to where she was sitting and bent down beside her. "Rosa's dead," he whispered into her ear. "Someone smashed in her head and trashed the apartment."

Ana doubled over in pain. "It can't be, oh dear God, not Rosa!" she said in a trembling voice. "Rosa!" A wave of sorrow ripped through her body. What could have happened?

She stared at Luis. She had never seen Luis cry. Probably he had never cried in his whole life. He wasn't crying now either, but she could tell from the way his face had settled into a mask that he was close to falling apart.

She was still trying to make sense of his words. "How do you know?"

"I couldn't sleep. I had a bad feeling, like something was wrong. I got up early and went to check on Rosa. When I knocked on her door, it swung open. You couldn't tell it from the hall if you were just passing by, but the door had been jimmied.

"I looked inside. Rosa sleeps on the couch near the door so I could see her right away, even

151

without going inside. Blood everywhere." Luis shuddered. "She was gone. Looked like she'd been dead for a while. I ran up here to tell you. I thought you should know. Carlito could be in danger. He could be next. So could you. But I don't have much time. I've got to go back. Fast. I have to find the body all over again and call the cops. So you got to decide now. What do you want to do? Do you trust the cops?"

Ana tried to think. Luis went over to the sink and stood there as if he was trying to unclog the drain. He heard something moving in the kitchen. "Ana!" he said in a sharp whisper. "Look!"

Carlito had come up behind them. He was standing there in his underwear, staring at them, and in spite of the heat, he was shivering.

"Oh God," Ana said helplessly. "What did he hear?"

"Ana, I got to go," Luis said again. He looked frightened.

Ana didn't know where to turn. She didn't know what to do. Luis had risked everything for her. But Carlito had collapsed onto his knees and wrapped himself around her legs, as if the very ground under his feet was about to give way. *"Mamí, Mamí, tengo que decirte algo,* I have to tell you something right now," Carlito sobbed.

"Luis, can you wait another minute?" Ana pleaded. Carlito was desperate. She could hear it in his voice. "Maybe he knows something about Rosa."

Nervously, Luis jangled his keys. "One more minute, Ana. Then I'm out of here, no matter what."

Rosa held Carlito close to her. "Tell me, what is it, *niño?"*

Carlito threw his arms around her neck, pulling her head down close to his until he could whisper into her ear. When he finished talking, Ana searched his face intently. What she saw in his eyes made her legs feel like rubber.

She grabbed Luis by the hand. "Luis, listen to me." When she told him what Carlito had said, Luis turned pale. Even his keys were silent. Ana told him what she was going to do. Luis nodded. "I'll take care of Carlito," she said firmly. "Go now, Luis," she said. "May God bless you. May God protect all of us."

Luis took off without another word.

Ana helped Carlito get dressed. Then she sat down with him at the table and began talking. "Carlito, listen carefully," she said in a low voice. "In a little while Luis is going to come back. We are going to follow him down to Rosa's apartment. When no one is looking, we'll leave by the side entrance. Once we're outside, I want you to run to the 'safe place' and wait for me there."

Carlito looked at her terrified. "No, *Mamí,* no. Not without you."

She took him by the shoulders and spoke to him sternly. "Yes, Carlito, you have to go without me. Try not to let anyone see you. Go as fast as you can."

Carlito started to cry again, even harder than before.

"Listen to me, Carlito," Ana said in tears herself by now. "You have to do what I tell you. Understand? For both of us."

He managed to nod.

"Make sure no one sees you," she told him again. "Go to the safe place in the storage building. You know what I mean?"

He nodded.

"Stay there until I come for you. Understand?"

"Si, Mamí, I understand," he said, still sobbing. He took her hand. She squeezed it tightly. "Stop

crying," she told him. "You have to be a man now."

She could hear Luis talking loudly to the officer in the hall. "Are you ready?" she said to Carlito. He nodded.

Ana opened the door. "What's the matter?" she said. "What happened?"

"It's Rosa," Luis told her. "I think she's dead."

Ana screamed. She started running down the hall, pulling Carlito along behind her. "I want to see her," she said. The cop was on the radio. Before he could stop her, Ana was running down the stairs with Carlito, heading for Rosa's apartment.

When they got there, Ana looked inside. "No," she told Carlito, pushing him away. "Don't look." She stood there, just outside Rosa's door, unable to move, her hand over her mouth, trying not to wail.

The cop came running up to her. "It's not safe here," the cop told her. "Go back upstairs. Lock your door. Stay there!"

"You stay here with me," he said to Luis. "I can't leave until the apartment is secured, understand? No one goes into this apartment, and I mean no one." He looked over at Ana, still frozen in place. "Get going, Ana. Your son may be in danger. Go! Now!"

Ana nodded and pulled Carlito by the hand towards the stairs. They ran up to the third floor, took the side stairway, and ran back down to the side entrance on the first floor. In minutes they were outside the building.

She bent down and kissed Carlito. She gave him a little push. "Run Carlito, run!"

Carlito could not make his feet move.

"Go on, Carlito," Ana said again. "You have to be brave for both of us. Now!"

Carlito took off like a rocket, weaving in and out of the bushes along the side of N. Building. He raced into the parking lot, pausing only to hide behind a car while two women walked through the lot towards the street.

There was the storage building, just ahead of him. His hands were shaking as he pulled away the chicken wire from the opening into the "safe place." He crawled inside and pulled the chicken wire back over the opening. Then he curled up on his side and closed his eyes. The minutes stretched out in front of him. When would she come?

Loud voices in the room woke him up. Terrified, he covered his ears. After a while the voices went away. He waited. He had to stay in the safe place until his *Mami* came to get him. He fell asleep again.

There was a noise near the opening. Someone was pulling away the chicken wire. Carlito sat up, too dazed to do anything but stare. A pair of black eyes looked straight back at him. His ears began to buzz. Then everything around him stopped moving.

38 | EARLY SATURDAY MORNING
Sandy Hills

WHEN SHE SAW CALI'S NUMBER on her cell phone, Maria took a deep breath. The way he'd treated her yesterday afternoon in Rosa's apartment still smarted. She didn't know what to expect. An explanation? Maybe. But not to hear him say that Rosa had been murdered. She never expected that.

She found herself sitting on the floor holding the phone like a foreign object.

"The door was jimmied," Cali was saying, "the apartment ransacked. They found Rosa's body on the couch where she sleeps."

"How?" She had to ask the question.

"Forensics hasn't...."

"Cali!"

"Looks like someone used a lead pipe. Mostly around the head. It would have been fast."

She heard herself talking in a thin voice. "Do we know who it was?"

"Not many details yet, but it doesn't look random. I'll be waiting for you at the station." Cali paused. "We'll get the bastard, you know that, right?"

"Right," she managed to say before she closed the phone.

Cali's words had been reassuring, reminding her that there were procedures in place. Her thoughts shut down. She stood up and walked down the hall into her bedroom. She got dressed and headed for the station. Only when she took the exit for downtown, did she became aware of her fingers, clamped cold and stiff around the steering wheel, the coils of tension winding around her neck.

She waited indifferently in front of the stoplight. No matter what time of day it was, the light was always red for her. She looked around. A drab procession of apartment buildings, bars, check-cashing stores, gas stations, and convenience stores lined the street in both directions.

She thought about the dog she'd reported to Animal Control. Someone had left a message on her desk yesterday. The dog was still available if she was interested. She was glad the dog was at the shelter. He would have food, water and a place to sleep. Beyond that she didn't care.

The sidewalks at the intersection were mostly empty except for a small group of people waiting at the bus stop to her right. One of them was a young woman in a white uniform, her black hair pulled back into a long thick braid.

Rosa Alvarez had worn her hair like that, a long thick braid down her back. Maria could still see her sitting at her kitchen table, dazed and weeping. Now Rosa was gone, beaten to death in her bed only hours after they'd spoken together.

Maria looked away. A new investigation had come to life. It would need her full attention. Anything else would have to wait.

She took a sharp turn into the parking lot behind the district station and parked the Jeep. As soon as she went around the corner and headed for the front entrance of the district station, she could hear the noise of the crowd. Keeping her head down, she pushed past the people blocking the sidewalk. How had so many people gathered there before eight in the morning? It seemed as if the entire *barrio* of Vereda already knew about Rosa.

One of the reporters in the crowd saw her and called out her name. Another woman with long blond hair and a low-cut blouse came rushing up to her and pushed a TV camera in her face.

Maria pushed past the camera and walked quickly into the station without turning around. She headed directly for the second floor. The sounds from the street were muted by the station walls into distant, blurred waves of static, but the angry voice of a woman speaking in Spanish over a bullhorn relentlessly followed her up every step.

"When will it end?" the angry voice on the bullhorn kept asking in the background. "*Hasta cuando durarà esta condena*? When will it end?" The crowd joined in, yelling along with her, "When will it end? When will it end? *Hasta cuando durarà esta condena*?"

By the time Maria reached the second floor, her shirt was damp with perspiration and sticking to her back. She went into the Squad Room and slammed the door closed. Immediately the woman's voice and the raucous chant of the crowd faded into barely perceptible ripples of sound, drowned out by the voices inside the room and the loud rumble of the air conditioners at the windows. The breezy noise from the windows blowing through the Squad Room day and night gave the impression of activity in the room even when things were slow, but this morning the crowded room was steamy with tension, like the inside of a pressure cooker about to explode.

Cali met her near the door. He pulled her off to the side. The expression on his face was grim. "How are you doing?" he said, for once not bothering to hide his concern.

She was silent, but her unspoken accusation was clearly visible in her eyes.

"I know you're upset about Rosa," Cali said, holding her gaze unapologetically. "We all are. But sometimes things get complicated in ways you don't expect." He hesitated. She could see he was struggling to find the right words.

"Rosa and Ramón" he said finally. "You worked hard for them, Maria. You did good work. It's a tough one, no doubt about it." He looked at her closely. "But what happened to them? It's got nothing to do with you. You got that? Nothing!"

Maria stared back at him. He was waiting for some kind of affirmation, but it wasn't in her to give. What happened to Rosa and Ramón had everything to do with her. She should have stopped to talk to Rosa on her way home, she should have spent the night with Rosa, she should have, she should have....The list was endless.

Joe came through the door and came over to where they were standing. "Cali, you need to start the briefing. Danforth will be here in a minute," he said. He sounded as if he had just run all the way up the stairs. He turned to Maria. "Come on, Maria, you and I are leaving."

"What are you talking about?" Her voice was shaking with anger. She looked at Cali. "What the hell are you talking about?"

Cali ran his hand through his hair, and she thought she saw something like an apology flash across his face. Then his eyes closed down, leaving two shuttered black holes. "Catch you later," he said briskly. "I got to go. Joe will explain." He left without another word and walked over to Danforth. Maria stared after him.

"Come on," Joe said again, taking her arm and moving with her towards the back of the Squad Room. "Let's use the back exit," he said. "Too many people out front."

"Let go of me!" she said angrily, pulling away from him.

"I'll explain in the car," Joe said without slowing down. "It's important, Maria. Trust me."

"Fine. I'll come with you. You don't need to hold my arm!"

"Fine. Let's take your car. You drive. I'll talk."

She looked at him coldly. "Where are we going?"

"To the Bosque trailhead."

They drove in silence until they got onto the highway. Joe reached into the black folder he had put on the floor beside him and pulled out some files. He started going through them. Finally he looked over at her. "Where do you want me to start?"

She wanted to know why Danforth was keeping her at arm's length and why Cali had treated her the way he did in Rosa's apartment. But first the case. She pushed away the feeling of betrayal burning in her chest and focused her attention on Rosa. "What happened to Rosa?"

"It's just guesswork at this point," Joe began.

"I know that," Maria said impatiently. "What does it look like?"

"Someone broke into Rosa's apartment. The way the apartment was torn apart suggests that the intruder was looking for something. Rosa was probably killed first." Joe hesitated.

"Go on," Maria said in a grim voice.

"Given the way Rosa was killed, or maybe I should say 'overkilled,' our best guess is that the intruder was Snake Baby, probably looking for Juan's evidence."

Maria took a deep breath. "Snake Baby went into the apartment to look for evidence, Rosa woke up, and he killed her? He beat her to death?" Just saying the words sent a shiver down Maria's back.

"We don't know," Joe said. "But it sure looks like Snake Baby's work. Every available officer in the area is out looking for that son of a bitch. This time he won't get away."

Maria nodded. "Rosa's murder, like Ramón's, must be linked to Gil's search for an evidence package, something Juan might have left with her or Ramón. Joe, you looked at the postcards. Was there anything in them that could have incriminated Gil?"

"I've looked at the photographs of those damn cards more than once," Joe said.

"And?"

"Nothing. As I said before, Gil was visible in the background of some of the photographs of Juan with his plane, but so what? We already know Gil runs the airport, owns the planes, etc."

"But it must have been Gil who sent Snake Baby to Rosa's apartment, right?"

Joe nodded. "Snake Baby would never have done this on his own, I'm sure of it."

"What have we missed? We checked out the school. Cali searched Rosa's apartment, and no one is better than he is!"

Joe shrugged, but the tautness of his face was in sharp contrast to the movement of his shoulders.

"What was Rosa doing in her apartment?" Maria said after a minute.

"She convinced Ana to help her. Told Ana she needed to be home for Juan in case he tried to get in touch with her. Because it was Ramón's birthday."

THE LADY IN BLUE

Oh, Rosa! What have you done? Maria thought to herself sadly. Joe nodded, as if he knew what she was thinking. "I know," he said. "This one really hurts."

Maria took Exit 6 off the highway for the Olde Road. At the end of the exit ramp, she turned left, pulled over to the side of the road, and turned off the engine.

"This is the closest highway exit for Riverside Park," she said to Joe.

Joe nodded.

"Why pick Ramón up from one place and then drop his body off a few miles away along the same road? They must have expected to find Ramón alive when they first picked him up, right?"

"That's the only way it makes any sense, especially if Ramón was to be used for barter in some way."

"OK, so let's say that instead of finding Ramón alive as they expected, they find a dead boy. Why not drop him off far away from here? It could have been days before we found him."

"I don't know. But we know that the place where they picked up Ramón was a few miles away from the closest exit onto the highway. One of Gil's lookouts probably saw a cruiser coming in their direction. Maybe Gil's boys thought the cops already knew that Ramón had been left along the Olde Road or that the cops were coming after them for some other reason. In any case, once they saw that Ramón was dead, they must have decided it was safer to get rid of Ramón right away rather than risk having their car searched somewhere along the exit ramp or the highway. If they were far enough ahead of the cruisers, they could have dumped the body and been back on the highway before anyone saw them."

"That's hard to believe," Maria said.

"Someone sure got lucky if that's the way it went down, "Joe said.

"But what else could have happened?"

Joe shrugged again. "I can't think of anything else," he said. "A stranger would have picked up Ramón and kept on going. Only an idiot like Angel would have thought of dumping the boy along the Olde Road and then scurrying back to his van, leaving it to Gil to pick up the boy without anyone noticing. Angel is stupid enough to accidentally overdose the boy. But Gil probably never imagined that the boy would be dead. What I can't believe is that when Gil's boys discovered that Ramón was dead, they somehow found a way to pick up the body in enough time to get rid of it and get back onto the highway without being seen."

Neither of them spoke for a while. "Where do you want to go now, Joe?" Maria said finally.

At first he didn't seem to hear her. Then he opened his hands in resignation. "To the trailhead," he said finally. "To the trailhead where they dumped Ramón's body."

Maria sat back in her seat.

"What's up?" Joe said.

"Before we go, I want more answers."

"Fire away," he said, turning to face her.

"Why did Danforth send us out here?"

"He wants us to take the lead on the Ramón Alvarez investigation. It's a messy one. Lots of press, lots of questions, and no answers that make sense. For example, what's the likelihood the boy was taken at random?"

"None," she said right away. "Even if there was a stranger in the woods at the exact moment and in the exact place Ramón disappeared, he had to have help disposing of the body, right? That takes planning as well as incredible luck."

"Then you think the murder was planned?"

"Impossible," she said again. "No way Gil would have used Angel to do the job. And how could Angel have known when Ramón would be alone? How could Gil have planned to pick Ramón up from the side of the road without being observed? He managed to get rid of the body by sheer luck, but you can't plan luck."

"I agree. So?"

"Ramón's death must have been an accident," she said after a long pause, "Angel decided to take Ramón if an opportunity presented itself. Then he told Gil, dropped off the body, and ran back to his van."

"My thoughts exactly. Gil's men pick up the boy, discover he's dead, and somehow manage to dump him out at the trailhead and get back onto the highway without being seen."

"If Gil had known the boy was dead, I think he would have sacrificed Angel rather than risk his men getting caught with a body in the trunk. Especially if the body was the son of his missing pilot. He could have silenced Angel before too much damage was done."

"Agreed," Joe said. "Let's say Gil doesn't know anything about Angel's plans until after Angel takes the boy. Angel tells him the boy is OK. Gil decides to help Angel out. Probably because of the big shipment coming into the Repository tomorrow night. He needs Angel.

"But to make things even worse, so far we haven't found a shred of evidence that ties Angel to Ramón's disappearance," he added after a moment. "Even his damn shoes and pants were dry. Angel must have done some heavy planning."

"He must have thought Gil wanted to use the boy as barter," Maria said. "The boy for the package, but who knows what Gil really wanted?"

They sat silently in the car. "What a waste," she said, turning her face away from Joe and looking out the window. "What a waste. Ramón was so hopeful. How could this happen to him?"

"All we can do is find something that proves Angel was lying when he said he took the pedestrian bridge back into the parking lot. Or else some sign in the woods or near the river that indicates Angel was there when he shouldn't have been. I plan to keep looking."

"I know," she said. "I know you're a sign cutter, a well-known one too. That's good." She leaned forward and looked at him intently. "But there's something else weighing on me, Joe. And I need some straight answers."

"I'll do my best."

"Carlito knows something important." She kept her eyes fixed on Joe's face as she spoke. "Why is Danforth keeping me away from him? I wanted to talk to Carlito yesterday. Instead he sent Cali out to take my place. I wanted to talk to Carlito today. Instead I'm out here with you. Carlito's life could be in danger? Why can't I talk to him?!"

"I know you have strong feelings about what's happened," Joe said. His expression remained carefully neutral, but his eyes were sympathetic. "But you need to cut Danforth some slack. The top brass, the Latino community, the board of Riverside Park, you name it, he's been meeting with it.

"The press is all over us, and who can blame them? The murders have people scared. People want answers. They're frightened. The press is pushing the idea that Ramón was taken by a stranger. That helps. So far everyone's been cooperating. But a lot of the kids who go to the trailers are illegal. Their families move around a lot. After the raid on the Repository tomorrow, if people think the cartel is involved, they'll walk away. Get out of town. Especially since school will be over for the year. Danforth has a lot of tough decisions to make. The pressure to solve Ramón's murder quickly doesn't help."

"What about Carlito?" she insisted.

"You know how good Cali is. You don't think he can talk to Carlito as well as you can?"

Maria didn't bother to reply. Why had she believed him? She started the car and headed for the trailhead.

"Cali knows his job," Joe said after a few moments. "There's nothing to indicate you could have prevented what happened to Rosa. I know how you feel though," he added. "I lost my informant. Sometimes it's hard not to second-guess yourself."

"What's happening with Ana and Carlito?" she asked.

"They're fine. Cali is checking up on them."

"Did Ana see Rosa's body?"

"She followed Luis and the officer down to the apartment. Why?"

"If Rosa was beaten to death, there must have been blood all over the walls, the sheets. I hope Carlito wasn't with her."

"I don't know," Joe said. "All I know is that according to the officer on the scene, Ana ran screaming out of Rosa's apartment as soon as she saw the body, and that neither Luis nor Ana touched anything in the apartment. But like I said, Cali is checking up on them." He paused. "Does it surprise you that Ana didn't stay around to talk to the detectives at the scene?"

Maria thought for a minute. "No, I don't think so. She's illegal."

Joe nodded.

They drove the rest of the way to the trailhead in silence. The road went uphill in a series of curves until they came to the drop-off area on their right. They could see the trailhead on the ridge just ahead of them. Maria pulled off the road and parked.

"Today the Olde Road is used mostly to access Riverside Park and the hiking trails," she said. "So since Ramon's body was found over there by the trailhead," she pointed to her right, where the road inclined slightly and then descended out of sight, "whoever dumped his body didn't have to worry much about other cars being in the vicinity."

"Let's go," Joe said unbuckling his seatbelt.

"Wait a minute," she said quickly. She looked at him, weighing her words carefully. "I'd like to take another look at the place where Ramon's body was found. She hesitated. "By myself. It won't take long. Can you start looking for sign here near the road?"

"No problem," he said, handing her the top file. "Take your time."

She took the photographs from the file and got out of the car. Her path took her through yellow and brown grasses up to the top of the hill. From there she could see the river. The early morning light, silvering the Blue Sierras in the distance, shadowed the thin line of cottonwoods along the river's edge. A short distance away from where she was standing, the hiking trail began its descent towards the river.

Maria looked at the photographs in her hand, then back at the trailhead. Yes, that was it, the place where Ramon's body had been found. The first photograph, taken from where she was standing, showed two small feet sticking out of the bushes.

Suddenly Maria felt dizzy with the effort not to remember. Not the newspaper articles. Not that day in Sandy Hills when she was seven. Not the way her adoptive mother had cried the whole time she was talking. She had listened dry-eyed to the story of her family, how they had died out in the desert, how she was the only one to be saved.

When she was older, she'd read everything she could find about what happened in the desert, but she had remained strangely unsatisfied. For her, reading all those articles was like reading a story, a fiction. Maria, the girl miraculously rescued from death in the desert, was like a character someone else had invented. She couldn't feel any connection.

She studied the other photograph. This one showed a child in a red and white striped shirt and dark blue pants lying on his back. A beautiful child, but what struck her was how peaceful he looked. Her work forced her to look closely at people who had died violently. The victim's pain and desperation were often as physically present as the blood and the bruises. She rarely saw anything like the serenity on Ramon's face.

Was it the killer who had thrown the boy's body into the bushes? Whenever she thought about it, someone dumping Ramón's body out of the car like so much trash, she felt a familiar fist of anger thumping in her chest.

She walked back to the car, going over the report again in her mind. They hadn't found any useful evidence at the trailhead. No discernible footprints. There were a few marks in the dust of the turnoff indicating that a vehicle had been there recently, but no identifiable tread marks or lines.

Not much useful evidence anywhere else either. The puncture wound on Ramón's arm and the traces of powerful sedatives in his blood told them how he had died. Someone had injected him with a syringe full of sedative. But there was nothing to indicate whether the overdose was accidental or deliberate.

Ramón would have lost consciousness immediately after being injected, but before that? There were no indications of a struggle. The boy's chest wasn't compressed, there were no signs of strangulation. And nothing to identify the killer. Ramón hadn't been molested. There was no semen. No skin under the fingernails. There were a few trace woolen fibers on the boy's clothing, but that was it. Even asking the public for information hadn't produced results. So far, no one had reported seeing anything unusual along this stretch of road.

She watched Joe walking slowly through the tall grasses near the trailhead. Once he bent down and picked up a cigarette butt in the palm of his hand, ripped a piece of paper out of a small notepad, and carefully folded up the cigarette butt inside the paper before putting it into his pocket.

"Find anything?" she asked him when he got back to the car.

He shook his head. "Just a cigarette butt," he said. "I'm through here." He studied her face. "You feeling OK?"

"I'm fine," she said. But she wasn't. A little boy on his first school trip to the park had been murdered and his body dumped under the bushes at a trailhead. And it didn't look like they would be able to put the killer in jail anytime soon.

"You really OK?" Joe asked again.

She nodded and gunned the car back out onto the Olde Road, leaving clouds of dust and the sound of screeching tires behind them. She was anxious to get to the park. That's where Ramon had been abducted. By the time his body had been tossed under the bushes on the Olde Road, his life was over. If she was going to bring his killer to justice, she needed to leave the Olde Road behind and move on.

39 | SATURDAY MORNING
Vereda

AL WAS DRIVING FAST, swerving in and out of traffic, but his thoughts were racing far ahead of him. Time was short.

He could hear police helicopters clattering overhead as he drove past the Hidalgo Housing Projects where Rosa Alvarez had been murdered. The noise of the helicopters brought him back to Lastup, the border town where he'd grown up.

Al and his friends had spent hours after school watching the helicopters fly over Lastup, swooping down to the ground, taking off again straight up into the air. Al liked the helicopters best, but he thought everything in the show along the border was spectacular.

As soon as he got home from school, he would grab something to eat and rush out of the house to join his friend, Gil, and the others. They stayed out for hours, sometimes not returning home until early morning. Their favorite viewing place was the roof of the pump house on Gil's property. They would jump onto the roof from the low-hanging branches of the tree next to the pump house.

From there they could see everything, the bright lights, the dark figures running through the desert, the cars in close pursuit, the helicopters overhead.

Sometimes just for fun, they would throw rocks at the illegals as they ran by the pump house. Sometimes they threw rocks at the Border Patrol Agents who were chasing the illegals. But Al and his friends never got caught. They knew how to get into the tunnel under the pump house. If anyone started after them, they would jump off the roof and run inside the pump house. Hidden under a floorboard was the entrance into a smuggling tunnel. They would drop into the tunnel and then follow it to a storm drain that opened into one of the fields owned by Gil's family.

The boys would carefully climb out of the storm drain and slowly merge into the grove of pecan trees planted in the field. Sometimes they would stay there in the shadows, watching the illegals try to slip over the border into the field.

Other times they would make their way into Lastup, less than a mile away. There were always people there in the center of town. Especially at night, Plaza Santa Teresa was full of people, walking, running, making love. Al still remembered those days as the best of his life.

On his fourteenth birthday, Al had gone into town with Gil and his other friends to see a new movie called *Safari*. The hunters in the movie drove fast cars and carried powerful rifles. They hunted animals that were brave and ferocious and sometimes faster than the wind, but in the end, the hunters always brought them down. During the movie, Al watched the hunters intently, cheering out loud every time they killed an animal, especially the lions. At first, he didn't even notice that Gil was talking to him.

"Clavito, Clavito," Gil kept saying in a low voice as he poked his arm. "I have something to tell you, Clavito." Gil had given Al the nickname, *Clavito,* Little Nail, and the name had stuck.

Finally Al had leaned over to listen to Gil, too distracted by the action of the hunt on the screen to notice the cruel set of Gil's mouth, the flash of maliciousness in his eyes.

As soon as he was sure Al was listening, Gil told him in a loud voice, "Clavito, Clavito, you're cheering for the wrong side."

Al had stared at him, bewildered. "*Que*? What are you talking about?"

"Clavito, don't you know you'll never be a hunter?" Gil said. By now other people in the theater were looking at them. Satisfied to have found an audience, Gil started to taunt him in earnest. "Clavito you'll never be a hunter! You're prey, Clavito, don't you know that yet?"

"Shut up!" Al yelled back at Gil, pushing his arm away. He turned back to the hunt on the screen and kept cheering on the hunters, but the excitement he'd felt earlier was gone. In its place, a vague uneasiness.

Over the next few weeks, the thrill of watching the action along the border began to fade as Clavito saw the border crossings with new eyes. The helicopters moving through the air, their blinding lights sweeping across the landscape, the uniformed men with their guns giving chase in their powerful vehicles, that part of the story was still the same. And it was still exciting. But now Clavito understood for the first time that along the border, the prey was human.

From then on, he followed Gil in everything. At least if he stayed with Gil, he would never be one of the hunted. He would never be prey. But Gil's protection came with a price, and by the time Clavito understood what it would cost him, it was too late.

With Gil, there could be no questions, no hesitation, only complete obedience. Gil had an answer for everything. If there was a bad situation, Gil never took the blame. Someone else had to take the rap. Usually it was Clavito.

"You were born to be a nail," Gil would tell him at those times. "*Naciste para ser clavo, acostúmbrate a los martillo.* Get used to being hammered, Clavito. Get used to being hammered, Little Nail."

And he had until that night in the desert. Al still had dreams about it, the cold sliding down his back, the ragged sky frozen into place. The screaming had set his head to pounding so hard, he'd felt something break inside. He'd understood immediately. Something that broken could never be fixed. Those bruised and bleeding lives left behind in the desert weren't the only ones to lose their souls that night. From now on, his was lost as well.

After that, he'd refused to work with Gil. He'd known it was only a question of time before Gil would mark him. Gil could not tolerate disobedience. But Al would not go back to him.

A week passed before Gil made his move. Al was walking home late in the afternoon when he saw Gil drive by slowly in his new red Camaro. Al had looked up and down the street leading to the trailer park where he lived, but there was no one in sight. He thought about running away. But where could he go? Who would help him?

Gil turned around and drove by him again. Then he pulled up to the curb and waited for him.

"Come here, Clavito," Gil called out. "I've been looking for you. Come see my new car." Two of Gil's friends were sitting in the back seat, grinning at him.

Al knew what was coming, but what could he do? Sooner or later, he would have to take his punishment. In a daze he forced his legs to walk over to the car. "Closer, Clavito, closer," Gil sneered at him as he came up to the car. "So you can see better."

Suddenly he felt Gil's hands around his neck, pulling him through the window. Before he could jerk free, Gil closed the window and stomped down on the gas. Al only managed to free one of his hands before Gil drove away, dragging him along on the ground. By the time Al could pull his other hand out, he'd lost two fingers.

Gil backed his car up to the place where Al was lying on the ground, holding his bleeding hand, screaming out in pain. Gil rolled down the window. "You are mine, Clavito," he said, drilling Al with his eyes. "My mark is on you...."

From then on Al found himself alone most of the time. After graduating high school, he decided to join the local police department. It was the only way he could figure out to get away from Lastup. He had a clean record, and he was smart. The local sergeant, an old guy who had seen everything, decided to give him a chance.

Al lost time at first. He had to learn how to keep his mouth shut, how to let the wetback jokes roll off his back. But once he understood the system, he was on his way.

He studied the people around him, the subtle operations of power, biding his time. If he didn't look right for a cop, he'd cultivate his own look, his own expertise. If working in narcotics would put him on the fast track, he'd do narcotics better than anyone else.

He quickly learned how to work undercover. Soon he got a reputation as an expert. No one could do undercover like he could. He didn't just work the street, he became the street. It got inside of him.

Three years later, he helped the feds bring down a major cartel. He moved to Ciudad Nueva and joined the CNPD. Things moved fast after that.

And all the time, he was learning, how to manipulate, how to betray, how to protect himself. Never let a camera in close. Never testify in open court. Never trust anyone, not even your friends, not even your wife. There was no time anyway. Shift work meant days would go by when they didn't see each other. He didn't think marriage could work for an undercover cop. He'd tried twice and failed. That was enough.

A lot of the cops he worked with developed a tough skin, but he'd gone one step further, developing a strategic and resilient indifference. If the guys in the unit teased him about the way he'd strip before going into his house, leaving all his clothes outside in the garage, it didn't bother him. He wouldn't have roaches or vermin in his house. His house was clean. He did his job and he did it well. Other people could do what they wanted. He didn't have to explain anything.

He'd busted his ass to get out of that crappy little town of Lastup, and he'd succeeded. By now he was used to his life. He liked wearing a three-piece suit. He liked it when important people asked for his help. And most of the time, he didn't have to answer to anyone but himself.

When he first joined the police department, he wondered how long it would be before Gil confronted him. What would be the price for Gil's silence? Gil would always have the upper hand, but what choice did he have? He would not spend his whole life being hammered, a poor man doing a poor man's work in a crappy little town. Being a cop was his only way out.

Gil kept his silence, and most of the time, he kept his distance as well. He called on Al whenever he needed a special favor. For the rest, Ál was free to do as he pleased.

The AC in the car was blasting, but Al could feel the sweat in his armpits, running down his back. He took out a cigarette and lit it, inhaling deeply, studying Gil's mark on his hand. In a fury, he smashed his hand against the steering wheel. His whole life was forfeited for that one moment of trying to do the right thing that night in the desert. Ever since, he'd had to struggle to keep his footing.

Now his future was compromised. Now he was the one being handled, being used by that *hijo de la chingada*, Gil Gomez-Gil. And if he didn't move fast to take charge of the situation, he'd go down and everything would be lost, just like that.

40

SATURDAY
Riverside Park

THE SIGNS POSTED ON THE ENTRANCE GATE into the parking lot read *Park Hours: Daily from 8:00 A.M. to Sunset*. The parking lot was completely empty.

"I guess you don't see the parking lot like this very often," Joe said to Maria.

"Never have," she said. "It's too soon. People are still afraid."

They left the parking lot and walked over to the island, their footsteps on the bridge like sad echoes of their visit to the park only a few days ago.

Once inside the park, they followed the river to the picnic area. A line of stunted willow trees leaning in all directions cast thin morning shadows across the sandy trail leading to the picnic tables. On their left, the gravel path gently climbed up to the lavender and brown Lav sitting on top of the hill.

Joe pointed to one of the tables close to the path up to the Lav. "This is the table where Angel served the ice cream," he said.

Maria stood next to him, following the path up to the Lav with her eyes. In the brush on the right-hand side of the path, crime scene tape marked off the place where Cortez had been knocked to the ground.

"Cortez must have seen Angel coming up the hill," Joe said. "He probably started down the hill to get help. Angel would have had time to take him by surprise."

"Why didn't Cortez use his cell phone?"

"Maybe he did, and no one could understand him. Or else he started off after Angel instinctively, feeling there wasn't time enough to call. He was supposed to watch the front and the back of the Lav. He could have been in the back checking out the woods while Ramón was waiting near the front of the Lav for Carlito."

"In that case, Ramón would have been alone and in plain sight when Angel looked up and saw him. But Ramón couldn't have been there very long. He would have started walking around the Lav looking for Carlito. Angel just got lucky. Again!"

"I know," she said, swallowing the bitter taste in her throat. "Unbelievably lucky. And we look like fools."

"You saved a boy's life, Maria. He was drowning. He would have died if you hadn't gone in after him. His life is worth something too."

Maria just shook her head. "But I knew the park would be dangerous, I knew it, and yet I let Rosa...."

"You talk to Angel today?" Joe interrupted.

"Every day," she said. "I want him to know he is never out of my mind."

"He say anything interesting?"

"Same as usual. He's working in his office. We can reach him any time. Today he said he was 'lying low.'"

"Gil must have told him that," Joe said. "Today Vereda will be saturated with cops and reporters."

"It doesn't matter. No one bothers Angel." She shook her head. "Gil must have connections that go all the way to the top."

"No one is immune forever, Maria. Let's see what we can do to rattle Gil's cage a bit. Finding some way to pin Ramón's murder on Angel would be a solid blow for starters!"

She managed a small smile. Joe had a way of making her feel encouraged even when they were up against what looked like a dead end.

"I'm going up to the Lav again," Joe said. "I want to look around there more closely."

Maria nodded and walked over to one of the tables close to the water's edge. She sat down and looked out at the water, thinking about Joe. She liked him. They'd talked on their way out to the park, and he'd opened up a little about himself. She was impressed. The only thing that had surprised her was his age. She'd seen him as older than thirty-three. Maybe that was because he worked outside a lot. The sun had left its traces on his face, especially around his eyes. Or maybe it was the kind of work he did. All he'd said was that he'd been in the Special Forces before joining the Border Patrol. He hadn't offered anything else, and she hadn't asked.

She put her thoughts away and looked out at the river, letting herself move with the water as it rippled, glistening in the sunlight. In the distance she could hear the guttural honking of cranes. A family of mallards swam slowly past her.

The heron was standing alone in the shallow water near the edge of the river. It was so still, she hadn't noticed it at first. The tall gray bird with its long legs and sharp bill was intent on the water, waiting for signs of a passing fish, waiting to feed. It seemed completely indifferent to her presence.

There was something about a heron with its wide wingspan and skinny legs that always gave her an unpleasant feeling. She had never been able to figure out why. But whether it was the heron or the unrelenting sun beating down through the trees, something was making her stomach churn. And she was tired. She hadn't been sleeping well. The heat in her bedroom was unbearable. And the image of Ramón in his red and white striped shirt, lying in a heap under the bushes where he'd been tossed, had burned itself into a repeating dream that kept waking her up.

Out at the trailhead, she'd asked Joe if he thought dreams were important. He'd looked at her warily, as if he'd somehow intuited she was also asking for herself.

"Life is hard enough," he'd told her. "Believe me, there are real nightmares out there, waiting to bring you down if you don't give them your full attention. If you want to bring about justice in this world, if you want to survive? You'd better put dreams aside."

Now Rosa was simply part of the Alvarez file lying on the table in front of her. Maria picked it up and started to go through it yet another time. The case was hard and frustrating. So far they had nothing on Angel. But there was always a missing piece. She had to believe that if she looked hard enough, she would find it. Once that was in place, the rest would follow.

SATURDAY
Riverside Park

MARIA WAS FINDING IT HARD TO CONCENTRATE. She couldn't shake the feeling that someone was watching her. She turned and looked hard through the trees in back of the Lav, trying to see into the darkest shadows, but nothing was moving. Nothing she could see anyway. Something flashed near the Lav, then was gone. Sun glinting off the metal window frames?

Joe was standing beside her. She hadn't heard him approach.

"You willing to go over our thinking one more time?" Joe said, sitting down next to her on the bench.

Maria nodded. "You start."

"The way I see it," Joe said, "Angel did have a plan in mind. But I don't think he ever expected things to fall into place the way they did."

"I agree."

"He probably couldn't believe his luck when he saw Ramón standing by himself in front of the Lav and the rest of us distracted by the kids in the water."

She nodded. "Why the hell didn't we see him?"

"We were focused on the kids in the water, lives were at stake there too, you know," Joe said. "Do you think I'll ever stop asking myself how we could have missed him?" His face was lined with fatigue and discouragement.

Maria was silent for a minute. "Cortez sees Angel. Maybe he tries to stop him, find out what he wants," she went on. "Cortez must have tried to call us to check things out, but with all the noise the kids in the water were making and that voice box Cortez had to use...."

"I know," Joe said. "Everything falls into place."

"So he smashes in the old man's head with a rock...."

"That wouldn't have taken more than a few minutes," Joe added. "Angel must have felt invincible."

"Angel gets around the Lav in time to see Ramón go into the woods. What do you think Joe? Why did Ramón go into the woods? Was he running away from Angel?"

"No, I don't think so. When I look at Ramón's trail, I see a boy running towards something, not dodging and turning, trying to keep out of sight. I think Ramón was following something that mattered a lot to him. Maybe a Blue Heron flying overhead? We'll never know.

"But whatever the reason, Ramón probably isn't paying much attention to his feet, he sees the river in front of him, and then suddenly it's too late. He finds himself inside a ditch. He can't climb out. It's too deep. So he passes the time by writing in the sand and calling out for help. When Angel appeared, it must have seemed like the answer to a prayer."

"He wouldn't have struggled. He would have been glad to see Mr. Angel," Maria said in a thin voice. "So no skin under his nails."

"And no scratches on Angel," Joe added. "He picks up Ramón and before the boy knows what's happening, Angel sticks the needle into his arm. Ramón would have fallen asleep instantly."

"At least he didn't die afraid," she said, staring blankly at the water.

The sad undertone of resignation in her voice hit Joe unexpectedly hard. He fought to regain his focus, but it wasn't easy. Maria got to him. There was no point in denying it. At that moment, all he wanted to do was hold her.

After a few moments, Joe went on in a carefully neutral voice. "Angel crosses the river with the boy in his arms, and again, he's lucky. No one sees him. Once he's on the other side, he follows the hiker's trail until he comes to the Olde Road. Angel has long legs, he's strong, and he's fast. He could make the road in five minutes even with a small boy in his arms. He leaves Ramón in the tall grass by the side of the road along with his wet clothes and the syringe, then heads back to the river."

"How could Angel have figured all this out?"

Joe was silent, but he knew what she meant. He had been asking himself the same question. Had Gil been calling the shots from the beginning? Or had they badly underestimated Angel?

"You think Gil told him what to do?" Maria said. "Did we find a phone anywhere?"

"There was a phone in the trash barrel in the parking lot, but it was a throw away."

Maria stood up and looked out at the river.

"Let's take another look at the ditch," she said.

They walked up the hill without speaking. The dappled trees in front of them were noisy with bird calls. Maria stopped to look down at the river shimmering in the distance, a slender ribbon of gold winding through the green leaves of the trees. Joe stood next to her. For the next few minutes, neither of them moved.

Near the irrigation ditch that Joe had marked off, yellow crime scene tape fluttered in the breeze picking up from the water.

"The ditch is not that deep," Maria said. "But it's deep enough. A child like Ramón wouldn't be able to get out on his own. Can we prove that he fell here?"

"The search party went tramping through the area before we could preserve anything around the ditch, but I think what's inside is enough. The writing in the sand in the bottom of the ditch, the scuff marks on the sides of the ditch. Ramón had a scrape on his arm that looks like it came from a fall. And there was sand under his fingernails and silt in his hair. All that strongly suggests he could have fallen into an irrigation ditch. This one."

The ditch was about ten feet from the river. "The river is shallow enough here," Joe added. "You can cross the river easily enough although you'd probably get your feet wet."

"Angel's feet were dry," Maria said. Her words were heavy with discouragement. "That doesn't help our case much, does it?"

Across the river from where they were standing the parking lot was clearly visible. "There's a fence around the whole lot," Joe said. "But it's cut in several places. Park staff says it's been like that for some time. Angel could have easily squeezed through one of the openings and made it into his van in less than a minute."

Maria nodded. The river seemed to float in front of them as quietly as a cloud.

Joe took a deep breath. "It would be nice if we weren't working a case."

She nodded unhappily. "The problem is there's always a case."

As if to emphasize her point, her cell phone began to ring. She spoke briefly, then closed up her phone.

"That was Al," she told Joe. "He wants to meet us in the parking lot."

Before Joe could protest, Maria went splashing through the water over to the parking lot on the other side. Joe followed her, swearing under his breath. Maria easily squeezed through one of the openings in the fence. He found it more difficult but finally made it through the fence without ripping his clothes. She was waiting for him in the parking lot. "Just wanted to test our theory," she said. "Now let's go see what Al has to tell us."

Al was standing next to his car. He was rubbing his scarred hand back and forth against his pant leg, and he looked exhausted.

"Let me tell you what happened," he said. "Maybe this time we got lucky."

Joe's face revealed nothing, but Maria could feel his hostility. Joe didn't like Al, that much was certain. Did it have anything to do with her? She doubted it. Probably it was simply Al's style that hit Joe the wrong way.

"What do you have for us?" Joe said, studying Al closely.

"You remember when you asked me where Angel used to live before he got squirreled away in the Repository?"

Joe nodded.

"And I told you he lived in a small house on Vista Drive, right?"

"Right," Joe said. "We checked it out. Angel's was a rundown old house like most of the other houses on the street. The only difference is that it was painted yellow. The other houses are white. Supposedly now it's used as a safe house for illegals. Immigration is keeping an eye on it. They told us to leave it alone unless we found a reason not to."

"Right," Al said. "Well I've been talking to my informants like Danforth asked me to do. This morning I went to check in with my regulars who live in the valley. One of them told me about a girl who had information about dog fighting. I didn't want her to change her mind so I started looking for her right away. When I found her, she gave me everything!"

"We're supposed to be looking for Snake Baby, not dog fights" Joe said. He couldn't help it. Dog fighting! What was Al up to?

"It connects," Al said looking at Maria. "It's important."

Maria took a deep breath. Bringing down a dog-fighting ring could be as dangerous and violent as busting a drug ring. Dog fighting took place in a close-knit world. They'd had an informant once, but he hadn't lasted long. They'd found his body in a shallow part of the river, a metal leash attached to the spiked dog collar around his neck.

"That girl who gave you the information, she has a lot of courage," Maria said.

Al nodded. "I know. She should get an award, but if she's lucky, no one will ever know what she did."

"Why is she doing it?"

"Believe it or not, because of a puppy," Al said. "She lives near the barn where they train the dogs. She and four other girls. They belong to Snake Baby. He calls them his *babies*."

Maria ignored the shiver running up and down her back.

"Runaways?" Joe asked.

Al nodded. "Most of the time they can do whatever they want as long as they stay away from the barn and are available whenever Snake Baby and his boys want them. So it can get boring and lonely. About a month ago, this girl finds a puppy along the road. She asks Snake Baby if she can bring it back to the house, make it a pet. And Snake Baby tells her, sure, go ahead. So she takes it in, and pretty soon, she falls in love with it.

"Last week, she's inside the house when she hears the puppy whimpering outside. She looks out the window and sees this guy making off with her puppy. And she recognizes him! It's Felix, one of Gil's top lieutenants.

"She asks Snake Baby about the puppy. He laughs and says he doesn't know anything about any puppy, but there's something about the way he's laughing at her that makes her mad. So even though the *babies* aren't ever supposed to go to the barn by themselves, this girl goes looking around the barn late one night after everyone else has left.

"She finds the puppy in a trash barrel. It was ripped apart but still in the mesh bag they use to bait the dogs. I guess something went off in her after that, seeing the puppy all torn up in the bag and all. So she decides she doesn't care how dangerous it is, she's going to keep her eyes open, start listening. All she can think about is how to hurt Snake Baby.

"She found out where the dog fights are held in Vereda. She said there should be all kinds of things around the garage, bloody cloths, dogs in cages, all the proof we need. And here's the best part. She says Snake Baby himself goes to the fights. That means we could get him, Maria, we could finally get him."

"That's big, Al. Really big! But right now? Today? I mean, we're supposed to be...."

"Can you convince a prosecutor to bring up charges against Angel?" Al said, staring deliberately at Joe.

"We know he did it," Maria said, "but..."

"Can you prove it?"

She shook her head. "We've got nothing, absolutely nothing, at least so far."

"You willing to hear my idea?"

"Why not?" she said. "What do we have to lose? Right?"

Joe nodded reluctantly.

"OK then, listen. There's just one thing in this world that Angel cares about as much as he cares about Gil. You don't know him, you've only just met him once, but I grew up with him. Not many people know this about Angel, but he's always been crazy about animals, especially baby animals, like puppies and kittens. Gil won't let him keep any animals in the Repository, but at night, Angel still sneaks outside to leave food for the strays that come around.

"So it hit me as I was driving back from the valley, what if it was Angel's house where the dogfights are held? Because that's what the girl told me, she said the dog fights are held in the garage of a yellow house on Vista Drive. Wouldn't that be something?!"

"Because?" Joe said.

"Because Angel wouldn't be very happy, that's why. The word on the street is that he hates Snake Baby. And I'll bet that if you brought Angel out to his old house and he saw what happens in a dogfight, he'd turn over Snake Baby faster than...."

"Are you crazy?!" Joe said. "We have a raid tomorrow night in case you've forgotten! No way anyone goes near Angel before then. And we're not even supposed to go near the house without a good reason...."

"I was thinking of Ramón," Al said defiantly. "I was thinking of Rosa. Angel is a very strange person. You never know what's going to set him off. But I wasn't suggesting you do anything with Angel before the raid. All I was going to say is that you might want to check out the house again. See if what the girl said is true. If there really is evidence of dog fighting around the place, and it turns out to be Angel's old house, you might have something to use against him. After the raid, of course," he added sarcastically, looking directly at Joe.

Maria looked at Al thoughtfully. "You're saying if we bring Angel to the place where the dog-fights are held, and he sees what happens there, he might crack?"

"Exactly. If we're lucky, if we handle it just right, we might be able to persuade him to give up Snake Baby. He might even own up to taking Ramón, you never know. As I said, he is one strange man.

"But remember, Maria, you got to leave me out of it," Al added. "Otherwise they can trace things back to the girl. If anyone asks why you went to the house, you have to say it's because Angel used to live there."

"Right," Maria said. "I know how it works, Al. Don't worry. I've never let you down yet, have I?"

"And the second thing," Al added over his shoulder as he turned to leave. "Be careful. I'm not kidding. Anyone could be in that house, even Snake Baby, and he would have all the advantages. Wear your vests."

Maria waved good-bye to him as she peeled out of the parking lot, ignoring Joe's stony silence, and headed straight for Vista Drive.

42 | SATURDAY
Vereda

JOE TWISTED UNCOMFORTABLY in the passenger seat as Maria gunned the car through the back streets of Vereda. He tried to argue with her. "You know Danforth doesn't want you involved with Snake Baby. What the hell do you think you're doing?" he said sharply.

"I'm going out to Angel's old house," she'd answered without even looking at him. "Nothing to do with Snake Baby. Looking for a way to break Angel for Ramón's murder is reason enough to give his old house another look."

"I'm calling Danforth."

"No," she told him. "You know what he'll say. Taking officers away from hunting Snake Baby just to look at an old house? No. I'll drop you off if you want, but I'm going ahead with or without you. If it pans out, I'll call Danforth myself."

"Maria, listen to me, Al lives in his own world. He does what he wants, he drives too fast, he smokes where it's not allowed, he's always late, he disobeys instructions. I know it's the kind of work he does, but he doesn't follow the rules. He takes chances! And informants aren't always straight. Everything I know tells me this is a setup." Joe was yelling at her.

"I'm going anyway," she said firmly.

After that, Joe stopped talking. He couldn't bail out on her, not now anyway. He stared out the window. He hated the *barrio*. It was hot and dirty. He felt suffocated.

They passed a mobile crime unit in front of a large rooming house. Most of the front windows on the lower floor had been smashed. A Rottweiler with a spiked collar around his neck stared out at them from behind a chain link fence.

"Officers canvassed the neighborhood around N. Building after Ramón's body was found, right?" Joe asked, mostly to break up the awkward silence in the car.

Maria nodded. "According to their report, some of the shopkeepers knew Rosa because she worked at a grocery store in the neighborhood. But no one knew Ramón."

"Anything strange in that?" Joe asked. "That no one around there knew Ramón? Or is that typical of the *barrio*?"

"I get your point, Joe," Maria said in an even voice. "You're not fond of this community, are you?"

Joe didn't say anything.

"Let me tell you something," Maria said. "The *barrio* is what folks in the north call a ghetto, a high-crime section of the city. Unfortunately there are more porn shops, sex workers, drug sales, and ongoing gang activity in Vereda than in a typical *barrio*.

"There are also law-abiding residents in Vereda. They don't go out much, especially after dark. One reason no one knew Ramón is probably because Rosa kept him home most of the time."

"And the law-abiding residents are?" Joe asked.

"Seniors, families, just like anywhere else," Maria told him. "The difference in Vereda is that there are also a lot of law-abiding, hard-working illegals, single men who sleep crowded into apartments and boarding houses. They like to go out, but it's more dangerous for them than anyone else. They can't go to the law for help."

"Why so many illegals?" Joe said. If he could just keep her talking, maybe he'd be able to get some sense into her before it was too late.

"Lots of agriculture in the south valley," she told him. "Lots of construction around here too. Most of the field hands and a good percent of the construction crews are illegals, and most of them live in Vereda."

"Why Vereda?"

"Vereda is safe from *La Migra*, for one thing," Maria said. "Immigration officials know better than to go looking for illegals in Vereda. People in Vereda keep their mouths shut. And the community used to be OK," she added after a minute. "Before Gil and his drug money took over. But it's going down fast.

"Last week we interviewed a man who lives over here, near Vista. He'd been mugged. He told me that people used to look out for each other in the old way. But now, he said, now you hear gunfire almost every night. Now the people who live here get killed."

"More people getting killed near the border too," Joe said. "Seems to me it's getting rougher all the time. That's one reason not to go into a dangerous situation without backup."

Maria ignored him and took a sharp left at the next intersection. There were a few decrepit houses at the beginning of the street, most of them with bars on the windows. The rest of the street was a long, empty lot filled with old tires and tall weeds.

"Southside Mall's at the end of the block," Maria said. "On the right."

"We're going to the mall?" Joe said.

She didn't bother to answer him. She drove into the far corner of the mall and pulled up next to an overflowing trash bin. As soon as she killed the engine, Joe unbuckled his seat belt and looked around.

They were parked in what looked like a war zone. Empty bottles, newspapers, and ripped cardboard boxes covered the broken asphalt, reduced by now to a series of cracks and holes. Most of the buildings in the mall were covered with graffiti.

An SUV sat parked near one of the buildings, the words Syringe Exchange painted across the back window. Teenagers, most of them wearing baggy jeans and baseball caps, were standing around the SUV. A few kids were sitting lined up on the curb nearby.

Joe shook his head in disgust. "Syringe Exchange. The guy who teaches addicts to use clean needles? The guy who tells addicts what to do when they overdose? And tells them when the cops are coming?"

"I don't know about that last part," Maria said. "All I know is if you want to keep infectious diseases from spreading, you need to keep users from getting sick in the first place."

Joe was silent. "I guess that's fair enough," he said after a moment. "But why park here in the mall, in such a public place? It's like you're saying using drugs is OK."

"I don't know," she said. "Usually he parks on one of the side streets. Maybe nobody wants drug users in their neighborhood," she told him. "Not even when it's their own kids using."

Joe gave her a cautious look. "Now what?"

"I know the driver," Maria said. "I want to check in with him, see what's happening around here before we go to the house. That safe enough for you, Joe?"

She got out of the car before he could answer and went over to the SUV. An older man with a gray beard stepped away from the van to talk to her.

"*Hola*, Oscar," she said. "I heard there were dog fights in a house over on Vista. I thought we could go over to the house and look around. What do you think?"

"I don't know," Oscar said. "If it's the house I'm thinking of, the yellow house?"

She nodded.

"Well then, I don't know."

"What do you mean?"

"I mean, some of the time the yellow house is used as a safe house. New illegals arrive almost every week, they're herded into the house for a few days, then cars come in at night to drive them away to pickup points all over the state. You know, wherever they want to go, to a new job or maybe where their families are. Next morning, the house looks as empty as it did the night before. You definitely don't want to go sniffing around when the illegals are there."

"Right," Maria said. "But..."

"But there's a new activity since a couple of months." Oscar looked around nervously. "It takes place in the garage. From the outside, just passing by the house, everything looks pretty much the same. Word is even *La Migra* hasn't caught on yet to what's going on in the garage behind the house.

"Gil's boys work hard to keep the two activities separate, you know? So one week it's a safe house, and the next week, it's the other activity in the garage."

Maria nodded.

"This is the garage week. Usually that means no one is around during the day. But this is Saturday, the biggest night of the week as far as betting goes, so people show up a little sooner. A lot of money changes hands on Saturdays, let me tell you. There are big crowds every Saturday night. You see people parking cars everywhere there's an inch of space around that house, sometimes as early as late-afternoon. That's why we're in the mall today. We try to stay far away from that stuff."

"Smart choice, Oscar," Maria said. "What you do is already dangerous."

"What I do is little enough," he said. "I owe you big, Maria."

"I was just doing my job," she said, embarrassed.

"You can say it however you want to," Oscar said. He took her hand. "But I don't want nothing to happen to you. So if you go to that house today, you got to keep your eyes open. Look around fast and then get out of there. You should be OK for a couple of hours. Word'll get back to the homeboys that a couple of cops are messing around in Gil's territory, but they don't want public trouble, if you know what I mean. They have private arrangements already in place. So if you find what you're looking for, make sure you clear things with your boss before you come back. And you better plan on coming back with a lot more than just you and the cowboy."

Maria laughed out loud. "Oscar, you are something else," she said. "There isn't much going on you don't know about, that's for sure...."

"See you later, Maria," he said. "And remember, watch your back."

"I always do, Oscar, I always do."

43 | SATURDAY AFTERNOON
The yellow house
Vereda

"WHAT THE HELL WAS THAT ALL ABOUT?" Joe asked when Maria got back in the car."

"Long story," she said. "He used to be in law enforcement."

"I don't believe it," Joe said.

"Believe it. Life threw him a couple of curve balls he wasn't expecting and left him for dead. I was able to help him out. I think he's going to make it."

Maria headed east and turned onto Vista Drive. There wasn't much action on Vista Drive anymore, only cars moving slowly up and down the road. She drove past the large apartment building known as *la finca*. It looked deserted. She kept driving. Joe pointed to the yellow single-family house on their left as they went by it. Maria nodded, but she passed by it without slowing down. Across the street from the yellow house, there was a fenced-in empty lot, filled with tall weeds and scrub. They went by two other houses on their left before Vista Drive ended in a cul-de-sac, dwindling into a dirt road that must have served as a driveway for the abandoned adobe house at the end of it. Behind the house, there was only desert.

By now the noonday sun was burning high in the sky. It sent a bright lemon light splashing across the large mural on the front of the house like an enormous spotlight. Maria pulled over and stared at the mural. Joe stared at it as intently as she did. She'd seen it many times before, but it was always difficult to pass it by without taking another long look.

In the center of the mural there was a large painting of a man's face and chest. Wings extended out from his shoulders, and his face and hair were surrounded by a brilliant halo of flames.

Painted next to the man's face were two large, interconnected hearts. One heart was surrounded by roses, the other by thorns. The rest of the mural was covered with graffiti. "*Esteban nunca te olvidaremos*". "We will never forget you Esteban, RIP 2005." "Only the good die young, RIP Esteban." "A true soldier is gone, RIP." "We miss you sooo much Esteban."

"Who the hell is Esteban?" Joe said.

"One of Gil's top lieutenants," Maria said. "He lived on this street most of his life."

"Most of his life?"

"He was eighteen when he died. Taken down by a rival cartel. In your neck of the woods, by the way," she added. "Not far from the border."

She looked again at the house that dead-ended Vista Drive. "A good place for the graffiti of death, don't you think?"

Joe didn't crack a smile.

Maria made a quick U-turn and drove back down Vista to the yellow house. She parked across the street and turned off the engine. She studied the house. So did Joe. He didn't like anything about it.

While they were sitting in the car, a steady line of cars moved slowly past the yellow house to the end of the street. There, after turning around, they started back down Vista Drive.

"You think they're coming to look at the mural?" Joe said sarcastically.

"What I think is that Al was right," she said.

"I agree," Joe said reluctantly. "Look at that fence." He had a troubled look on his face. "Look at the driveway."

A chain link fence with razor wire on the top surrounded the yellow house. Large bushes had been planted in a thick line along the length of the fence. Only a small part of the garage was visible from the street. The rest of it was hidden behind the house. But there wasn't even a trace of a driveway leading from the street up to the garage.

There was a packed dirt sidewalk from the street to the house which stood about two feet off the ground on rusting metal footings. There were bars on the windows and Venetian blinds pulled down inside."Let's get out and take a look," Maria said finally.

"No," Joe said. By then she had already opened the car door.

He followed her to the front of the house. Empty bottles of *Palo Viejo* and *20/20*, broken glass, and old newspapers cluttered most of the front yard.

Joe kept his hand on his gun while Maria went up the steps to the front door. A telephone began to ring somewhere inside the house. She knocked hard on the door. Nothing. She put her ear to the door. She couldn't hear anyone moving around inside the house.

She went down the stairs and started walking slowly around the house, Joe followed a few feet behind. She stopped in front of one of the lower windows in the back of the house. The Venetian blind covering that window was missing a slat. Maria looked through the opening into the house. "What do you think, Joe?" she said moving aside. "A safe house, right?"

He looked through the blind. The linoleum floor was covered with mattresses and cigarette butts. The only other thing he could see in the room was the oil drum in the corner with a small TV on top of it. The front of the TV had been smashed in.

"Looks that way," Joe said. "The illegals get dumped out here. Spend a night or two. Then cars come to bring them away. Just like your friend said."

The telephone was ringing again. Its persistent tone interrupted the silence around the house. Every time it rang, Maria started. "I don't know why I'm so jumpy," she said. "But that phone, it's like a broken record. It never stops. You'd think people would figure out...." She stopped midsentence, thinking.

"Joe, I have an idea," she said slowly. "Wait here for me, will you? But stay out of sight so you're not visible from the street."

He shrugged and nodded. It was all her show by now.

She pulled out her shirt so that it was hanging outside her pants. "Can I use your hat?"

He handed it over without a word. She put on the hat and her sunglasses and went back around the house to the front door.

Joe stood in back of the house near the corner. He could easily step out of sight if he heard a car approaching, but this way he could also keep an eye on the street.

Maria waited at the front door, ignoring the telephone that had started ringing again somewhere in the house. As soon as she heard a car coming down the street, she went down the steps, visibly talking out loud to herself. The car slowed down as it passed her, but it didn't stop. It went to the end of Vista, turned around, and headed back down the road.

Maria went back to the door. Another car was driving by. Again she turned around and went back down the steps, shaking her head as if she was confused about something. This time the car moving slowly down the street pulled up beside her.

"*No necessario tocar la puerta mamita,*" an elderly man in the driver's seat called out through the open window. "No use knocking, *mamita.*"

"What's happening?" she said. "*Que pasa? Hoy es sábado!*"

"*Si entiendo chulita, todos estamos poco confudidos. Pero el jefe dice que no hay nada esta noche,*" the old man answered. "The man at the top said tonight is cancelled."

"*Que huevos*!" she said. "*Yo necessitos,* I need....Oh, never mind," she said over her shoulder as she took off down the street.

"*Que buena está,*" the old man said appreciatively as he watched her walking before he drove away.

Once he was out of sight, Maria cut through the back lot and walked back to the yellow house.

"What's up?" he said.

"Here's your hat," she said. "Looks like we have a little more time to look around. For some reason Gil cancelled the fight tonight. Let's check out the garage."

The garage was a long rectangular-shaped building, twice as large as the house. The front door of the garage was padlocked. Piles of old tires and ripped up mattresses covered the ground along the back side of the garage. Red, yellow, and blue trash barrels were lined up next to the side wall. Boards were nailed onto the two side windows.

Maria pushed ahead of Joe. She wanted to see what was at the back end of the garage. As she rounded the corner, a fetid smell hit her in the face. It was coming from a rusted metal trash barrel, too full to be closed securely. Instead the cover sat precariously balanced on top of the pile of trash spilling out of the barrel.

Maria covered her mouth with her hand, bumping the barrel with her elbow. The barrel cover tilted and fell, clattering loudly on the cement. Now the stench was unbearable. Joe took out his flashlight and looked inside.

"Maria, you OK?" Joe said quietly.

She nodded, but it wasn't easy to look at the remnants of the last dog fight. Large packs of bloodstained gauze had been stuffed into the barrel together with empty bottles of hydrogen peroxide, syringes, and razors. Joe was breathing hard. He hated the sight of it too.

Maria started towards the back of the house, trying to get as far away from the barrel as she could. Joe followed her over to a thick planting of bushes.

"Look!" she said to Joe, pointing to the metal crates barely showing under the bushes where they'd been shoved.

He pulled out one of the cages. When he saw what was in it, he clenched his fists and looked away. Maria stared silently at the thing in the cage. It was a bloodied pit bull lying on its side, looking more dead than alive even though it was still breathing. One of its legs was raw and bloody where the skin had been torn away. Its eyes were swollen shut, and one of its ears was covered with dried blood where it had been ripped. There was a large, infected wound on its stomach.

"Those bastards!" Joe said. There was a hard look on his face. "Those bastards!"

"Let's go," Maria said, pulling him along beside her. As they approached the back of the house, Maria felt the hair on the back of her neck stand up. A blind at one of the upper windows was moving slightly, as if someone had just dropped it back into place. The telephone had started ringing again. Maria grabbed Joe's hand and pulled him close to her.

"Listen, Joe, keep walking towards the car, but slowly, looking into my eyes."

Joe started to grin. Then he saw the expression on her eyes. "What is it, Maria?" he said, keeping his eyes fixed on hers.

"The most important dog fight is always held on Saturday, right?" she whispered into his ear. "But not today. Why? What could be so important? It has to be something that just happened because no one was expecting it. People have been calling and coming by all day. What just happened, Joe? What?"

"Rosa!" he said slowly. He had turned towards her so that his face was hidden from the house.

"And Snake Baby," she whispered again into his ear, putting her arms around him. "What if Gil stashed Snake Baby in this safe house until he could find a better place? He didn't have a lot of time. He knew the roads would be covered. What if Snake Baby is in the house?" Her throat was dry. "If he's in there, he's probably been holding a shotgun on us the whole time we've been here."

"If he didn't shoot, it must be because Gil told him not to, hoping we would simply look around and go away. So that's exactly what we need to do, OK?"

Her voice was steady. "OK, Joe, let's go to the car. We can call in from there."

They walked towards the car hand in hand. Joe opened the front door on the passenger side before he unexpectedly pushed Maria down on the floor. "Stay low, call for back up. I'm going to cover the back door."

Before she could do anything to stop him, he was gone, zigzagging back towards the house. "You son of a bitch," she cried out after him just before a bullet went through the windshield scattering glass everywhere. She brushed the glass off herself and called in for backup.

Gunshots coming from the house splintered the air. She grabbed her gun and ran back to the house.

Joe was standing near the back door, his gun drawn. Just as Maria got there, a scar-riddled Rottweiler came hurling through the air like a rocket. The dog hit Joe hard in the chest, knocking him to the ground. Right behind the dog, a man wearing a sweatshirt and a baseball cap dashed out the door and took off.

Maria followed the running man with her gun. "Stop! Stop! Get down!" she yelled, keeping him in her sights. "Drop your gun!"

Snake Baby stopped short, turned, and pointed his gun directly at her face. She shot him just as he pulled the trigger, aiming for his legs. His shot went wide. Hers hit its target. Snake Baby screamed out in pain and dropped to the ground, holding his bleeding leg with both hands.

Maria looked back at Joe. He was in trouble. The dog's haunches were up in the air, its back legs were locked, and its head was down, ripping furiously with its teeth at Joe's arm, trying to get to his throat.

She didn't hesitate. They would find Snake Baby another time. Joe needed her now. She wheeled, aimed for the dog's hind legs, and pulled the trigger. The dog yelped and turned to attack her, its teeth bared. She aimed and waited until the dog was clear of Joe. The dog was almost on her when she fired again hitting him squarely in the chest. A pink mist exploded into the air and over Maria's face and clothes. She followed the dog with her gun as it went down. It collapsed into a heap, bleeding out fast on the ground. After a faint shudder, the dog went limp. Maria wiped the blood off her face and rushed over to Joe.

He was lying on his back. His eyes were closed, and his neck was bleeding heavily. She bent over him, looking closely at his face and neck. At least the blood wasn't pumping out of his neck. As she felt for the pulse in his wrist, she looked around. Snake Baby was nowhere in sight.

She looked down at Joe. His pulse was strong and steady. She felt a flood of relief.

He opened his eyes and looked at her. "Snake Baby?" he said slowly.

"I shot him, Joe," she said. "We'll pick him up soon. Now hang in there. You're talking. That's good." The bleeding from his neck was slowing. "Just hang in there, Joe," she said again. "You're going to be fine."

44 | SATURDAY AFTERNOON
The yellow house
Vista Drive

THE FRONT YARD OF THE YELLOW HOUSE looked like a parking lot. Squad cars lined both sides of the street. The windows on the lower floor had been smashed, and the front door was in pieces. The screaming sirens and sharp sounds of breaking glass had brought out a small crowd, watching the wave of uniforms moving in and out of the house.

Over by the garage, Danforth's unit stood talking or listening to words in static over their radios. Like everyone else, they were watching the cops in the TAC unit attack the garage door with sledge hammers. The door split open and crumbled into pieces.

Maria stayed on the street next to the ambulance while a young paramedic put the last strip of adhesive over the large gauze dressing on Joe's neck.

"I'm off," Joe said as soon as the paramedic had finished. Maria watched him go, leaning forward into a long-legged stride that carried him quickly towards the house. "How's he doing?" she asked the paramedic.

"Not bad," the paramedic said. "He's got some bruises, the cut on his arm is fairly deep, and it's going to take a while for his neck and arm to heal, but otherwise, he's doing OK."

Danforth was speaking to someone on his cell phone as he came up to Maria. "Good work," he said, holding out his hand to her. "Joe's a lucky man."

Maria could feel herself flushing as she took his hand. "Thanks, Sarge."

He nodded. "You OK?"

"I'm fine."

"You made the right decisions, Maria. Not easy to hit a moving target. Not easy to wait till your partner's clear before firing when the dog's a few feet from your throat."

Maria nodded, then changed the subject. "What about the dog? The one in the cage?" she asked.

Danforth shook his head. "They'll have to put him down."

"Were there others?" she asked.

"No, only the one. But the rest of the cages were soiled. They all look like they've been used recently."

"What was in the garage?"

"Just what you'd expect. Weights, short poles, a wooden fighting ring."

"The house?"

"A safe place for illegals to spend the night," Danforth said. "Mattresses everywhere, not much else. Plumbing's broken, the toilets are stopped up. Doesn't look like a group's been here lately. But the neighbors all agree on one thing. The garage was used for dog fights on a regular basis. They're speaking anonymously of course. No one will testify against Gil."

"We've been looking for the dog fighting ring," Maria said. "We didn't know whether it was a house or a garage, but Al keeps his ear to the ground, and he's been telling us for a while that there's a good-sized gambling operation running dog fights here in Vereda." She paused. "Where's Al? He seems more distant than usual."

Danforth shook his head. "I don't know. He's out there trying to figure out what's gone wrong with his informants." Danforth paused. "By the way, you want to let me know how you managed to stumble onto the safe house where Snake Baby was hiding?"

Maria hesitated briefly. Then she said, "Joe and I decided to check out Angel's old house, where he lived before he moved into the Repository. It looked like we might find something to use against him, to break open the Alvarez murder. We had no idea Snake Baby could be here. I checked first with our friend, Oscar, remember him?"

Danforth nodded.

"Oscar told me the garage was used for dog fighting and that the biggest game was on Saturday nights, but he thought we would have a few hours to look around before anyone showed up. That's all we wanted to do, Danforth, just look around. But as we were leaving, I saw someone at the back window, and all of a sudden, things started to add up. Why had Gil cancelled his most profitable fight at the last minute?"

Danforth nodded. "Good thinking."

"We got back to the car, we were going to call for backup, when that damn cowboy pushed me inside and took off again for the house. I barely had time to hit the floor before a blast took out the front window. As soon as I called for backup, I went back to help Joe."

Danforth tried to look severe, but he couldn't keep back a small smile. "I'm sure you two broke every rule in the book," he said. "We'll talk about that after the briefing. I want to see you both back at the station as soon as we finish up here."

"Right, Sarge. We'll be there," Maria said.

Someone was calling Danforth from behind the house. "Good work, Maria" he said again before starting off in the direction of the garage. "By the way, change that shirt before you go anywhere," he added over his shoulder.

"Sarge, wait," Maria called after him. He turned around and looked at her impatiently. "We may want to bring Angel back here after the raid, OK?"

"No problem."

"And two other things." It wasn't a good time to talk, she could see that, but she had to know. "Can I see Carlito later today?"

Danforth hesitated. Then he came back up close to Maria and started talking in a low voice.

"You want to do the right thing, Maria. That's OK. It's part of what makes you a good cop. The problem is, you got to keep your feelings out of cases, you got to keep things separate. The Alvarez murders, the drugs at the Repository, they're too important to load up with personal stuff. We've gone down this same road before, right? More than once?"

She nodded.

"A lot of cops give up on caring," he said quietly after a few moments. "Don't lose your edge, Maria. It's important. But keep things separate. You've got to find a way."

"I hear you, Sarge," she said. "The other thing I need to know, is there a problem with Al?"

"How did I know you were going to ask me about that?" Danforth said. There was a flash of sadness in his eyes. "Al's life is complicated right now. He's staying out of sight as much as possible. He thinks someone set him up deliberately, gave him bad information. His whole career is on the line."

She was silent.

"I got to go," he said. "Keep your edge, kid. See you at the briefing."

She watched him walk away before she headed for her car. She always kept a change of clothes with her when she was working. She would need them now. Her pants would pass, but the blue shirt she was wearing was splattered with dried blood.

By the time Joe came over to the car, she was ready to go. "You changed," he said as soon as he saw her.

She nodded. "Cali and I usually ride together," she said. "There's a clean shirt of his in the trunk if you want it."

When Joe pulled his shirt off, Maria tried not to stare, but Joe had the lanky, muscled body of a much younger man. It surprised her. Attracted her too. But when he pulled Cali's shirt out of the trunk and put it on, she had to work hard not to smile. "Never mind" Joe said looking slightly embarrassed. "What the hell size is this shirt anyway?"

Joe was well built and over six feet tall, but Cali's shirt seemed to engulf him. "You look fine," Maria told him as she pulled away from the curb. "A little undersized, but at least you're not covered with blood."

She was the most annoying person he'd ever worked with, but Joe couldn't keep from laughing along with her.

45

SATURDAY
Vereda District Station

SNAKE BABY COULD NOT STOP CURSING. His thigh hurt like hell, the bleeding wouldn't stop, and he'd lost his favorite shotgun.

"Ah shit, Snake Baby!" Felix said. "My fucking car! Hold your leg tight for Crissakes, you're bleeding all over my seats."

"So help me, I'll kill you if you don't get me out of here," Snake Baby yelled at him.

"That's why I'm here," Felix said. "To get you out of here. So when I see this guy trying to run on only one leg, spilling blood all over the sidewalk and cursing like a madman, I say to myself, Gil was right. No way Snake Baby could lie low, not even for one day. So I get you into the car just before the cops came charging after us, and we make it out of there by seconds. That's right, I get you out of there, and now you're getting blood all over my car!"

"Go to hell," Snake Baby shot back at him. But he knew Felix was right. His getting out of there had been a miracle. By now the traffic around the yellow house was blocked for miles. Curiosity seekers, the press, the neighbors, everyone wanted to see the place where Snake Baby had almost been taken down.

The traffic was crawling. "Why is everyone staring at us?" Snake Baby said nervously.

"Because you look like a wild man," Felix said. "Calm down, comb your hair, here, drink some water." He tossed a small bottle of water at Snake Baby. Without even thinking, Snake Baby threw it back at Felix, hitting him on the forehead.

"Geez, Felix, watch out, you just ran a light!" Snake Baby yelled at him.

Distracted by the bottle, Felix had missed the light. A few seconds later, a siren began to wail in back of them. Snake Baby reached for his Glock, a police special.

"No," Felix said, covering Snake Baby's hand with his own. "No. That's an order from the top. Gil will get you out of jail in two minutes. The cops have nothing on the Alvarez woman and only the female cop's word against yours. It's nothing. Listen to me, Snake Baby!! Are you listening? Look at me!"

Snake Baby turned and stared at him with such rage, Felix felt a small shiver run up and down his arms. But he kept trying to talk Snake Baby down. Gil's orders had been clear. "I don't want that wild man messing things up even more. Shoot him if you have to. It will save me the trouble later on."

"Listen man," Felix began again, this time his words all pouring out in a hurry because the cops were already approaching the car. "If you shoot a cop now, in front of all these witnesses, then there ain't nothing Gil can do for you. So cool it. Just keep quiet until the lawyers get to the station. I'm calling them now."

A young cop approached the car.

"Geez, will you look at that, a rookie!" Snake Baby said through the open window to the cop. "You'll regret this day the rest of your life, you miserable little asshole."

The next thing Felix knew, Snake Baby had jumped out of the car and was hopping down the highway, trailing blood behind him. The rookie chased after him and easily brought Snake Baby down.

"Looks like you're the one that's going to have regrets," the rookie said as he cuffed Snake Baby and pulled him to his feet.

"I'm bleeding, I'm going to die," Snake Baby kept screaming as the cop started to walk him back to the car.

"You're something else," the cop said, shaking his head, but he pulled out his radio to call for medical assistance. No point in taking chances. Besides, who wanted all that blood inside his car?

46

SATURDAY
Vereda District Station

JOE AND DANFORTH STOOD IN THE HALL in front of the administrative offices on the first floor of the station waiting for Maria. She was in the bathroom washing the dried blood off her hands and face. Danforth could hear his cell vibrating in his pocket, but he ignored it. Getting things straight with Maria and Joe was too important.

"She saved my life," Joe said. "With that dog coming straight at her and then having to face Snake Baby's gun?! To be honest, I knew she was a great shot and all, but sometimes when she talks, she gets so involved, I was afraid the situation might get to her, that she might lose her focus. Instead she was cool, in complete control."

"Calm down, Joe," Danforth said with a smile. "You're a quiet man, or so you say. But you've been talking non-stop since you left the yellow house. You're still in shock even if you don't realize it. Having a dog's teeth in your neck? That's no picnic either."

Joe grinned. "You're right, my stomach does feel like it's been turned upside down."

"It takes a while," Danforth said. "But you'll be fine. You might want to remember this about Maria though. It doesn't show at first, but she is very much in control. Think about it. One minute she's facing a lethal attack dog and the next, she's shooting at Snake Baby's legs!! Bet she wasn't feeling so cool inside. It can't be easy to hold your shot until the dog has moved out of your line of fire, especially when the dog is coming after you! And then she goes for Snake Baby's legs??! What was she thinking of? Is that supreme confidence or is she just nuts?"

Joe smiled. "I guess we'll never know. But she's amazing, there's no doubt about it."

Danforth nodded.

"And yet how many people even know that side of her?" Joe went on. He couldn't stop talking in spite of Danforth's advice to calm down. "She holds back so much!"

"You didn't hold back today, that's for sure," Danforth said in a friendly way.

They were both quiet for a few minutes. "I didn't think," Joe said. "I didn't want Snake Baby to get away another time. So I went after him. It was a stupid move."

"You're right, it was a stupid move," Danforth said. He dropped his voice. "Just between us, Joe, I'd have done the same thing."

"Thanks, Danforth" he said. "I mean it."

Danforth nodded.

He's one of a kind, Joe thought to himself. A supervisor you could count on to cover your back. Someone who's been in your shoes. He understands what it's like out there.

"Look, we shut down the dog fighting," Danforth said. "That's big. Any other time, we'd be celebrating. But Snake Baby getting away again..."

"We got something though," Joe said. "Maria shot Snake Baby in the leg while he was aiming at her. He was facing her, trying to kill her. His friends in high places won't be able to get past that one so easily."

"That is something," Danforth agreed.

"Anything new on Rosa?"

"Doesn't look like there are any prints in the apartment. But Snake Baby knows how dangerous prison will be for him. He's too much of a risk to Gil. Maybe we can persuade him to talk in exchange for some protection...."

"If we can catch him," Joe said. "He seems to have nine lives!"

"Even cats die sometimes," Danforth said. "Especially once they've been shot!"

Maria had come out of the bathroom and was walking towards them.

"Hey sharpshooter, you look even better without the blood," Danforth said teasing her. She had dark bruises under her eyes and she looked worn down, but she tried to smile back. "Think you might be willing to take a breather tonight?" Danforth added.

"Agreed," she said right away. This time she really was ready for a break.

"But first let's go over this report together," Dan said. "Up in my office."

As they walked around the corner, they could hear loud crowd noises outside the front door of the station house. Something big was going down. You could feel the crackle of electricity in the air.

"What the hell is that damn TV camera doing?" Danforth said as he watched the crowd try to push a large TV camera through the line of blue uniforms standing in front of the door. "What's happening?" he asked the desk sergeant, Don Miller.

"I been trying to call you, Sarge," Miller said right away. "This is big. They're bringing in Snake Baby!" Miller was pacing the floor near his desk, and his face was red with excitement. "The asshole got pulled over for running a red light, took off running on one foot, and they brought him down. They didn't even realize who they had at first!"

"Where's Snake Baby now? Why is everyone here?" Joe asked, unable to keep the excitement out of his voice.

To Maria, the whole scene looked like something out of a movie, as if a neon sign had suddenly lit up over the station door flashing out the words, "Snake Baby." An increasingly large wave of uniforms had surrounded the station house, the door, and was spilling into the first floor of the station, their overwhelming presence sending out the message, "This is our house, asshole. Now you're our guest."

Joe burst out laughing. "I've never seen anything like this before," he said.

Even Danforth was grinning. "We've been after this bastard for a long time! What exactly happened?" he asked Miller.

"What I heard is that the patrol officers called for an ambulance. Once they knew who it was, they wanted to be very careful, do everything by the book. So the medic comes, pulls Snake Baby out of the cruiser so he can work on his leg and puts a temporary bandage on the wound. Meanwhile the crowds around the cruiser and the ambulance are growing.

"I guess by then Snake Baby had lost a lot of blood so the medic tried to bring him over to the ambulance so that he could take him to the hospital right away. At that point, supposedly Snake

Baby smashed the medic in the face and screamed, 'I ain't going to no fucking hospital,' and then jumped back into the patrol car." Miller could hardly talk he was laughing so hard.

"What a psycho!" Maria said, grinning in spite of herself.

"So they're bringing him here," Miller went on. "That's what everyone's waiting for. Word travels fast."

"I wouldn't miss this for anything, not even your briefing, Sarge," Maria said with a determined look on her face.

"I wouldn't either," Danforth said with a grim smile. "Look, there he is!"

Snake Baby pushed through the line of officers in front of the door and came limping into the station with his hands behind his back, an officer on each side of him and two lawyers in back of him. The moment he saw Maria, he headed straight for her. One of the lawyers pulled at his arm.

"Get the fuck off me," Snake Baby yelled at the lawyer, using his body to push the lawyer backwards with such force that the lawyer stumbled hard against the wall, scraping his face.

Then Snake Baby lowered his shoulder and rammed the officer next to him with all his strength, breaking the officer's hold on Snake Baby's arm. "This time, I'm going to get you, bitch!" Snake Baby screamed at Maria, his voice thick with rage. Maria had her gun out, but Joe had already tackled Snake Baby, sweeping his legs out from under him. With his hands in cuffs, Snake Baby's face hit the floor hard. Blood poured out of his nose.

One of the uniforms pulled Snake Baby to his feet and held him in a stranglehold while two others tightened the cuffs. Only then did the officer let go of his neck. By then, Snake Baby's voice had been reduced to a faint, hiccupping hiss.

47

SATURDAY
G. Briefing Room
Vereda District Station

"SNAKE BABY'S QUITE A FAN OF YOURS, ISN'T HE?" Joe said to Maria as they pushed through the crowd and hurried upstairs into the briefing room.

She managed a small smile. Everyone was there except Cali. Probably he was still out at N. Building, and that worried Maria, but she deliberately put it out of her mind.

"We got Snake Baby today. How about that?" Danforth said in a loud voice. The room exploded into cheers. "And it looks like Maria might have a way to convince Angel to start talking. So we have some good news for a change. Here's a summary of what happened."

Maria tried to listen closely, but the newspaper she'd brought into work lay folded on the table directly in front of her. The photograph on the first page seemed to be staring directly at her. She couldn't stop looking back at it.

One of the teachers had taken the photograph Wednesday morning shortly after the buses dropped off the students at the park. It was a group shot of Charlie Medrano and some of his third graders. The newspaper had put it on the front page along with articles about Ramón's abduction from the park and the discovery of his body at the trailhead.

The children in the photograph looked like they would spring into action with the closing of the shutter. Their excitement leaped off the paper. There was Ramón in his red and white striped shirt, waving and smiling broadly at the camera. Carlito was standing next to him.

Maria pulled the newspaper closer and carefully studied the photograph. Carlito was taller than Ramon, and his light brown hair was straight and cut in a line across his forehead. But what caught her attention was how much older he seemed than Ramon. He was holding his hands behind his back, and the short-sleeved white shirt he was wearing pulled tightly across his chest at the buttons, but that wasn't it. It was the way he kept looking off to the side instead of at the camera, his dark eyes sober and wary.

What was he thinking? He'd known hardship, she could tell. His father was missing although no one ever talked about it. Carlito noticed things, his feet were very much on the ground. He had information for them, she was positive. She felt a sudden stab of anxiety. She had to talk to him. She would tell Danforth at the end of the briefing. She had to see Carlito today.

She walked over to the coffee machine and poured herself a cup of coffee. As she headed back to her seat, she became aware of a change in the room, a sharp shift in tension, like the snap of a guitar string. She looked up. Cali was standing by the door. And when she saw his face, she knew what was coming.

"Carlito Fuentes," Cali said. "Carlito Fuentes has disappeared."

Maria stopped short, sending her coffee sloshing precariously back and forth in the cup. She sat down, keeping her hand steady.

"I went back to check on Ana and Carlito after lunch," Cali said. "Earlier this morning, Ana told me Carlito was sleeping. I had no reason to doubt her. But something didn't feel right. This time I insisted on talking with him myself. This time Ana confessed.

"She told me that Luis had taken Carlito south, into Lastup or maybe into Mexico. They left early this morning in all the confusion surrounding the murder of Rosa Alvarez. No way to catch them on the road by now, but for what it's worth, I've sent out a statewide alert with a description of Carlito, Luis, and his car."

"Why didn't Luis come to us?" Maria asked, unable to completely mask her confusion.

"Ana insists she doesn't know. All she'll say is that Luis told her it was too dangerous for Carlito to stay in Vereda."

"And she believes Luis because?" Joe asked.

"He's her brother," Cali said. He looked grim. "Luis sent Carlito to hide in the storage building behind N. Building. Apparently there's a hidden compartment the tenants call 'the safe place.' They all know about it. Illegals go there to hide if they get the word that *La Migra* is on the way. As soon as the coast was clear, Luis took Carlito from the 'safe place' and they headed south. Ana says he has family in Purgatorio, just over the border in Mexico."

There was complete silence in the room.

"There's something else," Cali added. "Luis left us a message."

"What message?" Maria asked.

"Luis said he didn't know any other way to protect Carlito."

"What the hell does that mean?" Maria said.

There was another long silence. Maria had never seen Danforth so angry. "Do you all realize what's happening here?" he said finally. "We look like the keystone cops, like we can't do anything right. We work so damn hard, being open with the Feds, trying to balance ten different problems, and every time, something goes wrong, something unexpected brings us down. I knew it," he said bitterly. "I could see it coming, those hidden rocks just waiting to do us in. This is a complete disaster, I'm telling you. Goddamn it, I can't believe what's happened." And with that, he walked out of the room, slamming the door hard behind him.

There was a shocked silence.

"Why would Luis take Carlito in the first place?" Al asked.

"Ana is his sister," Cali said. "He's legal, she isn't, the boy was born here, at least according to Ana." He sighed. "What a goddamn mess."

"So we don't really know where Luis is going," Al said.

Cali shook his head. "That's right, Al. All we can figure is that Luis is trying to get Carlito as far away from Vereda as he can. We don't know why, but it sure doesn't feel good."

"What about Ana Fuentes?" Al asked.

"Ana is safe and under federal protection," Joe said. "We've also asked the Mexican *Policia Municipal* to allow us to look for Luis and Carlito in Mexico. They'll take us in if we want. I think we should go. We'll be down there anyway."

Al nodded.

"The Alvarez family is going to be buried in Lastup tomorrow afternoon," Joe went on. "All three of them. There's at least a chance Luis and Carlito will show up at the funeral. It's less than a fifteen-minute walk from Purgatorio into Lastup. Luis could decide it makes more sense to turn himself in than to keep on running."

Cali interrupted him. "Joe, I want you and Maria to leave for Lastup tonight. I don't care if the whole world is out there looking for Carlito. I want us to find Luis and the boy first. We've put too much into this case to let someone else take over. I want that kid in our custody. You OK with that, Joe? That going to make trouble for you?"

"We'll make it work," Joe said.

Cali looked relieved. "You know your way around Lastup, Joe," he said. "That gives us an advantage. You'll make arrangements with the *Policia*?"

"I'll take care of it," Joe said

"Good. Al will meet up with you and Maria sometime before the funeral. Al grew up in Lastup. Maria was one of Ramón's best friends. That might count for something. Carlito might be willing to talk to her."

Joe nodded.

"What about the funeral?" Maria asked.

"Juan Alvarez had a cousin in Lastup," Cali said. "He was willing to make the arrangements, but he couldn't afford to pay for three burials. The Catholic diocese in Lastup is going to cover the burial expenses."

"Will you be there?" Maria said.

"I'll join you as soon as I can. Lastup will be a furnace tomorrow. You and Joe, you're going to be OK? You've both had a full day."

"I'll be OK," she said. Joe nodded.

Once the briefing was over, Maria headed back to the Squad Room. It was strangely quiet. A few officers on late afternoon shift had settled in behind their computers. Otherwise the room was empty except for a small group of people standing in front of the monitor of the interrogation room. Maria stopped to look at the monitor.

Al and Snake Baby were standing in the center of the room, smoking and talking in voices too soft to be audible.

Joe came up beside her at the monitor. "You allow smoking in there?" he said after a minute. She shook her head. "But sometimes with Al...if he gets results."

"I guess Al needs a certain flexibility," Joe said. Maria glanced over at him, trying to read the expression on his face. His eyes, fixed intently on Al and Snake Baby, were deadly serious.

She looked back at the monitor. In the spot of light hitting the center of the room, the snake slithering down Snake Baby's arm seemed to leer out at her. She looked at Al. In that moment, the yellow in his eyes seemed more intense than ever.

It was as if she could read his mind. He hated Snake Baby with such passion, he wanted to strike him dead. Al looked directly at the camera. Maria felt drawn to him. He was engaged in such a lonely battle.

Joe was standing beside her. "Two snakes," he said under her breath.

"No, you don't understand," she said firmly. She had never seen Al so clearly. "It's the opposite."

Joe looked at her puzzled. She gave up. It was impossible to explain.

A man in a suit, looking more like a cowboy than a lawyer for the cartel, came into the room. He was holding a bloody handkerchief to his nose. After a brief exchange, Al left the room.

She could hear him coming up the stairs. He came into the Squad Room looking troubled and distracted, nervously rubbing his hand against his pants. When he saw Maria, he started to say something. Then he noticed Joe standing beside her and walked past them without speaking.

"Let's get out of here," Joe said. Wordlessly she nodded her agreement. She picked up her notebook and her car keys.

"Give me an hour, Joe. You'll pick me up in Sandy Hills?"

He nodded. "See you then, Maria. See you soon."

48

LATE SATURDAY AFTERNOON
On the road heading south

MARIA PULLED ON HER BROWN HIKING BOOTS. Then she stood up and clipped the undercover holster and spare magazine onto her belt. She would wear her shirt over the jeans to provide some cover for the gun. She closed the small traveling bag she would bring with her and pushed the Glock into her holster.

Joe was at the front door fifteen minutes ahead of time.

"Anything new on Carlito?" she asked him.

He shook his head. "You'd know if there was."

The road south took them back through the town of Sandy Hills. As they approached the outer limits of the town, a sign came up on their right. "DRIVE SLOW SEE OUR VILLAGE, DRIVE FAST SEE OUR JUDGE."

"I see breaking the law is a lot different here than in Vereda," Joe couldn't help saying.

Maria nodded. "You're right about that."

"You like living in Sandy Hills?"

"Yes," she said. "It's beautiful. And it's safe."

"Everything quiet at your house last night?"

She nodded. "Not like it was at N. Building, that's for sure."

Joe didn't say anything.

After a while she asked, "Snake Baby's in jail?"

"He's in jail," Joe said. "And he won't be out any time soon either. Bail denied."

"What's happening at the Repository?"

"It's very quiet. Angel hasn't come outside the building at all."

"The raid on the Repository is still set?"

Joe nodded.

"So you'll be bringing Angel in."

"Right. At least we'll be able to charge him with drug trafficking. That ought to put a dent in Angel's activities. And with both Snake Baby and Angel out of the picture, Gil will have some reorganizing to do. That should slow him down for a while."

"Gil isn't worried about Angel being arrested?"

"Gil's thinking, if you want to call it that, is unpredictable, but I think he knows that Angel is absolutely loyal. I don't think Angel will ever say anything about the Repository or any of Gil's other activities. And there will be lawyers waiting at the station to remind Angel to keep his mouth shut. And Angel isn't stupid. He's confused but not stupid. He knows that being in custody is dangerous and that if there's any sign that he's willing to talk, Gil will take him out, first chance he gets...."

"So we still have no way to get Angel for Ramón unless we bring him out to the yellow house and he sees the cages and the other equipment...."

"Right."

"But, Joe, if Carlito saw something we can use to pressure Angel into a confession, that's a whole new ballgame, don't you think? I mean, Angel is an odd bird. He would never knowingly betray Gil, I agree, but if he really does feel protective towards animals and small children, if we could get him to confess to taking Ramón...."

Joe gave her a dark look.

"I know, I know, but in Angel's contorted mind, he probably thought he was saving the boy. And if he confesses to taking Ramón, he could inadvertently bring Gil into the picture as well. Accessory to the murder of a child. Now that's a charge that will stick, even to Mr. Cartel Boss Gomez-Gil."

Joe nodded.

"Can you protect Angel from Gil once you bring him in?"

Joe nodded again, but his face was tight. She could see how tense the muscles were under his skin.

"You think Gil already knows about Carlito being on the run?"

"No doubt about it. And I think there's a good chance that finding that little boy has suddenly become Gil's number one priority. "

Maria looked out the window.

Joe glanced over at her a few times before he said, "One other thing, Maria. I've got a place not too far from Lastup, twenty minutes or so. We can stay there tonight if you want."

She barely heard him. "Let's see what happens," she said finally. The thought of Carlito falling into Gil's hands made her stomach turn. She looked out the window and stared at the waves of heat bending the road ahead of them. The burning sky hovered over the windshield. For a moment, it wobbled. Then she was back. It felt solid where she was sitting, Solid and cool. She closed her eyes and let herself be carried along by the silence in the car.

"Maria?" Joe was saying.

She could hear concern in his voice. "I'm fine, Joe," she said. "Just trying to make sense of things."

It was an hour before they left the highway for El Camino Real, the ancient road that four hundred years ago had been the main link between Ciudad Nueva and the cities to the north. Today El Camino Real was simply part of the state's modern highway system. They would follow it south through the mountains to Joe's place near Lastup.

They were the only car on the road. "Gil's men will be looking hard for Carlito," she said after a while.

"I know. We have to find him first."

"You think we'll find him in Lastup?"

"Probably unless they've already gone Southside."

She nodded. "It's hard to understand how the Gomez-Gil cartel operates out of a small town like Lastup," she said.

"I know. But prepaid drop phones and good internet connections make a difference," Joe said unhappily. "Most of the guys at the top live somewhere else anyway. Miami. Chicago. It doesn't matter. They stay far away from the actual business. They move easily around the country."

"How did you arrange the funeral in Lastup?" she asked.

"I contacted the local church, Santa Teresa, and they agreed to a funeral in Lastup, free of charge."

"Why Lastup?" The way she asked, it almost sounded like an accusation.

"Why not?" He let his irritation show. "Rosa and Ramón were in the refrigerator in Ciudad Nueva," he said deliberately. "You know the routine. They were at the medical examiners. No one claimed them. No one was going to claim them. What was left of Juan is still in Lastup. Juan's cousin couldn't handle the financial responsibility. Now the Alvarez family has a chance to have a decent burial."

He could feel her staring at him. He glanced over at her. Her face was pale, her hands clenched tightly in her lap. What was wrong with her? He thought she'd be pleased that he'd been able to arrange a funeral even if it was in Lastup.

"What?" he said. "You don't approve?"

"That's not it," she said.

After a while, she added, "You know how my family died, don't you, Joe?"

He nodded and waited for her to say something more, but she was silent, looking out the window.

Everyone in the country knew how her family died, Joe thought to himself. It had been front-page news for weeks.

Human traffickers, *coyotes*, had driven the Chavez family across the border into New Mexico. It should have been a routine crossing. Those years, illegals usually moved easily across the border during harvest season, and the young parents were seasonal workers who'd been promised jobs in the orchards where they'd worked the year before.

Yet from what the Border Patrol agents were later able to determine, the *coyotes* had deliberately gone past the normal pickup point. Instead they'd driven into a remote desert area near the mountains and forced all four of the Alvarez family out of the truck. After they had beaten the father and sexually assaulted the mother, they had driven away leaving the two small children alone in the desert with nothing but their gravely wounded mother, a bottle of water and their prayers to help them survive.

Two days later, a Border Patrol Agent driving home after shift noticed vehicle tracks leading into the desert. He decided to follow the tracks for a while. A mile later, he discovered foot sign that indicated a family wandering around in the desert. The sign was fresh, and night was rolling in. He called his Field Operations Supervisor to report what he had found, but no one at the patrol station was available to help with a search. The agent was on his own.

Unwilling to abandon a family that might be lost somewhere in the desert, the BPA had stubbornly continued to cut sign, scanning the ground ahead of him with his flashlight, trying to find the right angle to see the tracks. He went on cutting sign by himself under the moonlight until it faded. Finally, as the sun began to rise, he found the family. Under the pale sky of early morning, a sad little trail of discarded clothing led him to the lifeless bodies of the father, lying near the truck tracks, and then after about a mile, the body of the mother lying next to some ripped cactus, the flies already buzzing on her open mouth.

A short distance away, the agent found four-year-old Maria, crumpled up under some trees, delirious but alive. He picked her up and looked at her closely. She was severely dehydrated, her lips dry and cracked, the skin on her bare feet blistered from her walk across the burning sand. He dribbled some water into her mouth, asking her over and over again, "Can you hear me? Can you hear me?"

After a few minutes, she started moaning. "Stay with me now," the agent urged her. "Tell me, is there anyone else?"

Later the agent would explain that when Maria began to talk, her words were jumbled, non-sensical. He couldn't understand her. Suddenly she opened her eyes and looked directly at him. "*Papi, Papi,*" she cried out. Then she went limp in his arms. "Stay with me, stay with me," the agent pleaded, but she could no longer hear him.

He stood up with the child in his arms and made another quick visual of the area. The hard desert floor was empty except for the clumps of spiny mesquite bushes dotting the ground in all directions. A hot desert breeze was already licking at the sand. The girl's breathing was increasingly halting and irregular. She needed hospital help, and she needed it fast. There was no choice.

The agent ran for the car with the girl in his arms. Even going code, it was an hour's drive before he could get her to the nearest hospital. Barely in time to save her. A miracle, the doctors said. A question of minutes.

As soon as the doctors took the girl, the agent raced his Jeep back into the desert. He had radioed for help on his way to the hospital, and by the time he got back to the place where he'd found the girl, other agents were there. They'd found the two-year-old boy, his body under a thick growth of mesquite bushes. He was dead. The medical examiner couldn't say with any cer-tainty whether or not the boy had been alive a few hours earlier. All anyone could say for sure was that the girl had been saved.

In the borderlands, there were always new stories about the illegals, robbed, beaten by ban-dits, or left to die by the smugglers they'd paid to get them across the border, but those weren't the kind of stories newspapers wanted on the front page. This time, however, a Border Patrol Agent, an authentic American hero, had rescued a four-year-old girl from certain death. Sud-denly everyone wanted to know more about the Border Patrol and the young family abandoned to their fate in the desert.

The investigations that followed were also front-page news, but it was Maria that people wanted to read about. And when it was revealed that whatever horrors she'd had to face in the desert had left her completely mute, the story exploded in newspapers across the county. The public fell in love with her, this small, silent witness who stared out at them from the front pages day after day, her eyes alone speaking of what she had seen.

Less than a year after her rescue, Maria Chavez went to live with her adoptive family in the suburb of Sandy Hills, just outside Ciudad Nueva. Shortly after her fifth birthday, she found her voice. Only a few words at first, but soon she was talking like any other five-year old although she spoke Spanish and English interchangeably, using words from both languages in the same sentence. Even that confusion quickly faded away, however, and by the time she was seven years old, Maria Chavez was a fluent bilingual American citizen, making a new life for herself in the United States.

A few reporters persisted in trying to learn her story, but nothing ever came to light. Whatever evidence might have once existed was lost or buried. And the little girl remembered nothing.

"I did a lot of reading," Maria told Joe suddenly. "I wanted to understand what happened. My parents were lucky, you know. They were carrying identification so they could be buried along with my brother in the Mexican village where they'd lived. But you know what happens to most unidentified migrants when they die, don't you? The *no identificados*? The unidentified ones?"

Joe nodded.

"If they're not identified and returned to their country of origin, illegals end up buried in cemeteries along the border. Thousands of people every year go to a cemetery for indigents, to a pauper's grave wherever the town has land. Usually the same place they dump the trash.

"The illegals get a sheet, a plywood coffin, and numbered concrete markers. Sometimes you'll see the words, *No Olvidado*, Not Forgotten. Sometimes there are some plastic crosses. But that's all they get. No one mourns them. There's no priest. They're just dead illegals."

Joe didn't say anything at first. Then he began cautiously. "I don't want to argue with you, Maria,..."

"I don't either," she said, interrupting him. "And I don't excuse breaking the law. Illegal immigration is just that, illegal. But there are thousands of anonymous graves along our border. And there are children in those graves, and young men and old men, and women, some of them pregnant. And some of them were *mules* bringing drugs across the border in their backpacks, and some of them just wanted a job.

"What I'm trying to say, Joe, is that there are human beings buried under those markers, not just unknown bodies out of a refrigerator. We don't know who they are, so we forget about them. It's as if they never existed. All we see is a bunch of plastic crosses."

"I know it has nothing to do with our case," she said finally. "It just brought back memories, that's all."

49 | SATURDAY EVENING
Joe's Ranchito
East of Lastup

IT WAS EVENING BEFORE THEY REACHED the turnoff for Joe's *ranchito*. They had radioed the authorities in Lastup and across the border in Purgatorio. No one had found any sign of Luis or the boy.

The curving single-lane road made for a slow drive into the high plains of the valley. The landscape, a deep silver green under the passing cloud shadows, looked like the runoff from the mountains to the river. Broken up foothills, canyons, *arroyos*. Not many houses that she could see. Mostly range cattle and an occasional windmill.

"Tell me something about your home," Maria said. "Your *ranchito*."

"My little ranch?" Joe said. He settled back into his seat. It was the first time she'd seen him relax. "There's a house and a barn," he told her. "A couple of horses who keep each other company and the two dogs who keep me company, Smith and Wesson."

She looked at him. Joe was a good guy, and he was easy to look at. But dogs named Smith and Wesson?

"We need a little humor out here," Joe grinned. "There are a few cats as well if they can manage to avoid the coyotes. The real ones, I mean. All in all, I've got about five acres. When I come home from work, I can sit outside and look at the stars in the quiet."

"Sounds nice," she said. She meant it. "You live alone?"

"I do now," he said. "Divorced twelve years ago."

She waited, but he didn't say anything else. That's a long time to be alone, she thought to herself. Her own situation wasn't any better. We're both lonely, she admitted silently. We've left no room for anything but our work.

They drove for another ten minutes or so until they pulled up to his house. She could hear the dogs barking on the other side of the fence. Joe opened the gate and drove in. Two dogs came running up to them as they got out of the car, an Australian Shepard and a large crossbreed.

"Hey Smith," Joe called out to the Shepard. "This is Maria. And this is Wesson," he told Maria, pointing to the crossbreed. The dogs followed them into the house.

"You hungry?" Joe asked her when they were inside.

She nodded. They hadn't stopped anywhere for dinner. She was starving. "Who feeds the dogs?" she asked.

"I have a friend who looks in on them when I'm away," Joe said. He bent down to embrace both dogs. "They may look hungry, but believe me, they've been well fed. They just want some attention."

He stood up. "Why don't you go on out back?" he said. "I'll try to find us something to eat."

She went outside and sat down at the table near the back door. There were blankets, even a few pillows piled up on the benches. "He must spend a lot of time out here," she thought.

She felt something moving under the table. A black kitten with white paws and a white nose was rubbing up and down against her legs. "Where did you come from?" she said as she gently scratched him behind the ears. Stars and silence filled the skyabove her. A church bell was ringing faintly in the distance. The only other sound was the soft purring of the kitten under the table.

Five minutes later Joe came out with two bowls of green chili stew, a cactus salad, and a few bottles of Dos Equis. "You made *nopales*? Cactus salad?" she said, giving him a surprised look.

"Leftovers" he said. He looked embarrassed.

She took a few bites. "This is good."

After that neither of them spoke until they'd finished, but she studied him across the table while they were eating. She liked everything about him, the clear hazel brown of his eyes, the smooth color of his skin that shaded into a deeper tan in the folds of his arms. She liked everything about him except his work. No, that wasn't it. What she didn't like was the way his work turned him into someone with secrets.

The Feds were running the show. It was subtle, but she could tell. Danforth was taking directions from Joe, not the other way around. There was more going on in their investigation than anyone had explained to her. More than the Repository and the drugs, more even than finding Carlito. But what? It hurt her that Joe still didn't trust her enough to tell her the whole story. Was Joe trying to protect her or the investigation? Why didn't Joe like Al?

And what about Al? At times she had the feeling he was trying to protect her. Had someone from her past recognized her? She had no memories, she couldn't be a threat to anyone, but what if Al had picked up something on the street that someone had remembered her. If he thought she was in danger, and especially if he thought she was completely unaware of it, he was the kind of guy who might take it upon himself to protect her. There were cops who felt a calling to protect people, cops like Cali. Maybe Al was like that too, at least with her. They had some kind of connection. She didn't understand it, but it was there.

"Let's take a walk," Joe said.

"I'd like that," she answered. Ahead of them the hills abruptly faded into darkness, then emerged small and faint in the distance.

"The way it happens out here," Joe said. "The sunset just up and disappears into darkness before you know it." He stood up and stretched.

She stood up with him. They walked out into the darkness falling over the desert sky, their hands meeting involuntarily as they walked. Ahead of them on the right the land inclined upwards into trees and bushes. "Come on," he said heading towards the trees. "I want to show you something."

When they got to the top of the hill, he sat down on the ground. It was almost black where he was sitting, under the thick shadows of the trees. "You come out here often?" she asked, sitting down next to him. In front of them was a wide, unobstructed view of the gray hills and the darker spots where the land was split open.

He nodded. "When I'm not on the job."

"To watch the illegals?"

He nodded.

"But why? You spend all day arresting them, then at night you watch them walking to their pickup points? Why?"

"I won't close my eyes to what's happening in my own backyard, Maria." Then he added, "It's early. We can talk if you want."

He could see her trying to pull her thoughts together.

"The operation at the Repository," she said. "Gil has invested a lot in that."

"He must be very sure of his informant," Joe added. "With that in place, he's got an unusually secure operation. Only the fact of Ramón's murder made it possible for us to go as close as we have at the trailers."

"I still think that if Gil had an informant in place, he would already know about the raid."

"We can't explain it," Joe admitted.

Something still didn't make sense. "Joe, where did you get the original tip? About the Repository I mean?"

"I don't know."

She tried to see his face through the darkness. "Maybe you don't want to know."

He didn't answer.

"A Border Patrol Agent found the body of Juan Alvarez along with four other bodies?"

He nodded.

"Three of them were members of Gil's cartel, one was Juan, and the other was your informant, Pipé?"

Joe nodded again.

"Was Pipé an American citizen?"

"Why?"

"Just curious."

"Yes he was. So were the other three."

"Were any of them informants?"

"I don't know, Maria. Not my agency. But I don't think so."

"All of them except Juan were tortured. Horribly." She forced herself to continue. "If Pipé or any of the others knew about the Repository, they would have told Gil's men. But how did we learn about it?"

Joe was motionless in the shadows. "They'll be here soon," he said in a whisper. "Sound carries a long way around here."

"They won't see us?" she said. She felt a tightening of anticipation.

"Not if we don't move."

Dogs started to bark in the distance. She felt Joe's hand on her arm. Now she could see them, a single file of black silhouettes moving across the landscape. They were heading north. Soon they would pass almost directly in front of them.

She could see them more clearly as they came closer. Men, women, a few children, all of them dressed in dark clothing, most of them carrying back packs. Maybe forty people in all. They were walking fast. Quietly. They climbed steadily up the rocky plateau ahead of them, disappearing down the other side.

She looked back in the direction they had come from. Another group was coming into view.

Joe shook his head and pointed in the direction of the first group. She turned just in time to see the figures emerge onto the next hill. They descended, vanished, appeared yet again, tiny

207

heads bobbing like dots on the horizon. Then they were gone.

Another group appeared, faded, came back into view. Then another. They watched the dark figures walking up and down the hills for almost an hour. It seemed an unending line. Finally there were no more.

She stood up. She needed water. Her throat was dry.

"Do you know where they're going?" she asked.

"It's not a secret," he said. "We get information. We know where most of the pickup points are. We usually manage to get them before they can move on."

"Because you're waiting for them," she said. "They walk all night long, and when they get there, you pick them up and send them back. Because you already know where they're going."

Suddenly the thoughts she'd been holding apart in her mind came together with such force she could feel the pain ripping through her body. She stumbled, caught herself, stopped short, demanding his attention. "Federal agents were listening, weren't they?"

He flinched at the accusation.

"We listened to those men being tortured," she went on with a great effort, keeping her eyes fixed on his face. "Ramón's father was an innocent and an American citizen. He was buying postcards for his son from an old friend, that's all. He was taken by accident, but when he was murdered and later when your informant was tortured, we listened. We let it happen. We knew, and we didn't do anything." At that moment, the weight of her grief was unbearable.

She started walking. He caught up to her quickly. After a moment, he put his arm around her. He felt her hesitate, then settle in close to him, moving in rhythm with his stride.

"I didn't know anything about it," Joe said. "That's not an excuse, just making the facts clear. All I knew was that our agents had picked up a rumor about the Repository, and it turned out to be true."

"And that Juan might have left some evidence against Gil somewhere?"

"That too, but the first I heard of it was after the bodies were discovered. The investigators searched the house to learn more about the bodies. That's when they found evidence that the house was wired and traced it back to the agents who had wired the house. They admitted they had listened to the tortures and done nothing, and those agents were dismissed. They'll never work for the government again.

"But that's where we first learned about Juan's threat. That's where we learned about the Repository as well. I only found out about it a few days ago."

"And in all this time, the supposed mole has never told Gil we were onto the Repository?"

"Maybe he didn't know."

"But by now he must know."

"Yes."

"Why wouldn't he tell Gil?"

"Too dangerous, I already told you. It could reveal who he is. At least that's all I can figure."

"I never should have been a cop," she said after a while. "This is the wrong kind of work for me."

"Maybe," he said. "The job's not right for everyone. But remember, not everyone who goes to war is ready for it. What matters is what you do when you get there."

"The job's right for you."

He nodded. "I think so. But it hasn't always been an easy choice."

"What do you mean?"

He paused. "I almost got married again," he said finally. "Two years ago. She was the best thing that ever happened to me. But she had a large family Southside. They were involved in the smuggling. I had to choose."

By now they were back at his house. She headed quickly for the door, trying to get inside before things fell apart, but it was too late. She could not keep back her tears.

He took her face in his hands and explored her mouth, her cheeks, her neck, tasting the warmth and sweetness of her body. He reached for the blanket and spread it on the ground, pushing her gently to her knees, bending her head back and planting kisses along the line of her throat. She could feel a faint shudder run through her body.

She tried to say, "Not here," but it was useless, his hands and mouth were everywhere, and she found herself filled with an aching desire so intense she could think of nothing else. She arched her back to meet him, and he came into her with such passion that her breathing caught in her throat.

Afterwards, she lay beside him, breathing lightly. She felt happy, peaceful. She hadn't felt like that in so long, she'd almost forgotten what it was like.

When she heard the cry, she had to fight her way out of a deep sleep. She opened her eyes. The coyote trotted past them, unconcerned. By now the black kitten in its mouth wasn't moving.

She stood up, but it was too late. The coyote was already out of sight. Joe was on his feet too. She looked at him with troubled eyes. "Why?" she said simply. "Why?"

"Maria, the worst thing you can do is to keep trying to make sense out of things that don't make sense," he said touching her hair and her face, trying to help. "When you start looking at everything that way, you're in trouble. It paralyzes you. What you need to be afraid of is not that you'll do the wrong thing. It's that you'll end up not doing anything at all. There aren't a lot of answers for us out here, Maria. We're just the ones who show up."

She touched his arm. "I hear you, Joe. Let's go in and try to get some sleep, OK?"

He nodded.

She looked at him more closely. The wounds on his neck were bleeding heavily.

He followed the direction of her eyes and reached up to touch the bandage. There was blood on his hand when he took it away. "It's nothing," he said. "I'll put on a fresh one as soon as we go inside."

50 EARLY SUNDAY MORNING *
Joe's Ranchito

THE ONLY SOUND IN THE DARK SILENCE of the room was Joe's slow, regular breathing. Maria looked over at the bedside clock. The illuminated hands showed just after 4:00 a.m. It was too early to wake Joe, but she was restless. She couldn't stay in bed any longer.

She made her way outside, the dogs following closely on her heels. A thin band of light glowed on the eastern horizon. She sat down at the table near the back door. Wesson sat down next to her. "We'll need everything we've got today, Wesson," Maria said quietly to the dog. "Every pair of eyes we can find." Already she could feel the anxiety knotting up in her stomach. Would they find Carlito in time?

She started to scratch Wesson behind the ears. Then she stiffened, remembering the kitten. She glanced over her left shoulder. Something was moving in the darkness by the side of the house. Automatically she reached for her gun. She stopped mid-course. Now that he was closer, she could see that it was Al coming towards her. Behind him the western sky was still black. What was he doing in Lastup at four in the morning?

"You're not afraid of me, are you, Maria?" he said. No trace of a smile on his face. She shook her head, trying not to stare at him openly. "You startled me, that's all," she said. But it was more than that. The truth was, she barely recognized him.

She had never seen Al this way before, shabby, diminished. He looked like he'd been sleeping in his clothes, a pair of black jeans and a wrinkled blue T-shirt. There were dark bruises under his eyes and a thick growth of black stubble on his face. He hadn't even shaved.

What took her breath away was the tinge of hopelessness that colored his appearance. It shocked her. She'd seen hopelessness like that before. Most ex-cons wore it every day. But Al?

"You must have left the city early," she said to Al, trying to create some sense of normalcy.

"I didn't get much sleep," he said. He sat down at the table across from her and looked out at the sky. The sun hung low over the horizon like a burnished disc.

"Is Joe up?" Al asked.

"Not yet. We didn't get much sleep either."

Al turned to look at her with a curious expression on his face.

She explained. "There's a crossing trail near here, Al. There must have been over two hundred illegals coming through last night. We watched them walking into the early morning."

Al studied her briefly, then looked away. She found herself wanting to change the subject.

"You grew up in Lastup, didn't you?"

Al nodded.

"Any family left around here?"

"No one I want to see," he said.

"Did you know Angel when you lived here?"

"I knew who Angel was. He left school early, joined up with Gil and his boys. He had nowhere else to go. No family in town. Gil became his family."

"His parents left him?" Maria said.

Al nodded.

"When he was a child? Didn't anyone around here know about it?" she couldn't help asking.

"From what I remember, people did know Angel had been abandoned," Al said in a rougher voice than usual. She could tell that her words had upset him. "But you ought to know this by now if you didn't before. Knowing and being able to do something about it are two different things."

"What was Angel like back then?"

"I guess he was a lot like he is now. In my experience, people don't change much."

"But you worked with him, didn't you?" She'd always wondered. Might as well ask.

"I worked with him," Al said. "When I joined up with Gil, I worked with him for almost three years. But I never got to know him. Not really."

She nodded, waiting to hear what else he had to say.

"When I graduated high school, I joined the police department," Al said. "You knew that, right?"

"Right."

"I was able to develop Angel right away. With Gil's permission, of course. Angel and I made an arrangement. He gave me information about Gil's rivals. I gave him whatever money I could pry loose from the department. I thought... maybe he could put the money aside, get away, start over again somewhere else."

"But you were helping Gil."

Al paused. "Look, Angel's information helped bring down a cartel," he said after a minute. "The cops could never have done it without my information. And Angel got good compensation for that. Then I moved to Vereda."

She waited, but Al didn't seem to have anything else to add. "Why didn't you work with Angel in Ciudad Nueva?" she asked.

"I approached him. He wasn't interested. By then he was working full time for Gil. No one betrays Gil. He punishes anyone who betrays him."

"But you got away?"

Al nodded. "Gil let me off the hook," he said. "But I paid a price."

She nodded but didn't want to ask anything else. They sat without speaking. The silence felt sticky. "Anything new on Carlito?" she said.

Al looked at her longer than necessary, as if he was trying to send her a message. "No, nothing," he said finally. "Nothing that I know of anyway."

His words bothered her. What was he suggesting?

"It must be hard for Carlito, don't you think?" Al said unexpectedly.

"What do you mean?" she asked.

"I mean, think about what's going on in Carlito's mind right now. As far as he knows, he may never see his mother again. That has to be tough."

Al's words felt like a shove in the dark. She didn't know what to say. "I'll go see what Joe is up to," she began, but before she could get up from the table, Al caught her eyes and held them. He hadn't finished.

"Once early on, I ran into a situation like that," he said. "I saved the kid, but it cost me."

Inadvertently she looked at his scarred hand. He nodded. "That was the least of it."

In the distance, she could hear a faint rumbling. Cloud shadows were rolling over the hills. Otherwise it was quiet.

She heard the back door open and turned around. Joe was coming out of the house with a pot of coffee and three cups. It was a relief to see him. She had no idea what to make of Al, the way he looked, the way he was talking this morning. Maybe it was because he was in his hometown. But why would he say things like that about Carlito? Why would he say things like that to her?

51

EARLY SUNDAY MORNING
The Repository

WHEN THE TELEPHONE IN THE DESK RANG, Angel felt a surge of relief. At last! He had never gone so long without talking with Gil.

He drove out to the Nature Preserve. "What's up?" he said right away as soon as Gil answered the phone.

"Nothing good, that's for sure," Gil said in a nasty voice. He sounded mad as hell.

Angel waited. He had to be especially careful when Gil was mad.

"The cops have Snake Baby," Gil said finally, biting off his words.

Angel started to tremble. He didn't know if he was feeling good or bad, but he knew he was afraid. "What happened?" he managed to ask, stumbling over the words. Snake Baby! He couldn't believe it.

"Snake Baby fucked up again," Gil snarled at him. "That's what happened. All he had to do was stay in the house, stay quiet. But the cops checking out the house made him nervous. He was convinced they knew he was there, that they were going to call for backup. So when one of them goes back to the cruiser, Snake Baby shoots at her."

"Shoots at her?" Angel said. "When she's in the car?"

"Right through the windshield."

"Did he....?"

"He missed. She's down on the floor but manages to use the radio and then makes a dash back to the house to join the cowboy. So Snake Baby decides he has to make a break for it. He sends the dog out the back door and comes running out behind him. The dog takes down the cowboy, and Snake Baby takes off."

"So what happened?"

"What happened is that instead of getting to the side street where Felix was waiting for him in a getaway car, Snake Baby decides to shoot at the female cop."

"Again?!" Angel felt like his head was going to explode.

"Yes, again! And you know what Angel?" Gil didn't even pause for a response. "Snake Baby misses."

"Again?" Angel mumbled.

"You sound like a parrot, you asshole," Gil screamed at him. "Yes, again. And you know what else, Angel?"

Angel was silent.

"The bitch shot him!"

Angel felt his throat close up. Snake Baby shot?!

"Just his leg," Gil said, reading Angel's silence. "And Felix was there to pick him up."

"They got away?"

"Felix ran a light. The cops stopped the car. Man, I don't know what I'm going to do, I'm surrounded by assholes."

"Snake Baby will never talk," Angel managed to say finally.

"Damn right he won't," Gil said in a cold voice. Angel shivered in spite of himself.

"But that's not why I'm calling," Gil went on. "I got another problem."

Angel waited.

"You know the little kid? The one who might have seen you from the Lav?"

"No one was in the Lav," Angel said right away.

"Whatever you want, Angel," Gil said in a hard voice. "All I'm telling you is that now the little kid has disappeared along with Luis."

Angel fumbled for words, but nothing came out.

"You asking why?" Gil said.

Angel nodded.

Gil sighed. "Christ, I'm surrounded by assholes," he said again. "But here's the thing, Angel. You're asking me why? Well, the answer is I don't know since I wasn't there when you were rocking the old man." He paused. "You were there," he added sarcastically. "Why don't you tell me why?"

Angel was silent.

"The kid must know something, Angel, right? Because every goddamn cop in the state is out looking for him. The word is that he's holed up somewhere near the border, in Lastup or maybe just across the border in Purgatorio. My guys are looking everywhere. And we're following the cop and the cowboy. We'll find the kid, don't worry. This time I'm going to be there myself, just to make sure. But you need to be ready, Angel. The cops could come knocking on your door, just to do a number on you, you know what I mean?"

"About the kid?"

"Right. They still don't know anything about our business in the Repository. I'd know if they did. So you see what I'm seeing, Angel?"

Angel looked out the window. "No, I don't see anything."

"Damn right you don't. So let me explain. If you hadn't had the bright idea of snatching the Alvarez kid, there wouldn't be any cops knocking on your door. And here's my problem, Angel. Your door is my door too, see what I mean."

Angel felt frozen to the seat.

"OK, look, without the kid they have nothing, so calm down. We'll take care of the kid. If the cops come, keep your mouth shut. I'll get our guys to you right away."

"How will you know?"

"Shut up!"

"And the business?"

"You're a complication, Angel, no doubt about that, but I got a big shipment coming in, I can't wait. We'll put on extra surveillance. My source will know if we have to hold up. But for now, we're going ahead tonight. As long as the cops aren't keeping you company, that is."

"I'll be ready, Gil."

"OK, Angel, keep cool."

The phone went dead. Angel drove back to the Repository and practically ran up the stairs to his office. Then he went over to the couch and lay down, staring up at the ceiling. If only he could fly away.

52 | SUNDAY MORNING
Lastup
Purgatorio

AFTER JOE BROUGHT OUT THE COFFEE, they sat in silence for a few minutes, lost in their own thoughts. The first to speak was Maria. "I want to go to Purgatorio," she said.

"It's a waste of time," Joe told her. "You really believe anyone is going to tell you where Carlito is over there? You think Carlito is suddenly going to appear in the middle of the road?"

"What else can we do?" she insisted over his objections. "No one's seen them, no one has any idea where they are. What do you want to do, sit here and look out at the desert all morning?!"

"I'll have to find someone to go with us," Joe said before he grabbed the empty coffee pot and stalked back into the house.

"What do you think, Al?" Maria asked.

Al shrugged. "It won't hurt, but I think our best bet is to go to the smuggling trails. Luis may have decided that the trails are the safest way to get into Mexico. I'll start asking questions around here. We can hit the trails when you get back."

Joe came back to the table. "I talked to the local PD in Purgatorio," he said. He refilled their cups as he spoke. "The *Policia Municipal* will meet us at the Lastup Point of Entry at 8:00 a.m."

"You won't get much if the Mexican cops are with you," Al said. "Folks Southside aren't likely to talk to the *Policia*."

"I know," Joe said. "But those are the rules. Maybe we'll get lucky."

They drove through the official border crossing in Lastup, the POE where Juan Alvarez had crossed and then mysteriously disappeared. Three men were waiting for them on the other side, each in a new model SUV loaded with options. They were wearing dark military uniforms with gold braid.

"The *Policia Municipal*," Joe told Maria. "They'll be going Southside with us."

One of the men got out of his SUV and came over to introduce himself. He was small and lean with dark curly hair and a mustache. He told them his name was Eduardo López. He said he had spoken with Al Diaz, and they had agreed that only one of the *Policia* would go to Purgatorio with them. He would follow them in his own car.

Joe took the main road leading away from the border. It would bring them to Purgatorio. They passed an adobe trading post on their right with large handmade letters written on the side of the building advertising WATER AND FOOD FOR DESERT WALKERS.

"Not much of a secret, what goes on around here," Joe said. He sounded resigned.

An airport appeared on the road ahead of them. The sign on the road said "*El Aeropuerto Sureños.*" An arrow on the sign pointed towards the airport.

"Gil's airport?" she asked Joe.

"One and the same."

Islands of clouds sat motionless overhead in an ocean blue sky. At the airport, a worn orange wind sock hung limply from its pole. Nothing was moving on the ground.

They passed the airport and kept driving. Soon they began to see groups of pink plastic crosses planted in the red sand near the side of the road. They were on the outskirts of Purgatorio. Lopez continued to follow them in his official car at a short distance. They were the only cars on the road.

"Al was right. How am I going to learn anything with López in back of me the whole time?" Maria said as they approached Purgatorio. "No one will talk to me if he's there."

"Al said...." Joe hesitated. He began again. "This morning Al reminded me that *la mordida,* the bribe, is still part of doing business in these parts. He said you can try to persuade López to give you more room. I told Al I'd pass on what he said. But I have to be honest, Maria, it bothers me. A bribe is a bribe."

"I agree, no bribe. But we have to try and find someone who's seen Carlito and Luis," Maria said. "Someone who will talk to us. There's no choice. If Luis managed to smuggle Carlito into Mexico, someone in Purgatorio will know about it."

"Your call," Joe said.

Ahead of them, Maria could see three boys in jeans, tennis shoes, and baseball caps sitting along the side of the road, near a row of scrub pines.

"I want to talk to them," she said.

Joe pulled over and parked. Lopez pulled over not far behind them,

"Let's see what happens if I talk to them by myself," Maria said.

Joe nodded. He didn't look happy.

Maria got out of the car and walked up to the place where the boys were sitting. Two of the boys had already disappeared by the time she got there, but one of them was still in sight, standing where the trees ended in a shallow wash. "*No te vayas*, don't go," she called out to him. "*Estoy tratando de encontrar a un niño perdido, necesito tu ayuda*, I'm trying to find a lost boy. I need your help. I'm looking for a man with a six-year-old boy. I'm trying to help them. Have you seen them?"

The boy kept his distance, but he was listening. If only he would trust her. He shook his head. "We're just waiting for a ride," he said.

"Have you been here a long time?" she asked, also keeping her distance.

"We got here a few days ago," he answered. "No one like that has come by since we've been here."

The boy came a little closer. He looked hungry and tired. Skinny. A light brown fuzz on his cheeks.

"Two days ago we were at the church of Santa Teresa in Lastup," the boy told her. "We went there to ask the Lady in Blue for help crossing the desert. So the gangs don't find us. Or the cops."

A shiver ran down her spine at the mention of the Lady in Blue, and the image of Ramon running to greet her with his wide smile flashed into her mind.

"So what are you doing back here?" Maria asked, ignoring the throb of sadness in her throat at the thought of Ramón.

"A Border Patrol Agent got us," the boy said, dejected. "But I guess we were lucky. All he did was drive us back across the border. Said don't come back or else."

"So now what?"

The boy shrugged. "I don't know. We can't go home. Anyway, no one like the kid you described has come along this road since we've been here."

She thought the boy was telling the truth. Luis and Carlito had not traveled this road into Purgatorio. She pulled some bills out of her pocket and put them down on the sand with a few pebbles on top of them to hold them in place.

"Here's something for you," she said to the boy. "*Vaya con Dios.*"

When she got back into the car, Joe was silent, but she could feel his disapproval. "I'm not a cop in Mexico," she said defensively. "And if word gets around that it's safe to talk to me, we might be able to pick up some information before it's too late."

"What do you think Carlito knows?" Joe asked.

"I'm convinced Carlito knows something about what happened at the park," she said. "But all Gil knows is that Carlito has disappeared and that he may have valuable information connected either to the old man's death or Ramón's kidnapping. The fact that the borderlands are thick with law enforcement out looking for Carlito must confirm Gil's determination to find the boy first even if he doesn't know for sure why we're after him.

"Gil is probably trying to decide whether or not to close down the Repository operation. He doesn't want to cut and run if he doesn't have to, so he's weighing his chances. Can he get to Carlito before we do? If he finds Carlito first...." She paused. "If Gil finds Carlito first, he won't spare either Carlito or Luis to find out what they know. Joe, we have to find them before Gil does," she added with new determination in her voice.

He nodded. "We will."

A large gas station complex came into view on the right. There were three islands of pumps and a convenience store in an orange concrete building with a horizontal yellow band painted around the bottom. A car was filling up at one of the pumps. Several cars and an old school bus were parked near the store. Two men stood outside the building next to a pile of empty cardboard boxes tossed haphazardly onto the ground.

"Let's check this place out," Maria said.

Joe nodded. He drove past the gas pumps and pulled over just past the store. Lopez drove up to the front of the store and parked. Maria waited to see what López was going to do before she got out of the car. It looked like López was going to stay where he was.

She got out of the car and walked up to the men standing outside the store. They stared at her impassively as she approached them. The older man had very dark skin and a handlebar mustache. He stood with his shoulders back and his arms hanging by his side as if waiting for a firing squad to take aim. The younger one, who could have been as young as fifteen, wore baggy jeans and an oversized large blue and white rugby shirt that came down to the middle of his thighs.

"*Estamos buscando a un niño,* we're looking for a boy," Maria began to explain. But before she could say anything else, the older man said, "We don't know anything." He was missing most of his teeth. "Wait a minute," she said, but the two men had already disappeared into the store.

Maria stayed where she was, squinting against the bright sun glinting off the cars in front of the store, trying to decide if she should follow the men inside. She made up her mind. What was the use?

She got back in the car and slammed the door. "We'll never find Carlito this way. You were right."

"I think I know those guys," Joe said. "If I'm right, the young one's 'the Kid,' the other one is 'Smurf.' They're Gil's men. You don't want to talk to them."

Maria nodded, a tired expression on her face.

Joe picked up the radio. As soon as he connected, an excited voice at the other end started yelling so loudly, Maria could hear his voice from where she was sitting. Joe looked like he was about to jump out of his seat.

"They found the car," Joe said as he put back the radio. "Parked close to the border in Lastup. No sign yet of Luis or Carlito, but everyone is out looking for them."

"Gil's men too," she said, feeling the anxiety twisting in her neck. "Anything to indicate Gil already has the boy?"

Joe shook his head. "Word is they're still looking too. With any luck, Luis and Carlito are already far away from the place they left the car."

When they got back to Joe's station, Al was waiting for them. They decided Joe would coordinate the search around the trail where Luis had left the car. Al would go with Maria to check out some of the other smuggling trails. They would meet Joe at the station mid-afternoon. Joe and Maria would go to Lastup for the Alvarez funeral service at 4:00 P.M. Not Al. Without any explanation, Al made it clear he wanted to keep his distance from the Lastup town square.

Al took off fast along the dirt road that would lead them to the smuggling trails, sending the car jolting violently on the rutted bed of hard-packed earth. The land around them was broken, as if a giant club had split open the surface of the earth with a terrible blow, leaving gaping crevices, open gulches, gullies.

"That's not bad cover," Maria said. "Even moving floodlights wouldn't find it easy to pick up someone hiding in one of those ditches. No wonder so many illegals make it out of Lastup without being caught."

Al nodded. He was driving more slowly now, looking for anything that might indicate if Luis and Carlito had followed any of the smuggling trails in the area. Maria opened her window. The walking trails were clearly visible even from the car. The red sand near the road was covered with smudged footprints.

She scanned the landscape around them. It was a landscape covered with garbage. Plastic bottles and bags dotted the sand as far as she could see.

They drove past a small growth of willows. An old Chevy with the word "TAXI" painted on its side was parked off the road, just beyond the trees. Maria could see the driver inside the car. He was reading the paper and smoking a cigar, but she couldn't see his face. He didn't bother to look up when they went by.

They were approaching a cluster of shacks built close together on a hump of higher ground. Most of the shacks were made out of pieces of cardboard and cement blocks. Corrugated metal roofs sat haphazardly on top of the cardboard walls. On the shack nearest the trail, someone had spray painted in large letters, "No urinar aquí."

Three or four dogs were lying on the ground near the shacks. They were so thin they looked like they were starving. They didn't move when Al stopped the car.

Great patches of clouds moved swiftly overhead and disappeared. Maybe there were people inside the shacks, but there was no one outside. No one anywhere along the road either. It was as if the sweltering heat had dissolved any kind of movement on the ground. The only sound she could hear was the flipping of plastic bags caught on clumps of spiny mesquite, twisting in the air.

"Should we try to find someone inside the shacks?" she asked Al.

He shook his head. "No one there. Besides it's too dangerous. This is Gil's territory."

He kept driving. After a few minutes, he pulled off the dirt track to park. "We would need to walk from here to get to the trail where Luis left the car," Al said. "Down there. Unless you've changed your mind."

Maria didn't hesitate. "By now the uniforms are probably stumbling all over each other searching the area where the car was found. I don't think we'll find Luis and Carlito anywhere around there, do you?"

"Agreed," Al said. "We'll have a better chance of finding them near one of the other trails. Luis is too smart to leave his car next to the trail he was going to follow. The problem is we still don't know if Luis brought the boy into Mexico or if they doubled back into Lastup from the place he left the car. "

She looked over at Al speculatively. "Patrols went house to house in Lastup last night without finding anything."

"That doesn't mean much," Al said sarcastically.

Maria thought for a moment. "We have to start somewhere," she said to Al. "Let's go to the other trails."

As Al and Maria walked along the sandy bed that led to the border, thick clouds were tumbling into a line along the horizon, as if waiting for something to happen. The heat beat down on them relentlessly. Maria tried to breathe through her mouth. The stench of human excrement in the air was overwhelming. Now Maria could see the barbed wire fence that marked the border. On the other side of the fence, a packed dirt road ran parallel to *la linea* as far into the distance as she could see.

The fence had been cut in several places, leaving openings large enough to climb through. Ripped knapsacks, blankets, odd athletic shoes and huaraches, plastic bottles, even a pair of pliers lay tossed around on the ground near the openings in the fence.

"When people are running, they toss everything," Al said. "They don't have time to think about what they might need later. They just want to get away from the patrol agents. They don't want to be sent back."

"The pliers?"

"To pull out cactus spines," Al said. "In case you fall. Or get shoved."

Someone was walking up behind them. Maria turned around. A tall man in jeans, cowboy boots, and a black cowboy hat was coming towards them. He had a rifle in his hand.

"Ciudad Nueva PD," she said holding out her ID as the man came closer.

"Border Patrol," the man said looking back and forth from Al to Maria, keeping a firm grip on his rifle.

She was startled. "Border Patrol?" she said.

"Informal Border Control," the man said. He studied her ID before he put down his rifle. "John Higgins," he said, holding out his hand. "I help Border Patrol by keeping an eye on things around here."

Higgins had gray hair combed straight back, sideburns, and a full mustache that covered his upper lip. There were large bags under his dark eyes.

"Detective Al Diaz," Al said, shaking hands with Higgins. Maria didn't move. "Detective Maria Chavez," Al added, nodding in Maria's direction.

As he spoke, Al sent her a silent warning with his eyes. She understood what he was saying. He was telling her to keep on track. But it grated on her, the thought of Higgins on the hunt for illegal immigrants.

"I know who you are," Higgins said.

Maria looked at Higgins skeptically. "You help Border Patrol?" she said.

"There're looking at a new law in the state next door," Higgins said with undisguised satisfaction. "First good response of government in a long time. Local law enforcement can ask for papers. But even here I can make a citizen's arrest if I think it's necessary. I have the right to protect my property.

"You city folk are still fussing around, but here in the borderlands, we know that the law is long overdue. Sooner or later you're going to have to enforce it too, Detective Chavez." Higgins said her name with a sharp drawl that twisted her name into something almost unrecognizable. "Did I say your name right, by the way?"

Maria bit back a sharp retort.

"As I was saying, Detective Chavez," Higgins began again. "This is a long border, and there are a lot of trails that come right through my back yard. That means hundreds of illegal aliens every night. They cut my fences, leave their trash all over the place, kill my chickens, turn on the water faucets to the cattle tanks and never bother to turn the water off. They're animals with no respect for other people's property."

Maria stared at him without saying anything.

"What's the matter, Detective? You don't think I belong here?" Higgins said, staring back at Maria with hard, suspicious eyes."My family has been here as long as yours has. And we paid for our land."

"We have a US Border Patrol," Maria said calmly. "They wear uniforms. So does local law enforcement."

"I won't argue with you there," Higgins said. "We do have an official Border Patrol and official law enforcement. They do a good job. But the border with Mexico is 2000 miles long, and only a small part of that border is secure. The rest of it is open and available to any illegal who decides to sneak into our country."

"I expect Border Patrol can handle the job," she told him.

"You expect wrong," Higgins snapped back at her. "You think it's a straightforward operation for Border Patrol to track down the *pollero* and his *pollos*? The chicken hawk and his chickens?" Higgins' face was bright red. "You have any idea the kind of money smugglers can spend these days? What kind of equipment they have? Prepaid cell phones, global positioning systems, two-way radios, infrared night-vision goggles. They have everything they need to sneak in."

"I don't know about the smugglers," Maria said. "But I know that most of the migrants come for jobs. And I know there's a lot of business in this country that couldn't function without illegal workers."

"The illegals bring drugs," Higgins said. "They bring terrorists. And they have plans."

Maria kept a neutral expression on her face. "Plans?"

"Think you're so smart, Detective?" Higgins shot back. "Think you know everything? Then let me tell you something about the reoccupation of these United States."

Maria looked over at Al. "We have to go," she said. "We have work to do."

"You don't know what I'm talking about here, do you?" Higgins said, baiting Maria.

"We don't have time," she said, turning away from him.

"You mean you won't take the time," Higgins said.

"We can make some time," Al said. "Go ahead, Mr. Higgins."

Maria turned around, glaring at Al.

"You can write me off," Higgins said looking at Maria. "But it won't change what's happening, Miss Detective. The fact is, illegal immigrants are making plans to combine Arizona, New Mexico, Texas, and California, with the northern part of Mexico. You know why? Because when there are more of them than there are of us, they think they can form a new country, a Hispanic country."

Maria was finding it hard to contain her anger. "Higgins, do you really think day laborers running for their lives across the border have anything like that in mind?! That's just propaganda, and you know it."

"You think you know everything," Higgins said in a cutting voice. "Listen to me, Chavez, I'm telling you, there's a movement out there. They want to create a new state, a Chicano homeland. The Aztlan Nation." Higgins said the last words very slowly and loudly. "The Aztlan Nation," he repeated. He glared at Maria. "Over my dead body."

"We can always learn something, Mr. Higgins," Al said in a neutral voice.

"I appreciate that, Detective Diaz," Higgins said. "But I believe your partner has a few things to learn about life in the borderlands. Anything can happen out here."

He turned to leave, tipping his hat. "I'll be on my way now," he said. He started walking back down the road, his rifle held firmly in his hand. "Good day, everyone."

"Where is he going?" Maria asked.

"Back to his taxi," Al replied.

"To his taxi?!" She looked at Al in surprise.

"It's his car, Maria. It's his land. He can park the car wherever he wants to on his land."

"He's waiting for people to come," she said, unable to contain her contempt. "He's waiting to trap them."

"He's not breaking any law at the moment," Al said, tensely rubbing his scarred hand on his pant leg. "We're the ones who are trespassing on his land. He could have made a point about that, and he didn't. We're out of our jurisdiction, remember. Let's leave it at that and get going. You said it. We've got work to do."

53

SUNDAY
The Smuggling Trails
Lastup

MARIA AND AL SLOWLY MADE THEIR WAY BACK to the car under a white hot sun. They found several brush outs where the walkers had used branches to sweep the sand clean of footprints, but no sign of Luis or the boy. There was no one else anywhere in sight either.

"Too many people around here know Gomez-Gil," Maria said in a tired voice. "They're afraid. Maybe Luis will find us at the funeral." She didn't sound hopeful.

Al nodded. He had been unusually quiet on the trails. She didn't know why. He wouldn't talk to her. Wouldn't explain. Answered all her questions with a shrug. Whatever it was that had led him to open up to her earlier that morning had long since disappeared.

When they reached the car, Al took off in a hurry. Maria looked out the window at the empty plastic bottles scattered everywhere. Luis and Carlito could be around there somewhere, walking under the burning sun without water, just like the old walkers across the desert.

"Poor Ramón," she thought. "How he loved the idea of exploring. He loved those old postcards too." She gave a start. The thought sent a bolt of electricity down her arm. "Al! I know where Carlito is!" she said. She could scarcely catch her breath. "I know it, I'm sure. He's gone to the Church of Santa Teresa, to the Lady in Blue."

Al blanched and slowed down. He looked past her, his eyes flat, as if he had pulled into himself, waiting for her to finish talking.

"Al! We need to go to Santa Teresa right away."

This time when he looked at her, his eyes were clear. "We agreed you would meet Joe at the station, that you would go with him to the funeral from there."

"There isn't time. We need to go now. Carlito is waiting for us. We have to get there before Gil."

"OK, Maria," Al said finally "I'll try to get you there. But it won't be easy, you know that. Let me check our tires. We'll have to go the back way."

She was scarcely listening. She couldn't wait to call Joe. She picked up her cell. When he answered, she said, "Carlito is in the Church of Santa Teresa, I'm sure of it." Before she could say anything else, Al reached through the window and smacked the cell phone out of her hand, quickly closing off the transmission.

"Christ, Maria, what have you done?" Al said. The color had drained from his face, and the flickers of fear were back in his eyes.

She stared at him, still shocked by his reaction. "You don't trust Joe?"

"I don't trust phones," he said. "Christ, now we're in for it." He jumped back into the car and gunned the engine. They bounded down the rutted washboard road so fast she had to hold onto the door handle to keep from being thrown around in the front seat.

"It's a dirt road, and bumpy, but at least it skirts the town," he said. "And there are trees. Makes it hard for the spotters to get a clear view of the road. Gives us more of a chance to avoid meeting up with Gil's men." He paused. "They'll try to slow us down, Maria, you understand that, right?"

"Gil would take a chance on messing around with law enforcement?"

"They have to get to Carlito before we do," Al said. "Gil's men have probably been following us since we left Vereda. Once Gil understands we're on our way to Santa Teresa, he'll tell his men to get there ahead of us."

Maria thought about what Al was saying. It frightened her seeing him this way, nervous, off his stride. But two things were clear. He didn't want to meet up with Gil, and he wanted to get to the boy before Gil did. That's what she wanted too.

Al took a sharp right into a heavily wooded area, then stomped on the brakes. The dirt trail in front of them was full of rocks. It looked more like a hiker's path than a road. "I'll have to go slowly here," Al said as the car hiccuped along the trail. "The last thing we need is a flat tire."

The branches scratching at the car windows were covered with thick, hairy leaves that looked like they were made out of velvet. "Chinquapin oaks," Al said, reading her curiosity from the expression on her face. "Supposedly they can go a long time without water."

Again she thought about Carlito and Luis. What if they were in the desert without water? If only they were in Lastup instead of somewhere along a desert smuggling trail.

"Al, what would you have done if you were Luis?"

"I don't know. Why?"

"I was wondering whether Luis had an escape route already mapped out, even before Rosa was killed. His sister was illegal, and he worked at the projects, Snake Baby's territory. Not exactly a secure situation."

"I don't think so. Luis couldn't have expected anything like what happened. Rosa's murder and cops swarming all over the place. For some reason, he panicked. Not because of Ana. She stayed behind. So it had to be because of Carlito or maybe Rosa, although we still don't understand why. Luis didn't have time to contact someone or set things up. He just wanted to get away. At least that's how I see things."

"So you think he just took off, hoping for a break somewhere?" she asked. "Like the funerals in Lastup?"

"Exactly."

She looked troubled. "I still don't understand the hit on Rosa," she said.

Al rubbed his hand back and forth on his pant leg for a few minutes. He put his hand back on the steering wheel just as the rocky trail ended at a wider dirt road. Al turned left and stepped down on the gas. "This is a better road," he said. "Now we can move faster."

She didn't say anything.

"I haven't forgotten your question," he said. "I don't know who ordered the hit on Rosa. I don't know why. But I agree, Gil's still trying to figure out his next move. He must have a plan in place to shut down the operation at the Repository fast, but he's not sure yet. He doesn't want to give up a good thing if he doesn't have to. And...it's complicated with Angel in the middle of everything."

"Where do you think Gil is now?"

"I would guess Gil's been having a lot of intense phone conversations with Angel since yesterday, but for sure Gil is around here in Lastup somewhere. He wants to know. What did Carlito see? How? When? Gil's people are looking everywhere for the boy. They're keeping a close eye on us too. It won't take Gil long to track us down, but maybe going to the church this way will give us a little breathing room."

Maria looked in the rearview window. No one else was on the road. "You mean because of the cartel scouts? Because of the spotters?" she said.

Al nodded. "Almost anywhere there's elevation around here, you're likely to find cartel spotters with their scopes," he said. "They track movement back and forth across the border 24-7. They watch the main roads, the POE, the shifts coming in and out of the Border Patrol Station. They signal any opportunity they find for the smugglers to move without being detected."

"Such as?"

"Sometimes an opportunity means getting a truck through the POE at the right time, when a 'friendly' agent is on duty. Or it can be an unexpected opening for the smugglers to move the *mules*, the illegals carrying drugs across the border. Maybe the agents are busy with something else. Or maybe the cartel has decided to put someone in place with a machine gun until the *mules* get across.

"An opportunity can be anything. The point is, when the right moment comes, the smugglers move. And they move fast. It's not just guns and bribes anymore, Maria. The smugglers have drop phones, not to mention the internet. The new weapons of choice."

A solitary gasoline pump in the middle of an empty lot came into view on their right. Al slowed to a crawl. Maria looked back. A black pickup kicking dust and veering from side to side was coming up fast behind them. Al swung into the empty lot, stopped, waited by the gasoline pump. The pickup went gunning on past them.

Al pulled back out onto the road. By now they were riding up a hump of hard-packed dirt. As soon as they started downhill, they saw it, a red car parked on the side of the road. Two men stood next to it with rifles pointed in their direction. Maria recognized them immediately. One was the man with the handlebar mustache. The other was the kid in the baggy jeans. The same two men she had seen at the gas station.

Al downshifted and braked hard. The car squealed to a halt. He started to turn around, but by now the black pickup truck was directly behind them, blocking the road.

Maria felt paralyzed by the thought that now they would never get to Carlito in time. The image of Carlito in Gil's hands squeezed her throat like a vise.

The clouds overhead had thickened, moving more slowly now. Cloud shadows darkened the road. With the wind picking up, the tumbleweed began drifting in waves across the open land on both sides of the car. She felt strangely absent from what was happening, as if she were somewhere else watching a film.

The sun moved out from behind the clouds, clarifying the landscape. Maria looked back. Small sand hills stretched out behind her, some covered with cacti and yucca plants as tall as eight feet. A tall man she had never seen before was standing by the pickup truck. Questions pounded in her head. Were there other men behind the cacti and yucca plants? She looked over at Al. He looked back at her, sending her a wordless message. No way out.

A third man got out of the back seat of the red car. He was noticeably smaller than the other two. He was wearing a white-brimmed hat and pointed cowboy boots. The medallion around his neck was a leather circle on a cord. His gaze swept the road, taking in Al and the car. Then his eyes came to rest on Maria. He started walking towards her, his arms swinging freely at his sides, his hands visibly empty.

Maria opened the car door part way and stood behind it. She pulled out her gun. "Stay where you are," she yelled at the man walking toward her. She held the Glock firmly in both hands and pointed it at the man's chest.

Al got out of the car at the same time as Maria, his gun pointing at the two men who had remained standing in front of the red car. They hadn't moved. With his hand on the trigger of his gun, he yelled at the man approaching Maria, "You heard her. Stop where you are. Now!"

The man stopped short in his tracks, a few feet away from Maria, and cut his eyes at her. "You won't need that," he said to Maria, looking at her weapon. "You must be Detective Chavez." He held out his hand. "My name is Gil Gomez-Gil."

54

SUNDAY
On The Road To Lastup

"YOU MUST BE DETECTIVE CHAVEZ," Gomez-Gil said again. "I understand you're looking for a boy." His words sliced the air. He had her full attention now.

She stared back at him, a short, stocky man with a thick neck and protruding forehead. His deep set eyes, flaring nostrils, and wide cheekbones had carved a permanent expression of anger and surprise on his face. There were deep folds in his skin. He seemed reptilian, ageless.

"As anyone in Lastup will attest, Detective Chavez, I'm a law-abiding citizen of this town," Gomez-Gil began. "But you should know, John Higgins isn't the only one around here who protects his assets." Gil's eyes narrowed. "We address anything that threatens our interests. The information from your phone call has been invaluable. My men are already on their way to Santa Teresa."

"Maria, behind you!" Al cried out, his eyes focused on something in back of her. Maria heard the unmistakable sound of a shotgun being racked behind her. She froze. So did Al. The message was clear. The man from the pickup truck had a shotgun pointed at her back. If Al made any move to help her, she would go down.

Gomez-Gil was sneering at her, his eyes blank and cold. "Put your gun down, Detective Chavez. You're the one who's covered now. Put your gun down or he'll fire."

Maria ignored him and kept the Glock pointing steadily at Gil's chest. She remembered Cali's warning. "Don't let the old scars take you down. Be ready for the battle when it comes."

Lowering her gun was not an option. The only negotiating she was going to do would be over the barrel of her gun.

"Your gun is useless, Detective," Gil went on. "Even if you kill me, my men will get you and Al. And then we'll take out the boy. Is that what you want?"

Maria remained silent.

"No? Then listen. You're heading to Lastup, correct? You want a ride? We can stick together like best friends!" He burst out laughing.

Her heart racing, Maria tried to think through her options. No matter what Al did, whether he went after Gil's men by the red car or the man with the shotgun, Maria would die. That much was certain. Al might have a chance if he was lucky, but she knew he would never try to save himself at her expense. Worse, with the shotgun pointed at her back, Al was also helpless to protect himself.

231

She felt a sharp stab of pain but quickly put it aside. There was no time for fear or guilt. She would need all her strength. Impassively she held Gil's eyes without flinching.

He stared at Maria, evaluating. Then he shook his head. "I should shoot you right now," he said in a voice filled with hatred. "You hurt my boy, Snake Baby. But you can be useful to us for a while longer, Detective. Carlito will come to you sooner or later. And when he does, we'll be waiting for him. But make no mistake, today is only a temporary reprieve. You're going to be looking over your shoulder for the rest of your short life."

"There is one more thing I need to do before we go," Gomez-Gil continued, as if they were having a casual conversation about the weather. "We consider betrayal the greatest of sins. We punish it accordingly. And your friend over there, Al, he doesn't play by the rules. That's not acceptable."

"I didn't know Snake Baby was in the yellow house," Al said defiantly. "We were working on something else."

Gil's gaze shifted over to Al. "It doesn't matter. You gave them the yellow house. You gave them Snake Baby. I warned you, *Clavito*. Don't ever get in my way. You broke the bargain. Now you'll pay the price."

Al looked from Gomez-Gil to Maria, and then to the man behind her with the shotgun. There was no expression on his face, but she could feel his desperation. For a few moments, no one said anything. The silence was excruciating.

Al had the strange sensation that he was back in high school, waiting to walk over to Gil's car, knowing there was no escape. Something seemed to go out of him. He shuddered and dropped his gun on the ground. Then his face closed down.

As if they'd picked up the barely audible click of a starting gate, the two men by the car started moving towards Al. Before they could reach him, Al lunged forward and grabbed the man with the mustache around the throat. Furiously he wrestled the man to the ground, using his fists to smash against the man's face and dig into his stomach. The kid in the baggy jeans had a thin smile on his face as he watched them roll back and forth on the ground.

When the smaller man went limp, Al struggled to his feet. That gave the kid the chance he'd been waiting for. He aimed a vicious kick at Al's back. Al went down like he'd been shot. As soon as he hit the ground, he curled up into a ball, but by now the first man was on his feet again. Slowly, methodically, the two men began kicking. With each blow, Al cried out in pain.

Gil was enjoying himself. "Are you having fun too?" he said to Maria, looking at her closely. By now he was standing next to her. The contempt in his eyes was obvious, for her apparent helplessness, for the visible suffering on her face. The gun was still in her hand, but they both knew it was useless with the shotgun aimed at her back. Gil looked away from her and went back to watching the fight.

The sound of sirens in the distance cut through the air. The men stopped kicking. Al lay motionless on the ground.

"They're coming, boss," one of the men said to Gil. "You want us to slash her before we leave?"

Maria felt Gil's eyes look through her. He shook his head. "No need," he said. "She's already marked. My sign is on her." He followed the scar on her forehead with his finger nail.

Maria ignored him and held her ground. Gil hesitated. Then he decided. "She's already marked," he said again. "Let's go. I'll take care of her later."

The sound of the sirens grew louder. "Don't try anything, Detective," Gil said as he walked over to his car. "See you in Lastup." He was still laughing as they drove away.

232

Maria stood in place until the car and the pickup truck were out of sight. Then she ran over to Al. She bent down beside him. His eyes were swollen shut, and his hair was matted thick with blood.

She stood up and took out her cell phone. "Joe, we've got a situation here," she said. "Hurry!" She felt a hand curl tightly around her ankle.

"Al, what the hell are you doing?" she said, struggling to free herself, but his curved hand gripped her leg like pliers. She looked down at him. There were flies buzzing around his head. His mouth was moving, and it sounded like he was saying, "Don't call 911," but she couldn't be sure.

She bent down next to his face. The gold flecks in his eyes were swimming in pools of tears. "What is it, Al?" she said. "What?" He was too weak to answer, but as she looked into his eyes, she felt an old pain ripping through her chest, pulling her backwards in time. The buzzing of the flies grew louder.

55

SUNDAY AFTERNOON
Church of Santa Teresa

MARIA STOOD NEXT TO AL waiting for Joe to arrive. The small group of trees on her left seemed to expand into a misty cluster of dark wood. Only the top branches were light. A crow flew by so low, she thought she could see its feathers white under the sun.

She stared at the clouds filling the sky. Images of Carlito filled her mind. She saw him standing in an unfamiliar room, holding out his hand to her just before fading away. She saw him in a bright blue sky hung with stars, flying freely with his arms stretched out, his white shirt open, the sleeves billowing out like wings. When the walls of the sky began to crumble, she started running towards him, calling out his name. She wanted to warn him, to shield him from what was coming. But before she could reach him, the sky collapsed, and Carlito disappeared beneath the rubble of broken sky.

She had never wanted anything so much. "I have to find Carlito before Gil does," she kept saying to herself over and over again like a prayer. The thought of Gil's cold eyes and cruel hands on that boy was unbearable.

Joe had told her over the phone that several Border Patrol Agents were already on their way to Santa Teresa. 'Don't worry," he'd insisted. "They can handle Gil's men."

By now the sun was buried under a cover of thick clouds.

"They really hurt Al," Maria told Joe when he drove up a few minutes later. "But he doesn't want us to call the local ambulance."

"A friend of mine, a paramedic, will be here in a few minutes," Joe reassured her. "He's not a doctor, but at least we can trust him. He can take care of Al."

"I'm going ahead to the church by myself," Maria said. "As long as I know Al will be OK."

"Take my car," Joe said, for once not giving her any argument. "I'll be there soon."

Maria bent down to look at Al. His eyes were closed and his breathing was ragged. "He'll need some care," the paramedic told her when he arrived a few minutes later. "But don't worry. I'll bring him to my clinic. He'll be safe."

It took Maria less than half an hour to get to the little town of Lastup. The once bright afternoon had turned dark. Maria parked the car on a side street off of Plaza Santa Teresa and looked around.

The entire right side of the Plaza was formed by the colonial mission church of Santa Teresa. The church had been constructed by the Franciscans in 1790. The pure simplicity of its architecture and the loveliness of its plain facade and single bell tower still attracted tourists.

The native village surrounding the church had grown into the sprawling town of Lastup, but the church and surrounding square had remained at the center of town life. People came to celebrate the mass, but also to congregate in the square, especially in the late afternoon. Even today, in spite of the threatening sky, the square was full of people.

There were shops selling everything from clothes to colorful souvenirs and postcards. Most of the activity swirled around the street carts and vendors that lined the covered sidewalks around the church.

Before Maria got out of the car, her mind turned to Al, bruised and bleeding on the ground, Gil's men dogging her every step, the feeling of Gil's finger on her forehead, and most of all his words, "I've put my mark on you."

What did he mean by that? She'd never even met him before. All she knew was that his words had set off an old tape in her head, weighing her down with fear and guilt. "*Mea culpa, mea culpa, mea maxima culpa*, my fault, my fault, my most grievous fault."

It was time to get going. Carlito's life was in her hands. With a great effort, she pushed all other thoughts aside. She would deal with them later. She summoned up the energy she would need to search for Carlito and opened the car door. She would go into the church first and then to the cemetery.

Earlier that morning, Joe had explained that most of the activity in Plaza Santa Teresa took place in the cemetery behind the church. There were always gravestones to be swept, fresh flowers to be laid with a prayer at the resting place of the departed, and candles to light. And always, there were always new graves. According to Joe, mourners filed into the cemetery on a daily basis. "Death is a big part of everything that happens around here," he told her. "The church bells are never silent for long in Lastup."

Maria took a deep breath. She looked around the square one more time. Then she walked over to the church. It took a few minutes for her eyes to adjust to the semidarkness inside. When she could see clearly, she felt her heart constrict. The chapel where the statue of the Lady in Blue should have been standing was empty.

Careful not to let her feelings show, Maria glanced casually around the entire sanctuary. There were a few people in the church, but they looked like tourists. She didn't see anyone that looked like he could be one of Gil's men, but it was hard to know for sure.

She headed back outside and walked along the side of the church where a long row of women were sitting under the portico, their wares spread out on blankets in front of them. In spite of the intense heat trapped under the clouds that covered the sky, most of the women wore dark headscarves and shawls.

There were candles and incense burners for sale as well as mounds of flowers piled up on the blankets. Some of the flowers were in tall tin cans that looked like they had once held beans or tomatoes. The labels had been removed and the cans filled with water. Other cans were painted a deep blue.

A short flight of steps led from the back of the church up to the cemetery where the Alvarez family would be buried later that afternoon. Under an increasingly dark sky, Maria climbed the narrow steps into the graveyard.

In front of her the cemetery stretched upwards into a sparsely wooded area at the top of a hill. The whole cemetery looked congested and worn out. There were a few marble headstones, but mostly there were rectangular cement blocks, sometimes as many as four or five laid one on top of the other. Most of the tombs were dark with dirt and candle drippings, hardened into thick, gray-black deposits of old wax. Everywhere she looked, there were vases of flowers and tall white candles that flickered and flamed, sending thin wisps of gray smoke to dissolve into an already gray afternoon. Incense burners filled the air with the scent of copal.

The figure of a man standing by the benches caught her attention. He was waiting for her.

"Cali?" she said tentatively as she came up to him.

He gave her a broad smile.

His solid, dignified presence, in such contrast to the gray confusion of the cemetery, reassured her. "Do you know how Al is?"

"Al's at the clinic of Joe's friend. He seems to be OK, but he needs X-rays and some lab work. He should stay at the clinic overnight. We've posted a BPA there just to be sure Gil doesn't try anything more with Al. You never know with a son of a bitch like Gil."

"Good," she said. "I'm glad Al's safe."

"You held your own with Gil," Cali said.

Maria could feel herself flushing. "That's what we do," she said. "That's my job."

"You went well beyond that," Cali said. "In my village, we used to say that a man like Gil has the evil eye. People are afraid of his powers. But according to Al, you didn't let him see your fear. That probably saved your life. And Al's." Cali looked at her with respect.

For a moment Maria had to turn away. Words like that from Cali. He didn't say things like that very often. She didn't know why Cali was acting more like himself again, but whatever the reason, she was relieved.

"What does it mean for me, that Gil confronted me that way today?"

"I don't know. Joe is convinced that right now, the only thing Gomez-Gil wants is the boy. You're a secondary interest unless you get in the way. But no doubt about it, Gomez-Gil isn't used to people standing up to him. You shot Snake Baby. Gil's a prideful man. He may well decide to come after you, simply to make a point."

"And?" she said unhappily.

"And Dan has already made arrangements to post officers at your house."

"I don't want that," she said.

"I know," Cali said. He looked at her sympathetically. "You'll have to talk to him when we get back to Vereda."

She was silent, considering.

"What are your plans?" he said.

"I have one," she said in a low voice. She looked around. No one was within hearing distance. "I have a plan, Cali, but I need your help."

He nodded.

"Inside the church, in the first chapel, there should be a statue of the Lady in Blue. I looked into the church briefly before coming back here, and the chapel was empty. I think Carlito will be looking for the Lady in Blue. Can you find out where they store pieces of statuary in this church, and can you do that without anyone knowing? I can't do anything without Gil's men watching me like a hawk."

"No problem," Cali said.

I'll go to the funeral mass, but at a certain point, I'll slip out and go to the place where they've stored the Lady in Blue. That is if you can find it and let me know where it is. And if you can distract Gil's men if any of them come after me...."

"Sounds like a good plan, Maria. Joe should be here soon. He'll be in the church during the ceremony along with me and several others from our unit. There are already several undercover Border Patrol Agents in the square, going from store to store, mixing in with the crowd. We're looking for the boy with everything we've got."

"About the funeral mass," she said after a minute. "Even if you haven't been able to locate the Lady in Blue by then, I'm planning to leave before the end of the service. I want to be in the cemetery before they bring out the coffins."

"Agreed. We'll cover you."

She nodded. "But not too close. If Luis is anywhere around here, and he sees three of us approaching, he may lose his nerve."

"I know," Cali said. "Just don't take off anywhere so fast we can't stay with you."

She nodded again.

"Something's already going on in the back of the cemetery." She pointed up the hill. "I want to check it out. The Alvarez procession won't be going into the church for another half hour or so. See you there?"

Cali nodded. "We'll be around if you need us."

Maria began to make her way through the candles and flowers that took up every square inch of ground in the graveyard. In the far distance, she could hear the voices of children calling out to each other, the faint bumping sounds of a ball against the cement. She passed an old man sweeping off a gravestone with a broom he'd put together from old flowers. He nodded solemnly in her direction.

When she got up close to the woods in the back, she looked around. For some reason, the cemetery was now mostly empty. Only here at the far end of the cemetery were there still mourners. Three women, as still and silent as shadows, were standing in front of a cement tomb. The tall, white candles surrounding it were all lit. One of the women had her head bowed and was murmuring a prayer.

Off to the right there was a large opening in the ground. Three caskets could fit in there easily, Maria thought to herself. She walked over and looked for a marker of some kind. Nothing was there, but she was convinced. This is where the Alvarez family would be buried.

A brown dog with a white muzzle and white paws lay stretched out on top of a nearby tomb, staring straight ahead into the distance. That too seemed to be a new grave, but as far as she could see, there were no mourners. Only the dog.

Maria walked over to the three women, keeping a respectful distance from them. Now that she was closer, she could see that one of the women was very old. Her face was a mass of wrinkles. One of the other women looked to be in her forties. The third woman was young. A family, Maria decided. Grandmother, daughter, granddaughter.

She waited until the young woman glanced over at her. "Excuse me," Maria said, holding out her ID. "I'm looking for a six-year-old boy, Carlito Fuentes. He's probably traveling with a man, Luis Santiago. Have you seen either of them?"

The young woman shook her head. Maria tried again. "Have you seen any children around here?" she asked. "Children looking as if they were lost? Maybe sleeping in the cemetery? There's no trouble," she added quickly.

"Grandmother," the youngest one said in Indian dialect to the old woman. "The detective is looking for a lost boy."

The older woman studied Maria silently.

"We can't help you," the youngest one said to Maria. She pulled at her grandmother's arm. "Grandmother, we should go."

"Wait," the old woman said. She shook off the younger woman's grasp and turned to Maria. "There is a boy," she said. "They say he sleeps in the back of the church somewhere. He is *loco*, not right in the head. But no one bothers him, and he doesn't hurt anyone. You should leave him alone." Then she turned to the young woman. "Now, granddaughter," she said. "Now we can go."

The women filed away without looking back. For a few more minutes, Maria stayed where she was. Then she decided she might as well go back to the church. There wasn't much more she could do in the cemetery.

As she walked towards the church, the voice of a child drifted towards her from behind one of the tall marble tombs on her right. The voice was singing over and over again, *La vida baja por el dren, como tierra en el fregadero.* "Life goes down the drain, like dirt in the sink." Maria looked hard in the direction of the voice. By now the cemetery was deep in blue shadows. There was a stir of movement. A boy in a white shirt stepped out from behind the tombs to look at her, then quickly disappeared again.

"Who's there?" she called to the boy. "Come out where I can see you."

The voice stopped singing, and a boy slowly moved out from behind the tombs. He was wearing a long, ripped T-shirt and shorts, and he was as thin as the starving dogs that haunted the outskirts of the town. He stared at her vacantly. In the flickering candlelight, he seemed more like a lost soul than a real child. He looked nothing like Carlito. It was all she could do not to let her disappointment show.

"Here," she said, holding out some money to the boy. He came up just close enough to reach out and take the money into his hand. Then he moved back into the shadows.

The church bell was ringing. It was time for the funeral mass.

As Maria headed towards the church, she could hear the boy singing again somewhere behind her, "*La vida baja por el dren, como tierra en el fregadero.*" The smell of candles and incense in the dark heat of the late afternoon began to close in around her. She couldn't wait to get out of the cemetery and into the fresher air of the church square.

She got around to the front of the church just in time to see the funeral procession come through the square. People emerged from the shops, strange, remote faces turned curiously towards the church. Soon a large group of spectators had gathered in the square to watch the procession. Even where death is common, three coffins were a spectacle, especially if one was the coffin of a child.

Maria stood by the front entrance, scanning everyone in the square. She couldn't see Carlito or Luis anywhere, but she quickly recognized Gil's men marching in the front of the procession. There were also two men wearing hats with the initials AS on the front. For *Aeropuerto Sureños* she thought immediately. The men must be pilots.

Charlie Medrano, looking smaller than ever, was walking next to Ana Fuentes. Both were surrounded by protective BP Agents. They were positioned just in back of the priest, an altar boy, and an older couple she didn't recognize, probably Juan's distant relatives in Lastup.

As soon as the small white coffin vanished into the vaulting darkness of the church, Maria went inside. At first she stood near the door to study the people sitting in the church. She didn't expect to see Felix or Gil. They could hardly show themselves at the church with Border Patrol Agents and local law enforcement looking for them everywhere. But there were three men she'd never seen before, darkly still and silent, standing in the back, scanning the people seated in front of them. Gil's men, she was sure of it.

Cali was standing on the other side of the church. Maria stepped outside and took out her cell phone. "We saw them," Cali said. "You're covered. Wait for me by the door."

When he came up to her, he spoke softly into her ear. "The storage areas are all in the back of the church. We went through them, but there was no sign of the Lady in Blue."

Maria nodded. Cali went back to his position midway towards the front of the church. Joe had positioned himself near the front. The three caskets had been placed before the altar with burning candles surrounding them on all sides. It was time to remember the Alvarez family. Maria took a seat in the back row and joined with the rest of the worshippers in the requiem mass.

Three times after every lengthy prayer from the priest, the congregation responded, praying,

"Hail Mary, full of grace, *Dios te salve, María, llena eres de gracia, el Señor es contigo.*

Bendita tú eres entre todas las mujeres, y bendito es el fruto de tu vientre, Jesús.

Santa María, Madre de Dios, ruega por nosotros, pecadores, ahora y en la hora de nuestra muerte. Amen."

When the mass was almost over, Maria got to her feet and made her way to the door. Before she went outside, she looked back. The priest had begun to sprinkle the coffins with holy water.

She walked quickly around the church towards the back. As she passed the line of vendors sitting along the wall, one of the women, her face almost entirely hidden by her headscarf, motioned with her hand in Maria's direction. Maria went up to her and picked up one of the candles spread on the blanket spread out in front of her. "How much is this?" she asked.

The woman opened up her scarf. It was the old woman from the cemetery. Her eyes were like tiny black beads in a mass of wrinkles.

"Come here, daughter," the woman said to Maria quietly.

Maria bent down to listen.

"You said you were looking for a child?"

Maria nodded.

"Someone is hiding inside the church. In the back. "

Maria nodded. She could hear footsteps approaching.

"How much is the candle, Grandmother?" she asked quickly.

"It is for you, daughter," the old woman said. "No charge."

"*Gracias, Abuela,*" Maria said. She straightened up. Two men were standing there, studying the candles. As she walked away, she could feel them watching her with suspicious eyes.

She bumped into Cali as she went around the corner. "I'm going to check out the back part of the church," she said quietly.

"We already did that," Cali said. "Just a few minutes ago."

"I know, but I want to give those rooms another look."

"Be careful, Maria. We'll be close behind you."

She headed towards the back of the church. The thick clouds piling up overhead had blanketed the sun. Candles winked in the cemetery off to her right. The back wall of the church was indistinct and fuzzy in the darkness. She was almost past the door before she saw it. She pulled sharply at the handle and slipped inside.

The door quietly clicked shut. Maria stood there motionless, her chest tight. Moments later, she heard the men walk by. Only when their footsteps retreated into the distance, did she let out her breath and look around. She was standing in what seemed to be a long corridor running along the back of the church.

Dim lamps hanging overhead from the wooden ceiling sent a pale light into the hallway. Maria moved down the corridor as quietly as she could. She passed one door on her left and then another. At the end of the corridor, there was an arch. She passed under the arch to find herself in front of a brick wall with swinging double doors in the center.

She turned around to stare into the long, dark corridor behind her. It was empty. No movement of any kind. Absolute silence. She was alone. Now she had to decide. If Carlito and Luis were hiding in one of the rooms, and they heard her coming, would they disappear again? She had to choose carefully. The first door she opened could be her only chance.

She spoke softly into her cell phone. She had to risk it. "At the end of the corridor, through the double doors. I'm going in now."

56

SUNDAY
Church of Santa Teresa

MARIA PUSHED THE DOORS OPEN and stepped inside. She stood still, listening intently for anything that might signal the presence of someone else in the room. Nothing was moving. The room was silent and dark. Only faint leaks of light came through the low, shuttered window on the outside wall. Cautiously she edged towards the window and pulled open the shutters a few inches. Outside the cemetery was glowing with pinpoints of candlelight against the heavy gray afternoon sky.

She turned around to look more closely at the room. The pale light from the window revealed white plaster walls and a dark, square tile floor. She shivered involuntarily as she looked more closely at the walls. Strange, grotesque faces stared out at her from all directions. The walls were covered with masks. The floor space near the walls was filled with stacked paintings, life-sized statues, and other religious objects. Was the room a museum of some kind? Or simply storage for the objects used for traditional feast days and processions?

She scanned the room again, looking for some sign of Carlito and Luis. Nothing. No movement, no sound.

A large crucifix covered with painted drops of blood leaned haphazardly against the wall just beyond the window. She touched it lightly. The crucifix was plastic, not wood. This was no museum, she decided. And the room was crowded enough with stored religious objects to serve as a hiding place. At least for a small boy. She would have to go through the room carefully.

A group of life-sized figures standing motionless in the front of the room caught her attention. She would look there first.

She moved slowly towards the figures, looking closely at the objects on the wall. A mask of the Virgin Mary with black slits under her eyes looked out at her indifferently as she passed by. Hanging on the wall next to the Virgin Mary there was a mask of an Indian child wearing a feather headdress. The child's black eyes seemed to follow her as she passed by.

There was a niche in the wall near the masks. Inside the niche stood a half-life, half-death statue, a figure split down the middle. Half of the statue was a boy, the other half the skeleton of the boy. In the shadowy half-light of the room, the boy's grinning skull seemed to mock her fading hopes for Carlito.

Once she was close enough to the human-sized figures in the front of the room to see them more clearly, she recognized them immediately. Mary, Joseph, the shepherds, the Three Kings, they were the figures necessary for an elaborate life-sized Nativity scene. They must have been stored in the room to wait until Christmas.

Now, in the low light of the room, the figures seemed almost human. Was that why she kept feeling someone else was in the room? Again she listened intently. Nothing.

Light suddenly streamed in through the window. She looked up, startled. Outside the cloud cover was breaking up. The sun had come out again. She went up to the manger. A baby doll wrapped in swaddling clothes lay in the cradle still filled with dry hay. She looked over at the Three Kings holding gifts, silent and unmoving, their arms stretched stiffly out in front of them. Nothing there either.

As she turned to go back to the door, this time examining the other wall, she glanced over at the shepherds one more time. A shepherd boy with unwinking, jet black eyes looked straight back at her. She jumped. Carlito! Wordlessly she went up to him and put her arms around him. He was trembling, but he made no effort to get away. "Hold on, Carlito," she whispered. "We're going to get you out of here."

She spoke softly into her cell phone. "Cali, he's here. Hurry!"

She took the boy's hand and started for the door. "Come on, Carlito, hurry." But it was already too late. Shadowy shapes were coming into the room through the doors. Then a voice. "No noise. Get rid of her. Bring the boy. Hurry."

She pushed Carlito away as the man with the handlebar mustache lunged at her out of the shadows. She sidestepped and smacked the palm of her hand onto the bridge of his nose. She felt the shift of cartilage and heard a small dull pop. He wavered slightly. She'd caught him off guard, but she knew he was only momentarily stunned.

She followed up with a hard kick at his groin. He managed to shift his hips back quickly enough so that she only hit his inner thigh, but he was still off balance. As he slid back, his head came down just enough to expose the back of his skull. She came down with both fists on the back of his neck, simultaneously dropping her body weight through her fists onto his neck. Her timing was off, but it was enough. His body slammed down prone on the floor. If her first strike had not broken his nose, the impact of his face on the floor surely would have. He was out for the moment.

The kid in the baggy jeans was almost on her. He thrust at her with his knife, narrowly missing her neck. She dodged, kicked him hard. He screamed and fell back into one of the three kings. All three of the kings toppled, carrying the man with the handlebar mustache down to the ground with them. One of their crowns rolled noisily across the room.

She looked for Carlito. He was still standing against the wall, looking at her with large frightened eyes. Just as she reached out for him, she heard someone coming up behind her.

She turned. The kid was back on his feet, knife in hand, and he was closing in on her fast. There was a flash of metal. One of the shepherds was swinging at the kid with a key ring. There was the sound of metal smashing flesh and bone. The kid fell moaning to the floor, blood spurting out of his face. The shepherd grabbed Carlito's hand and started for the door, but now there were more men coming into the room.

"Get back here," she called out to Carlito as she drew her gun. Suddenly the sun disappeared behind the clouds, and the room went dark. All she could see were shadowy figures running everywhere. She heard Carlito crying somewhere behind her. She took aim at the figures coming towards her, but there were too many of them. She'd be lucky to get two shots off.

There was a loud crash at the door. Something large and fast had come into the room. Cali was moving through the room like an enormous club, smashing into Gil's men at full force, sending them flying through the air and crashing to the floor.

Then it was over. Joe had his knee on the Kid's back as he locked the cuffs into place. Cali was standing like a concrete watchtower over the men lying on the floor as uniforms poured into the room and began to cuff them one by one.

Carlito was crying hard. Maria sat down on the floor next to him and took him into her arms. "It's OK now, Carlito. Everything is going to be OK."

The shepherd with the key ring came up to them, grinning down at her from under his headscarf.

"Not bad, wouldn't you say, Detective Chavez?" Luis said.

"Not bad Luis," she told him. "Not bad at all."

57

SUNDAY
Church of Santa Teresa

MARIA STOOD IN FRONT OF THE SHUTTERED WINDOW. She pulled the shutters open and stared out at the cemetery. She could see the mourners from the Alvarez funeral in the back of the cemetery.

Joe walked over and stood next to her. "All set?" he said.

"I'm going back there," she told him.

She thought he would argue with her, but all he said was, "I'll go with you."

They left the storage room and started down the hallway. "What's happening with Danforth?" she asked.

"The raid on the school goes down late tonight," Joe said. "He doesn't want to wait until tomorrow. He'll call us when he knows the schedule. Until then we can stay at my place if you'd like."

"What about Al?"

"Al is on his way back to Vereda, at least as far as I know."

She looked stunned. "Do you know why?"

"He refused to stay at the clinic. Nothing Sam said could persuade him to stay."

"He must be worried about Gil. Even at the clinic."

"I don't know," Joe said.

She let it pass. "And Gil's men?"

"They're in jail, charged with assaulting a police officer. Supposedly they'll be held without bail. Let's hope it sticks."

Once they were outside the church, she could feel the late afternoon heat pressing down on them. The promise of rain had come and gone. She took the short flight of stairs up to the cemetery. Joe followed her.

From the top of the stairs, Maria scanned the dark cemetery in front of her.

"You want to find that boy," Joe said. "The one you saw before, the one who lives in the cemetery."

She turned around to look at him. His eyes had darkened, and he had a tired expression on his face. "Rescuing Carlito wasn't enough for you?" he said in a tight voice.

"You want to walk away and leave that boy here?" she said, defensively.

"And you want to rescue the world? Do you really think that will bring back your brother?

247

Make things right somehow?"

His words made her so angry, she almost slapped him.

He took her arm and held it. "Maria, we have to talk. Now."

She drew a sharp breath and moved away from him, but he kept his hand on her arm. "Let's sit down for a minute," he said. "It's important."

Reluctantly Maria went with him over to one of the benches near the entrance. They sat down. "What's your problem, Joe?" she said. Her face had gone tense.

"We found Carlito, didn't we?" Joe said looking at her steadily.

She nodded.

"Cali is bringing him back to Ciudad Nueva," Joe continued. "Luis too. Federal Witness Protection has been approved for all of them, including Ana. Al was hurt, but not so badly he couldn't drive himself home. Gil's men are in jail. Tonight we go into the Repository. We're going to bring Angel in, and with Carlito's testimony, there's a good chance we'll finally learn what happened to Ramón."

Maria stood up abruptly. "Joe, we don't have time to sit here and congratulate ourselves."

"Maria, sit down. I mean it." He was deadly serious.

She sat down again slowly. "What is your point?" she said in a cold voice.

"It's over," he said forcefully. "It's over. Why can't you accept that?"

She turned her eyes away from him, searching the cemetery for some sign of the boy.

"My job," she said. "And none of your goddamn business."

"Don't give me that bullshit, Maria. What's going on?" he repeated.

Maria kept staring straight ahead, looking for the boy. She caught a glimpse of him, a white shape crouching behind the tombstones off to the right. A sweet, thin voice rose up though the dusty air. The boy was singing again. This time the words seemed like echoes of memory. *Una camisita te voy a poner, el día de tu santo....* With a little shirt, I will dress you on your birthday...."

A chilling image. A sharp flash of pain and loneliness. Black insects began to swim through the filtered evening light falling on the gravestones. Her memory slammed shut. She shivered and bent over, holding her head in her hands.

Joe put his arm around her, unsure what to do next. After a while, Maria straightened up and looked at him. She was deathly pale. "What is it?" he said.

She hesitated. "I don't know," she said finally. "There are flashes, that's all, like unconnected pictures. And there's something about that song. I think my mother used to sing it to my brother, but I'm not sure. It's like following a thread somewhere. When it snaps, I don't know how to find it again."

"Try to remember," he urged her. "What do you see?"

The candlelight was making her dizzy, lightheaded.

Joe waited.

"I was with my brother in the desert," she said after a while, surprised to hear herself talking. It was like she was speaking through plastic, the words almost too thick to push their way out.

"Then I was crawling on the sand. I fell asleep. The next time I opened my eyes, a man was giving me water. My throat hurt. I tried to talk to him. 'My brother,' I told him. 'My brother.'

"But the man drove away. I remember hearing the car door slam. I left my brother there all alone, Joe. And he died."

Joe took her hand. "Maria, you were four years old. It's not your fault."

"Then why did he leave? Why didn't the man get my brother?"

"Maybe he didn't understand you."

"What do you mean?"

The boy in the cemetery was singing again. "There's one answer," Joe said.

She looked at him questioningly.

"Listen," Joe said. "The boy's singing in Spanish, isn't he? Maybe it's just that simple. Maybe the agent didn't understand you because he didn't understand Spanish. Or maybe what you were saying didn't make any sense. You were delirious, remember? You were dying. The agent had to make a choice, that's all."

"Not my fault then?"

"Maria, what the hell is wrong with you? Can't you see that's not the point?"

She shook her head.

"I'll tell you, what seems off to me," he said, trying to contain his frustration. "Why are you so quick to blame yourself?"

She was silent.

He felt as if he was reaching out to her across an endless distance. "Dammit, Maria, what about the men who left you there?" he said. "You talk like you somehow landed mysteriously in the desert, as if you dropped down there from outer space. But someone brought you there. A real person left your family there, a real person raped your mother, a real person killed your father. Why don't you blame them?! Why don't you blame the men who hurt your family?"

She tried to stand up.

"No you don't," Joe said, pulling her back down on the bench. "You don't get off that easy. Stop trying to save the world, Maria. That won't fix what happened. Make your peace with it."

She tried to make sense out of what he was saying, but in the smoky twilight everything around her seemed to expand into a brooding silence. There was a flash of something white. Now the boy was standing only a few feet away from them, seemingly absorbed in his own thoughts. The dog with the white muzzle and white paws that had been lying on the gravestone was sitting next to him. As Maria stared at the boy, the dog stood up stiffly and stretched. The boy put his arms around the dog's neck and hugged him.

Unexpectedly the image of the boy and the dog sent shock waves racing through her body. She felt the shiver of discovery. All this time she had been trying to rescue them, but she was the one trailing a broken leash, still trying to find her way back home.

The boy looked at Maria. "*Yo te perdonaria,* I would forgive you," he told her. Then he turned and started moving towards the woods at the back of the cemetery, the dog close behind him. She followed them with her eyes until they were swallowed up by the trees.

58 | SUNDAY
Joe's Ranchito

THEY LEFT THE CEMETERY and walked across the plaza to the car. Several street carts selling souvenirs were set up in the plaza. As they neared one of the carts, the man standing next to it seemed to recognize Joe. He looked at Joe and started to say something, then stopped and looked away.

"Pipé had his stand around here," Joe said, nodding in the direction of the cart. "His friends want to know what happened to him. But in Lastup, it's dangerous to ask questions."

Before she got into the car, Maria took a last look at the Church of Santa Teresa. The white bell towers glowed against a clear crimson sky. It was a warm evening. The clouds had passed. People were walking around the plaza much as they had been before the Alvarez funerals. Death in the midst of life. It was a familiar rhythm. Certainly no reason to stay home.

They drove out of Lastup and headed north towards Joe's ranchito. Joe called in. Danforth told them he was keeping the news of Carlito's rescue under wraps until he could set up the raid on the Repository. He would call when it was time for them to return to Vereda.

Maria kept thinking about what they would find when they went into the Repository. Would Angel be there? Working? Sleeping? The large heaps of black pilings and barren hills sliding monotonously past the window provided little distraction.

She caught sight of a long freight train in the distance, so far away its tiny colored cars moved along an invisible track. The train's destination was identified, its arrivals and departures scheduled. Instead her destination remained unknown. Her life had switched tracks somewhere in the past, leaving her to circle endlessly through a paper mache landscape like a toy train with a broken switch.

She leaned back against the headrest and closed her eyes. She thought about Joe's ranchito. She thought about the land around his home, the vaulting sky over miles and miles of silence stretching from his back yard into the distance. She thought about the dogs, Smith and Wesson, waiting for them at the gate. Smith would be running back and forth, panting, her tongue hanging out of her mouth. Wesson would be sitting at attention, listening.

"Thinking about home?" Joe said, interrupting her thoughts

"How did you know?" she said, startled.

"Trains have a way of doing that," he said. "Making you think about home, I mean."

She managed a small smile. "But I was thinking of your home," she said.

"I thought you might be," he said, smiling back.

Ahead of them, the mountains had carved the horizon into a jagged edge. Maria swallowed hard.

"You want to talk about those mountains?" Joe said, reading her mind again.

"I know a patrol agent found my family somewhere near those mountains."

Joe nodded.

"Do you ever go there?" she asked.

He looked over at her. "You want the truth, Maria?"

She nodded.

"The truth is, I can't even begin to tell you how many bodies have been found in those mountains. There are bandits everywhere. They rob illegals, and if they don't get what they want, they beat them up and leave them there. A lot of illegals don't make it after that. " He paused. "I'm sorry about your family, Maria."

She looked back at him. "Thanks, Joe." She knew he meant it. "What do you think happened to my family?" she said finally.

He was quiet.

"I'd like to know what you think," she said.

"From what I know, I think what happened to your family was unusual," Joe said slowly. "More like a deliberate assault than a robbery. There were at least two smugglers driving a pickup truck. Your father must have died almost immediately. His body was found near the place the truck was parked.

"Your mother must have searched until she found you. She went as far as she could with you and your brother. Gave you two all the water. When she died, you were on your own."

"But why? Why did they do that to us?"

"Sometimes evil just happens, Maria. No reason. Just opportunity."

They were coming up to a white Chevy Tahoe marked with the green insignia of the U.S. Border Patrol. The agent in the Tahoe was driving slowly along the shoulder of the road, his head hanging out the driver's side window, a flashlight in his left hand. He was staring down at a smooth drag running parallel to the road. Joe flashed his lights. The patrol agent straightened up and waved at them. They pulled around him and drove on.

"What's he doing?" she asked, trying to put the thoughts of her family behind her.

"He's on patrol," Joe said. "Sign cutting from his vehicle. He's driving slow so he can cut fast. If you have a smooth drag, you can get it cut faster, cover more area. When he's got his head out the window like that, we say he's 'looking at dirt.'"

Maria looked back at the Tahoe, then at Joe. "What you do out here, cutting sign, looking at dirt, that's not what we do in Vereda," she said.

"I don't know about that," Joe said. "A Border Patrol Agent gets to know his area of operation, the features of the terrain and the traffic patterns, just like a cop in Vereda gets to know the streets of the *barrio*. You're just working another kind of beat, that's all. The big difference out here is that when you're cutting sign, most of the time you're working alone."

"Why do you call it cutting sign?" she asked.

"Sign is anything we see that's not natural, anything out of place," Joe explained. "Sign can be something small and subtle, like a bent twig, a broken branch, stones or pebbles that look like they've been moved. Or sign can be something obvious, like footprints.

"A good cutter can tell a lot from the sign," Joe continued. "If he's tracking smugglers, he can tell how many people are in a group. The smaller the group, the more accurately he can read the sign. That's because large groups of illegals usually walk in single file to hide their numbers."

"And the drag?"

"Picture it this way," Joe said. "Four or five tires lying next to each other, yoked together by a heavy steel pipe or bar. A chain attached at each end of the bar is designed to loop over a trailer hitch ball so that the drag can be towed behind a patrol agent's vehicle. When you drag the tires that way, the bar in front helps to hold them down and keep them from bouncing around. That's how we get a smooth dragging surface.

"Like I said before, the idea is 'to drag slow and cut fast.' What I mean is, you pull the drag along slowly, creating a smooth surface that's as wide as the five tires. No one can jump over a drag that wide. You can't cross it without leaving some kind of a mark or sign. The cut is what you go looking for, some disruption in what was a smooth surface. We can make a drag any-where, but we try to make drags in the shoulder area where there's usually good cutting."

"Is that how the patrol agent found my family?"

Joe nodded.

"I'm ready to know more," she said after a few minutes.

"No problem," he said. "I like to tell you about what I do. But where your family's concerned, I can only guess at most of it."

"That's OK," she said. "I need to start somewhere."

Joe couldn't help smiling at her. "That's big," he said. "I think you're on your way."

She nodded.

"OK, one thing I know for sure," he said. "The patrol agent who found you was going back home after shift. He was off duty. He didn't have to do anything. But he saw vehicle tracks across the smooth surface of his drags in an area where normally there wasn't traffic of any kind. He wrote that in his notes."

Maria nodded.

"And the vehicle tracks were leading cross-country into the desert. So the agent would have asked himself, why is someone driving into the desert this way? Kids messing around? Joyrid-ing? That's a possibility.

"But my guess is, the agent was worried about smugglers, and he decided to follow up. And that's not unusual, by the way. Whether it's out of dedication or persistence, the fact is a lot of patrol agents won't go home until they've made their cuts. And if they find something, espe-cially if it looks like children or a family could be in trouble, they won't ignore what they've seen."

"So he wanted to know why the tracks were leading into the desert."

"The only reason why *coyotes* would drive into the desert when they could follow a road to a drop-off point is so that the people they have with them can't make it back to safety," Joe said reluctantly.

"So it wasn't an accident," she said.

He nodded. "The agent followed the vehicle sign until he saw where your family was forced out of the pickup truck, where the truck was parked before the smugglers drove away. He found your father's body. He found foot sign that told him there were still three people out there, two of them children.

"The desert is dangerous, especially for children. They dehydrate really fast. He knew you were in trouble. He called in for assistance. That's on the record too. But no one was available. So he set out to find you by himself."

"What else?"

"I don't know what the patrol agent saw that night, Maria. But I can tell you what I know from my own experience."

"Go on, Joe. I want to know."

"As soon as you begin to find things like discarded outer clothing, you know someone's in trouble. As you follow the sign, you begin to discover more discarded things like backpacks, shirts, pants. Do you want me to go on, Maria?"

She nodded again.

"Another indication of trouble is when sign doesn't go in a fairly straight direction. Groups of illegals usually pick a point on the horizon and march towards it for long periods of time to avoid getting off the trail and becoming lost. When the sign begins to wander sort of haphazardly, becoming more irregular, even circular, the more this is an indication of trouble."

He stopped talking.

"What else, Joe?"

"The footprints of children," he said after a minute.

She waited.

"Sign for children, smaller tracks or footprints, indicates that the adults are in trouble. Little kids are usually carried so they don't slow everyone else down. If kids are walking, it means the adults no longer have the strength to carry them."

Children stumbling across the desert at night. The image lay before her like a trap. The darkening sky seemed to widen dangerously in front of her. Then she heard the dogs barking. They were home.

Their lovemaking that night was solemn, almost chaste after the hungry coupling of the night before. They moved well together. She curved and fitted herself against his tall, lanky body. And Joe was a surprise, making love. He held nothing back.

She could love this man. But the way he loved her made her afraid. She felt vulnerable in the face of his passion. And he believed in things. She knew there was nothing to believe in. Maybe that divide was too large for any kind of a permanent crossing.

The phone was ringing. "Danforth wants us back in Vereda," Joe said. He got up to get dressed. She buried her head in his pillow and breathed in the scent of him. She didn't want to think about being without him.

Joe drove the car north along dark roads. She listened to distant sounds cracking the night while a cold, white moon sliced through the windshield.

59

MONDAY BEFORE DAWN
The Repository
Vereda

WHEN JOE DROVE INTO THE CENTER OF VEREDA, the stream of moonlight that had followed them on the dark roads north from Lastup disappeared into streetlights, head-lights, and flashing neon lights. The center of Vereda was an explosion of light. Everything on the street was illuminated, the thumping cars driving slowly back and forth, the woman lighting a cigarette in the doorway, the group of gangbangers standing on the corner.

Danforth's unit was meeting at the old church of Santa Maria on the outskirts of Vereda. Once the confusion of the central district was behind them, Maria directed Joe down a series of nar-row streets, dark and quiet.

"We're here," she said after a few minutes. They passed a line of squad cars parked along the street. Then two tall bell towers rose up in front of them, like silent sentinels standing guard over the walled parking lot of the church. The lot was empty except for the vans parked in the shadows near the trees. Joe pulled up next to the vans and turned off the engine. They had arrived.

The SWAT team stood together near the vans. Danforth's unit, together with the uniforms, stood in a smaller group a short distance away. Everyone in Danforth's unit was wearing dark shirts, dark pants, and standard-issue work boots. Most of the shirts were workshop freebies with things like Tac Op School written on the front. On Cali's shirt, there was a picture of a lawn-mower spitting bullets, the word YARDWORK written in large letters just below the lawnmower.

Maria and Joe walked over to their unit. Danforth was furious. "We're still waiting for the canine unit," he told them. "Goddamit, they went to the wrong church. If they don't get here by 5:00, we're going in without them. I have to talk to the SWAT unit. Joe, I want you to come with me."

Maria watched as Danforth and Joe went up to a tall man standing in the center of the group. Like the rest of the SWAT team, he was wearing blue battle uniform. The flak vests, helmets, and side arms were waiting for them inside the vans.

Cali came up to her. "How you doing?" he said, looking at her closely.

"I'm OK," she said. "Who's the guy talking with Danforth?"

"That's Vetrano," Cali said. "He's in charge of the SWAT team."

"I wonder what he wants with Joe."

Cali shrugged. He seemed tense and distracted. Probably because of the lost K-9 unit.

She remembered the brown dog. "Cali, did you happen to check with Animal Control?"

"The dog's still there, Maria. If you decide you want him."

Al was limping across the parking lot in their direction. As he came closer, she could see that his arms were covered with bruises and one of his eyes was black. The cigarette in his hand was mostly ashes.

"You get checked out at the hospital?" Maria asked as soon as Al joined them.

"Haven't had time yet," Al said. He tossed his cigarette onto the ground and stepped on it. Then he turned to Cali. "Carlito's with his mother?"

Cali nodded.

"How is she doing?"

"She's doing well," Cali said.

"Good. And you did good work too, Maria, finding the boy like that," Al said.

"Thanks, Al. I guess I got lucky."

Cali kept looking over at Danforth, as if he were waiting for something to happen.

"You were able to interview Carlito?" Al said to Cali after a long silence.

Without taking his eyes off Danforth, Cali said, "Carlito saw Angel rock the old man."

"So Carlito was in the Lav," Al said. "Just like Maria said."

Cali nodded at him.

"Why didn't Carlito tell Medrano what happened?" Al said.

"I don't know," Cali said. "We still have a lot of questions for Carlito and our friend, Angel."

"Such as?" Al said.

"Such as how did Angel get rid of the body, for one."

Al rubbed his hand back and forth on his pants. "Too bad Snake Baby got it before he could tell us anything," he said after a few moments.

"Snake Baby dead?! How?" Maria said in a shocked voice. "That's the first I've heard of it."

"The voice on the street is that Gil wanted to tie up loose ends," Al said.

"But Snake Baby would never give up Gil. He knew his life would be worthless if he did that," Maria said. She looked over at Cali. "Did you know?" she asked him. "Why didn't you tell me?"

"I was planning to talk to you," Cali said. "There hasn't been a lot of time."

She noticed Danforth looking over at them.

"Me?" Cali said pointing to himself.

Danforth nodded.

Cali left them to join Danforth and the SWAT team. Joe was still there talking with Vetrano.

In the parking lot, the darkness was fading but so was the moonlight. No sun yet either. In the faint light of dawn, Al seemed deflated. He started to pace back and forth, nervously studying Danforth and Cali, his discomfort palpable. Maria looked at him, puzzled. Something was wrong.

"How are you doing?" Maria asked.

His eyes flickered gold, softened. "I've felt better," he said. "No sleep though. That doesn't help."

Maria nodded. Gil's men had hurt him. Then the long drive back to Vereda. He had to be in a lot of pain.

Danforth was calling out to them. "Maria, Al, all of you, get over here. You too," he said to the uniforms. When they were in one large group, he said, "Here's an update on the briefing I gave you earlier.

"The K-9 unit is going to meet us at the entrance to the Repository when they get here. At the moment they're still on the road. That means we're going in without them. We can't wait any longer.

"Vetrano agrees there shouldn't be a problem with the initial entry. Surveillance has been up and functioning for several days now. We have access to the cameras that cover virtually every corner of the Repository, inside and out. From our perspective, the operation inside the Repository is essentially transparent. That should give us an edge.

"There are the usual delivery trucks parked at the rear entrance of the Repository. The drivers are already inside the building, along with some others who help with the unloading. We think there are five men in all plus Angel. Based on what we've seen this week, it looks like they unload on a regular basis, slow but steady, every other day. The operation's been foolproof up until now so we believe that no one will be expecting us, that the drivers will be as relaxed as they were two days ago. They have a designated guard while they're moving the stuff from the trucks into the Repository, but once they're inside, everyone unloads, including the guard.

"According to surveillance, they've just finished bringing the packages from the trucks onto the main floor. We believe that within the next five to ten minutes, they'll begin putting their packages inside the freight elevator that goes down to the restoration area of the basement. The five men from the trucks should be in the basement when we get there.

"There is a secondary access to the basement through a small rear entrance, to the left of the loading docks. We'll have men posted there in case any of the drivers attempt to escape that way.

"We don't know where Angel is, but we believe he's inside his office on the second floor. We saw him at the window of his office this morning. No one has seen him leave. Gomez-Gil hasn't come anywhere near the school, but then we didn't expect him to show up for a routine unloading operation. He never does.

"I want patrol cars visibly stationed at the front and back entrances of the industrial park. No one gets past them except the K-9 unit. If they ever arrive, that is," Danforth added with a furious expression on his face.

"My unit? We're going to help cover the exits." Danforth looked at his watch. "Vetrano's got the TAC brief. Then we're off. In exactly six minutes."

60

MONDAY BEFORE DAWN
The Repository

LESS THAN TWENTY MINUTES LATER, the Repository had been secured. The SWAT team was bringing the drivers and the other men outside, five in all. Al recognized them. "They're all part of Gil's organization," he told Danforth.

"Where's Angel?" Maria said.

"We couldn't find him," Vetrano told her.

She flinched involuntarily.

A dark blue van pulled up near the rear entrance and screeched to a halt. The K-9 unit had arrived.

Everyone who had been inside the Repository was now outside. Vetrano looked over at Danforth and nodded. "Our turn," Danforth said immediately. "Cali, I want you to take charge of the interviews here. The rest of you, take the goddamn place apart. I want the evidence. And I want Angel!"

Most of the team went with the canine unit into the basement. Danforth went up into the dusty silence of the second floor with Maria and Joe. They went straight into Angel's office. It was empty.

"No one's here," Maria said, looking around. Her voice was tight with frustration. "Vetrano was right. Angel isn't here."

Al stuck his head into the room. "The part of the basement under the stairs is stuffed with packages," he said. "There are secret compartments everywhere, under the ceiling panels, behind the wall boards, under the floor boards, behind the supplies on the shelves. It's a warehouse made to order."

"How big are the compartments?" Joe asked.

"Some of them could hold a man from what I've seen." Al said. "No doubt about it. Maybe the dogs can pick up Angel's trail." Then he disappeared.

Danforth's face was red, and he was perspiring heavily. "Goddamit, where is Angel?" he muttered looking around the room over and over again. "Maria, Joe, go on down to the basement. Angel must be down there somewhere. I'm going outside. Maybe Gil's men can tell us where Angel is."

Maria was searching the compartments in the basement with Joe when she heard someone yelling far away. She heard two shots.

She raced up the stairs with Joe just behind her. By the time they got into Angel's office, Angel was lying on his back, bleeding heavily from his head. A gun lay on the floor next to his hand.

Al was on his knees, bending over Angel. He was closing Angel's eyes.

"What are you doing?" Maria yelled at him. But Al didn't seem to hear her. It was as if he were speaking only to Angel, saying over and over again in a low voice, *"Dios te cuide, Angel, Dios te cuide."*

"What are you doing?" Maria said again. This time Al heard her. He whirled around, his arms spread out like wings, as if to somehow shield her from the sight of Angel's body sprawled across the floor.

Maria could not stop staring. Al looked like a bird with tiny legs and wide wings settling slowly down to earth, using his wings as ballast. Something clicked in her memory.

Then Al's eyes skittered and yellowed. In the distance, Maria heard Danforth say in a thin, tinny voice, "...Al, come outside with me." She felt Joe grab her around the waist as her knees buckled. She struggled to regain her balance, but everything in the room grew smaller and smaller. Finally the room itself faded into the darkness and disappeared.

61 | MONDAY MORNING
Repository
Sandy Hills

MARIA OPENED HER EYES. She was lying on a cot on the main floor of the Repository. It was dark except for the row of fluorescent lights humming overhead. The room felt strangely silent after all the noise of the SWAT team, the dogs, the yelling and cursing, the gunshots. Now the space felt empty, as if all the life had been sucked out of it.

Joe was watching her from the shadowy chair next to the cot. "So you decided to join us," he said when he saw that her eyes were open.

She tried to sit up.

"No, don't move," he said, turning his chair slightly so that he could talk to her more easily. "There's no hurry. Things are winding down anyway."

She heard Cali coming towards them from the other side of the room. His footsteps had a comfortable beat all their own. She always recognized his approach. He came up to her, and to her surprise, he bent down and gave her a quick kiss on her forehead, the same place where Gil had made his mark on her with his finger.

She looked at him. His face was worn with fatigue, but he was smiling at her. "You OK, Maria?" he said, looking deep into her eyes. When she looked back at him, she could feel the warmth in his eyes go directly to the aching spots inside her. "You OK, Maria?" he asked again. All she could do was nod.

"I'll see you later. Have to talk with Danforth." Then he was gone.

"I don't understand Cali," she said to Joe. She could already feel the first press of anxiety in her chest. "In the parking lot before the raid, he seemed indifferent, distracted."

Joe nodded. "It was confusing. You were caught in the crosshairs of a bad situation. All we could do was try to make the best of it."

Maria sat up before Joe could protest. "I'm fine," she said. She looked around the room. Desks had been tossed against the wall, chairs ripped open, file cabinet drawers left slanting from their metal frames. Suddenly the image of Al bending over Angel's body threatened to swallow her up. She felt the color leave her face. "I need some answers, Joe," she said, keeping her face so rigid it began to hurt.

"Trust me on something?" Joe said quietly.

"It depends," she said. "I want to know about Al."

"Al's been suspended, pending the investigation," Joe said evenly. "As far as I know, he's gone

261

home. That part's routine." He paused. "As far as the rest of it, where Al is concerned...." He paused again. "Cali wants to be part of that conversation, Maria. It's important. Can you wait for the rest of it until we bring you home?"

"Why?"

"Maria, trust me," Joe said, forcefully this time.

"That's not good enough," she said.

"Look, Vetrano's team is through here at the Repository," Joe said. "They've already left. Our unit is at the station processing the drivers and the evidence. We got everything we need to shut down Gil's operation for a long time. Danforth's pleased with the way things went. He's planning to brief the whole unit tomorrow morning at 8:00. Till then, we're supposed to get some rest. I said I'd take you home. Cali's coming too."

After a moment, she nodded. "I'll wait on Al, but I want to know everything else now."

"You've got a deal," Joe said. His shoulders relaxed.

"How long have I been out?" she asked.

"Not more than five minutes."

"Cali got here fast."

Joe smiled. "He sure did."

"What about Angel?"

"He's gone, Maria."

A feeling of abject discouragement swept over her. She closed her eyes. "Then we'll never know about Ramón," she said in a faint voice.

"Not true, Maria. We have Snake Baby."

"What do you mean?" she asked, her eyes wide open now. "Al said Gil put out a contract on him."

Joe shook his head. "Danforth has Snake Baby in safekeeping. And this time he's going to talk. In exchange, we'll find him a relatively safe prison."

She started to say something else, but Joe interrupted her. "Time to go, Maria."

She stood up.

They walked by the line of trailers, dark and empty. Cali was waiting for them by the car. "I'll sit in the back," he said when they got there. They pulled out of an empty parking lot and headed down the interstate.

They rode in silence until the turnoff for Sandy Hills. "How many officers did Danforth post at the house?" Maria asked uneasily as they approached the center of town. She was still uncomfortable with the idea of her home under surveillance, but she hadn't forgotten Gil's words, "... you're going to be looking over your shoulder for the rest of your short life."

Joe shook his head.

Maria looked at him in surprise.

"Gil is dead," Cali said unexpectedly, his voice rumbling around in back of her. "They found his body in the old pump house. Somebody used a nail gun to kill him. Not the nicest way to die."

Cali paused. "You wanted answers?"

She nodded.

By the time they got to Sandia Drive, Cali had finished talking and Maria had no more questions. As Joe drove down the dusty road to her house, Cali's words faded into a distant conversation she'd heard a long time ago. Maria felt the sudden impulse to pull down the visor and look at her face in the mirror. Did she look as old as she felt?

She stared at herself. There were new, unfamiliar lines around her mouth, and the eyes that stared back at her in the mirror seemed to belong to a stranger.

"I'll see you tomorrow," she said as she got out of the car.

But Joe had already turned off the engine and was coming around the car to stand beside her. Cali climbed quickly out of the back seat to join him.

She stopped midway to her front door and stared at them. "What's up?" she said in a tight voice.

"Stay in the house and lock the door," Cali said looking at her intently. "Joe and I are going to stick around for a while."

She started to protest, but Joe interrupted her. "Not negotiable, Maria."

She was too tired to fight. "I'll see you later," she said again. She went into the house and locked the door. She could hear Cali and Joe talking outside. "I'll take the front?" Cali said.

"Good. I'll be out back," Joe said. She heard his footsteps on the gravel fade away as he headed for the graden.

Maria went into the living room. She pushed the couch up close to the windows and lay down. Sunlight slowly filled the room. Leafy shadows floated lazily across the dark red tile floor. Was there a breeze this morning, rustling through the trees?

She closed her eyes. In the garden, a spiral of smoke, so thin as to be almost invisible, was snaking its way through the dappled sunlight. By the time Joe had made his way back around the house to take up his post in the garden, the smoke had disappeared entirely.

ᏬᎧᎧ

Al sat absolutely still under the trees. He knew how to make himself invisible. Soon he would have to make his move. But he had always prided himself on being strategic. First he had to review his options.

He needed time to absorb the knowledge that he was free of Gil. He still couldn't believe it. He had never imagined that he could kill Gil and get away with it. Only now did he realize that the beating he'd endured in front of Maria had shattered the framework of his life. At first, in the immediate aftermath of the beating, all he'd understood was that he could never again submit to Gil's control over his life.

Joe's friend had staunched the heaviest bleeding and helped him clean up. Then Joe had walked him over to his car. "You sure you're OK to drive?" Joe had asked him, preoccupied. But Al had insisted, ignoring whatever advice Joe was calling out to him as he drove off. He wanted to get as far away from Gil as possible. Beyond that he couldn't think.

Without any warning, he'd inexplicably pulled over to the side of the road and started sobbing. He hadn't cried like that since the night in the desert so many years ago. Now he found he couldn't stop.

In a daze, he'd turned the car around and driven back to the fields and the pump house that belonged to Gil's family. It was there that he and Gil and their friends had spent most of their boyhood nights watching the immigrants cross *la linea* with Border Patrol vehicles following in furious pursuit.

Back then, the diesel motor in the pump house steadily pumped over 3000 gallons of water a day into a three-to-four feet wide steel culvert that began under the pump house and narrowed as it went deeper into the ground. From there, the water flowed through black plastic tubes into irrigation canals in the surrounding fields.

The boys called the covered tubes their secret tunnels. In fact, the tubes were only thirty-six inches in diameter so even as boys, they'd had to tunnel through the tubes on their hands and knees like small, blind moles. It was hard, and it was dangerous because they had to carefully time their tunneling to avoid the flow of water through the tubes.

But it was worth the risk. The boys would slide out of a tube and push up through the sandy soil into a field heavily planted with groves of pecans. The field ran along the border with only a cut wire fence dangling on the ground to mark the boundary.

The boys would sit in the field and watch the flight of illegals through the fence at such close quarters, it was like being in the first row at the movies. So much was happening, it was hard to take it all in.

By the time Al graduated high school, Gil's family had stopped any pretense of farming. The motor sat silently in the pump house. The irrigation canals were dry. Gil's family had more important business to take care of than growing strawberries or pecans.

The land on Gil's side of the wire fence soon became nothing more than a dry, abandoned field surrounded by clumps of brush and low trees, but for a long time it remained an important part of the smuggling trail. The smugglers and their straggling flocks of *pollos* would finalize arrangements in the field on the Mexican side of the wire. Then they would cross the border into Gil's field to wait under the trees for someone to pick them up and drive them to safe houses throughout the state. Later the field was abandoned as a meeting place. It had become too well known to *La Migra* to be effective. Today the deserted field was simply known as Wino Alley.

Al headed towards Wino Alley. He parked the car behind some mesquite bush a short distance away from the field. Then he grabbed a cell phone out of the glove compartment, stuffed it into his pocket, and got out of the car, pulling his baseball cap down over his eyes.

He walked slowly, unsteadily down the road. The abandoned field was just ahead of him. It looked much the same as it had when smugglers had used it as a meeting place. Sand and juniper bushes, plastic bags caught on the branches, broken bottles and beer cans on the ground. A large cardboard box that must have been used as a little hooch by some inebriated vagabond during the colder months had been pushed up against the juniper bushes by the wind, but it didn't look like anyone was around now.

Al stumbled over to the cardboard box and looked inside. All he could see was some empty rum bottles and a pile of black plastic bags under a large rock. Sometimes panhandlers sold plastic bags like that as raincoats. But today was dry, in spite of the clouds, and the owner of the cardboard box didn't seem to be around.

If he stayed away from the border, Al told himself, away from the sensors in the ground and the surveillance cameras, he might have a chance. It wasn't easy to cross the line these days. Now there was a tall steel barrier along the border.

No matter what he did, Border Patrol would see him. They were watching him now, but as long as he stayed clearly on the Northside of the line, they might see him as just an old drunk, looking for some quiet place to pass out for the rest of the afternoon.

Al grabbed one of the rum bottles and started searching the field carefully, weaving back and forth on his feet, as if he were looking for something on the ground, like a cigarette stub or a can with a few swallows of beer still left inside. He laughed and stumbled as he searched, chanting to himself in a loud voice, *muy borracho, muy borracho*. Anyone looking at him would see him as very drunk.

Finally his foot bumped up against something hard. He sat down and casually pushed the sand away with his hands. As soon as he saw the black plastic, he knew he'd found the irrigation tube, the secret tunnel to the pump house. It was still there, under a layer of sandy soil that looked like it hadn't been moved in years.

He took a swig of air from the empty bottle and looked around again. Still no one in sight. The sky was heavy with clouds, and the floodlights along the border were still dark. He would have to take a chance. By now there was no going back.

He stood up and then stumbled, falling forward on his stomach like a drunk in a stupor. He lay there without moving for what seemed like hours. Nothing happened.

Slowly he began to push away the sand covering the opening of the tube. By the time he'd cleaned out the opening, his hands were raw and he was exhausted, but there was no time to lose.

Quickly he wiggled backwards on his hands and knees until he was completely inside the tube. He held his breath and listened. Nothing. He tentatively put out his hand. Again nothing happened. He took off his hat and left it just outside the opening so that the brim was barely visible. Then he pulled some of the sand back over the opening. The thin covering of sand and the hat wouldn't fool anyone who looked closely. All he could hope for was that the Border Patrol Agents had seen him as a drunk who'd crawled into some kind of opening in the ground to take a nap. He was Northside after all. No one ever crawled into a ditch to sneak south.

Painstakingly he turned himself around and began inching forward, crawling and sliding through the dark, narrow tube that would take him to the pump house. If he was lucky.

It was completely black inside the tube. All he could do was sniff the air for smells that might warn him that someone else was in the tunnel. Every few feet he would stop and listen for sounds. When his hand touched a pile of empty plastic bottles, he froze. Empty water bottles? Was that a sign that the tunnel had been used recently? By Gil's *mules*? The thought brought back a rush of old fears. He crouched in the darkness, paralyzed, unable to move. If there were drug runners using the tunnel, he was lost.

But illegal immigrants looking for work also used the smuggling trails around Lastup, Al reminded himself quickly. Maybe some of them had stumbled onto the tunnel by accident. If that was the case, they wouldn't have told Gil or anyone else about the tunnel. No one was supposed to cross *la linea* near Lastup without paying Gil for permission to cross.

Al forced himself to struggle forward, a few inches at a time. When he finally found himself in the culvert, ten or fifteen minutes later, he was more surprised than anything else. He was almost there! But he would have to work quietly. What if someone was inside the pump house?

Carefully he pushed up against the wide, wooden floorboard that covered the entrance to the culvert inside the shed. It wouldn't budge. He pushed harder, with all the strength he could summon up. Still, it wouldn't move.

He fell back in exhaustion and with something like horror, he found that he was weeping again. What if the floorboard door had been nailed down by someone inside the pump house? He would be lost!

But there was a chance. Maybe someone had locked the door from inside the culvert. He and Gil and Angel used to do that. They had made a lock so that no one could follow them from the pump house into the tunnel. It was a simple lock but effective. Four hooks, one on each side of the door.

Al felt around the edges of the door. The hooks were there, but they were hanging loosely, unattached.

He started back again, frantically pushing at the floorboard, but it remained unmovable. Increasingly desperate now, he began beating on the wood, ignoring the noise and his bleeding hands. Finally he was able to move the door slightly to the side. He saw a small crack of light. He put his fingers into the crack and clawed frantically at the wood until he'd forced an opening wide enough to get his arm through. When he had made enough space to pull himself up into the pump house, he squeezed through the space and collapsed on the pump house floor.

He looked at his watch. It was smashed beyond repair. He pulled out his cell phone. At least that still worked. Not much more than two hours had passed since the beating. It seemed impossible.

He crawled to his feet and looked around. Several large barrels filled up most of the floor space inside the pump house. One of them had been sitting over the floorboard, probably by pure chance.

Al forced himself to walk over to the pump house door, grimacing with every step from the sharp stabs of pain in his legs and back. He opened the door and looked outside. No one was around. He shut the door and began to examine everything in the pump house. Then he punched in Gil's number. He didn't know what he was going to say, but the words came out smoothly, flawlessly. He must have been planning this for a long time and never even known it.

"Clavito, you little shit, you must be crazy calling me like this," Gil yelled at him over the phone. "Do I have to come back to get you and beat your ass again?"

"*Cállate la boca*!" Al yelled back, shocking both of them. "Shut up!" he yelled at Gil again, enjoying the sound of the words in his mouth.

There was silence at the other end of the phone.

"Listen to me, Gil," he said. "Meet me at the pump house in fifteen minutes. Come alone. If you bring anyone with you, you're dead."

"What the hell are you talking about?" Gil said. He was laughing hard as he spoke, but Al could tell he was listening.

"You're looking for the boy?" he said to Gil.

Gil was silent.

"I can tell you where he is," Al went on. "They're driving him to a safe house. I know where they're going. The boy for my freedom, Gil. That's the deal."

"Clavito, don't fuck with me," Gil said. He was still laughing, but there was a serious quality to his voice that hadn't been there before. "I can find him without you."

"You won't find him, Gil," Al said with absolute certainty. "I know where he is. The boy for my freedom."

In the silence that followed, Al held his breath. His whole life hung in the balance. Would Gil buy it? The Gil of many years ago wouldn't have believed him. But the older Gil had become arrogant. This was a slower Gil who no longer used his hands. He just gave orders. That made a difference.

And Gil had a lot riding on the Repository operation. The uncertainty was making him nervous, and a nervous Gil could make a mistake. Especially if Gil thought his Clavito was down and out.

As the silence continued, Al began to regret the strength of his first words. He shouldn't have said, "*Cállate la boca*!" to Gil. Clavito wouldn't have dared to tell Gil to shut up!

A moment later, Al realized that his words hadn't made any difference at all. Gil was already taunting him. "I didn't think you could even make it into your car," Gil was saying. "A little shit like you. Sounds like you need another beating to straighten you out, Little Nail."

Al held his tongue, willfully silent, refusing to let Gil take control. After another long silence, Gil said, "I'll come to the pump house alone, Clavito. For old time's sake." His voice was acid, dismissive. "But I'll be armed," he added for emphasis, "and my men will be waiting for me outside. If I don't come out in a few minutes, they'll take you apart."

"Your word is still good?" Al said in a deliberately timid voice. "You always said, no matter what, your word would be good."

"You can count on it, Clavito," Gil said, sounding surer of himself now. This was the Clavito he remembered, the fool who was always ready to follow his orders.

In any case, Gil told himself, it was time to clean things up. He'd already given up a profitable business on Vista Drive just to divert attention away from Al. Pipé's disappearance had been uncomfortably close to Al's conversation with Pipé. Maybe no one even saw them. But if they did, for Al to learn that Pipé was an informant and then for Pipé to disappear the next day, well, it was just too close for comfort.

And Al had done good work, Gil had to admit it, convincing Pipé that he was working together with the cowboy. But enough was enough. You couldn't count on someone forever, even stupid little Clavito. It was time to get rid of him. The pump house was as good a place as any. If his information about Carlito was good, he would allow Clavito to die quickly.

"You can count on it," Gil told Al again. "I'll be there."

62

MONDAY MORNING
The Pump House

AL KNEW IT WOULDN'T BE LONG before Gil and his men arrived at the pump house, but he didn't need much time. The pump house was well supplied with boards, barbed wire, and nails, lots of nails.

As Gil's car headed for the pump house, the driver argued with Gil, as he had been doing the whole time they'd been driving. "This is crazy, boss" he kept saying. "Let us go in. Clavito will tell us what we want to know. Why do you want to risk everything? If you're alone, he could hurt you before we can get inside."

Gil shook his head. "No, you don't know Clavito the way I do," he said. "Clavito is tired. He's tired of me always being there, giving the orders. He knows I probably won't let him off the hook, but he's hoping. If he sees the three of you coming in, he'll take himself out."

"So what? That's no great loss. We'll find the kid anyway."

"No, I can't risk it. If they get to the kid and then to Angel before I can do anything, they could get to me," Gil snapped back at him. "I can't risk it. Besides, Clavito is a coward, and he's stupid. He'd never dare hurt me. He'll tell me where the kid is and then hope. He's hoping that maybe I'll let him go. Maybe he can hold a gun on me until he gets back down in the tunnel. If he can't, he knows a quick bullet to the head would be better than always looking over his shoulder, wondering when the next beating is going to come along. I could see it in his face today. He can't take it no more."

"So if he gets into the tunnel, you're going to let him get away?"

"Asshole! Who do you think will be at the other end of the tunnel? My boys are already there. Now pull up here. I'm going in. If you hear anything that sounds like trouble, come in fast."

"You going in without a piece?!"

Gil laughed. "I'm not Clavito, asshole. I've got my piece right here in my front pocket. Clavito knows I'd never come in unarmed. But first we're going to talk. He *needs* to tell me a few things. He *needs* to go out with a little dignity, something you don't know anything about. Now shut up and get out of my way."

Gil walked into the pump house, his hands empty.

"Shut the door," Al said in a frightened voice. "What I want to say is private. His face was pale, and even his hands were shaking.

What a fool he is, Gil couldn't help thinking as he shut the door.

Before Gil could turn around, Al had the garrote he had fashioned out of barbed wire around Gil's neck and had pulled it so tight, Gil couldn't get a word out. Instantly Al locked the door and pushed Gil down on his back, immobilized on the dirt floor of the pump house, blood oozing from his neck. Gil struggled to breathe, staring at Al with horror and disbelief.

"Everything OK in there?" the driver called out.

"*Callate*," Al said. "We're finalizing. He told you before, shut up! You're interrupting things."

The driver didn't respond, but Al could hear him pacing around outside the door.

Quickly he put his knee down on Gil's chest, holding tight his grip on the wire around Gil's neck. He put Gil's right hand on top of one of the boards he had found in the pump house. Then he picked up the nail gun. "These are big nails," he told Gil. "For you from your *Clavito*."

As Al nailed Gil's other hand, and then his feet, he kept looking at Gil's eyes, and he kept talking to him, reminding him of all the cruelty he had inflicted on other people, especially Maria's family. When he placed the nail gun on Gil's forehead, he finally saw what he had been looking for all along in Gil's eyes, submission and penitence. "Now my mark is on *you*," Al said as he drilled in the last nail.

Gil's men were banging on the door. Al slipped into the tunnel and locked the trapdoor. He could hear Gil's men break down the door, screaming, furiously pulling at the trap door into the tunnel, but it wouldn't budge. They tried to pull Gil's body away, but it was nailed to the boards, and the wooden structure was too large to fit through the door.

All of them except the driver took off for the field where the tunnel ended, waiting for Al to emerge. Al carefully raised the trapdoor just an inch. His first bullet got the driver in his eye. He went down without making a sound.

No one else had stayed behind. No one paid any attention to him as he walked back to his car and drove away. No one noticed him on the highway. Only Al watched himself, nailing Gil in the pump house, driving away, as if it was all a dream, completely disconnected from the world around him and from everything that had just happened.

63 | MONDAY
Sandy Hills

MARIA WAS LYING ON A WIDE EXPANSE of sand under a partly cloudy sky. Patches of light played across her skin. The sun felt warm on her face. She could hear a plane overhead, and she knew it was trailing a banner just for her, floating a message in large letters through the sky. She would read it later.

As she let herself sink back into the sand, she slowly became aware that she was dreaming. There was no sand. She was sleeping on the living room couch. The sun she felt on her face was pouring in through the large windows along the back wall. It felt good lying there in the quiet sunlight. And for once, she'd slept heavily, well into the morning. Maybe she should always sleep in the living room.

She sat up slowly and opened her eyes.

Al Diaz was sitting in a chair in front of the couch. He was clean shaven and dressed in a three-piece suit. Even his hair, held together in a neat ponytail, seemed to be freshly washed. But there was a Colt .38 Super Caliber automatic pistol on his lap, and he was staring at her with an intensity that reached her bones. She sat in place, as if she'd been turned to ice. Only her heart was still moving, leaping around in her chest with a loud banging noise.

"What are you doing here?" she demanded as she shifted around on the couch, trying to steady the trembling in her legs. "How did you get in?"

Al was silent.

"You had a key. You made a copy of my key!"

After a moment, he nodded. "I was waiting for you," Al said tonelessly. "I waited in the woods. I knew Joe would step away at some point. Once he was out of sight, I ran through the garden and came into the house through the back door."

"You've been waiting in my house?!" Her head was pounding. "Where were you, Al? Where were you waiting?"

"In the kitchen," he said quietly.

"I don't believe you," she said. "How could you know I wouldn't go in there?"

"I didn't know," he said. "I took a chance. But it was hours since you got here. I figured it was long enough you'd be asleep. I came in here. You were sleeping."

She shivered in spite of herself. "I don't believe you," she said, glancing out the window as she spoke.

Al picked up the pistol, moving his thumb along the outside edge of the ivory grip.

"We have to talk."

"You wouldn't shoot me." The words slipped out before she could stop herself.

Al's eyes seemed to yellow. "I would shoot Joe without thinking twice, and I'll have the advantage. Is that a chance you want to take?"

She felt sick. She didn't doubt for a minute that Al would do exactly what he said. Even if she could somehow get Joe's attention, if he came into the house unprepared, Al would kill him. She was on her own. She had to focus all her attention on the man sitting in front of her, holding a pistol in his hand.

She studied him, sitting there like a statue, unmoving, staring at her as if part of him was somewhere else. Even his eyes looked empty. All the gold flecks seemed to have disappeared into a flat yellow, like the flat eyes of a snake. She shivered again.

"You frightened of me, Maria?" he said coldly.

"I'm not frightened of you, Al" she said. "But I want to know why you've been following me."

"What?" He seemed startled. "What are you talking about?"

"Joe matched your DNA."

Al looked at her skeptically. "Don't bullshit me, Maria. You can do better than that. My DNA's not on file."

"When we were in Lastup, Joe picked up some of the swabs his friend used to wipe the blood off your face."

"So what?"

"Joe picked up your cigarette butts, Al. From Riverside Park and from the elm trees out back. He sent them to the lab days ago. Yesterday he sent the swabs along. A positive match. You've been watching me. Why?" She tried furiously to keep the hurt out of her voice.

A shadow passed over Al's face. "Danforth knows?" he said.

She nodded. "Why?" she said again. "Were you wondering if I'd finally remembered that night in the desert?"

"I was looking out for you, Maria." Al said evenly. "I always have. I think you became my responsibility that night in the desert. And no, I didn't think you'd remembered anything or that you ever would. Only last night at the Repository, I could see it in your eyes...."

"I remembered the words," she said in a daze. "I didn't know why at first, but I suddenly remembered your voice and those words. Just like in the desert. I remember you, Al. You were there. I remember. Who were the others, Al? Gil and Angel?"

Al nodded. "But that's in the past, Maria. Now I'm the one who needs help, your help."

She shook her head. "No."

"You owe me." His eyes were fixed on hers, willing her to listen, to connect to him once again. "I saved your life, Maria. Gil wanted to kill all of you. I stood up to him. And it cost me my life."

"You made choices, Al," she said. "You chose to take illegals across the border with Gil."

"And you came across the border."

"I was four years old!"

"And I was in high school, Maria. Just a kid. I didn't know what Gil was going to do."

"You chose to stand up to Gil," she went on, as if he hadn't said anything.

"That's right. I draw the line at killing kids," he said, his words demanding her sympathy.

"And you also chose not to tell anyone that we had been abandoned out there in the middle of nowhere with nothing but a bottle of water," she said forcefully, rejecting his claim on her feelings. "If you had told someone what you'd done that same night, my brother would still be alive."

"You don't know what you're talking about," he told her coldly. "Telling someone was never a choice. I'd have gone to jail. I'd have been Clavito stuck in Lastup my whole life. That was no choice."

"Is what happened to you any better?" she threw back at him. "Your whole life was a lie. Gil controlled everything you did. There was a choice, Al. You made the wrong one."

"It's not over yet, Maria," Al said after a moment. "I don't know exactly what's going to happen now, but I don't think there's enough evidence to convict me of anything. All I have to do is take off, disappear somewhere Southside."

"Then why haven't you already disappeared?" she couldn't help asking.

"Because I'm not sure," he said. "How much do they know?"

"They found Gil."

"What are you talking about?"

"They found his body, Al, in the pump house. Someone took a nail gun and ended his life."

"I wouldn't know anything about that," Al said.

"Well, whoever was in the pump house left a lot of blood on the floorboards," she went on, ignoring his comment. "And someone left some clear tire tracks where his car was parked near the entrance to one of the old irrigation canals. The one that leads into the pump house, by the way."

"That's not proof, Maria. And even if all that did point to a specific person, what jury would convict someone who put a creep like Gil out of business? Whoever took out Gil deserves a medal, not a jail term."

"Maybe if that's all there was to it, a jury might buy it," she said. "But there's a lot more than Gil at someone's door."

"What do you mean?"

"They have Snake Baby," she said. Now she was the one relentlessly holding his gaze.

He jumped back as if he'd been bitten.

"That's impossible," he said. "Gil put out a contract on Snake Baby."

"Danforth had Snake Baby in a safe place all along, Al. Danforth had his doubts about you from the beginning."

"Thanks to your friend, Joe," Al said bitterly.

"Thanks to you," she snapped back at him.

Al's eyes narrowed. "You're pushing me into a corner, Maria."

"Your choices, your corner, Al," she said without missing a beat, checking his hands as she spoke, trying to read his intentions.

He moved his finger over the trigger.

"Tell me about Angel," she said. "Whatever happens, you owe me that much."

At the mention of Angel's name, Al's face closed down, as if a curtain had fallen over him, separating him from everything else around him. "Go ahead then," he said in an expressionless voice, taking his finger off the trigger and letting the pistol fall back onto his lap.

"Why did you help Angel get rid of Ramon's body," she said. "How could you?"

"I believed Angel. He said it was an accident. The boy was already dead. I didn't want Angel to go to jail. That would have been a death sentence, and a painful one. Even in jail, they don't like people who hurt little kids."

"I don't buy it," Maria said coldly. "You're sure you weren't hoping to get on Gil's good side? Maybe get a bargaining chip for your freedom?"

He was silent.

"Is that why you didn't tell Gil about the Repository?" Maria asked. "Is that why you didn't tell him we were on to his operation? You were hoping we could get rid of Gil for you?"

Al nodded.

"You killed Angel at the school," she went on. By now Al had the pistol back in his hand, his finger back on the trigger. "How did you do it?"

Al didn't say anything.

"You warned Angel about the raid, didn't you? You told him to hide in the secret room under the floor. You told him the K-9 unit probably wouldn't come in with the SWAT team." She interrupted herself. "You did that too? Sent the K-9 unit astray?"

Al shook his head. "That was blind luck, Maria. Just blind luck. I didn't know what I was going to do at the school."

"But you knew you were going to wait until we were all in the basement," she said. "You knew you would go back to his office and tell Angel it was safe to come out." She paused. "And you knew you were going to shoot him. Why, Al? Why did you shoot Angel?"

"I thought there was no one else around to know about me," Al said tonelessly, avoiding her gaze. "Gil told me Snake Baby was dead." He looked directly at her. "But Gil and Angel were bad guys. They deserved to die."

"And what about Rosa?" she said attacking him furiously with her words. "Was Rosa a bad guy too?!"

Al stared at her as if he had suddenly been struck dumb.

Now it was her turn to wait silently.

Al lifted up the pistol. "I didn't know Snake Baby would kill her," he said. "All I wanted him to do was take the box of postcards."

"You saw the photographs mixed in with the postcards? You were afraid there was one of you?" she said sadly.

Al nodded. "I'd already been into the boy's basket," he said. "In the trailer, just before you and the cowboy got there. There were photographs of me with Gil and Angel in the card for the mother. We were in the background, but there I was, talking with Gil and Snake Baby, with maps spread out in front of us.

"I took the photographs out and sealed up the card again. But later in the apartment, when I saw photographs mixed in with the postcards, I thought there might be more." He looked out at the mountains. "I was wrong. I found out later. Snake Baby took all the photographs. There was nothing."

"Then what happened to Carlito? What spooked him when I was trying to find out what he'd seen at the park?"

"The only thing that could have set the kid off was the photo of Gil and Angel talking, not far away from Juan and his plane. Maybe seeing Angel like that, so close to Ramón's father, maybe it just set the kid off, remembering how Angel rocked the old man. Who knows what Carlito saw when you were talking to him."

"How did you know about that," Maria asked dumbfounded.

"News travels fast in N. Building," Al said. "Even Cali knew something had happened. He was trying to keep you away from me. He thought if Carlito had seen something important and you knew about it, you might tell me. But it was all for nothing. All for nothing."

He looked at Maria from someplace far away. "A long time ago, I saved your life, Maria. All you have to do is forget what you know about the postcards, about Rosa. Tell them that you've remembered how I saved your life, how I stood up to Gil. It will make a difference, I know it. They'll pull back, give me some breathing space so I can get away. A few days, that's all I'm asking for.. I'll disappear, and you'll never see me again. That's a promise. Give me back my life, Maria. I gave you a chance. Give me a chance now. You owe me."

She could feel the perspiration rolling down her back. She had to think. Time was running out. "What is it you really want Al?" she said slowly. "Absolution? For me to say it's OK, that it all evens out in the end?"

He was silent.

"You want me to do what you did, don't you?" she said unbelievingly. "You want me to be your silent partner, tell everyone I've remembered how you saved my life, but keep quiet about the other things I know, like why Rosa was killed and how you helped Angel by dumping Ramón's body while you were pretending to look for his killer. You want me to keep this conversation secret, even help you get away! That's what you want, isn't it? You want me to live out the rest of my life as a lie, just like you did. But I won't do that, Al, never!"

"I'll never go to jail," he said, lifting the pistol up off his lap.

"Al," she said desperately. "You've spent your whole life on the run, trying to play it safe. But you can't escape yourself in the end, you know that."

"I can try," he said, and pulled the trigger.

275

64 | TUESDAY
Vereda District Station

THE DUSKY MOUNTAINS AROUND CIUDAD NUEVA pushed into the silvering sky, as if to signal her attention, but this morning Maria wasn't interested in the view. She turned on the car radio and scanned the stations until she found Jim Croce singing *Time In A Bottle*. She turned up the volume and settled back in her seat for the drive into the city.

Usually she liked to drive in silence. It was a good time to think about the cases that had been suspended as well as the investigations that were ongoing. But this morning she needed some company, even if it was just a grainy voice and the chords of a guitar on the car radio.

It was different yesterday. As soon as the necessary questions had been asked and answered, the physical evidence collected, and Al's body removed from the house, she had insisted on going for a long walk by herself in the bosque that lined the Rio Poderoso in Sandy Hills. Yesterday she had needed to be alone.

Danforth had objected at first. Finally he'd agreed, but he'd made it clear that he would assign some officers to keep her company, no matter how she felt about it. They would keep their distance, but he would not allow her to take a long walk along the river by herself.

She hadn't been able to speak with Cali before he left the house, but she knew he had volunteered for the job. And she knew that by the time she reached the bosque, he would already be there, positioned to watch her back. For Cali, being constantly on guard was a necessity, not a choice.

Joe had left for the bosque with Cali so there wasn't time, but he would have listened if she had tried to explain things to him. "Who's left?" she would have asked him. "Except for Snake Baby, carefully locked up someplace far away, they're all dead, aren't they? Juan, Ramón, Rosa, Angel, Gil, and Al."

Especially Al. Just saying Al's name made her chest ache.

She could have said all that to Joe, but there hadn't been time. All she'd been able to say was, "I'm going for a walk by myself. I'll see you tomorrow at the briefing."

Now she was on her way to the briefing by herself, and she didn't like it. She felt too alone with her memories, Al dressed in his suit talking to her, Al pulling the trigger sending streams of blood and pieces of his brain to splatter against the living room window in slow motion.

She took the exit for Vereda and headed for the district station. As she drove through the streets of the *barrio*, she noticed that everything around her was strangely transparent, as if a strong wind had come up during the night and blown away the dust that usually hovered over the streets and sidewalks. The pale early light slanting onto the objects around her seemed to diminish their solidity, and she felt the acute absence of anything solid in herself, as if an essential part of herself had been blown away along with the dust. Even the familiar sounds of the barrio seemed to fall through the air like echoes, the buzzing whine of a motorcycle in the distance, the mailman's whistle, a child's voice floating across an empty parking lot.

A dog barking at the passing cars reminded her of the lost dog she'd seen at the intersection. She was through waiting for the right time. She would call Animal Control as soon as the morning briefing was over to tell them she'd be picking up the dog on her way home.

It was summertime. Children had sprouted up everywhere, in rows and clumps, running along the sidewalks or riding bicycles. Some boys were playing soccer on an empty lot. On one corner, two little girls holding dolls in their arms were watching a group of older girls jumping rope. Nearby a group of older boys stood talking and watching the cars go by.

Maria raced up the steps to the Squad Room, but once she got to the second floor, she stopped to catch her breath. She found herself walking more and more slowly across the gray, linoleum floor, past the doors to the bathrooms, past the snack and soft drink machines into the briefing room.

No one said anything when she walked into the room, but she could feel their stares. She sat down and glanced around the room. Joe gave her a quick smile. She nodded at him, then turned to listen to Danforth.

When the briefing was over, she followed Danforth into his office. "Shut the door, Chavez," he said. He waited until she sat down. "You wanted to talk to me?"

She nodded.

"Go ahead, Maria," he said quietly.

For a moment she couldn't speak. In the pale fluorescent light that substituted for sunlight in his office, the lines on Danforth's face looked deeper than ever. He looked old, vulnerable. She couldn't believe it. Danforth vulnerable? She'd never even imagined it.

She searched for a different way to begin. "You think I'm a good cop?" she said finally.

He nodded. "You are a good cop, Maria. And you're getting better all the time. You're doing all the right things, you know. Those problems you think you've got? They're in your head, that's all."

"It's not that simple, Sarge. I was never a believer, you know that, don't you?"

He nodded.

"I saw the truth about what we do a long time ago," she said, trying to find the words that would make him understand.

"Go on."

"What people really want from cops is a good stage show. They need to believe that we can protect them and that the bad guys will go to jail. It's just an illusion up there on the stage, and we're just the props, but I accepted all that as part of the job." She paused.

Danforth was silent, waiting for her to go on.

"What we do is very clear to me," she said, still searching for the right way to put her thoughts into words. "But here's the problem, Sarge. At least for me."

She hesitated before she went on. "There's too much death," she said finally. "We keep it off stage, in the wings, but it's there, and we have to deal with it. That's our real job. People need cops because they want someone to stand in for them, to see what's really happening out there on the street. They need someone to look death in the face so they don't have to. We do what they can't do.

"But we see all that, what people do to each other, the violence, the death. We see it and then it's in us, and it stays inside us even if we learn not to recognize it. I don't want to do that any longer. No more separations. No more secrets."

"Is it living with secrets that's the problem?" Danforth asked her. "Or is it living with guilty secrets?"

"What's the difference?" she said, forcing back tears. "How can you trust anyone in a world where everything is an act and everyone wears a mask?"

Danforth studied her for a few minutes. "You're talking about Rosa."

She nodded.

"I won't accept responsibility for that," he said evenly.

"Because you follow orders," she said, unable to keep the anger out of her voice.

Danforth shook his head. "You've got it all wrong, Maria. Keeping you away from Ana and Carlito was the only way I could keep them away from Al. The strategy was a good one. I agreed with it."

Maria could barely look at him. "That's not true, Danforth. If you hadn't sent Cali out to Rosa's apartment, if I had been able to interview Carlito that night..."

"Two can play at that game," Danforth interrupted. "If you had checked in on Rosa later that night when she was supposed to be at Ana's...."

Maria gasped at the cruelty of his words.

"Here's something else to consider," Danforth continued. "Someone has to take responsibility for Al. I've been asked to resign."

"That's not fair," she said, trying to keep her voice steady.

"No, it's not fair," he said. "And I'm going to fight it. I have no intention of being run out of here. The job is too important."

"I don't understand you," she said in a tired voice. "Why bother?"

"I'm not sure I can answer that," he said. "I know a good deal about death in the wings, as you put it, but I'm not sure about evil – what it is or how it works. Still, though it's mostly guesswork, I have a strong suspicion that evil has been with us from the very beginning, and I'm convinced that there are evils out there I've yet to come up against.

"But what I do know for sure is that I seem to have a calling. And I can tell you this much, Maria. Someone has to show up. Otherwise, evil wins. The way I see it, hell isn't fire and brimstones and all that sort of thing. Not at all. On the contrary, Hell's a pit of absolute emptiness."

Maria stared at him, too shocked to speak.

"Why so surprised, Maria?" Danforth said with a tired smile. "You didn't think I could talk that way?"

She could feel her cheeks burning.

"I can't tell you what to do, you know that, right?" he said gently.

She nodded.

"I can give you are a few words of advice. If you want them."

She nodded again.

"Investigators come in all sizes and shapes," Danforth began. "There's not just one mold for a good cop. And you've got something, Maria. You're engaged in what you do. And that's no small thing. Cops who don't give a damn about their work, who see it as just a paycheck or to use your words, as a useless stage show, get bored very quickly, and boredom is fertile ground for cheating, anger, even cruelty. It's the kind of attitude that brings down a lot more cops than you could ever imagine. You're one cop who will never have that problem. More important, though, the job is what it is. That's true for all of us. You either have to walk away from it or commit to it. It's your choice, Maria. It's up to you."

Danforth stood up to leave. She followed him with her eyes. When he opened the door, she caught a glimpse of Joe and Cali staring in her direction. Danforth turned and looked back at her. His body filled the doorframe, blocking her view.

"When you're ready," he said. "When you're ready, we'll be waiting for you."

Then he went out to join the others in the Squad Room, closing the door firmly behind him.

9372717R0

Made in the USA
Charleston, SC
07 September 2011